YOKAI
Enchantments

by

Margaret L. Carter

Anthology

YOKAI Enchantments

Cover Art by *The Wild Rose Press, Inc.*

The Wild Rose Press, Inc.
PO Box 708
Adams Basin, NY 14410-0708
Visit us at www.thewildrosepress.com

Publishing History
First Edition, 2021
Trade Paperback ISBN 978-1-5092-3962-7
Digital ISBN 978-1-5092-3963-4

Published in the United States of America

Yokai Magic

When Val unearths a Japanese scroll and a cat figurine inherited from her grandfather, magic invades her world. The statuette, actually a cat spirit named Yuki—a yokai—enchanted into that form for her own protection, comes to life. With her old high-school boyfriend, she searches for a way to vanquish the threat from the spirit realm, while facing the attraction they thought they'd long since put behind them.

Kitsune Enchantment

On the verge of losing her job, Shannon leaps at the chance to sell her graphic novel series to a major publisher. She'd love to have a closer relationship with her artist collaborator, Ryo, but how can she count on a man who keeps disappearing with the flimsiest of excuses?

Ryo feels the same attraction to Shannon, but he isn't sure how she'd react to the truth. He's a kitsune—a fox shapeshifter—prone to transforming at awkward moments. When a wannabe wizard follows him to a science-fiction convention, Ryo's secret, liberty, and budding romance with Shannon are all threatened.

Kappa Companion

Two years after her husband's sudden death, Heidi hopes to make a fresh start with a new love and a new home. But she hasn't planned on sharing her century-old house with her son's not-so-imaginary friends—a ghost child and a Japanese water monster. At least the creatures aren't dangerous—or are they?

Praise for Margaret L. Carter

"Margaret L. Carter has created a unique story that will bring a smile to one's face with the antics the characters are involved in. The reader will enjoy learning all about what a Kitsune Fox is, and what the fox's habits are. The author did an excellent job with the description of the fox and how it shifts. This is a fun read for everyone!"

~InD'tale Magazine gives
"Kitsune Enchantment" 4 stars

"Val is a wonderfully developed character who rolls with the punches that life has thrown her way. I admired how she took the fact that she has magic infused in her house without screaming in panic and running away. . . . The plot was very enjoyable and rather different. I always enjoyed learning about a different culture. The novel teaches about different yokai and other legends."

~Long and Short Reviews gives
"Yokai Magic" 4 and a half stars

Acknowledgments

With special thanks to Karen Wiesner for her invaluable help as a critique partner.

Yokai Magic

by

Margaret L. Carter

Chapter One

Dust and cobwebs coated the box marked "Granddad's mementos from Korea." Climbing onto a stepstool, Val swept away the mess with a broom before lifting the box down. It had probably sat undisturbed on the basement shelf since her family had bought the house, when she was twelve years old. She lugged her find upstairs and set it on a newspaper spread on the kitchen table. Her cat leaped onto the chair next to hers and stared as if supervising the job. With a paring knife, she slit the crumbling tape that barely sealed the box top.

After pulling out handfuls of wadded-up packing paper, she came upon a pile of letters with exotic stamps and a military return address. A separately bound bundle of envelopes looked like her grandmother's reply letters. Val squashed the temptation to start reading them on the spot. If what she needed wasn't loose in the box, she would riffle through the envelopes. From another nest of paper, she dug out a porcelain figurine of a white, green-eyed Japanese good-luck cat wearing a red scarf around its neck. She set the statuette on the table. The next layer in the box revealed a cylindrical package swathed in more paper and bound with tape.

What's this? A picture of some kind? As she sliced open the wrapping, the knife slipped. The blade nicked her finger, and a drop of blood fell onto the package. *That'll teach me to use scissors next time.* She dug a tissue out of her jeans pocket and wrapped her fingertip. For a second her vision blurred. *What's that about? Too long since lunch?* The weird sensation faded, and she dismissed it from her mind.

To her relief, when she stripped the wrapping off the package, she found only a barely visible bloodstain on the very edge of the object inside—a Japanese painted scroll. After shoving aside the heap of mail and the porcelain cat, she unrolled the scroll on the kitchen table. It portrayed a small, red building with a freestanding, rectangular arch in front and a peaked roof. *Maybe a shrine?* A slender, white cat wearing a red scarf that resembled the one on the figurine sat in a demure pose in front of the gate. In the background, next to a flowering cherry tree and a sketchy outline of a stream, hovered a misty figure of a woman in a lavender, floral-printed kimono. She wore a scarf like the cat's around her neck and something black on her left hand—a ring? A column of Japanese characters ran down the upper right side of the picture.

Val rubbed behind the ears of the long-haired, charcoal-and-silver tabby sprawled on the adjacent chair. "What do you think, Toby? Could I sell this for a small fortune and get the roof replaced?" Her pet blinked at her. "No, that's what I thought."

She sighed over the pile of mail. Sure, it would be interesting to read the letters her grandfather had written during his Army service in Korea in 1951, but would one of those envelopes contain what she was looking for? She'd hauled the stuff upstairs in search of a receipt for two Japanese ivory figurines that had adorned the fireplace mantel for as long as she could remember. Much as she hated the thought of giving them up, the websites she'd checked suggested their value would take a healthy bite out of the roof cost. She couldn't legally sell ivory, though, without proof Granddad had owned it before the ban on possessing it existed.

After popping into the ground-floor half-bath to bandage her finger, she returned to the kitchen to finish emptying the box. It took her a minute to notice something missing from the table. "Hey, what happened to the cat statuette?" She glanced at Toby as if he might have an answer. He leaped to the floor and strolled away, plumed tail waving. With a shrug, Val peered into the box, in case she'd replaced the figurine in it without thinking. "Not there. Then where did I put it?" She flipped through the remaining papers, although there wasn't enough debris left to hide the object. She glanced at the floor, where she would have seen obvious shards of porcelain if the cat had knocked the thing off the table. "Hope I'm not losing my mind. I might need it again." *Ridiculous. If I were going to have hallucinations, I wouldn't start by imagining random Asian artifacts. Better quit for now. Definitely way past dinnertime.* She stowed the items back in the box for safekeeping and cleaned off the table, then rummaged in the refrigerator for leftovers to heat up.

After supper, she strolled into the back yard, carrying a colander to harvest the newest batch of ripe tomatoes. Since she'd set the plants out late this year, they were still bearing in August. In this part of Maryland, summer heat lingered well into September. Maybe she'd whip up a pot of spaghetti sauce this weekend. Tall grass tickled her bare calves. *Time to mow the lawn again already.* Although she would miss the home where she'd lived off and on for nineteen years, shedding the burden of house and yard care would come as a relief.

Just as she finished filling the colander with tomatoes, the back door of the house on the right banged open. Mrs. Garrett, her gray hair slicked back into a tight ponytail and a loose blouse flapping around her thin torso, marched down the steps of the rear deck and across the lawn to the fence. "Valerie Sherman, here you are!"

Val suppressed a sigh. *Right where I usually am at this time.* "Hi. What's up?"

"That cat of yours has been in my garden again. Your mother would never have let that happen."

Val suppressed the impulse to snap, "Well, Mom isn't here, is she?" Instead, she said as meekly as she could manage, "Toby got out and went into your yard just that once, two months ago, and it hasn't happened since."

"I definitely saw a cat just a minute ago."

"It wasn't him—he." Because in her prime Mrs. Garrett had taught English at the local high school, Val still felt intimidated by her regardless of the passage of time. Even Mrs. G.'s Facebook posts bristled with grammatical correctness. The fact that Val had dated her son, Thad, from tenth through twelfth grade didn't help. *Get a grip. That ended thirteen years ago.*

"There it is again." The older woman jabbed a pointing finger at the low hedge on the other side of her lawn.

A lithe, white shape darted out of the shrubbery and dashed into the shadows at the corner of the house. Just before it vanished, Val glimpsed the shine of green eyes in the twilight.

"That's a white cat. Mine is gray. He hasn't been in

your yard." She inwardly cringed at the defensive tone in her voice, as if she weren't a gainfully employed woman of thirty-one, but a teenager Mrs. G. had the power to flunk out of AP English.

Mrs. Garrett sniffed. "All right, my mistake. But see that he doesn't do it again anyway."

After a "goodnight" that her neighbor grudgingly returned, Val went inside wondering why the stray cat had looked familiar.

The brief conversation started her thinking about Thad for the first time in at least a week, since she'd last seen a Facebook post by him. She'd friended him just to prove to herself that casual communication between them was no big deal. She could "like" his posts and see him "like" hers in return without her pulse racing and her stomach fluttering. That was how she knew about his recent assignment to teach at the Naval Academy. He would be living in town for the first time since his graduation and commissioning. Surely he would drop by his parents' house often. *Which means I'll have to see him. I can handle it. I'm a big girl now, right?* Since the end of high school, they hadn't talked to each other aside from an occasional breezy "hi" when they couldn't avoid it. The memory of the last time they had any contact less casual than a wave across the yard on his visits home still made her cheeks flush with heat. Both of their final close encounters, in fact, woke echoes of feelings she wanted to forget. As much as the breakup had hurt, winding time in reverse wasn't an option, so why dwell on that old pain? *Thirteen years ago, remember? You got over it a long time ago, right?* On the other hand, what woman didn't cling to memories, fond or otherwise, of her high school boyfriend and the senior prom?

****

Saturday night, in the wee hours after the post-prom pancake breakfast: A pair of hot-blooded eighteen-year-olds, they snuggled together in the back seat of Thad's subcompact car in the parking lot of a playground—one location where they could hope not to get chased off by a patrolling security vehicle. The oaks that overhung the far corner of the lot shadowed them from the floodlights. Through the half-open car window drifted the chirps and buzzes of insect choruses. The scent of his spicy aftershave mingled with the aroma of newly mown grass. As overachievers and Honor Society members focused on AP courses and college applications, Val and Thad seldom drank, but in honor of the occasion he'd scored two single-serving bottles of champagne. Sipping the bubbly, over-sweet wine, they wiggled around in the cramped space to get as close together as possible. She ended up on his lap, her turquoise gown crumpled up to her knees and her blue-dyed carnation corsage half crushed. In spite of the night breeze, humidity plastered her hair to the nape of her neck.

Swallows of champagne alternated with deep kisses that made her insides quiver. Every stroke of his tongue seemed to zap electric shocks to places untouched by anyone but herself. He skimmed over the bodice of her dress, the friction through the satin making her nipples tingle. His hands wandered below her waistline more boldly than ever before. He and Val were both too straight-arrow to risk pregnancy, but they'd avidly explored other possibilities. While one of his hands roamed under her skirt and the other cupped her breast, he nuzzled her throat and the cleavage above the V-neck of the dress. The wine and his hot breath on her bare skin made her head whirl. As his growing hardness pressed against her, her body responded with a flood of heat. She yearned to give herself to him as much as their ingrained caution would allow.

She couldn't help arching her hips when he targeted the sensitive spot she'd never allowed him to touch before. Her sighs turned to moans, and waves of pleasure surged through her.

When she caught her breath, she unzipped his tuxedo trousers and returned the favor with her fingers wrapped around his handkerchief. He shuddered and muffled his groans against her breasts. Her head whirled with the thrill of driving him to ecstasy. *We belong to each other—forever. Oh, God, please let it be forever.* So what if they were only eighteen?

Hugging her so tightly her ribs ached, he whispered, "I love you more than—more than anything. You believe that, don't you?"

The intensity in his voice twisted her stomach into knots. "'Course I do. Why wouldn't I? I love you twice as much."

"I love you thrice."

She giggled, still lightheaded from the champagne. "Love you fice."

The aftermath of that night hadn't turned out the way she expected…

The next day, Sunday, he came over to visit her after lunch. Although still fuzzy-headed from dragging herself to church with her folks after too little sleep, she remembered the night clearly enough to blush at the sight of Thad. He lowered his eyes and mumbled a greeting that conspicuously lacked the loving tone she'd hoped for. *What's wrong with him?* Her qualms only increased when he said, "Let's go someplace we can talk. I've got something important to tell you."

He wouldn't say anything more while they mounted their bikes and rode to the community beach, deserted this early in June. By the time they were sitting together on a bench that overlooked the Chesapeake Bay, her heart was racing and her stomach churning. When he clasped her hand, his palm felt as sweaty as her own. "Okay, what's the big thing you couldn't tell me on my front porch?"

He blurted out a sentence that made her head ring as if he'd punched her.

"What? You've got to be kidding. You did not just say that."

He repeated the statement more slowly and distinctly. "I've won an appointment to the Naval Academy."

Inside, she wailed in protest. Aloud, she said only, "What happened to our plan?" For a year and a half, they'd discussed attending the University of Maryland at College Park together. They'd both been accepted, and she'd taken for granted that their immediate future was settled. "Since when did you apply to the Academy? Without one word about it to me?" From her sister Linda's husband, a Naval Academy graduate, she knew acceptance came at the end of a long, multi-stage process. Thad couldn't have taken this step on a sudden impulse.

He stared at his feet instead of meeting her glare. "You knew I used to think about following my uncle into the Navy."

"Yeah, but I thought you dropped the idea ages ago. You're supposed to go to College Park and become an engineer."

"I can be an engineer in the Navy, too." Now he turned to face her. "I didn't tell you about applying because I knew how you'd react. Getting in was such a long shot that I figured, why mention it until it was a done deal? I'd probably get turned down, and you'd never have to know I tried."

"Of all the underhanded, cowardly—" She sprang to her feet. He pulled her back down onto the bench, and she let him, but she snatched her hand out of his. "So you sneak around, plotting this behind my back, and then spring it on me out of nowhere. After last night!"

His face reddened. "I didn't want to spoil the prom by bringing it up beforehand."

"Or spoil the make-out session afterward?" She couldn't suppress a flash of satisfaction when he flinched.

His voice roughened. "I didn't want to get into a giant fight. What's so horrible about this, anyway? I'm not vanishing off the face of the earth. I'll be right here in Annapolis."

"I know enough about plebe year to know I'd be lucky to see you more than an hour at a time until next May. Besides, why would I stay in a relationship with a guy who's headed for a Navy career? The last thing I want is to end up like my sister." After all she'd heard from Linda, ten years older and a Navy wife for the past seven years, about the trials and tribulations of military families, Val had rejected any idea of following that path. *Abandon my home, family, and friends, maybe lose any hope of a steady career?* Not that she and Thad, at eighteen, were officially engaged, but they'd discussed sharing a life, if only on a fantasy level so far.

"Does she make it sound that bad?"

"Oh, she just gripes in a humorous way, but I can read between the lines. Leaving everything and everybody I know, moving every couple of years? No, thanks." She stood up again, and he didn't try to stop her. "Have a great summer, what little of it you'll get to enjoy."

He matched her cold tone. "So we're leaving it like this?"

"What else is there to say?" She turned her back on him and grabbed her bike. Tears stung her eyes as she pedaled furiously home. She had the sense, even racked by clashing emotions, not to burden him with her deeper qualms. It wasn't as if he could say anything to soothe her fears. *People in the service can die!* A friend of Ron, her sister's husband, had been killed in Afghanistan only a month ago. Linda's e-mails had revealed how shaken the event had left her, even though she'd said little about it. *What if we do end up married and then Thad goes out and gets himself killed?*

Over the following week, Val avoided Thad as much as living in adjacent houses would allow. She didn't return his tentative greetings across the yard. At graduation on Friday evening, she didn't speak to him, to her parents' bewilderment. Less than two months later, he reported to the Academy for plebe summer, essentially boot camp for future officers. Later in his first year, when he was allowed contact with the outside world, she refused to see him on his weekend visits home and ignored his phone calls and e-mails. She had her own college freshman year to adjust to, and why complicate her life by setting herself up for heartbreak?

****

She'd gotten over her outrage at what she'd seen as Thad's betrayal, but she hadn't changed her mind about the breakup. What would be the point of starting down a road that couldn't lead anywhere? Why risk falling in love again with a man whose lifestyle she didn't want to share? *Is there actually a risk of that? Can't we go back to being friends?* The memory of his passionate words and kisses, though, threatened to sabotage that possibility. Locking away those unwelcome thoughts, she signed onto her computer in the spare bedroom she used as an office.

She peered through her silver-rimmed glasses at the latest e-mail from her sister. Linda currently lived in Florida with her Navy pilot husband and four children. The message reprised a familiar refrain: "Any new developments about selling the house?"

Val clicked Reply, typed, "If there were, I would've told you," deleted the sentence, and started over. "Just what I told you right after the Realtor looked at it. It'll need a ton of repairs before we can put it on the market, starting with replacing the roof. Big bucks."

After five minutes of scanning the contents of the in-box, she received a new message from Linda: "Thought about a home equity loan?"

Since their mother had used part of their father's life insurance to pay off the mortgage, they owned the property free and clear. Val's budget would stretch thin to make payments on her half of a loan until the proceeds of a sale could pay it off, though. She pointed out this problem to Linda, adding, "And I don't think you really want to commit to that, either, do you?"

With a sad emoticon as punctuation, her sister replied, "True that. Every extra dollar goes to Walt's college fund. Which is why we need the house sold ASAP." Well aware of that need already, with her oldest nephew starting his senior year of high school the following month, Val sent a brief upbeat response. Linda shot back, "BTW, on Facebook I noticed Thad's stationed in Annapolis now. Planning to see him?"

Val sent, "Not if I can help it," and closed the e-mail program to evade any forthcoming sisterly advice.

Just as she switched off the computer, a yowl from downstairs made her jump with alarm. She scurried to the living room. Toby crouched in the middle of the carpet, his ears flattened and tail lashing. He glared at the corner where the television sat in its niche, flanked by shelves of DVDs. His cry segued into a drawn-out growl she'd never heard from him. She tiptoed closer, reaching out but afraid to touch the fur that bristled along his back. Following the direction of his stare, she asked, "What's wrong with you? Something behind the TV?"

He paid no attention to her. She sidled around him and peered into the corner. With only a single end-table lamp lit on the other side of the room, she couldn't get a good look. *I hope it's not a mouse. Or, dear God, a snake.* Behind her, Toby's growl modulated into a hiss. She thought she glimpsed movement behind the TV case. Did something rustle? With the cat making so much noise, she couldn't be sure. There—the electric cords moved as if something had disturbed them. She straightened up and glanced at Toby.

He leaped at something that darted from behind the TV. All she saw was a flash of white, gone so quickly it could have been an optical illusion. The cat sprinted through the dining room into the kitchen. Val ran after him. When she got there, she found him in the middle of the linoleum floor, the tip of his tail flicking from side to side and his fur still standing up in a ridge along his spine. She saw no sign of his quarry, though. Naturally, the door leading into the garage was closed. If the fleeing creature, whatever it was, had veered off to the dining room or the den, Toby would have chased it there. With a flashlight, she checked under the stove and behind the refrigerator. Nothing but dust.

"Way to go," she said to the cat. "You flushed out some kind of creepy-crawly and then lost it. Now I have to spend all night worrying if it's loose in the house." He sat down and licked his front paws, each in turn, with his ears twitching as if he acknowledged her scolding but couldn't bother with a response. "Best case, it was just a big, white moth. I could live with that."

After one more scan of the kitchen and a survey of the dining room, just in case, she succumbed to second thoughts and checked the den and laundry room as well. Nothing. In the den, she did notice that the high-backed, rattan papasan chair, another souvenir her grandfather had picked up in Japan, was sitting in the middle of the floor instead of where it belonged. She'd taken photos of it the evening before to compare with online images of furniture of similar origin and age, in case it might be valuable enough to bother selling. Probably she'd repositioned it for better lighting and absentmindedly neglected to move it back. She shrugged at her own flakiness and tugged the chair into its usual corner.

After pouring herself a glass of Riesling, she settled on the living-room couch to watch a nature program she'd recorded earlier in the week. Toby curled up next to her with his plumed tail over his nose. She stroked him to calm herself.

Halfway through the life cycle of dolphins, she glimpsed movement from the corner of her eye. *Is it back?* She glanced up and located the disturbance above the fireplace. The two ivory figurines on the mantel, which her grandfather had bought in Japan, the ones she'd been seeking documentation for, twitched their limbs. The dragon spread its lacy batwings and glided to the edge of the hearth. The octopus stretched its tentacles and crept down the fire-guard screen. Toby uncurled his long, fluffy body, flexed his claws, and hissed.

Val slowly pulled herself to her feet, clutching the wing-backed end of the couch. "You see that?" she whispered. *Maybe that's what happened to the cat statuette. It got up and walked away, too.*

The dragon and octopus scrabbled onto the carpet, their respective legs and tentacles clicking like a handful of dice. The cat lashed his tail and hissed again. Her breath caught in her throat. *This is not happening.* She flapped both hands at the animated figurines. They halted, the dragon's wings vibrating and four of the octopus's limbs suspended off the floor. Toby sprang at them. They both skittered up the screen to their places on the mantel.

Val collapsed onto the couch, trembling, with her face in her hands.

When her pulse slowed, she peeked between her fingers. The dragon and octopus sat in the positions they'd occupied ever since her family had bought the house. Toby jumped onto the cushion beside her and licked his tail. "That didn't happen, right?" she asked him. He blinked at her. "I dozed off and had a really weird dream." After her hands stopped shaking, she gulped the rest of her wine, turned off the TV, and went upstairs, where she lay awake staring into the dark until exhaustion silenced the turmoil in her brain.

Chapter Two

She woke in the middle of the night, not an unusual event, since she still hadn't become completely used to sleeping in her parents' bedroom. Even after replacing the mattress and redecorating with new drapes, bedspread, and linens, she'd needed a while to nerve herself to the logical step of moving out of her cramped, ten-by-twelve-foot childhood room. Now and then she still imagined the lingering ghostly fragrances of her mother's cologne and bath powder. This time, though, she had the impression that something besides her own restless brain had awakened her. She sat up, straining her ears. Did she hear a rustling sound from the attached bathroom?

"Toby, are you in there?" She shuffled into the bathroom. No sign of the cat or any other living creature. After using the toilet and flushing it, she jumped at a noise from behind the shower curtain. Not a rustle so much as a slither.

The plastic rippled. She grasped the edge of it. "Toby?" She swept the curtain open.

A screech burst from her. She stumbled backward and collapsed on the bath mat, with a jarring thump to her rear end. "What the holy hell is that?"

A hunchbacked creature about two feet tall was huddled in the tub. Brick-red, naked except for a ragged loincloth of the same color, it had a mop of stringy, black hair and elongated fingers and toes with nails like claws.

It was licking the tile walls with a long, sinuous tongue like a frog's. Its saucer-like, black eyes stared at her. With a stifled "eep!" it blinked out of existence.

Trembling, Val clutched the edge of the sink and hoisted herself upright. She scurried into the bedroom and dove under the covers like a child fleeing the boogeyman.

She lay there with her lids squeezed shut until her pulse slowed to normal. *I did not see that, I did not.* She opened her eyes and gazed into the darkness, softened only by the night light from the open bathroom door. "What is with these crazy dreams all of a sudden?"

"You are not dreaming." The feminine voice sounded as if it came from somewhere in the middle of the room.

Val sat up with the sheet pulled to her neck. "Who's there?" She switched on the bedside light.

A slender, white cat leaped onto the end of the bed. The animal had emerald-green eyes and wore a red scarf around her neck. "Greetings and profound thanks for your hospitality. I assure you this is not a dream."

Val bent her knees to keep her feet out of the phantom feline's reach. "Is too. I must be still asleep. If not, how did you get in the house?"

Demurely seated at the foot of the bed, the cat curled her tail around her paws. "I have always been here. I was bound to the magic of the scroll, and your blood released that magic."

"You were in the scroll?"

"I was the statue. The scroll's enchantment locked me in that shape."

So the figurine did walk away by itself. Perfect dream logic. "Why?"

"I was enchanted for my own protection."

"Protection from what?" It couldn't hurt to have a polite chat with this figment of her imagination, even if her brain had concocted the whole scene. *Her mouth movements look like meows, but she speaks English. More dream logic, I guess.*

For a couple of seconds, the cat's shape wavered and became translucent. "I cannot remember."

"Not that it matters, because you aren't here. I'm dreaming." The cat vanished. Val said with a shaky laugh, "See, I told you so."

****

It was becoming difficult for Val to convince herself she'd dreamed all three strange incidents of the previous evening. By the time she finished getting dressed the next morning, though, she'd managed that feat. After all, otherwise she'd have to accept that either her house was haunted by supernatural entities, which she'd never believed in, or she was losing her mind. *Definitely dreams, then.*

The condition of her bathroom didn't support this conclusion, however. The stains on the grout between the shower tiles had disappeared overnight. In fact, closer inspection revealed that every surface except the ceiling looked freshly scrubbed. On a hunch, she checked the upstairs hall bathroom. It looked equally pristine although she hadn't cleaned it in a week, since the previous Saturday. She'd never sleepwalked in her life, and even if she'd started now, she doubted she would be sleep-cleaning. *So it's magic? Come on!* If her hallucinations wanted to do the housework for her, though, she wouldn't complain. Laughing and shaking her head to dismiss the notion, she headed to the kitchen for breakfast.

"What do you think, Toby?" she said a while later as she set her cereal bowl on the floor to let the cat lap up the dregs of the milk. "Is there a ghost cat around here?" She had to admit he'd been acting nervous that morning, prowling along the baseboards and staring into corners as if tracking invisible prey.

"If we have been invaded by a feline spirit," she mused aloud, "what does that have to do with a goblin that cleans bathrooms?" A quick glance at the half-bath off the den revealed that it had received similar treatment. *Whatever happened, I'll have less housework to do this weekend. I'd rather have a fairy godmother than a goblin, though.*

Certain she would think of a more rational explanation after fresh air and human contact, she scribbled a grocery list and headed for the car. Outside, she waved to Mr. Garrett, a retired accountant, getting into his own car with a golf bag. He seemed to spend all his free time at the course, weather permitting—and occasionally in weather Val wouldn't think of enduring for a mere game. She resisted the impulse to ask whether Thad had started his assignment at the Naval Academy yet. She would learn his status soon enough whether she wanted to or not.

After her usual Saturday morning routine of shopping, cleaning, and lunch, she delved into her grandfather's box again. She rummaged through stacks of letters she wanted to read sometime but unearthed no documents relevant to the ivory pieces. Giving up on the search for the present, she repacked most of the contents the way she'd found them and shoved the box to one end of the kitchen table. She set aside the letters to take upstairs for bedtime reading. *Maybe I should scan the most interesting ones and e-mail them to Linda.* Unable to invent any other excuse to avoid tackling the overgrown lawn, she rolled the mower out of the garage. The August heat and humidity, which dampened her hair and made her T-shirt stick to her skin after a few minutes of shoving the machine through the thick grass, tempted her to postpone the chore until the following day. But she knew she wouldn't feel any more like mowing then, either, so she forced herself to persevere. Weeds tickled her ankles, and she itched from perspiration and stray blades of grass. Less than fifteen minutes after she'd started, the machine sputtered to a halt.

Muttering a curse, she turned off the motor and knelt on the ground for a closer look. She didn't need gas or oil, since she'd topped them off the last time she'd mowed. Maybe the blades were clogged. She tilted the mower onto its side and started pulling clumps of grass from the undercarriage.

At that moment, a forest-green sports car parked at the curb in front of the Garretts' house. Thad got out and immediately waved to her. She tossed off a casual "Hi," hoping he wouldn't pause for anything more. No such luck.

"Having mechanical problems?" He strode across the yard to loom over her.

"Not sure. I hope it's just clogged." What a time for him to show up, when she was sticky and grubby, dressed in faded shorts and grass-stained tennis shoes. Not only that, her sweat-dampened hair and bangs needed a trim and even more than usually resembled what Linda called a "shaggy sheepdog cut." Not that Val wanted to impress Thad with her ravishing beauty, but did he have to look so cool and sharp by contrast, in a polo shirt and crisp khaki shorts? She couldn't claim he hadn't changed a bit since the age of eighteen. If anything, he'd improved. His lean swimmer's build had filled out without making him musclebound. The boyish face she recalled had firmed up. Lines were etched in the tanned skin around his hazel eyes, probably from sun exposure at sea. He wore his thick, seal-brown hair shorter now, though not in an extreme military buzz cut. She got to her feet, brushing off her knees. At six foot two, he stood a head taller than she.

"Want me to take a look?" Without waiting for an answer, he examined the blades of the mower, then turned it right side up to check the exposed parts. He asked about gas and oil, and she assured him both had been freshly filled. "Could be the spark plug," he said. "You might have to replace it, but if we're lucky, it'll just need cleaning. Do you happen to have a spark plug socket? Brake cleaning fluid?"

"Heck if I know." Of the tools and supplies stacked on the garage workbench and the shelves above it, she could have identified roughly half.

"I'm sure my dad has what we'll need. Hang on, I'll be right back."

She waited, finger-combing her hair and blushing at the realization that she came across like a helpless female who needed a man to rescue her from malfunctioning machinery. *But, hey, I'm a librarian, not a mechanic.*

He quickly returned with a spray can, a couple of tools, a rag, and a wire brush. She sat on the ground, arms wrapped around her bent knees, to watch him as he detached a wire from the spark plug at the front of the mower. "I was sorry to hear about your parents," he said.

"I can't imagine how rough it must have been to lose both of them before they even made it to seventy."

Her mother, who'd died the previous year, had almost made it that far. Her father had died six years earlier, in his mid-sixties. "Yeah, it was way too soon. Both of them smoked all their lives and couldn't quit no matter how many times they tried. We didn't know there was a thing wrong with Dad. He just dropped dead one day—heart. Mom had a series of strokes and never completely recovered from the last one. Then pneumonia hit her, and that was it." Val had to pause to swallow a lump clogging her throat. A trace of tears blurred her vision, although she thought she'd exhausted her need to cry months before. *It's not fair! Not when they were just getting to the stage where they could relax and enjoy life. They wanted to travel to Europe. They wanted see me get married and have children.* She knew *not fair* sounded like the cry of a little kid waiting for a turn on the playground slide. Yelling at God or Fate, though, suited her better than the alternative of blaming her parents for smoking themselves into early graves.

"Sorry I couldn't make it to either funeral. I would've, but…"

She shook her head, brushing her bangs off her damp forehead as an excuse to wipe her eyes clear. "Don't apologize. You were stationed thousands of miles away." He'd sent flowers and a card each time.

Thad unscrewed and removed the plug. After squirting it with liquid from the can, he scrubbed at the threads with the brush. Meanwhile, she flipped the mower over again and worked at the grass clumps in the blades. "I heard from Mom that you work for the state government," he said. "What happened to the library career?"

"That hasn't changed," she said. "I'm a librarian for the Department of Legislative Services downtown."

"Oh, haunting the corridors of power?" His lips quirked in a teasing smile.

She laughed. "More like haunting a cubicle in the basement." *This isn't so bad after all. We can talk like old friends. Nobody grows up to marry the boy next door nowadays, anyhow.*

Within ten minutes, he dried the spark plug, set the mower upright, reattached the part, and reconnected the wire. "Try it now," he said.

The engine started right away. "That's great, thanks." She couldn't brush him off with no more than that after he'd gone out of his way to help her, could she? "I don't feel like finishing the lawn right this minute. Would you like to come in for a glass of tea?" To her annoyance, her pulse accelerated as she raised her voice to talk over the engine noise.

He switched off the mower and met her gaze for a second, then shifted his attention to the supplies he was gathering up. "Sure, why not?" He set aside the tools and clasped her hand to help her up.

Shivers coursed up her arm. She blushed, broke the contact as quickly as possible, swept grass off her shorts, and headed for the house. "Let's sit in the den." The formality of the living room would lend the encounter too much importance. She led the way through the gate into the back yard and across the patio to the sliding glass door that opened onto the den. The chill of the air conditioner rushed over her heated skin. While he washed his hands in the half-bath, she cleaned up in the kitchen sink and splashed cool water on her cheeks, then poured two glasses of iced tea. When she walked into the den, where Thad was already seated on the couch, she noticed the papasan chair looked a couple of feet out of place. *I definitely put that back where it belonged, didn't I?*

Accepting a glass from her, he waved at the small television across the room from him. "Don't tell me that's the same TV we used to play video games on?"

She nodded, taking a seat at the other end of the couch. The worn cushions sagged under her weight. "We never had a reason to get rid of it. Of course, if I play anything at all now, it's on the computer."

"Do you still have your fantasy trading cards, too?"

"Sure." Torn between love for the collection she'd spent so much money on and reluctance to face the memories it held, she'd compromised by storing it in a box on her closet shelf. A pang pierced her as images of their countless games in this very room floated to the surface of her mind. She had no desire to linger on their shared past, though, any more than to unpack and sift through those decks of cards. Instead, she congratulated him on his Naval Academy assignment. "You must be awfully busy getting ready for fall term." *Could I sound more like I memorized that line from an etiquette book?*

"Classes don't start until the third week of August, so I've got a couple of weeks for orientation meetings, setting up my office, stuff like that."

"What about a place to live? You aren't moving in with your parents, are you?" That idea hadn't occurred to her until this moment, and she hoped her horror at the thought didn't show on her face.

He raised both hands in a warding-off gesture. "You've got to be kidding. Hell, no, and I decided not to live in quarters, either. I've rented an apartment two blocks from the main gate. In decent weather I can jog to work, then change in the gym." Scanning the room as if comparing it with his memories, he paused at her teenage swimming trophies gathering dust on a bookshelf. "Do you still belong to the community pool?" He must be groping for safe conversation as desperately as she was.

"Sure, even if I don't have as much time for it as I used to." As teenagers, they'd competed on the neighborhood swim team together several seasons in a row and, in the summer before their senior year, had worked as lifeguards at the pool. She'd been slender and fit then. Now, at over thirty, only occasional swimming and regular exercise-bike riding kept her waistline in check. Did Thad like her curvier adult body as much as he had her eighteen-year-old one? *Stop that. Wrong thinking!* Projecting teenage passion into the present didn't fit into the uncomplicated friendship she wanted. *If I keep telling myself that's all I want, it'll be true, right?*

He grinned. "Remember the first time our families went swimming together?"

"How could I forget? We were thirteen years old, and the first thing you did was throw my flip-flops into the deep end."

"Yeah, good times." His smile widened.

She relaxed a little. They had plenty to reminisce about without revisiting that last fight. "We did have some good times, even if I don't count frantically swimming for my sandals as one of them."

"Like the gaming club."

He'd talked her into joining, one of only two girls in the group. She had enjoyed collecting the cards, although more for the art than the competition. "And that Halloween party in our senior year, when we dressed up as our favorite characters from a galaxy far, far away." He'd made a dashing interstellar smuggler. "You kept telling everybody not to quote you the odds."

"You looked great in that princess costume." Did a wistful note creep into his voice?

She evaded his gaze and tried to lighten the moment with, "Only if the princess had strawberry blonde hair. Mom wouldn't let me dye it dark brown, and I couldn't find a decent wig." Back then, her hair had been long enough to wind into a pair of buns. She preferred its current low-maintenance length. How had they wandered onto this byway of memory lane, anyhow? She'd forgotten how many strands of her teenage experience had been intertwined with his...

What's that? A movement in the corner of her eye snagged her attention. The cat? Toby was nowhere in sight. Did the papasan chair spontaneously shift a couple of inches? *No, that did not happen. I didn't see a thing.*

"What's wrong?" Thad leaned forward, his glass cupped in both hands. "You drifted off for a second."

"Nothing. Just woolgathering." She didn't need him to think she'd gone bonkers.

"So maybe we'll be seeing more of each other for a while. You planning to live here permanently?"

She shook her head. "Too much house for me. I can't afford to buy out Linda's half and handle the maintenance and taxes. Anyway, Linda needs the money for her kids' college and stuff, and I could use it, too." After their father's death, his life insurance had gone to pay off the house and other debts. Val's mom herself hadn't carried a very large policy, and it had been gobbled up by funeral expenses, leftover medical bills, and balances on the two sisters' credit cards. Thad didn't want or need to hear any of that dreary stuff, though. "The thing is, before we can sell the place, it needs a ton of repair and renovation, especially the roof. That's why I dug out my granddad's souvenirs from Japan."

Thad straightened up and set his glass on the coffee table. "Japan? What kind of souvenirs?"

"Right, you used to have a thing for Japanese culture—anime and all that."

"Still do. I got more into it while I was stationed in Yokosuka for a couple of years."

"You might remember the ivory dragon and octopus on the fireplace mantel upstairs." The ones that did *not* go for a stroll the night before. "First off, I was looking for an invoice or whatever so I might be able to sell them online. I need to get the roof fixed before I can even think about putting the house on the market."

"You know, I get the feeling you don't really want to give up the place."

She started to blurt out a denial but forced herself to answer honestly. "Maybe not. I admit I'm not crazy about the idea of leaving the home I've lived in most of my life. It feels like cutting my ties with Mom and Dad. Silly, huh?" She forced a smile and shrugged. "It's not as if I have much choice, though. Like I said, I can't handle the upkeep on a house this size. Besides, we need the money, especially Linda. Anyhow, getting back to Granddad's souvenir box, I didn't find the paperwork I was looking for. The main thing I came across was some kind of scroll." No point in mentioning the cat figurine, which still hadn't turned up. "Wait here. I'll show it to you."

She hurried to the kitchen and came back with the scroll.

He stood up and leaned over her shoulder while she unrolled the picture. His breath tickled her neck, sending shivers rippling through her. She edged away. When she glanced at him, his face reddened. "Cool," he said, looking away from her to fix his gaze on the scroll. "It's a wall hanging, maybe from the nineteenth century. Probably not worth enough money to bother selling it." He trailed a fingertip over the shadowy figure of the woman.

The papasan chair scooted across the floor and halted beside him.

Val went lightheaded for a second. *I'm not dreaming now. So I'm definitely losing it.* She could have dreamed the talking cat, walking figurines, and tub-crawling goblin the night before. She could have turned into a somnambulist overnight and scrubbed the bathrooms in her sleep. But this? Maybe she'd better visit her doctor for a referral to a neurologist. *Or a shrink.*

Thad whirled around and stared at the chair. "How did you do that?"

"Do what?"

"Come on, since when does your furniture move by itself?" He rapped his knuckles on the rattan chair-back.

"Wait, you saw that?"

"Well, yeah. Hard to miss."

"Then I'm not crazy?"

"Not unless it's contagious." He set down the scroll and made a show of examining the chair, even flipping the seat cushion. "No wheels, no wires."

A washing machine with an unbalanced load could shuffle across a floor like a monster from a mad scientist's lab, but ordinary furniture couldn't. "It might've been a minor earthquake." If he'd seen the anomaly, too, there had to be a natural explanation.

"I didn't feel a tremor, did you? Anyway, how often does Maryland have earthquakes?"

"Not very," she conceded.

"Plus, one strong enough to cause that would have knocked things off shelves. I've served in California and Japan, so I know quakes. That wasn't one." He carefully took a seat in the chair. Nothing happened.

"Then what else could've caused it?"

"Magic? If I weren't a hardheaded engineer, I might wonder if this place was haunted." His grin assured her he wasn't serious.

She managed to smile back at him. "By what? This is an ordinary two-story-plus-basement tract house, less than forty years old. My parents were only the second owners. And I'm pretty sure the developers didn't desecrate an ancient native burial ground." The impulse to tell him about the other incidents flitted across her mind. *No, those didn't happen. They can't have anything to do with this.*

As if reading and refuting her thought, he said, "Your granddad bought this chair in Japan, too, right?"

She nodded.

He dug his wallet out of a side pocket and produced a typical Navy calling card printed with his name and rank only. "Got a pen handy?"

"In the kitchen."

He followed her to a kitchen counter where a coffee can crammed with an assortment of pens and pencils sat next to the phone. He jotted his number on the card. "That's my cell. If you need help with researching

Japanese artifacts or—or anything, give me a call."

"Thanks." Her pulse accelerating when their fingers brushed, she pocketed the card. "Now, thanks loads for the repair job, but I'd better finish the lawn."

On the way to the front door, he said, "I'm staying for dinner with the folks. Why don't you come over?"

Aargh, how awkward would that be? "No, thanks. I wouldn't want to impose on your first evening home. Maybe some other time." *After Hell freezes over, so we can go on an ice-skating date.* She inwardly cringed at the thought of facing his parents across the table while they speculated on Thad's and her potential relationship.

Did he cast a disappointed look over his shoulder before his nonchalant "Bye"? The expression faded too fast for her to be sure. As she went outside and restarted the mower, she wondered whether he hoped they might get back together. *After all those years of water under multiple bridges? Definitely not in the cards. Magic or not.* She plowed the mower through the thickest clump of stubborn grass and let the roar of the engine blot out all such thoughts.

****

While Val rode her exercise bike in a corner of the den that evening, watching an episode of a vintage cozy mystery series on her tablet, Toby slinked into the room and hissed at nothing she could see. "Not again! What is it now, poltergeists?" That was an idea she hadn't considered before. She could believe in a poltergeist shifting figurines and furniture more easily than she could accept outright magic. The papasan chair, if nothing else, had moved in full sight of a presumably sane second person, so *something* was going on outside her own head.

The cat stared at the couch, his tail lashing and fur puffed up. A white shape darted from behind the couch and dashed across the floor. Toby pounced and missed. Yowling, he chased the thing out of the room.

With a sigh, Val dismounted from the bike and hurried after him into the kitchen. He crouched, emitting a long, low growl, in front of a creature huddled against the door that led to the garage. A cat—the white, green-eyed cat she'd "dreamed" the night before—shimmered and turned translucent.

Chapter Three

"No, don't disappear. I've got to know whether you're real." The cat's form solidified. Val stooped to shoo Toby away, apprehensive about touching him in this mood. He backed up inch by inch and finally sprinted into the den. She closed the door behind him, then turned to the white cat. "Did you actually talk to me last night?"

The strange feline stalked into the middle of the floor and sat with her tail curled around her front paws as her bristling fur gradually smoothed. "Certainly. After all, we are both rational beings."

"We are? I've been having doubts about that."

"Is magic unfamiliar to you?"

Val plopped into a chair at the kitchen table. "Most people in this country don't believe it exists."

"How odd."

"Uh—would you like something to eat?"

"That is kind of you. I do not need food, but I can enjoy it."

What to give her? She seems too sophisticated for cat food. Val opened a can of tuna and served a bit on a saucer, placing it on the floor next to a bowl of water. After nibbling the tuna and lapping at the water, the cat licked both of her front paws in turn. "I wouldn't have expected a ghost to eat," Val said.

"I am not a ghost. I am a *yokai*." The animal leaped onto a chair and gazed up at Val.

Yoke-eye? "A what?"

"A kind of spirit, you would say, I suppose, but not of a dead creature."

"If you're a Japanese spirit," Val asked, "how are you speaking English?"

"I am not, as far as I know. I believe we understand each other because your blood awakened me."

"I'm beginning to think this is really happening. If not, it's one fascinating dream." She picked up the dishes from the floor and rinsed them. "You don't remember why you got magicked into that scroll?"

"I have remembered part of it. Not enough to be certain whether I am safe from whatever the danger was or whether I have brought danger to you."

"Let's worry about that later. Tell me what you do know, please." Val returned to her seat at the table and gazed at the cat, half afraid the animal would vanish at any second.

"My name is Yuki. Before I was bound to the scroll, I dwelt in the shrine of a minor *kami*."

"What's a *kami*?"

"You would say a god, I suppose. This was a very small god, the spirit of a stream that flowed beside the shrine. I guarded the place from vermin. An *onmyoji* named Hiroshi often visited to pray to the *kami*." As if anticipating Val's next question, she said, "A worker of magic. He was also a gifted painter. We grew to love each other. When he learned of the danger that threatened me, Hiroshi painted the magical scroll you now possess and enchanted me into the form of a statue. As long as I remained in that form, my enemy could not harm or even find me."

This sounds like a fairy tale, a man falling in love

with a cat spirit. But if it's more than that… "So it's my fault you're exposed to whatever this danger is," Val said. "Who's your enemy?"

Yuki flicked her tail in apparent frustration. "I still cannot remember."

"Maybe he's dead. How long ago did all this happen?"

"I have no way of knowing. While under the spell, I had no awareness of anything, including the passage of time." Yuki meditatively licked a paw, then asked, "Where are we, and when is now?"

"The United States of America, twenty-first century." Val told her the exact date.

The cat's whiskers twitched. "Alas, your measurements of years mean nothing to me. The only clue I can offer is that, when I was last aware, Emperor Ninko ruled our land."

With Val's limited knowledge of Japanese history, she'd never heard that name. "He's not one of the emperors in my or my parents' lifetimes."

Yuki lay down in a disconsolate puddle of white fur, her tail drooping over the edge of the chair. "Then Hiroshi must certainly be dead by now. Yet I would still wish to go home if I could." She raised her head to meet Val's eyes. "I should be able to tell you what has become of the magic in the scroll. Where is it?"

"Right here." Val opened the box that still sat on the table, where she'd replaced the artifact after showing it to Thad. She took it out and unrolled it.

The cat placed a paw on the corner where the droplet of Val's blood had spotted the silk. "As I thought, most of the magic has leaked out and taken up residence in your home. Just enough remains to tie me to the vicinity of the scroll. I discovered that yesterday, when I tested how far I could wander."

"Oh, that's why you were running around Mrs. Garrett's yard."

Yuki's mouth formed an almost human smile. "The elderly lady who chased me away? Quite so. Unless I find someone who can break the remnant of the spell, I must stay near my painted image."

Val touched the picture of the cat in front of the shrine. "That's you?"

"Yes, and the painted woman also. My kind can assume human form for brief periods."

"And my house is infested with magic?" *I have a feeling it won't be as easy to eradicate as roaches.* "That's why knickknacks and furniture have started walking around?"

"Yes, the unleashed enchantment affects objects that came from my place and time."

Val decided that if she wasn't suffering an elaborate hallucination, that hypothesis explained a lot. "Where does the red goblin in the bathroom come in?"

"You saw the *akaname*? Its whole purpose for existence is to clean baths. I am not surprised the magic is attracting other *yokai*."

"I don't mind housecleaning spirits," Val said, "but I don't like the idea of getting invaded by a horde of random creatures. Or having to capture wandering chairs before I can sit on them."

The cat stretched. "Why did you not tell your man about me when he witnessed the chair moving?"

A blush warmed Val's cheeks. "Because I didn't want him to think I'm a raving lunatic. Anyway, he's not my man. We're just old friends. You saw him?"

"I was hidden under the sofa. I considered showing myself but decided not to interrupt. It appeared to me that you shared more than friendship."

"That's over. We were kids then. We'd already been friends a long time before it turned into—something more. His family moved next door to mine the summer we were both thirteen, about to start the eighth grade. Riding the bus together to middle school, naturally we got to know each other fast." Noticing Yuki's blank stare, Val realized she'd lost the cat at *bus* and *middle school*. "Things have changed a lot since you were in any condition to be aware, I guess."

"I wonder how long it has been. I would prefer to know the worst."

"That should be easy to check online." Val walked upstairs, half expecting her visitor to pop out of existence and reappear in the office. She padded up the steps in the normal feline way, though.

She sat on the floor staring up at the computer as Val signed on and navigated the search engine. "How wondrous, a box that makes pictures and sounds. Yet I do not sense magic."

"No magic, just science. Electronics. Bits and bytes." She shrugged. "Don't ask me to explain. I'm a librarian, not a techie." She connected to a page on Emperor Ninko. "His reign ended in 1846, so that's the latest year you could be remembering. About a hundred and seventy years ago."

Yuki emitted a soft mewl of distress and lay flat on her stomach with her forepaws crossed in front of her. "There may be nothing left of my home," she whispered.

"It can't be as bad as that. Japan is an ancient country with loads of history." Val entered a search for

"Images, Japan" and clicked through a dozen pictures.

The cat watched in a posture of wary tension, her ears and whiskers slanted back. She exclaimed at one point, "What is *that*?"

Val enlarged the image. "The Tokyo Tower." Studying the white and orange lattice-like construction that reminded her of the Eiffel Tower, with a needle point of an antenna on top, surrounded by urban high-rises, she realized why it must come as a shock to her visitor. Yuki edged away from the desk as if she expected the building to come to life and leap out at her. "But it's not all like that." Val kept clicking until she landed on a photo of a shrine similar to the one pictured on the scroll.

The cat stood on her hind legs and placed one paw on Val's knee. "Then some traces of my old world survive."

After running through a slide show of shrines, Val displayed an image of Mount Fuji. "See, the land itself hasn't changed."

The cat vanished, leaving a ghost of a whispered "Thank you" behind.

Her head spinning, Val sagged in the chair and let out a long breath. *Did that really happen?* The browser on the computer still showed Mount Fuji, so she had run the search she remembered, at least. She went downstairs and opened the door to the den. Toby stalked into the kitchen, with his tail held high and the tip flicking to declare his indignation. To atone for offending him, she fed him the rest of the canned fish. "So that's what you've been trying to tell me. We have a supernatural incursion."

Could the conversation with Yuki have been another

dream? Val couldn't cling to that hypothesis, not after such a concrete, detailed incident. Besides, the saucer in the sink, still containing traces of tuna, validated her memory. *I met a talking spirit cat.*

She knelt to stroke Toby. "Now what? She doesn't want to stay here forever, and I suspect you'd take a dim view of having her in the house. But I can't just throw her out. She'd be lost in this century."

****

A peal of thunder woke her. The digital alarm clock read 3:17 a.m. Seconds afterward, lightning flashed, with another thunderclap in its wake. *Funny, the weather forecast didn't mention a storm.* Without turning on the lamp, she groped her way to the window and peeked between the drapes. The frame rattled in a gust of wind. Another lightning bolt flashed, followed almost instantly by thunder. *Good grief, it's right on top of us.*

Brightness flared in the back yard. She blinked her dazzled eyes and struggled to focus on the thing—a globe of blue fire that zipped from tree to tree. As it collided with each obstacle, sparks shot from it. *Ball lightning.* She had read about the phenomenon but never expected to see it.

Yet another roll of thunder left her ears ringing. The bedside clock and the bathroom night light switched off. *Oh, great, power failure.* In the darkness outside, a second glowing object appeared. More ball lightning? No, this new apparition looked like a huge, white wolf outlined by blue fire. It chased the globe around the yard like the Hound of the Baskervilles playing with a basketball. She rubbed her eyes, wondering whether the blinding flashes of light had triggered some kind of optical illusion.

The wolf launched itself into the treetops, electric blue flames crackling around it. The creature lunged at the window. Val staggered backward with a screech and landed on the bed.

"*Raiju*," a voice said beside her.

"Huh?" She glanced wildly around. In the darkness, barely relieved by intermittent flashes from the globe and the wolf-thing, she faintly made out the shape of the white cat sitting on the pillow. "What did you say?"

"That is a *raiju*. It is harmless."

"You guarantee that?"

"You have nothing to fear from it. Be grateful much worse things do not intrude on your peace." Yuki vanished.

The thunder and lightning abruptly cut off. "Must you pop in and out like the Cheshire Cat?" Val tiptoed to the window and peered out. The deserted yard looked perfectly normal. As far as she could see, the storm had come and gone without a drop of rain. Just as she turned toward the bed, the bathroom night light switched on, and the clock started blinking. *Thank Heaven for small favors.*

****

The next morning, a glance out the window revealed no sign of the previous night's weather anomaly except a few broken branches. While dressing for church, eating breakfast, and feeding Toby, she was half relieved and half annoyed that Yuki didn't show up. Val would have liked to ask her more about that *raiju* creature. *Maybe it was a fluke and won't come back.* If it existed at all. She was beginning to revert to the hope that she'd dreamed or imagined at least some of the weirdness. *On the other hand, would coming mentally unhinged be much better than a magical infestation?*

Bleary-eyed, she trudged to her car and flinched when Mrs. Garrett's front door opened. Val slid into the front seat a second too late to avoid the older woman's greeting. *This is ridiculous, being afraid of a neighbor I've known most of my life.* She answered with "Good morning" and a sketchy wave.

Mrs. Garrett halted in the middle of her front lawn with her arms folded. "Valerie, did you get a dog?"

"Good grief, no. Why would I do that?" She stepped out of the car and leaned on the open door.

"I didn't actually think you would, but it was running around your yard last night."

Val barely stopped herself from saying, "You saw the wolf with the blue flames, too?" Instead, she asked, "You mean that big, white dog?"

Mrs. Garrett nodded. "It was tearing around in circles during that freak thunderstorm. The couple on the other side of you have one, don't they?"

"Not that kind. Jake and Shawna have a little dachshund."

"Then it must have been a stray. If it shows up again, someone should call Animal Control."

"Good idea," Val said, glad to hear a remark she could agree with. "Anyway, I'm glad the electricity didn't stay off for long."

"You lost power? We didn't."

Lucky me, I had the magical power failure all to myself. "Really? Odd." With a farewell wave, she got into her car and started the motor before she could get mired in further conversation.

She wasn't sure whether to feel thankful or sorry to have confirmation of the wolf creature's reality. If it existed, maybe the other bizarre events weren't dreams or optical illusions, either. Her mind kept revolving in that hamster wheel of alternatives until she reached Saint Anne's downtown at the head of the half-mile, brick-paved Main Street. Since the historic church had no parking lot, she had to park over a block away, as usual. The walk to Church Circle made a pleasant stroll on a sunny summer morning, although not so welcome in rainy or freezing weather.

Reliving the conversation with the white cat left Val little brain space for concentrating on the rector's sermon. During the choir's offertory hymn, she mused on what he would say if she asked him about *yokai* and *kami*. Was it heretical or blasphemous to entertain belief in the god of a little shrine beside a stream? After some reflection, she tentatively concluded that a minor spirit of a place wasn't anywhere near on the same level as the Creator of the universe, and there was no contradiction in believing in both of them. Not that this idea brought her any closer to deciding what to do about Yuki. If the cat was bound to the scroll, she wouldn't leave unless the artifact were taken somewhere else. Val felt she could hardly just unload the thing at random, quite aside from her attachment to it as a souvenir of her grandfather.

Driving home, she wondered whether she would walk in the door to find more household items wandering around under their own power. Surely not, because Yuki had said the magic affected only objects from her place and time, hadn't she? In the driveway, Val paused to collect the Sunday paper and noticed Shawna in the side yard with her little girl, Dani, not quite two. At the sight of Val, their dachshund, Otto, scurried over to the chain-link fence and assailed it with frantic leaps. The young mother, with her hair in long braids the same tawny shade as her skin, picked up the toddler and walked over to greet Val. "That was some crazy storm last night, huh?"

"Yeah. My power went off. Did yours?" Val knew she might be getting obsessed with comparing notes on the weirdness but couldn't resist asking.

"Nope. Funny. Hey, did you see that huge, white dog streaking through the back yards? He jumped the fence from yours into ours. Otto freaked out, barking at the patio door."

Dani glanced down at the dachshund. "Where big doggie?"

"Not here anymore, hon," her mother said.

Well, that's another independent confirmation, Val thought as she parted from Shawna and went inside. Neighbors on both sides had seen the dog, wolf, whatever. Val wasn't sure whether to feel glad she probably wasn't losing her mind or horrified that reality as she knew it was shattering around her. It didn't help that when she walked into her bedroom to change clothes, she glimpsed a flash of movement in the bathroom. When she charged through the door to investigate, the brick-red goblin-thing stared at her for a second before it vanished with a squeak of alarm. Scanning the room, she noticed the black mildew spots on the ceiling above the shower had disappeared.

After putting on shorts and a T-shirt, she was hanging up her dress when Toby slinked into the bedroom, his fur puffed up. She followed the direction of his fixed glare. The white cat stood in the middle of the queen-size bed. "Why do you keep appearing out of thin air? Why don't you just hang around?"

Yuki stood and stretched. "My presence alarms your cat. I would not want to cause him constant distress."

"True, there is that." Val shooed Toby into the hall and closed the door.

"Besides, it takes a great deal of energy for me to maintain physical form. I think it has something to do with the spell that binds me to the scroll."

Val sat on the edge of the bed. The cat padded over to sit beside her and allowed Val to stroke her soft fur. It felt exactly like a normal animal's. "The bathroom goblin came back a minute ago, but it blinked out. It acts scared of me." A detached corner of her mind marveled that she'd passed beyond gibbering confusion to calm conversation with a feline spirit about impossible phenomena. *One shock too many and I've gone numb, I guess.*

"*Akaname* are indeed shy creatures. They do not like to be seen by humans."

"Should I be leaving him payment, maybe a saucer of milk or something?"

"No, his kind exist only to perform their work. They regard the task as its own reward."

"Oh, like the elves and the shoemaker." As soon as that story came to mind, Val remembered that fairy-ish beings tended to clear out if offered any reward, even clothes. "When it vanishes, is it still lurking around, invisible?" Her skin prickled at the thought of that grotesque thing creeping in corners, maybe leering at her from the shadows.

"No, it is simply gone," Yuki assured her.

"What about you? When you disappear, where are you?"

Yuki flicked her ears. "Nowhere. It is as if I fall into

a dreamless sleep. Should you ever wish for my presence, call me and I will—wake up, as it were."

Recalling scraps of the previous night's conversation, Val said, "You mentioned you can take human form."

"Easily." A white mist surrounded the cat. When the fog cleared, a woman in a lavender, floral print kimono perched on the edge of the mattress. She wore a red scarf identical to the one around the cat's neck. "My time in this shape is limited, though."

"You look exactly like the picture on the scroll."

"Of course. Hiroshi painted me from life."

Val glanced at Yuki's left hand. "Even the ring. Interesting design."

Yuki spread the fingers of her left hand to display the ring's rectangular stone. Its glossy, black surface was etched with a delicate, gold-toned spray of flowers and leaves. "It is called *shakudo*. A gift I received from a would-be suitor, long before I met Hiroshi." A wistful smile flitted across her lips.

"So his painting included a spell to bind you to the scroll. Does that mean wherever the scroll goes, so do you?"

The woman nodded with a graceful bow.

"So if I sent it far enough away, the magic would leave along with it?"

"As would I."

"It's a tempting thought. I won't be able to sell the house if it's effectively haunted." *But how could I get rid of the scroll? I can't just advertise it online and palm it off on an unsuspecting buyer.* On the other hand, if she admitted the haunting up front, some people might jump at the chance to own a magical artifact festooned with a flock of spirits. On the third hand, twinges of guilt pricked her at the idea of shipping Yuki away like an unwanted package. The cat-woman-spirit was a sentient being, after all. "If you had a choice, what would you do?"

"I would wish to go home."

Yuki's yearning tone and lost expression squeezed Val's heart. *No way can I throw her out alone in this strange century.* "If I shipped the scroll to Japan, you'd tag along with it, right?" *Except I don't know anybody over there to take custody of the thing.* Besides, that twenty-first-century nation wasn't Yuki's Japan. Unless she managed to find a new home in an antique shrine, she might feel almost as lost there as here, and how could she do that, tethered to her portrait? "I'll bet that ring is valuable. Unless you have a sentimental attachment to it, maybe if you got unbound from the scroll, you could sell the ring to buy a plane ticket." *Not that I have the slightest clue how to unbind her.*

"No, I would not mind parting with it. Plane?" The woman's eyebrows arched in puzzlement.

"Airplane. A machine that flies. When you get over there, you could try to find your old home or something like it."

"There are machines that fly like birds, and your people ride on them?"

"Not exactly. The wings don't flap, and we sit inside them. Like in a carriage." Yuki's face looked even more confused. "Never mind, I'll show you pictures if you want."

The woman flinched. Her form blurred and reverted to feline. "Another time, perhaps. Thank you." She vanished.

"Can't blame her for not wanting to face another barrage of what looks like bizarro world to her." Val rubbed her eyes, walked over to open the door, and peered up and down the hall. "Coast is clear, Toby. Where are you?" She hoped he hadn't panicked and hidden.

A second later, a furious yowl ripped through the silence. She hurried down the steps to the living room. Toby crouched in the middle of the carpet glowering at the ivory octopus, which scuttled crabwise a couple of feet from him. Meanwhile, the dragon dive-bombed him, swooping out of reach whenever he shifted his attention from the octopus to try a claw-swipe.

"Stop that right this instant!" Val snatched up a throw pillow and waved it at the dragon. The octopus inched closer to the cat. She grabbed another cushion and pitched it at the crawling figurine. It skittered backward. The dragon whirled around for another pass. She swatted it with the pillow she still held. "Back off! I don't want to break you. You're supposed to be my new roof."

Flapping erratically, the dragon skimmed a foot above the rug. Toby sprang at it. It launched itself upward and glided in circles around the lamp on the table at the end of the couch. "Get away from there!"

Her cat leaped onto the couch. "Toby, no!" She lunged toward him and tripped over the octopus. She fell forward onto the floor. Pain slammed through both knees. Cursing, she blinked tears from her eyes and levered herself upright. The cat jumped onto the back of the sofa and swatted at the dragon, which looped out of reach. Toby's paw hit the lamp and knocked it over. The bulb shattered with a tinkle of glass, while the dragon spiraled to a halt next to the cowering octopus. Toby jumped down and ran under the coffee table.

Val waved the cushion at the two figurines. "Get back where you belong. Shoo!" To her surprise, the dragon soared up to the mantel and alighted there, while the octopus crawled up the brickwork to take its usual place.

"You know," she said to Toby as she set the lamp upright on the end table, "if you keep freaking out, you're just encouraging them. And you!" She pointed at the figurines. "Stay put and behave yourselves, or you're going in a box." She stomped into the kitchen for a broom, dustpan, and bag to clear up the fragments of the broken bulb.

After the clean-up and a few minutes of soothing her indignant pet, she ran an Internet search for *shakudo*. The jewelry style, she read, was fashioned from an alloy of gold and copper specially treated to produce the dark patina. Gold, silver, or copper formed the inlaid decorative patterns. She found several images almost identical to Yuki's ring. On the auction sites, some sellers were asking four thousand dollars and up for similar pieces. Val realized she hadn't thought of asking Yuki whether the ring could be removed. Was it permanently attached to her finger by the magic of the painting? If so, selling the jewelry for plane fare was out. She would probably have mentioned that problem if it existed, though. *Moot point anyway, since I don't know how to set her free.*

Chapter Four

Another thunderstorm struck that evening at twilight. As Val sat reading in the den, a flash dazzled her eyes. Rubbing them, she walked over to peer through the sliding glass doors. No rain fell, but wind whipped the tree branches. Thunder boomed, and a neon-blue globe of ball lightning rolled onto the patio. It transformed into the white wolf she'd seen before, its outline etched in an electric-blue glow. The creature flung itself at the glass. Val emitted a stifled shriek and stumbled backward. Her heartbeat raced.

Behind her, Toby hissed. She whirled around to find him on a chair, poised to attack, with his fur bristling. "I don't blame you a bit," she said, annoyed at the tremor in her voice. *This should be routine for me by now, shouldn't it?*

When she turned back to the patio door, a second lupine shape charged across the lawn. This one had ash-gray fur streaked with autumnal brown, a bushy, white-tipped tail, and glowing, crimson eyes. It pounced at the other wolf. The blue-white one, the *raiju*, turned to snap at the grayish beast. The two creatures leaped into the air and chased each other from tree to tree, sparks flying from their fur, claws, and fangs.

"Yuki!"

The white cat materialized at Val's feet. "I am here."

"What is *that*?" Val pointed with a shaky hand at the second wolf. "Now I've got two of them?"

"That is not a *raiju*." Yuki's voice came out weak and tremulous. "That is—" She curled up and covered her eyes with the tip of her tail.

Val knelt beside her. "What is it? What's wrong?"

The cat raised her head. "It is an *okuri-okami*. I remember it now."

"A what?" Val glanced outside. The creatures were still charging and ripping at each other.

Another peal of thunder rattled the house. A crash sounded from above. "What was that?" She sprang to her feet and dashed for the stairs. Toby ran after her, trailed by the white cat. In the living room, he jumped onto the back of the couch to stare out the front window, while Yuki kept pace with Val. Just as Val reached the foot of the staircase, the doorbell rang. She caught her breath and hesitated with a hand on the knob. *What's to be nervous about? Spirit wolves probably don't ring bells before they barge in.*

She opened the door to find Thad on the porch. "What are you doing here?" *Way to be polite. Mom would give me ten lashes with a wet noodle.*

"I was hanging with the folks after dinner when I heard thunder. I looked outside and saw a limb break. I think it hit your house."

"I heard a noise and was just going to check. Come on in."

She stepped aside, and he followed as she hurried upstairs. "Hey, did you notice," he said, "that there's no wind anywhere except your yard?"

"Why am I not surprised?"

Glancing into her room and the office, she didn't find any damage. Thad called from the spare bedroom, "In here."

He'd turned on the overhead light. Wind gusted through a hole in the single window. The end of a branch poked through the jagged gap, and shards of glass littered the hardwood floor. "Oh, damn." She stalked to Thad's side and folded her arms, glaring at the mess.

He peered through the remains of the window at the gathering darkness. "What the hell are those?"

She looked out, too, disappointed that the wolf-things hadn't vanished. "What do you see?"

"You may not believe this, but I see two wolves with glowing fur zipping around in the trees."

"Thank God." She expelled a long sigh. "I thought either the whole world was going nuts or I was."

"If you're going, reserve me a seat on the same flight." He turned from the window toward her. "So you know what they are?"

She swallowed before working up the nerve to answer. "Would you believe a pair of Japanese demons conjured up by a magic scroll my granddad brought back from the Korean War?"

He held her gaze for a long span of seconds, then shrugged. "It's as good an explanation as any, given that I don't believe in shared hallucinations." He pulled his cell phone out of a pocket and snapped several pictures of the window. "I'll send you these. What's your e-mail?" She recited it, and he entered it into his phone. Taking a careful grip on the branch, he shoved it out the hole inch by inch. "I want to hear all the spooky details, but first we need to cover this so you won't get water damage if it rains. Got some kind of plastic I can tape over it?"

"Be right back." On the way downstairs, she noticed for the first time that Yuki had dematerialized at some point. Toby lay on the living room couch washing himself in a disgruntled manner. Val collected duct tape and a plastic garbage bag from the garage. As she reentered the kitchen, the lights blinked off. "Double damn." She groped in a drawer for a flashlight, switched it on, and climbed to the second story again.

"Power failure." Thad looked through the window toward his parents' house. "The lights are on over there, so it's probably not natural." When he took the bag and tape from Val, their fingers brushed. She mentally cursed the sudden racing of her heartbeat. *This is no time for that.* Nor was it the right time to analyze the sense of comfort she got from his matter-of-fact competence and his calm acceptance of the incredible phenomena. "I'll take care of the hole," he said, "while you call your insurance company."

"There doesn't seem like much point. The repair is bound to cost way under the deductible. But I guess I should get it on record anyway."

"Right, in case there's other damage you don't see till later."

She crept to the bedroom for her cell phone, then to the office for the number of her homeowner's insurance provider. Only then did it occur to her that she'd left Thad in the dark, except for stray illumination from the nearby street lamp and the flashes of lightning. So she headed back to the guest room and propped the flashlight on the dresser while making her call.

He finished the patching job before she got through to a representative and explained her problem. After arranging for an adjuster to come and check on the window the following afternoon, she said to Thad, "Thanks. No need to hang around in here with broken glass all over the floor. I'll sweep later, when I can see what I'm doing." *Good grief, we're in a bedroom together.* Not that the setting exactly qualified as romantic, what with the black plastic on the window and a flashlight instead of a candle.

"No, we might as well get comfortable. I figure you've got a long story to tell me."

"Okay, but don't blame me if it sounds too wild to believe. I didn't ask for this." On the way out of the room, she closed the door to keep Toby from walking on the shards of glass before she could clean them up.

They fumbled their way downstairs by flashlight. She picked up a candle and matches as she passed through the kitchen. In the den, she and Thad stared out the glass patio doors, transfixed by the spectacle. Globes of ball lightning careened around the yard, followed by crashes of thunder. The two wolves collided in an explosion of sparks. The grayish one broke off first and streaked skyward. The white one charged after it into the upper limbs of the nearest tree. Abruptly the wind, thunder, and flashes stopped. Val sagged onto the couch, her legs trembling.

She set the fat candle on the coffee table and lit the wick. The flame shed vanilla fragrance and a halo of wavering light.

The papasan chair scooted up to Thad. He flinched but gingerly took a seat in it. "Does all this have something to do with that scroll?"

She nodded, sagging onto the couch with a sigh. Now that the uproar had stopped, her muscles felt like melting with weariness. "Short version, I cut my finger, bled on it, and woke up the magic. At least, that's what the cat said."

"The cat." His eyebrows arched. "The plot thickens. Your cat started talking?"

"No, not Toby. A porcelain lucky cat figurine from the box of Granddad's stuff came to life. Also, those two ivory sculptures in the living room have been flapping around. And I've got a reddish goblin thing—aka-something—scrubbing my bathrooms." She clenched her fingers on the edge of the seat cushion and waited for him to burst into laughter or run away from the babbling lunatic.

Instead, he pulled out his phone and started searching. "That rings a bell. Yeah, here it is. *Akaname.* Bathroom-haunting *yokai*, attracted to dirt." He showed her a picture, which bore a clear resemblance to the creature she'd glimpsed.

"The cat used that word. Yoke-eye?"

Thad spelled it for her. "A spirit or demon, but not quite what we mean by *demon.* They're not necessarily evil. Can you tell me about this talking cat?" She couldn't decide whether she heard polite skepticism in his voice or not.

"It would be easier if you met her. We can be crazy or hallucinating together." She glanced around, half expecting the cat to appear on her own. "Yuki? Please come out."

Yuki materialized in the middle of the braided rug on the den floor.

Thad half-rose, clutching the arms of the chair. He opened his mouth, closed it, heaved a deep breath, and greeted the animal in what sounded like Japanese.

"I am honored to meet you, Thad Garrett." Yuki bowed with her forelegs stretched in front of her.

Thad returned the bow and lowered himself into the

chair. "She's real." He visibly swallowed. "Then it's all real." He cast an apologetic smile at the cat. "I didn't catch all of that. My Japanese is limited to a few standard words and phrases."

"Say what? I'm hearing her in English. You aren't?"

He shook his head.

"Then it's like she told me, I understand her and vice versa because my blood activated the magic." A question Val hadn't thought of before popped into her head. "When the thunder beast—the *raiju*—showed up before, my neighbors saw it as just a big dog. How come you can see it and the other wolf as they really are?"

Yuki padded over to the couch and jumped up. "I believe he has a clear vision of the *yokai* because he touched the scroll."

"Makes sense," Val said. "As much as anything does." She gave Thad a quick summary of what she knew about Yuki's past. "I'd like to find a way to unbind her from the scroll so she can go home, not to mention un-magic my house. But I don't have a clue where to start. Yuki, when the second wolf appeared, you said you remembered more."

A shiver rippled through the white cat's slender body. "I remember everything." A silvery mist enveloped her, then dissipated to reveal her human form.

Thad blinked. "Wow."

Val translated the cat's last remark for him. "She says she remembers everything now. Yuki, what happened back then that's scaring you now?"

Yuki folded her hands in her lap and spoke with only a faint tremor in her voice. "The *okuri-okami* is besieging your house because it wants to destroy me. As I told you, my beloved Hiroshi was an *onmyoji*—a magician—as well as an artist. A rival *onmyoji* visited the shrine and beheld me in this human form. Lust overwhelmed him, and he determined to possess me. When I rejected him, he conjured the *okami* and sent it after me. Frightened that if I continued my resistance, the *okami* would destroy me, Hiroshi devised a plan for my protection. He transformed me into a porcelain cat, as you saw, and painted guardian magic into the scroll. He hoped to find a way to banish the creature, and then he would release me from the spell."

Val summarized this account for Thad, then asked Yuki, "Do you know what happened to Hiroshi and the other magician after that?"

"No. Until your blood released me, I had no awareness of anything. It was like dreamless sleep." Tears shimmered in her eyes. "But of course, now I know both of them died long ago. The *okami* must have become aware of my existence as soon as I awoke, and it continues to obey its master's last command."

Val handed a tissue from a box on the coffee table to the other woman. "Oh! It's my fault you're in danger, then."

Yuki dabbed her eyes with the tissue. "Please do not blame yourself. You had no way of knowing. If anything, I am at fault for bringing the danger upon you."

After Val translated this exchange for Thad, he said, "Forget about whose fault it is. Sounds to me like the dead magician is who you should blame. Question is, how do we get rid of the *okuri-okami*?"

"And why hasn't it invaded the house? Does it have to be invited in like a vampire or something?"

"I do not know this word *vampire*," Yuki said, "but I believe the remainder of the magic infused into the scroll keeps the *okami* at bay for the present. Perhaps the spell summoned the *raiju* to protect us."

"So no matter how scary the *raiju* looks, it's not a threat?" Val said.

"No, it is an ally." A clicking noise interrupted Yuki. All three of them turned to watch as the ivory dragon and octopus scrabbled into the room and climbed onto the coffee table. "These wish to serve you also."

Thad leaned forward for a closer look at the now-motionless figures. "Walking chairs, a talking cat, animated ivory—now I've seen everything."

"Don't say that." Val held up both hands with fingers crossed. "That's just asking for something else to happen."

"Point taken. What were you two saying just now?" She told him.

"Okay, I say again, how do we get rid of the *okami*?"

Without much hope, Val asked Yuki for suggestions. The woman shook her head. "It is a creature of the night, so you need not guard against it by day, but it will surely return after each sunset. An *onmyoji* with power equal to the summoner's would be able to banish it. Otherwise, I do not know."

"The obvious next step is research." Just as Val spoke, the patio light blinked on. "Good timing." She stood up, turned on a lamp, and blew out the candle. "Come on, the computer's upstairs." Yuki resumed her cat form, and both she and Thad followed Val to the second floor. In the office, Val took her seat at the computer, and the white cat leaped onto her lap. After the machine cycled through the rebooting process and admonished her that she hadn't shut it down properly, she called up the search page. With Thad's help to figure out the spelling of *okuri-okami*, she accessed images of the creature. She lingered on one drawing in which a terrified man with flapping robes fled down a path, while a pair of gray wolves menaced him from behind. Their jaws gaped open, bristling with sharp teeth.

Yuki placed one paw on the edge of the desk. A shudder convulsed her slender body. "That is it." She vanished.

"Can't blame her for bailing, with that beast after her." Val rubbed her eyes. "I don't know if I'll ever get used to the disappearing act."

Thad, leaning against the desk, said, "I hear you. If it weren't obvious you're seeing the same things I am, I'd be running in circles, gibbering in panic." His wry smile downplayed the claim.

"A rational engineering type like you?"

"All the more reason not to let things like that into my world. I'm amazed at the way you're holding yourself together." He placed a hand on her shoulder.

A wave of heat radiated through her. Every touch reminded her too vividly of countless touches and kisses they'd shared all those years ago. "Well, I've had a little time to get used to it." She subtly shifted position, and he removed his hand. Trying to ignore the warmth of a blush on her cheeks, she clicked links until she found a page of *okuri-okami* legends.

"Since it's not chasing us down a lonely road through a forest," Thad said, "this information may not too relevant."

"Let's see how to defeat it." She skimmed the text. "It won't attack as long as you don't trip and fall. That's it? That's how you protect yourself against the big bad wolf? Don't trip?"

"Wasn't planning to," he said. "Okay, make a note of that. Don't trip. How about protection against evil in general? I seem to remember something in Japanese folklore about beans."

"Are you sure you're not making that up?"

Bending over her, he entered "banishing evil beans" into the search box. Even when she leaned away from him, his breath tickled the nape of her neck. Shivers danced over her skin.

"Here it is." He straightened up. She hoped he didn't hear her letting out a shaky breath. "To invoke luck and banish evil: Throw roasted soybeans to the four cardinal directions while chanting, 'Come, good fortune; begone, demon.'"

"That simple, huh? There must be a catch. Well, we want the demon gone, and even if this doesn't work, it sounds harmless."

"Then we should pick up some roasted soybeans and give it a try," he said.

"Actually, I think I have some." She levered herself out of the chair, her skin twitching at Thad's nearness. *Back off, won't you?* She couldn't think of a polite way to say that aloud, especially since she couldn't explain why. She couldn't very well confess to the flock of butterflies that fluttered inside her whenever he got within arm's reach, as if she were eighteen again. "I'm pretty sure there's an unfinished snack pack of soy nuts in the kitchen, and they're really just roasted soybeans. I guess it won't matter that they're salted, will it?"

She found the bag in the cabinet where she recalled leaving it, and the two of them walked through the den and out onto the patio. Opening the bag, she said, "This has got to be the silliest thing I've done since—since my teens." She'd almost said "since I broke up with you." *Not going there!*

"Granted, I do feel like an idiot, but as you said, what can it hurt?"

Val scooped out a handful of soy nuts to give him. "I hope your parents don't happen to glance out here and notice what we're doing. They'll think I've lost my mind for sure."

"If they ask, I'll tell them we were feeding the birds."

"At this hour of the night?" She cast a mock scowl at him. "How does that anti-evil charm go?"

"Come, good fortune; begone, demon."

She sighed. "I can't believe we're doing this. Okay, here goes."

Facing north, south, east, and west in turn, they chanted the phrases four times in unison. No sparkly magic, no spray of rainbow light—not that she'd expected any visible result. "Come to think of it, if you told your folks we were feeding birds, it wouldn't be a lie. They're bound to peck up these nuts eventually, if the squirrels don't get here first." She brushed salt grains off her hands.

On the way in, Thad said, "The magic is attracted by the scroll, right?"

She nodded.

"Have you thought of renting a storage space isolated from residential areas and locking it in where the wolf *yokai* won't bother you or anybody else?"

"Actually, no. Now that you mention it, that might work, except for one problem." She headed for the kitchen to put away the half-empty bag. "That wouldn't do a thing to keep the wolf from trying to kill Yuki. I can't have that on my conscience."

"How so?"

They strolled toward the front door as Val answered, "Because I messed with the scroll and woke up the magic, even if it was an accident. I can't just abandon her. Did I mention that she wants to go home to Japan?"

"Understandable."

"I thought about shipping the scroll overseas, after we get rid of the wolf, but that seems too chancy when I don't know anybody there to take care of it. I thought I might be able to sell her ring—*shakudo*, it's called—to pay for a plane ticket." She told him what she'd discovered about the item's probable value.

Thad whistled. "Yeah, that would more than cover it."

"It's moot, though, because, again, wolf demon."

"I'll do some digging," he said, "in the Naval Academy library and online, and get back to you if I uncover anything useful. And please call me if you find out something important or need help again." When they reached the front door, he paused with it half open. "Do you have any idea how much I've regretted the way we broke up?"

"We were eighteen, for heaven's sake. Of course we were clueless." The stricken look in his eyes sent a pang through her. "Okay, I admit it, *I* was clueless. I shouldn't have cut you off like that." A deep breath brought her a whiff of his sandalwood-scented aftershave. *He's changed his brand since high school. I wonder what else has changed about him.* Ignoring the surge of lightheadedness that swept over her, she kept her voice steady. "Looking back, I'm sorry I acted the way I did, even if I still think it was rotten of you to spring your plans on me like that."

"I hear you. It was terminally stupid of me not to tell you in advance. You wouldn't speak to me for the rest of the summer even long enough to let me apologize. Then after I got settled into plebe year, I phoned you multiple times. Still no connection." He brushed a hand lightly over her hair.

"I should've talked to you, at least." She held herself rigid so he wouldn't notice how his touch unsettled her. "Being busy with freshman year of college myself, I had an excuse not to look back." She'd continued to ignore his e-mails and dodge him whenever he'd visited home on weekends. By the time her indignation and hurt had worn thin enough that she could see him without risk of falling apart, they'd reached the point of exchanging nothing but casual pleasantries when their paths crossed.

"I wish I'd pushed harder." He stroked her jawline with his thumb. "By the time I got up the nerve, I knew you had to be dating other guys. So I played the field, too, with what little time I had for a social life."

Struggling to keep her voice steady, she said, "Actually, Dad and Mom were sort of relieved we'd broken up." At his look of dismay, she added, "Oh, they liked you fine. They thought I was too young to get so attached, that's all. Given that I'd never really dated anybody else, they'd always been a little worried that I didn't have a basis for comparison."

"I won't ask how I stacked up to the competition." He punctuated the remark with a wry smile.

None of the other guys, not even the one she'd almost gotten engaged to in college, had measured up to her memories of Thad. She couldn't bring herself to tell him that and risk opening a door she might not be able to shut. "Then I won't ask the same of you."

"If you did, I hope you'd like the answer." He leaned closer and brushed his lips over hers. She gasped, and he seized the opportunity to deepen the kiss. Swaying toward him, she reached up to steady herself with a hand on his shoulder. His mouth tasted like coffee and wine.

She caught herself stroking the dense pelt of his close-cropped hair. With a shaky breath, she broke off and took a step back. "Time out. This is a mistake." That door could open onto the verge of a trap she might fall into—and end up in love with him all over again before she could climb out.

His hand dropped from her head to her shoulder. "No, a mistake would be letting this chance go by. But I won't push—yet."

After he left, she leaned back against the closed door, hugging herself. If he sincerely wanted to start over, would she? *No way. I still have no desire to be a Navy wife.*

When she trudged up to her room, though, a nostalgic impulse overcame her. She tugged a chair over to the closet and plucked a taped-up box from the high shelf. She sat on the bed for a minute with the box on her lap before reaching for a pair of nail scissors in the nightstand drawer. Cutting the tape and opening the lid felt like unlocking a portal to the vault of memories she'd sealed. Right on top lay the pack of rare cards Thad had given her for her eighteenth birthday. With trembling hands, she ran her fingers over the slick surfaces. Tears blurred the iridescent colors. *That chance he mentioned—could it be real?* She set the box next to the bedside lamp and dragged herself to the shower.

Later, as she crawled into bed, a sullen rumble of

thunder sounded. She didn't look out the window to check whether it was a natural storm or a return engagement for the two spirit wolves, the snow-white-and-electric-blue *raiju* and the ash-gray *okuri-okami*. *I've had enough for one night.*

Chapter Five

Monday afternoon, Val left work an hour early to meet with the insurance agent. Having inspected the window, he made arrangements for the repair two days later, which, of course, would come out of her pocket because the estimated cost fell below her deductible. Thad's snapshots of the branch poking through the hole helped, since the weather report didn't mention the freak "storm." Later, after changing into cutoff denim shorts, with numbers and dollar signs buzzing in her head, she carried a colander out back to harvest any new tomatoes that might have ripened.

Amid fallen branches, all the vines lay limp on the ground, leaves shredded and fruit smashed.

Tears burned her eyes, and her pulse hammered in her temples. She raced into the kitchen and flung the colander into the sink. With clenched fists, she pounded on the counter and let out the yell that had been choking her. "It killed my tomatoes! This means war!"

The white cat appeared on the floor next to her. "I feared something like this might happen."

Panting, Val brushed her hair back from her sweat-dampened forehead. "Say what?"

"I observed what you did outside last night. The *okami* is too powerful to be banished by the charm you performed. It only provoked the beast to anger."

"I wish you'd mentioned that before we did it." Val slumped onto the floor with her back braced against a cabinet.

"You did not ask me."

"For one thing, I didn't know you were there. How about giving me a heads-up when you decide to drop in?" Val glared at her but had to concede the cat had a point. "So, any suggestions on what to do next?"

Yuki thoughtfully licked a paw. "We can expect further attacks. Keep in mind, however, that the *okami* has not yet gained enough power to enter the house. And, as I mentioned, it is active only by night. As long as you stay inside after dark, you will be safe."

Val levered herself upright. "Let some monster-spirit-thingy trap me in my own house? The hell with that!" She leaned against the sink to peer at the destruction outside. "Think it over and let me know if you come up with a better idea."

"Very well." The cat stood and stretched. "There is one simple way to protect yourself and your home. Remove the scroll to some other location."

"That has crossed my mind. Thad suggested it, too. But you'd go with the scroll and the wolf would follow you, right?"

"That would be the expected result. You would be freed from the curse."

"You wouldn't, though. It would keep attacking and maybe kill you, if you can be killed."

"Yes, I can."

"It's my fault this creature showed up in the first place. You woke up because of me, and the wolf would never have found you if that hadn't happened."

"True." Yuki's voice remained cool.

Val knelt and stroked her. "There's no way I can throw you to the wolves, so to speak. I have to find out some way to destroy the demon-thing or at least banish it."

"Thank you for your kindness. You owe me nothing. Rather, I owe you a debt for allowing me to take sanctuary here." The cat vanished.

Should I call Thad and bring him up to date? He'd volunteered to help, after all. On the other hand, considering that kiss, she didn't want to give him the idea she was encouraging a relationship.

As if she'd telepathically alerted him, the phone rang, showing his caller ID.

"Are you doing okay?" He sounded genuinely anxious about her.

"I'm fine, except that the back yard is a war zone." She told him about the ravaged tomatoes. "The soybean charm didn't do any good. In fact, Yuki said it probably just made the *okami* madder."

"Then we'll have to dig up something more powerful," Thad said. "Meanwhile, at least let me try to help you with the scroll. Let me take it to my place and see what happens."

She sighed. "I've gone through that argument with you and Yuki, too. I won't abandon her to her doom."

"Don't be so all-or-nothing dramatic. Where's your spirit of experimentation? Give me the thing for just one night so we can find out if the plan works at all. You can always take it back, depending on the result."

"Spoken like a true science guy. Why are you so determined on this, anyway?"

"Because the next step could be the *yokai* hurting you instead of trees and vegetables. Damn it, why won't you let me try to protect you?"

"I don't need protection." Her skin heated, and she

caught herself clenching her fist around the phone. While she might not "need" protection, the idea of seeking shelter in his arms tempted her more than she wanted to admit. "I've gotten along just fine without you for the past thirteen years."

"Yeah, and you're just as stubborn as you were thirteen years ago."

"Stubborn!"

"So much that you wouldn't listen to my side then, and you won't now, either."

She choked down the angry rebuttal trying to spew out of her mouth. *Maybe he has a point.* Shouldn't she have outgrown automatically lashing out and cutting him off? "Oh, all right." She drew a deep breath and softened her grudging tone. "You can borrow the scroll for a night, just as an experiment."

"Great, I'll come over to pick it up tomorrow after work if that's okay." To his credit, he didn't sound as if he were gloating over her concession.

"Why not tonight?" *Did I really ask that?* she silently groaned. She did not want to seem eager to get together with him.

"I was planning to wait until I have the *ofuda* I ordered."

"Whoa! Back up. The what?"

"Magical symbols drawn on paper, usually by a Shinto priest. They're supposed to protect homes and other buildings and dispel evil. Even if it doesn't drive the *yokai* away, I figure it can't hurt."

"Are you sure about that? The soybean ritual didn't work out so well."

"But we're amateurs," he said. "Maybe we screwed it up somehow. I ordered a batch of *ofuda* online from a site that had good reviews for authenticity. Couldn't find a Shinto shrine in the area to buy them in person."

"You can order magic charms online?"

He chuckled. "As you should know, you can get anything online. Uh—I hope you don't mind that I didn't check with you first."

"No, it's okay." He meant well, and she couldn't deny she welcomed the help.

"On second thought, could I see you this evening after all? Let me sweep you off your feet and take you away from all this—just for a couple of hours."

"Away? What did you have in mind?" *Red alert! Is he asking for a date?* One date could lead to another, and before she knew it, she would have to deal with the attraction that kept sneaking up on her every time they met.

"Sushi downtown. You need to get better acquainted with Japanese culture, given your current predicament."

"Sushi? Raw fish?" Although she considered herself an adventurous eater, she'd never tried Japanese cuisine.

"Please. Common misconception. Raw fish is sashimi. Sushi means vinegared rice balls, which can have almost any kind of filling. Let me take you to dinner and demonstrate."

"Well…" She wanted to see him again, a sound reason to avoid doing just that. On the other hand, they needed to plot their defense against the *okuri-okami*, and she had to eat regardless. Surely she could enjoy one meal with Thad without getting trapped in a web of relationship complications. She almost giggled at the image of him as a spider. "Okay, we can have a dinner strategy meeting."

"Just strategy?"

"Right, absolutely not a date." In that case, she ought to offer to split the cost, but she knew he wouldn't go for that plan.

"I hear you. In no way a date. You might as well bring the scroll with you."

They ended the call after settling the time for him to pick her up. Upstairs, she noticed that the toothpaste blobs she'd dripped in her bathroom sink that morning had been wiped off. *I'll actually miss the akaname when it moves out.* She stood in front of her open closet, ruminating on what to wear. Dinner downtown rated better than her usual slopping-around-the-house or grocery-shopping clothes. Yet she didn't want to dress up enough to look as if she'd made a special effort. On the third hand, she did like the idea of showing Thad what he'd lost, so to speak. *Aargh, am I turning into some kind of tease or what?* Besides, from what she remembered about their evenings together in high school, he hardly noticed her clothes one way or another, aside from lingering gazes at the neckline. *Stop obsessing. Not a date, remember?* She picked out a miniskirt and a peasant blouse with a paisley print, which showed just enough cleavage for a casual dinner.

After showering and dressing, she called for Yuki, who instantly appeared on the bed. "Thad and I decided to try moving the scroll to his place just for one night to find out what happens. Is that okay with you?"

The cat said, "I have no objection. But you realize this change will only transfer the danger to him?"

"Yeah, that's one major glitch in the plan. He insisted we should do the experiment, though."

"Then I shall be honored to be a guest in your man's home."

"He's not my man!"

Yuki blinked out of sight with no further comment.

Thad's green sports car pulled into the driveway promptly at six, as punctual as she'd expect from a naval officer. When she went to meet him without waiting for him to walk up the sidewalk, he got out of the car and opened the passenger door for her. She couldn't remember the last time a man had done that. Certainly not her college boyfriend.

"I thought we'd run by my place first," he said, "and drop off the scroll."

Ten minutes later, they crossed the low bridge over Spa Creek into downtown Annapolis. After they passed City Dock, Thad drove parallel to the Naval Academy campus for a couple of blocks, then turned onto a one-way side street barely wide enough for a single lane of traffic. He pulled into a driveway next to one of many circa-1900 houses converted into apartments. "I've got a quarter of the first floor," he said. "You wouldn't believe the rent for a one-bedroom place that size."

"Sure I would. I lived on my own a long time before Dad died and I moved back in with Mom." She declined Thad's invitation to come inside while he stashed the scroll in whatever safe nook he'd chosen for it. Somehow entering his bachelor pad would feel more intimate than having him in her house, which he'd visited countless times in their teens. Her mind wandered to the hours they'd spent in the den playing video games, guzzling cola, and sharing a bowl of popcorn or potato chips. She had to rub her eyes to dispel a mist of nostalgic regret for the loss of that comfortable companionship.

On Main Street, they had the luck to find a curbside parking space in the middle of the street's half-mile length and strolled along the brick-paved sidewalk to the restaurant Thad had chosen. A miniature, rock-lined waterfall adorned the closet-sized foyer. The host showed them to a table for two in the small dining room, decorated with wall scrolls that reminded her of the one she'd inherited. Thad ordered green tea and two bottles of sake. The porcelain sake decanters, Val was relieved to see when they arrived a minute later, were smaller than beer bottles. She wanted to hang onto her composure, what was left of it. Thad poured some of the drink into the pair of tiny, handle-less cups that came with it.

She took a tentative sip of the warm liquid. "I always thought sake was supposed to be super high in alcohol content."

"Don't know where that stereotype comes from. It's about like a light wine."

Scanning the menu, she said, "Since this is supposed to be a strategy meeting, what's the chance you'll let me pay my half?"

He grinned. "Zero."

She decided not to argue. Why give him another excuse to call her "stubborn"? In the same spirit, she let him pick sushi platters to share. The meal came with individual bowls of rice and clear soup. When the sushi arrived, Thad demonstrated blending the green blob of wasabi into a pool of soy sauce. Remembering she'd never been a fan of scorching hot spice, he cautioned her to stick to a tiny fragment.

"In Japan, they'd look at you sideways for mixing them, but that's how most Americans eat it. Start with the California roll and cucumber roll—no raw fish, I swear." He showed her how to position a pair of chopsticks between thumb and first two fingers.

Encouraged by his instructions, she fiddled with the chopsticks until she managed to pick up a roll. She dubiously examined the bite-sized rice lumps wrapped in black seaweed before putting one in her mouth, but she had to admit they weren't bad. After sampling a few other types, she let him persuade her to try the raw tuna option. The flavor turned out to be mild, not at all "fishy." "Okay, you've officially expanded my horizons. I actually like this."

"Now, about the scroll," he said after drinking the last of his soup straight from the bowl. "If moving it from your place to mine doesn't cure your magic problem, what next?"

"First off, I'm more concerned about what to do if the *problem* just leaves me alone and infests your apartment instead. That wouldn't solve anything."

"Assuming the *ofuda* I ordered get here tomorrow, we can test their protective power wherever the *okami* shows up. Think of it in flow chart terms." He gestured with his chopsticks as if pointing to an invisible diagram in the air. "Does the magic follow the scroll to my apartment, yes or no? If no, I'll return it to you, and we'll reevaluate the situation. If yes, I'll hang up the *ofuda* to guard the premises, including the porch and shrubbery. Does that keep the *okami* outside those boundaries? If yes, we're done. If no, we plan the next step."

"Hold on, not done. All that's okay as far as it goes, but I don't like the idea of staying strictly on the defensive," she said. "We need to find a way to banish the *okami* permanently or destroy it if there's a way to do that. Otherwise Yuki will never be safe, not to mention my house and yard."

"Like I said, I'll dig into whatever books on Japanese folklore I can find in the Academy library."

"And I'll search online for banishing spells. Also, it couldn't hurt to ask Yuki again." She nibbled on a sliver of the pink ginger that garnished the plate. Its tang freshened her mouth with a slight but not unpleasant burn. Although surprised at how quickly the sushi variety platter had filled her stomach, she decided she had room for green tea ice cream, another novelty she discovered she liked.

As she finished her dessert, he topped off their teacups from the nearly empty pot. "Speaking of expanding horizons, could you expand them wide enough to consider we might pick up where we left off?"

"I don't see how. We're not eighteen anymore."

"I know, it's water under the bridge after the horse escaped from the barn, as your dad used to say. So belay that suggestion. Forget about going back—could we make a fresh start going forward?"

She sipped her tea, stalling, before she answered. "It's been a heck of a lot of water. We've changed. At least, I sure hope we have in thirteen years." For one thing, she hadn't known then what a naïve fantasy it was, to expect plans made at age eighteen to work out exactly the way she'd daydreamed them.

"That's not a bad thing. I think I've learned a few things since high school. And I know you haven't spent all this time in an enchanted sleep waiting for me to ride back into your life on a white charger," he said with a wry smile. "You must have dated, had relationships."

"Sure." She shrugged. "Only one that was serious, though, in college. It morphed into a long-distance thing when we moved on to different grad schools and

73

eventually ended almost painlessly. What about you?" She lightened her tone. "Girl in every port?"

He laughed. "The womanizing habits of the average naval officer are much exaggerated. On deployment, you go to bars and clubs off duty, but if you've got any sense of self-preservation, you're careful. Not that the Shore Patrol in every port doesn't round up plenty of sailors with a conspicuous lack of sense, but that's not me. Stateside, I've dated, of course, but I've never been stationed in one place long enough to get serious."

She didn't pursue the topic any further. While she knew he couldn't have led a totally celibate life, she didn't need details. They finished their drinks and emerged onto the sidewalk in the deepening twilight, illuminated by the lit windows of shops, restaurants, and bars.

On the way to the car, he reached for her hand, and she let him take it. When he bent to open the passenger door for her, he brushed her shoulder in passing. Her skin rippled with a fleeting chill despite the warm, humid air. *Doesn't mean a thing. It's the novelty factor, that's all. If I got used to him again, a simple touch wouldn't affect me like that.* A voice in the back of her head retorted, *Oh, yeah? Who do you think you're kidding?*

At her house, he challenged that theory by clasping her hand again on the way up the front walk. Her stomach fluttered along with her pulse when he paused on the porch to put an arm loosely around her and smooth her hair. She couldn't resist leaning toward him when he cupped the back of her head. She considered evading his mouth when he lowered it to hers, but she couldn't force herself to move. Instead, she parted her lips to welcome the kiss. When his tongue teased her, waves of heat and cold coursed along her nerves. Her body remembered their kisses on prom night and what that embrace had led to, even if her brain advised her to forget it. For a few seconds she allowed herself to bask in a cloud of sensual warmth. She rested her palms on his chest, tempted to let her fingers wander to his open collar and savor the touch of his skin.

No! She pushed him to arm's length. "Enough. Too fast."

"Not fast enough for me." His lips quirked in a hint of a smile. His breath came as ragged as hers. "You don't know how often I've thought about you since we separated."

"Don't expect me to believe you've spent the past thirteen years pining away."

"Not pining, but definitely remembering. When I got transferred here, it escalated to hoping. But as long as we're moving ahead instead of astern, I can live with it."

"Ahead at half speed, please. I have the house and my job. You'll be getting transferred again in a couple of years."

He let go of her arms. "I'm starting to realize why you don't want to sell the house."

She took a step back from him. "What do you mean?"

"You've got your safe nest here. Maybe you're afraid to strike out into the world. No guts, no glory."

The pulse pounded in her temples. "I don't want glory."

"No, you just want to hide in your burrow like a rabbit."

"Where do you get off, talking like you know me

inside out?" Her breath came fast and harsh. "We've hardly seen each other in thirteen years, and suddenly you think you can read my mind?"

"Whose fault is that? After prom night, I tried enough times to connect with you. Are you surprised I finally decided to cut my losses?"

She planted her fists on her hips and glowered at him. "Losses? That's how you see it? And suddenly I'm the bad guy in all this?"

"I didn't mean—"

"I don't care what you think you meant. You've got enough gall to divide into three parts."

His lips tightened. "Then I'd better go."

"Good idea." As soon as he reached the front walk, she slammed the door, not caring how petulant that gesture made her look.

After he drove away, she collapsed on the living room couch, where Toby jumped up and stepped onto her lap. She ran her hand over him from head to tail while she fought to rein in her rapid breathing and racing pulse. Toby rubbed against her hand, purring. She nuzzled him, grateful for the comfort of his furry bulk. "You're probably glad to have Yuki gone. I'll sort of miss her." If the change proved to be permanent, anyway. Scanning the room, Val found the ivory dragon and octopus, last seen on the coffee table, on an end table. She returned them to their place on the mantel and dragged herself upstairs for a hot shower. As much as she might need a cool one to quench the molten heat that lingered in the pit of her stomach and sharpened the ache in her head, she wanted the relaxing effect of hot water.

"No unnatural thunderstorm," she said to Toby fifteen minutes later, when he strolled in as she was slipping on a nightgown. "No flashing lights or howling demons. Peace and quiet."

While she brushed her hair, the phone rang. Her heart stuttered at the sight of Thad's caller ID. With the memory of their argument tying her insides in knots, she was half tempted to ignore him. Shaking her head at her body's undisciplined response, she answered the call.

"I don't want to leave things the way we did." His tentative tone wrenched at her heart.

"Neither do I." She tried to sound cool.

"I shouldn't have said what I said. Can we erase it from the record?"

"Maybe." How could she forget just like that? "Let's not talk about it anymore for now. More important, what's happening with the scroll?"

"The white cat's here with me," he said, "sitting on the couch at this moment. And the two wolf things, the *okuri-okami* and the *raiju*, are battling outside."

Over the phone, thunder boomed in her ears. "Then it worked."

"So far, anyway. I'll touch base with you again sometime tomorrow." Although he didn't try to prolong the conversation, the caressing tone of his "Goodnight" did nothing to calm her.

After distracting herself with a novel for a while, she went into the office to check e-mail one last time before bed. She figured she owed Linda an update on the status of their grandfather's memorabilia, while censoring details that would make her sister think she'd come unhinged. Val started with the easy part, the contents of the box and the fact that she hadn't found documentation on the ivory's provenance. She didn't mention the cat figurine, since it had permanently transformed into its animated counterpart. "Last night a short thunderstorm blew through here and broke a window in the guest room. Don't worry, it's getting fixed, and I can scrape together the bucks. Thad was visiting his parents and dropped over to help out…" Val feared if she didn't say anything about seeing him, the news would somehow leak to Linda, who would give her grief for leaving out that detail.

Walking down the hall to her bedroom, Val glimpsed movement in the bathroom. When she peeked in, the *akaname* whipped around to face her, then flashed out of sight. "Why are you still here?" Wasn't all the magic supposed to follow the scroll to its new location?

Shoving the question to the back of her mind, she headed for her room, turned off the light, and lay down. As soon as she settled under the sheet, memories of the goodnight kiss rushed into her head and swamped the residual anger from the shouting match. Heat flooded her body. She threw off the covers, and her skin prickled in the cool draft from the air conditioner. Brushed by the satiny fabric of her nightgown, her nipples peaked. She wrapped her arms around herself and let out a faint moan. Why had she let herself taste him when her better judgment warned she couldn't enjoy the full feast? Yes, she longed to relive the intimacy they'd shared in the distant past, but they couldn't rewind time and become teenage lovers again. Fitting that intimacy into their adult lives would present a challenge she wasn't sure she could face.

After she finally sank into unconsciousness, thunder jolted her awake. A glance at the clock revealed that she'd slept a little over an hour. She lurched to the window and looked out. No sign of the ash-gray *okami*, but the white wolf, outlined in blue flame, zigzagged from tree to tree.

"What are you doing here? Why aren't you keeping tabs on the *okami*?" Val closed the curtains and stumbled back to bed. *I'll have to tell Thad the cunning plan didn't work after all.*

Chapter Six

In the morning, the ivory dragon and octopus had migrated into the dining room and settled on a shelf of the china cabinet. Toby stretched on his hind legs, sniffed the edge of the shelf, and lashed his tail but didn't fly into a rage. "Getting used to them?" Val asked, scratching behind his ears. He shook his head as if to dislodge a flea and stalked off.

She phoned Thad for a status update. "The thunder and fireworks lasted until after midnight," he said. "Everything's been quiet since."

"The *raiju* showed up back here, and the rest of the magic hasn't left, either. You might as well give me the scroll. What's the use of having two different locations infested with *yokai*?"

"Roger that." He proposed returning the scroll to her downtown at lunchtime.

After a moment's hesitation as she recalled the brief fight, she accepted the suggestion and agreed on a meeting place. "I have to admit I sort of miss Yuki," she said.

"She'd probably rather be near you anyway, considering you can talk with her and I can't."

On her lunch break, Val took a five-minute stroll in the muggy heat to the coffee shop on Main Street where she and Thad had arranged to meet. Tempted to quicken her steps when she got near the café, she quashed the impulse. Why give him the wrong impression by acting eager to see him? *Even if I am.* He'd staked out a table for two by the window. Her stomach fluttered at the sight of him in his summer whites. *Come on, I'm too old to get swept off my feet by a cool uniform.*

As soon as she sat down, he handed her a plastic bag containing the scroll. An iced coffee and what looked like a gyro wrap sat on the table in front of him. "I didn't know what to order for you. What'll it be?" Nothing in his voice or expression hinted he was thinking of the way they'd parted the night before.

She suppressed a sigh in her relief that they wouldn't have to revive the quarrel. "I'll buy my own this time, thanks. No argument, please." Leaving the bag with her purse on her chair, where he could keep an eye on the artifact, she went to the counter and placed her order. Shortly she returned to the table with a latte, a sandwich, and, after some internal waffling, a scone.

"According to the tracking info on the website," he said between bites, "the *ofuda*—protective charms—I ordered should be there when I get home this afternoon. Then I'll bring them over to your house to hang them at strategic points."

"Let's hope that works better than soybeans. Have you had a chance to check the Academy library like you mentioned?"

He shrugged. "No shortage of books on Japan, but the ones I skimmed weren't of much practical help. Long on cultural background and folklore, short on specific instructions. The legends are mostly cautionary tales along the line of, *Don't go near this stuff in the first place, you idiot, or you're doomed.*"

"It's a little late for that."

"Granted. A far cry from the way we used to spend

time together, huh?" He changed the subject to reminisce about hanging around downtown in their teens, buying ice cream cones at a shop that still occupied a storefront three doors up Main Street, viewing Fourth of July fireworks or the Blue Angels flight exhibitions with their families. Gradually the butterflies in her stomach went dormant enough to let her eat. She enjoyed the conversation on safe topics and finally glanced at her watch with surprise at how fast the time had fled. She gathered up her things to head back to work with a tinge of unexpected reluctance. Thad promised to phone to let her know whether the charms had arrived and, if so, when to expect him at her place that evening.

In her basement cubicle in the building on State Circle opposite the State House, she tucked the bag containing the scroll into the bottom drawer of her desk. She was checking her work e-mail when Yuki appeared next to her computer. "We are not at Thad-san's home. What is this chamber?"

Val looked around with alarm, hoping nobody had noticed. "You can't be here," she whispered. "This is the Legislative Services library."

"Ah, a place of learning. You are a scholar."

"Sort of, I guess. Now make yourself scarce. I'll wake you when we get to my house."

Just as she spoke, another librarian walked past. Yuki vanished. The woman stared at Val's desk and blinked. "Were you just saying something?"

"Talking to myself, that's all. Cursing the spam."

"For a second I thought I saw a cat." She pointed at the spot next to the computer.

Val forced a giggle. "How would a cat get down here?"

"You brought in a stuffed animal, maybe?"

"Nope." Val kept a bland smile in place until her coworker walked away, shaking her head. Val released a sigh. While she had no desire to make her office mates doubt their sanity, better that than try to explain vanishing cats.

****

When she arrived home that day, after changing out of her work clothes—resisting the impulse to pay special attention to her outfit for Thad's planned visit—she took the scroll into the living room. She set it on the mantel between the two ivory figurines, which had returned to their usual place sometime during her absence, and said, "Yuki, you can come out now."

The white cat appeared on the coffee table. "I am glad to be here. This place holds a certain familiarity."

"Maybe you somehow sensed your location even when you were a porcelain model?"

"Perhaps. The ways of magic are inscrutable."

Val sat on the couch. "Speaking of that, do you have any idea why the *akaname* and the *raiju* didn't leave here? Well, the *raiju* did for a while, but it came back. And the ivory animals moved by themselves again."

Yuki meditatively groomed her front paws and slicked back an ear. "After the scroll has rested here for so many years, even dormant, perhaps your dwelling has become imbued with some portion of the enchantment. I conjecture that the *raiju* feels an obligation to guard this place. When the *okami* ceased to attack Thad-san's home last night, the *raiju* may have come here to ensure that the threat did not return to you."

"That's thoughtful of it and all, but what I really want is to stop the supernatural shenanigans completely.

No offense." She skimmed a hand over the cat, who leaned into the touch with a low purr.

"None taken. Have you a plan?"

"Thad has ordered a batch of *ofuda* to protect the house and yard." Val sighed. "Other than that, we've got nothing until I do some more research."

"The idea is sound," Yuki said, "but I fear the presence of *ofuda* may provoke the *okami* to attack with more determination."

"Then we'll have to find a way to banish it permanently before the wards lose their effectiveness. Any suggestions?"

"Only that I suspect what you require to cancel the wicked *onmyoji's* curse is another adept of equal power. And where would you meet such a person in this strange land?"

"Good question. Thad couldn't find a Shinto shrine anywhere in the area. He had to order the *ofuda* online."

Yuki looked puzzled.

"On the computer, to be shipped through the mail."

"Ah, yes, the magic box with pictures." She jumped down and sauntered out of the room, tail gently waving.

Val went up to the office to run a search on the "magic box" for demon-banishing spells. As she waited for the first website to load, it occurred to her that she could post a request for a Japanese sorcerer to exorcise the wolf. She laughed aloud at the thought of the flood of replies she would probably get from assorted weirdos.

She came across a nature magic incantation that looked promising and copied it: "Spirit that threatens in this place, fight water by water and fire by fire. Every power of thine erase, until thy evil force expire." Although from the wrong cultural background, it was a general enough invocation against evil that she hoped it might have a positive effect. Other websites recommended colored candles for various uses, including black for protection and magenta for exorcisms. Salt, holy water, and burning sage also came up frequently in her search. Salt was no problem, and she had a bottle of dried sage in the spice cabinet. Multicolored candles, though, didn't form part of her standard household supplies. Clinging to the premise of "can't hurt, might help," she texted Thad to ask whether he could track down a few black and magenta candles before coming over, as well as a source of holy water.

He replied with a row of question marks followed by, "Your wish is my command. Will see what I can do. Maybe get holy water at St. Mary's downtown."

She called for Yuki, who materialized next to the computer. "Did you find answers in the magic box?" the cat asked.

Val explained what she'd decided to do. "Do you think it will work?"

Yuki flicked her tail and slanted her ears back. "It may, since these charms belong to the lore of this country. I doubt the wisdom of such acts, though. As I said about the *ofuda*, if you fail to banish the *okami* by these means, it may attack even more fiercely."

"I know." Val's shoulders sagged. "But I have to try. There's no guarantee it wouldn't eventually break through into the house and hurt you. Anyway, even without that, if we don't get rid of it, I could be stuck with it howling around the yard every night forever."

"That is indeed possible. You must do as you think best." Yuki leaped to the floor and walked out of the room.

When Val logged onto her computer, an instant message from Linda popped up. "So you've been hanging with Thad? Come on, juicy details!"

"No details," Val shot back. "Nothing juicy, just casual friends."

Linda retorted, "Yeah, right. You expect me to believe you're not tempted to revisit auld lang syne?"

"Not one bit," Val typed, blushing at the lie. "In a couple of years, he'll be moving on, so what's the point? After what I've heard from you about the Navy wife lifestyle, I have absolutely no desire for it. So why risk getting tangled up with him?"

"Chicken, neener, neener, neener," came the retort. "What could I possibly have told you to make you run scared like that?"

"Who said anything about scared?" Linda's zinger stung the same tender spot as Thad's accusation.

"Why else would you let my occasional gripes dictate your whole future? Sure, being a military wife has downsides, but it has upsides, too. I wouldn't trade our years of traveling and living all over the country for anything."

"That's not what I got out of listening to you," Val replied.

"Just because I have some complaints, that's not all there is to it. Geez, if I can't vent to my little sister, who can I vent to?"

"As for the moving around thing, I have a job right here that I'm happy with."

"Enough to tie yourself down to it forever? You can be a librarian anywhere, can't you?"

"I'm not thrilled about the idea of leaving our home town or the house I grew up in, either."

"We're unloading the house, remember?" Linda countered. "Don't use that for an excuse. Or maybe you're dragging your feet on selling because you don't want to give it up?" Another echo of Thad. *If two people tell me the same thing, maybe I should consider they have a point.*

"Come on, I need the money as much as you do, and I know I can't afford to keep up this place long term. But, yeah, maybe there's some of that. Thad has his folks' house to come home to. In the Navy wife scenario, I'd be coming home to a house with strangers in it."

"More excuses." Val could almost hear Linda's sharp tone through the words on the screen. "His parents won't live forever, and even before that, they might move into a senior community. Face it, you're just evading your real feelings."

"Thanks a bunch, Ms. Freud. It isn't only the constant uprooting or the other so-called gripes I've heard from you." Val hesitated before typing the next part but plunged on. "People in the Navy die. Remember Ron's classmate, the Marine who got killed in Afghanistan during my senior year in high school? Don't try to tell me that didn't shake you up. And a couple of years ago you mentioned a sailor on Ron's last ship who died."

"That one didn't even happen in combat," Linda messaged back. "It was an accident. News flash: People can die anytime, anywhere. They don't have to be in the military. Life doesn't hand out guarantees."

Don't you think I know that? Dad and Mom died on us. That was enough for one decade. Val couldn't say that to her sister, though. By now, her stomach was churning. "Why did we get on this subject, anyway? I've talked to Thad a few times, that's all. I'm not dating him and don't have any plans to." Although that claim wasn't completely truthful, she couldn't share the whole story without delving into the enchanted scroll problem. *I can barely imagine what she'd say if I told her the house is haunted by Japanese spirits.* She made an excuse to end the conversation and switched over to e-mail.

Just as she finished skimming her in-box, her phone announced a text from Thad. "Got the supplies you asked for. Picking up pizza on the way. You still like green peppers?"

She texted back a Y. The revelation that he hadn't forgotten her topping preferences brought an unexpected lump to her throat.

Half an hour later, he rang the doorbell. He'd changed from his uniform into shorts and a "Go Navy" T-shirt. They spread out the pizza on the kitchen table, and she produced a couple of beers from the refrigerator. He'd remembered to order pineapple on her half, an ingredient he'd often labeled "an abomination against nature."

He pulled a partly filled plastic water bottle out of a shopping bag he'd brought with him. "I snuck into St. Mary's and got some holy water. Good thing nobody caught me and asked if I was planning to fight vampires or something."

She nodded at the bag, which bore the name of a shop on Main Street. "Any luck with candles?"

"Aye, aye, Captain, I snagged an assortment of black and magenta, like you said. Magenta is that purplish color, right?"

With a light slap on his arm, she said, "Don't pretend you don't know what magenta is." She peeked inside the sack anyway and confirmed he'd bought the right shade.

"And I stopped at my place to pick up the package with the *ofuda*." He dug in the bag once more and held up a padded envelope.

"Let's eat. The *okami* won't show up until after sunset." She set out plates and napkins, and they dug into the pizza. Halfway through the meal, Toby padded into the kitchen. Thad dropped a scrap of pepperoni on the floor for him. "Hey, who authorized that?" Val said.

Thad cast a sheepish smile at her. "Against the house rules? What can one time hurt?"

Toby stretched on his hind legs to place his front paws on Thad's lap. "See," she said, "that's what. Now he'll be expecting treats from the table." She shooed the cat away. "I'm surprised he's not hiding to punish me for letting Yuki back into the house."

"He doesn't like her?"

"He seems to take a dim view of anything supernatural, and who can blame him?" She shook her head. "I can't believe I'm accepting it this calmly myself. I still have moments when I think it's a dream I'll wake up from any minute."

"If this is a dream, I don't mind sharing it with you." For a second his smile looked almost wistful.

Val took refuge in a swig of beer. *I'm starting to feel I wouldn't mind sharing a lot more, but I can't think about that now.*

By the time they finished the meal and cleaned up, daylight was fading. Thad dug a roll of packaging tape out of the shopping bag. "First, we should guard the windows and doors. I made sure of getting plenty of *ofuda* to cover every entrance."

The charms consisted of white paper rectangles smaller than dollar bills, with Japanese characters drawn on them. Val took a handful along with tape from the kitchen drawer and fastened one *ofuda* each to the front and back doors and the frames of all windows on the main floor. In the living room, Toby darted behind the couch when she entered. "Don't like this routine, huh? Don't worry, it's supposed to make things better." Meanwhile, Thad had gone upstairs to do the same thing to the windows there. They met on the lower level to tape *ofuda* to the windows and the sliding door.

Next they carried the supplies outside, where lightning bugs flitted through the grass of the back yard in the deepening twilight. Thad attached paper charms to a pair of trees, one on each side of the patio. They fluttered in a gentle breeze.

"They won't last long if we get rain or a windstorm," Val said.

"Let's hope you won't need them after tonight. Now, how about the candles?"

He arranged them on the patio table, and she lit them. Last, she spaced four shot glasses evenly on the table between the candles. Thad poured the holy water into them.

The breeze quickened, making the flames dip. At some point, Yuki had materialized. With her whiskers and ears slanted, she scanned the yard. "This does not feel right."

Val folded her arms against a gust of wind too chilly for August. "Less right than it's been ever since I activated that scroll?"

Having finished the preparations, Thad turned to her. "Now what?"

"Now I guess we recite that spell I found and hope sheer desperation makes up for neither of us being any kind of wizard." Thank goodness the shrubbery around the patio made it unlikely the neighbors would notice the two of them performing arcane rituals.

They took their places on opposite sides of the table. Thad reached for her hands and clasped them in a warm, solid grip. Together they chanted, "Spirit that threatens in this place, fight water by water and fire by fire. Every power of thine erase, until thy evil force expire."

The wind howled. A second later, another kind of howl, the cry of a wolf, echoed it. Val glanced up. The ash-gray beast with glowing eyes crouched on the limb of a tree. It glowered down at her with bared fangs. "The spell," she whispered. "Let's try it again."

She started the verse, and Thad joined in. The howls of wind and wolf swelled in counterpoint. The *ofuda* flapped in the rising gale that whipped Val's face and hair. Thad squeezed her hands. Yuki crouched under the table, growling low in her chest.

The *okami* leaped from one tree to another and seized an *ofuda* in its jaws. It tore each of the charms from that branch, then launched itself across the yard to the other paper-festooned tree. It shredded all those rectangles as well.

"They're not working!" Thad shouted over the wind.

"You think?"

The beast dove to the ground and charged at the patio. Val tugged her hands free of Thad's, sprang away from the table, and backed toward the door. Yuki emitted a wordless yowl that struck Val as a summons. *Is she calling the raiju?*

Thunder answered the cat's cry. The *okami* lunged at Val, who stumbled and fell to one knee with a jarring thump. The creature's burning eyes and gaping maw raged at her. An odor like charred wood stung her nose. Thad jumped in front of her, grabbed a shot glass, and splashed the holy water in the *okami's* mouth. The beast halted with a roar. Val dragged herself to her feet and snatched up another glass. When she flung the water at the *okami*, it shook itself but, instead of backing farther away, slunk toward her.

The trees rattled with thunder and wind. Lightning flashed. Val risked a quick upward glance. An orb of blue flame hovered in mid-air. It zipped to a tree, rolled down the trunk, and transformed as it hit the ground. The white wolf, outlined in an azure glow, howled a challenge.

Snarling, the *okami* cast a baleful glance at the *raiju*. Instead of rushing to meet the new attacker, though, the ash-gray wolf stalked closer to Val. Her pulse hammering in her temples, she threw another glass of holy water at the thing. Thad picked up the last of the four shots and did the same.

The *okami* swiveled toward him, its growl becoming deeper and louder. "We're out of ammo," he said. As he spoke, the beast sprang, knocking over the table with a clatter and a roar. Candles scattered on the stone patio and snuffed out.

Thad shifted to stand between Val and the *okami* again. When he raised his arms to ward off the attack, the creature's jaws clamped onto his left forearm. He fell, barely catching himself with his free hand and dragging the beast to the ground with him. Her vision blurred, and her stomach lurched. "No!" She grabbed the nearest lawn chair, staggered toward the wolf, and slammed its rump with the chair.

"Are you out of your mind?" Pain roughened Thad's voice. The wolf let go of him and whirled in Val's direction. She whacked it across the muzzle.

The *raiju* chose that moment to leap onto the *okami's* back. By the smoldering glow of the *okami's* eyes and the bluish shimmer around the thunder-beast, she could make out the two spirit animals biting and clawing at each other. The *raiju* sank its fangs into the other's neck. The *okami* broke free and launched itself into the air. The blue-white wolf soared after it. Amid a flash of lightning, the two disappeared into the trees.

A second later, the lightning stopped, and silence fell.

Her knees trembling, Val clutched Thad's unhurt arm. "Come inside. Got to fix you up," she panted.

Together, they stumbled into the den, and she closed and latched the sliding glass door. "Oh, God, it could have killed you!" Tears scalded her eyes.

"Right back at you. What got into you, attacking a supernatural monster with patio furniture?" The papasan chair shuffled up to him. After a dubious backward glance, he sagged into it. Blood trickled from slashes in his left forearm.

"You wanted me to let it tear you apart? No way! I'm not finished with you yet." *Good grief, did I say that out loud?* Maybe he wasn't listening carefully or, with luck, would chalk up the remark to the panic of the moment.

That luck didn't hold. He captured her hand and raised it to his lips, his breath making her skin tingle. "Not finished, huh? I can't wait to find out what you're planning to do with me next."

Oh, God, I wish I knew, myself. She tugged her hand free. "First off, clean that bite. Don't move. I'll be right back."

She rushed to the half-bath off the kitchen and came back with gauze pads, first-aid tape, antiseptic spray, and paper towels. Kneeling beside Thad, she wiped off the blood, then sprayed and bandaged the wound. When she'd finished, he caught and squeezed her hand. "Thanks."

Warmth spread from his fingers up her arm and through her body. A flush heated her face and chest. "What's to thank me for? I'm the reason you got attacked in the first place." She looked down at her free hand and crumpled the stained paper towels in it. "Let me get rid of this stuff." She scurried to the bathroom, threw away the trash, and stowed the first-aid supplies. At that point the pain in her scraped knees forced itself on her attention. She blotted away the traces of oozing blood and stuck bandages on the worst of the abrasions.

After a stop in the kitchen for two glasses of ice water, she returned to the den. She was sure Thad let his fingers brush hers on purpose when she handed him one of the drinks. "Just what we need, trying to explain to your folks what the heck is going on over here." She pointed to his injured arm. "What are you going to tell them? That a dog bit you?"

"No way. They'd freak out and insist I report it, and I'd have to get rabies shots." She couldn't help laughing at the idea of getting rabies from a wolf demon. "I'll concoct some not-too-farfetched explanation, maybe that I was helping you clean up the yard and got cut by a broken branch."

"Then your mother will know it's my fault you got hurt. I don't think she likes me."

He stared at her as if she'd announced the Earth was flat. "Where in the name of the Great Horn Spoon did you get that idea?"

"The what of the which?"

He grinned. "Something my first CO used to say in situations too extreme for profanity. You were one of Mom's favorite students."

"You'd never know it from the red ink all over my senior term paper on *A Midsummer Night's Dream.*"

"Are you kidding? She came home bragging about how brilliant that paper was. She has high standards, that's all, and she's never believed in over-praising kids. She acted the same with me."

Val had to mull over this mind-boggling notion for several seconds before she could frame an answer. "Well, I always did assume she was a perfectionist."

"You assumed correctly." He caught her hand again. "But she definitely approved of you. She thought I was an idiot for letting you go." He lifted her hand and brushed his lips over her fingers. Heat and chill rippled through her. "She was right." He reached out to thread his fingers through the hair at the nape of her neck. Standing, he lowered his mouth to hers.

Chapter Seven

She couldn't resist parting her lips and darting out her tongue to meet the teasing flicker of his. But only for a second—a sense of being watched jolted her back to rationality. Turning away from Thad, she met the cool gaze of the white cat, seated near the patio door.

"I beg pardon for this interruption." Yuki bowed her head in greeting. "I have made a circuit of your property and confirmed the *okami* and the *raiju* have both departed for the present."

"Uh…thanks." Val drew a deep breath, trying to tame her racing heart.

The cat padded over to them and rubbed against Thad's legs. "I trust you are not seriously injured."

He cast a quizzical look at Val, who translated.

"No, I'll be okay," he answered.

After passing on that reply, Val headed for the stairs. "Yuki, how about a treat? You deserve it." The cat and Thad followed her up to the kitchen, where they found Toby crouched by the refrigerator. He hissed at the sight of the spirit cat but didn't run away. *That's some improvement, anyhow.* Val opened a can of tuna and dished the contents into a pair of saucers, which she set on the floor at opposite ends of the room. She added two small bowls with a slosh of milk in each. Yuki murmured her thanks and settled to nibbling on the tuna. Toby took wary bites from his share, watching the white cat with his ears laid back. "See, she's a friend," Val said. "She's helping us figure out how to chase away the big bad wolf."

Yuki glanced up with a twitch of her ears. "I can hardly claim to have given much help. This ritual has provoked the *okami's* wrath anew, and it will surely return with a fiercer attack."

"Then we'll have to think of another plan," Val said with an attempt at a confident tone.

Thad's wry smile suggested he saw through her façade. "Yeah, we have not yet begun to fight."

"What's the standard rebuttal to that saying? There's always somebody who didn't get the word?" She walked toward the living room, leaving him little choice but to follow. "Yuki was right all along. We're just making things worse. We don't have any magical power of our own, and on top of that, we're trying to fight a Japanese demon with Western rituals."

"So we'll find a different angle. I'm sure as hell not giving up." He stretched out his lacerated arm. "My honor's at stake now."

In the foyer, he wrapped his arms around her before she could dodge. For a second, she let herself lean into the hug. Somehow, she felt safe there, strange though that seemed after so many years of clinging to the idea that he'd betrayed her. *It would be so easy to stay this way.* Nevertheless, she ducked when he bent to kiss her. "You should go."

"Do you really want me to?"

"It's not a matter of *want*. It's a matter of being sensible."

"It wouldn't be sensible not to make up for lost time while we have the chance." His hand skimmed up and down her spine and came to rest on her bottom. He nuzzled her neck. Her pulse stuttered as he nipped his way along her jawline to her mouth.

This time she didn't evade the kiss. For only this moment, she yearned to rewind reality to their last kiss so long ago and imagine they were still in love, still anticipating a happy life together. *Is the love part all imagination?* Closing her eyes, she tilted her head back against his embracing arm and opened her lips to the exploration of his tongue. He'd changed from the hot-blooded but awkward teenage boy she remembered. Somewhere along the way, he'd learned to lick, taste, and savor in ways that made her tingle with pleasure. At the thought of his probable interludes with other women, a ridiculous twinge of jealousy stung her. The next second, a surge of sensation obliterated it as he deepened the kiss. His firm clasp on her rear felt like a burning brand even through two layers of cloth. In front, a hard ridge pressed against her, igniting flames that radiated through her core. She melted. He moved his other hand from her neck to wander down her arm, up her ribcage, and over the lower curve of her breast. Her nipples peaked with an ache that wrung a faint moan from her.

He pressed still closer, molding his body to hers and trapping his hand between them. Her back thumped against the front door. He winced at the bump to his wounded forearm.

She opened her eyes. Flushed with a blend of passion and embarrassment, she said, "Good time to put on the brakes."

"When we were finally shifting out of first gear?" He massaged the center of her back and skimmed a thumb over one breast, not quite touching the nipple.

"Not now." She gasped out the words, struggling to

breathe. She planted both palms on his chest in a too-tentative shove.

He took the hint anyway and stepped back. "Too soon?" His breath came harsh and rapid.

She nodded. "Too soon. Too fast."

His eyes held hers in a grave stare. "So when? Do you think we'll be able to pick up where we left off? Or, better yet, start over and move forward? Do normal things like stream movies and go swimming at the pool?"

"I'm not saying a definite *no*. But I can't think about anything like that while my house is under siege by a monster."

Not quite smiling, he said, "I get it. As an officer and a gentleman, I yield to my lady's wish—for now."

"Thanks. For one thing, how late do you want your parents to see you leaving here?"

He stroked her cheek and smoothed an errant strand of hair. "That excuse won't work forever. We're all grown up."

"As Scarlett says, I'll think about that tomorrow. Or maybe later. Meanwhile, what do I do now? I may be stuck with that beast forever."

"You mean, what do *we* do? No way will I let you to face this alone. I'll see you tomorrow." He brushed a light kiss on her lips. "And every day until you're safe again." Leaving her with that echo of her own thoughts, he walked out.

She leaned back against the closed door, hugging herself and trembling. A flashback to the moment when she'd thought the wolf's fangs might slash Thad's throat instead of his arm rushed over her. *People die. But not here and now, not him.* She wiped her eyes and drew a deep, shuddering breath.

The white cat strolled into the room, tail waving, and rubbed against her ankles. Val bent over to stroke her, then abruptly stopped. A twinge of awkwardness pricked her as she remembered the cat was also human, at least sometimes. "I never thought to ask you if it's okay to do this."

Yuki stretched. "Of course. I am a cat first of all."

"Where the wolf thing is concerned, do you think we're all right for now?"

"As far as I can tell. You should be safe inside your home unless the *okami* grows strong enough to break through the protection of the lingering magic from the scroll."

"Could that happen?"

Yuki's whiskers twitched. "I cannot say for certain that it will not."

"The beast already had enough power to tear down the *ofuda*, so we can't depend on those to keep it away." With the Yuki stalking beside her, Val walked to the kitchen to clean the cat-feeding dishes. "All the Western-style magic we've tried has been a bust. Any ideas?"

"I will think upon the problem."

After Yuki disappeared, Val finished loading the bowls in the dishwasher and made a circuit of the house, checking locks and turning off lights. She glimpsed the *akaname* in the downstairs bathroom using its tongue to scour hard-water stains from the sink. As usual, it vanished at the sight of her. She sighed. "If you're that afraid of me, I guess I can't count on you to help fight off a wolf *yokai*. Not that anything has much chance to beat it if the *raiju* can't even take it out."

****

When she stepped out her front door the next

morning, she found a tree branch blocking the sidewalk. Cursing under her breath, she shoved the limb out of her way. *At least it didn't hit the car or smash another window. Or punch a hole in the roof, thank God.*

Just as Val reached the car, Shawna and her little girl walked down their driveway to collect the newspaper. While Dani picked up the paper, her mother sketched a wave at Val. "Another freaky storm last night, huh? Crazy-ass wind and thunder but no rain. Maybe it's climate change."

Val shrugged. "Who knows?"

"And that huge stray dog was running around again, too."

Dani grinned and piped up, "Big blue doggie."

Val forced a weak smile. "Wow, that's some imagination." Waving goodbye, she drove off before she had to invent any more feeble replies.

She had to reprise the subject of the "freak localized thunderstorm" again that afternoon, when she left work early to meet the glazier hired by the insurance company. She answered his good-natured puzzlement in the vaguest terms she could manage. At completion of the job, she gritted her teeth and handed over a card for payment, mentally calculating how much or little credit she'd have left after subtracting the repair cost.

After a session of collecting fallen limbs in the back yard and cleaning up furniture, candles, and broken glass on the patio, she poured herself an iced tea, sat at the kitchen table, and called Yuki's name. When the white cat appeared next to her chair, Val said, "I've been thinking about why we can't exorcise the *okami*. The *ofuda* by themselves obviously weren't enough. Thad and I don't know any Japanese demon-banishing spells, and since we're not sorcerers anyway, they might not work for us even if we knew them."

"That is a fair assessment of the problem."

"What we need is a genuine Japanese magic-worker. But if Thad couldn't even find a Shinto shrine in the whole mid-Atlantic region, tracking down a sorcerer in the next couple of days doesn't look like a reasonable prospect. Posting a query online would bring the delusional and the con artists out of the woodwork in droves."

"I know not why such folk would be lurking in the walls to begin with, but I share your reservations." Yuki stretched, then resettled herself, seated with her tail curled around her paws. "If only Hiroshi were here."

"Yeah, too bad that's impossible." Val took a sip of her tea. "It is, isn't it? I mean, he must have gone wherever in the afterlife good magicians go."

"It may not be truly impossible." The cat spoke so quietly Val could hardly hear her.

"You mean we could maybe call him back from the dead?"

"That depends on whether he has moved on, to either his next life or the Pure Land. If his spirit lingers on this plane of existence…"

"Are you suggesting a séance?" Val plunked down her glass with a rattle of ice. "That sounds risky." In every horror movie she'd watched, summoning the dead never turned out well.

"If he were nearby and chose to answer," Yuki said, "he would surely have benign intentions toward me and toward you as the keeper of the scroll. The question is whether we could make contact with him at all."

"Do you honestly think we should try?"

Yuki lay flat and bowed her head on her paws. "I do not wholly trust my own thoughts on this matter. That is why I have not made this suggestion before. It would be such a consolation to see him once again. But if I called and got no response…"

"What have you got to lose by trying? No guts, no glory." *Sheesh, did that just come out of my mouth? I've been listening to Thad too much.*

"You speak wisely."

Val bent over to stroke the cat. "If his spirit answered us, would he be able to vanquish the wolf *yokai*? Before, all he could do to keep you safe was turn you into a statue."

Yuki looked up. "Since then, he has had the rest of his mortal life as well as over a century of afterlife to grow in power. We will not know unless we make the attempt."

"Okay, do you know of anything we'll need?"

"*Shikigami*."

Val blinked. "What's that?"

The cat leaped onto a vacant chair. "An *onmyoji* performs his art by conjuring minor *yokai—shikigami—*into physical vessels, often figures cut out of paper."

"Any special kind of paper or figures?" Val took a long gulp of her tea and got up to put the glass in the sink.

"The shapes are usually those of animals. As for the paper, almost any kind would do, but red is an auspicious color. It stands for power."

"Luckily, I think I have a batch of red construction paper." Val walked upstairs to the office, followed by Yuki. In the closet, she unearthed the box she remembered stashing there after volunteering as a Sunday school assistant the previous year. "Here we go.

I knew I had some left over from making Valentines." She opened the search page on the computer to find instructions for calling up spirits of the dead.

After sifting through several pages that cautioned against trying any such thing, she scanned a few sites with more practical suggestions. "White candles and a mirror. What do you think of that?"

"Those implements do not seem likely to open a gate for evil forces," Yuki said.

As lukewarm as that endorsement sounded, it would have to do. "This page says the optimum number of participants is three. Counting you as one of them, we have enough. Now, do I have three white candles?" She headed back to the kitchen to root through the cabinet where she kept supplies for electrical outages. Turning up three thick, vanilla-scented white candles, she said, "Good, I won't have to send Thad to buy any." She plopped into a chair, setting the candles on the table. "If he'll go along with this. I haven't even asked him yet."

Her pulse stuttered as she called his number. After they got through this crisis, would he still want to revive their relationship? Would she? Her heart was softening toward the idea, even though her brain kept poking holes in it. *Suppose it's only the excitement of fighting demons together that's making me feel this way? Then what happens when the fight's over?*

When he answered the phone, she explained the séance plan.

"Is that safe?"

"Compared to what?" she said. "Combatting a wolf demon on our own? The way I see it, we'll get one of two results. Nothing will happen, so we'll be no worse off. Or Hiroshi will answer the call, and he'll defeat the thing."

"There's a third possibility. He could show up, and it could beat him."

"I'd rather not think of failure as an option. What happened to *don't give up the ship* and *I have not yet begun to fight*?"

He chuckled. "Okay, we'll sail in with guns blazing—figuratively, of course. I'll come over around seven-thirty, when it starts to get dark."

After hanging up, Val stroked along the cat's back and sighed. "If this doesn't work, I don't see what else we can do."

"In that case, you must remove the scroll from your home," Yuki said, "to some isolated location, as you considered before. To have myself alone under attack from the *okami* is better than having it torment you and your neighbors as well."

"Even when we moved the scroll, residual magic stuck around here. Suppose it never goes away? I wouldn't be able to sell a house that's essentially haunted." She picked up the pile of red paper, got a pair of scissors from a desk drawer, and went back to the kitchen where she could spread out the supplies on the table. "So failure isn't an option. Now, what kind of animal shape do we need?"

Yuki tilted her head sideways in a feline shrug. "That matters little, as far as I know."

"The *okami* flies around, so maybe we should use something with wings. Birds should be easy enough." Since Val didn't have any pretensions to artistic talent, *easy* was an important factor. *Fast* counted, too. She tore a piece of notepaper from the pad by the kitchen phone, folded it double, sketched half of a bird with its wings spread, cut out the shape, and unfolded it. "Looks birdlike to me." She began tracing multiple copies of the pattern onto the red paper. "How many of these will Hiroshi need to work his magic?"

"I believe it varies. Seven is a fortunate number."

"Hmm. To be on the safe side, how about a multiple of that? Three times seven?"

Yuki purred agreement.

"Okay, twenty-one it is." Val proceeded to draw and cut out paper birds, with a break for a sandwich at dinnertime. Finally, she had twenty-one cutouts stacked in three piles and the scraps cleared away.

Thad showed up promptly at the agreed time. Even before joining the Navy, he'd always been a model of punctuality. He'd replaced the original bandage on his arm with a neatly taped-on gauze square. "I touched base with Mom and Dad before coming over here and told them the 'jagged branch' story. I got a lecture about doing yard work in dim light, but at least they bought it." He grinned and planted a light kiss on her cheek before she could dodge. "And like I said before, they're totally in favor of us getting back together."

She flushed. "Wonderful. If we do start dating, they'll be watching our every move. Let's get through the next hour first." *Did I really say "if," not "no way"?*

"Okay, how is the séance going to work?"

She showed him her pile of paper cutouts. "I figured we should do it outside because the *okami* can't come in the house. If Hiroshi's spirit does appear and try to fight off the thing, it would help to be where it hangs out." She glanced at Yuki, who had materialized at some point after Thad's arrival.

The cat responded with a nod and a slow blink.

Together they carried the paper birds, the candles, a hand mirror, and the scroll onto the patio. In the humid twilight, punctuated by flashes of lightning bugs in the grass, Val ignited the three candles, placed at the apexes of an imaginary triangle. She set the mirror face up in the center of the table, encircled by the red cutouts, which she tucked under the edges of the mirror in case of wind. "I thought having the scroll here would be good because of its connection to Hiroshi." She laid it next to the mirror.

"That may help," Yuki said. "Ultimately, however, I suppose it will depend on whether he is able to hear my cry for assistance and is willing to answer. These objects and your concentration on our need will serve to focus my appeal. The precise elements of the ritual matter less."

"Sounds reasonable," Thad said. A dry laugh escaped him. "How did we get to the point where the word *reasonable* belongs in the same world with summoning a ghost? So what do we do now?"

Val shrugged and took a seat. "In movies people always form a circle and clear their minds." She reached out with one arm. Thad pulled up a chair, and the white cat perched on another. Thad clasped Val's offered hand, while both of them touched Yuki with their free hands. The cat quivered under Val's fingertips.

Closing her eyes, Val slowed and deepened her breathing. Her mind was far from clear, her head buzzing with memories of the previous night's attack. She forced herself to home in on the sound of Thad's inhaled and exhaled breath. She relaxed her taut shoulder muscles and let her hand lie loosely in his grip.

A breeze sprang up. Yuki meowed, then began to

speak. "Hiroshi," she whispered. "Hiroshi, are you near? Can my words reach you?"

The wind grew cooler and brisker. An indrawn gasp from Thad broke the rhythm of their synchronized breathing. Val opened her eyes. The reflected flames in the mirror dimmed and vanished, obscured by thickening darkness. A purplish-black cloud swirled in the glass.

"Hiroshi, your spell has been undone," Yuki continued more loudly. "I have been awakened, and I am calling for you."

The dark blot on the glass coalesced into a shape with eyes and teeth. Within a couple of seconds, it became the ash-gray wolf *yokai*.

Thad muttered, "Maybe we should abort this mission."

Val squeezed his fingers. "We can't give up yet."

"Hiroshi!" Yuki cried. "I need you now. Come to my aid."

A rose-tinted light flashed in the mirror. The wolf's head melted away, and a man's face, faint and amorphous at first, sharpened into focus. Middle-aged, with receding but still black hair, he wore round spectacles with tortoiseshell rims. The cat sighed his name again. His head floated upward from the mirror, followed by the indistinct outline of his body. He drifted away from the table and solidified to stand beside the chair where Yuki sat. Slender, well under six feet tall, he wore a black, hip-length jacket over a kimono.

The white cat stood on her hind legs, front paws resting on the back of the chair, and meowed at him. He bent over to nuzzle her fur, and she licked his chin. "Yuki-chan," he whispered, stroking her. If he was a disembodied spirit, how could they touch? Of course, she was a kind of spirit, too, so physical limitations probably didn't apply. He straightened up, blinking as if to banish tears. "Who are your friends? What and where is this place?"

"Hiroshi-san, may I present Thad-san and Valerie-san? Perhaps she can best explain what has happened."

Val clutched Thad's hand tighter. It was one thing to try summoning a ghost, something else altogether for the summoning actually to work. She swallowed. "We're in the eastern United States, twenty-first century. I'm the one who activated the spell and woke up Yuki by accident." She sketched the main outlines of the situation.

Thad looked from her to the spirit with a puzzled frown. "Translation, please?"

Val had momentarily forgotten he didn't have her magical advantage in understanding the conversation. She summarized what they'd said.

"You have made a valiant effort," Hiroshi said, "but your rituals would not have defeated the *okuri-okami* even if you were adept in them."

"Now that he's here," Thad asked, "can he fight the *okami*?"

Val passed on the question, fair enough since the magician hadn't dared face it in his lifetime.

"My power has grown during my time suspended in the void," Hiroshi said. He ran his fingers along Yuki's spine, and she arched her back with a low purr. "I could not leave this plane of existence until I knew you were permanently safe. Now I am prepared to ensure that." He looked at the paper birds on the table.

"Will those work for you?" Val asked.

"They will serve," he said with a grim smile.

"What should we do?"

"If you can, keep the candles alight." A small brush appeared in his right hand. After sketching a pair of characters on one of the red cutouts, he murmured a phrase under his breath. A black mist shot through with silver swirled up from the writing and wafted over the circle of paper figures. Identical writing appeared on each one.

As he recited another incantation, the wind picked up, lashing the trees and making the candle flames waver. Shivering, Val again tightened her grip on Thad's hand. His frozen stare revealed the same fear that constricted her own chest.

The brush in Hiroshi's grasp dematerialized. Thunder rumbled, and the scraps of paper rose into the air in a miniature whirlwind. The magician intoned one more syllable. The red birds fluttered out of the formation to fly independently. Their crudely trimmed beaks lengthened and sharpened.

A mass of black fog oozed down from the clouds. The *okuri-okami* emerged from it and alighted under a tree. With a snarl, it looked from Yuki to Hiroshi. It bared its fangs and slinked toward them.

Chapter Eight

The magician shouted aloud, this time in words Val understood. "No! You shall not touch her." He chanted one final sentence in that other, incomprehensible language.

"He is calling his *shikigami*, his spirit servants." Yuki whispered.

A shower of golden sparks enveloped the paper birds. They enlarged and filled out, no longer two-dimensional silhouettes. Golden eyes gleamed in their heads. They flapped toward the *okami*, which leaped up to snap at them. Thunder boomed with a simultaneous flash of lightning. The *raiju* dove out of the treetops.

Val's dazzled eyes glimpsed movement at the edge of vision. She glanced sideways in time to see the patio door sliding open by itself. The *akaname* slithered out. Behind it clattered the ivory dragon and octopus. Like the birds, the ivory figurines grew bigger, swelling almost to the size of the two wolf *yokai*. The *okami* growled more loudly. Yuki sprang forward and hissed at it, her fur bristling.

Hiroshi opened his mouth to protest but closed it without a sound. Instead, he gestured at the *shikigami*. They dive-bombed the *okami*, stabbed it with their beaks, and scratched it with clawed feet they hadn't possessed a moment before. The octopus skittered up to the wolf and twined its tentacles around one of the beast's legs, while the dragon's talons raked its eyes and muzzle. The *akaname* slinked around the periphery of the fight as if in search of the perfect opening.

Meanwhile, the wind howled with a chill like an October gale. The three flames sputtered under its assault. Val leaned over the table, and Thad, immediately catching on, did the same, trying to shield the candles.

The *raiju*, neon-blue sparks sizzling around it, clamped its jaws onto back of the *okami's* neck. The ash-gray wolf twisted around to bite the attacker. Thunder and lightning overlapped, making Val's ears ring and her eyes burn. The *okami* wrenched itself free of the *raiju's* grip to snap at the flock of *shikigami*. Each time the wolf *yokai* shredded one of the cutouts between its teeth, the figure crumpled to the ground, merely paper again. More of them kept mobbing the *okami*, but at this rate they wouldn't last long.

One candle blew out. The *okami* shook off its tormentors and lunged closer to the patio. After several seconds of fumbling with the lighter, Val got the flame reignited. The wolf halted, and the other *yokai* and *shikigami* redoubled their attacks. Silver blood dripped from the slashes in its pelt.

The wind snuffed out another candle. While she struggled to light it, the *okami* stalked closer despite the creatures biting and clawing at it. Val's pulse hammered in her temples, and the hand clutching the lighter shook. The wolf's bared fangs, scarcely two yards away from her, made her head spin as she choked down rising panic. Waving his arms and yelling, Thad leaped between her and the *okami*.

"Stop that!" *Oh, God, not again! It could've killed him last time. What is he thinking?*

The *akaname* jumped into the melee and lashed the

wolf with its prehensile tongue. The beast whirled around to repel this new threat. Snarling, it chomped down on the *akaname's* neck and flung the creature across the patio. After a snap at the *raiju*, the *okami* turned its attention to the human watchers and charged at Hiroshi.

With a siren-like yowl, Yuki sprang in front of the magician. When she raked her claws along the wolf's chest, Hiroshi cried out in protest. The cat rolled sideways and leaped out of the *okami's* reach. Growling, it pivoted toward her. Hiroshi flailed his arms in complex gestures that left tracks of golden light in the air. They streamed over the remaining *shikigami* and seemed to infuse them with fresh power. In a single mass, the red birds swarmed over the *okami*, pecking its eyes and clawing its muzzle. While they distracted the wolf, which bit and shredded each one it could catch, the *raiju* leaped onto its back and seized its neck again. The *akaname* crawled over to whip its tongue around the *okami's* forelegs. The octopus tangled its rear legs. The dragon ripped into its belly.

The *okami* collapsed, enemies clinging to every part of its body. At another sharp command from Hiroshi, the last of the *shikigami* tore open its throat. Yuki sprang in to sever the exposed artery with her needle-keen fangs. Silver blood gushed out.

A shudder convulsed the *okami*. Its body crumpled in on itself and disintegrated to ash. A gust of wind blew the dust into the air, where it dissolved into nothing along with the splashes of ichor.

Yuki shook herself and smoothed her disheveled fur with her tongue. The *akaname* vanished. The octopus and dragon shrank to their normal size, becoming lifeless ivory, while those birds not already torn to shreds reverted to flat paper silhouettes. Thunder and lightning ceased as the *raiju* also disappeared.

Her knees trembling, Val grabbed Thad's arm to steady herself. "Is the storm wolf gone for good, too?"

"It is not likely to return," Hiroshi said. "The destruction of the *okami* absorbed all the magic."

Yuki shimmered from feline to human form. Hiroshi stepped over to her and touched her cheek. "You are safe now. I am content."

She sighed. "If only you could stay."

"You know I cannot."

"I know that very well. It would be wrong to chain you to the material world."

He ran his hand over her hair, then rested it on her shoulder. "Is there anything more I can do for you?"

"The scroll's magic binds me to its vicinity. Would it be possible to change that so I can roam at will?"

"Easily." The calligraphy brush reappeared in his hand. Bending over the table, he added a pair of characters to the column of writing at the side of the scroll. "Now you can travel wherever you wish and maintain physical form as long as you desire. You still have limits on the time you can remain in human shape, because that is part of your inborn nature, but otherwise you have complete freedom."

She bowed to him. "My profound thanks, Hiroshi-san."

His arms encircled her. She swayed toward him to lean against his chest.

Val, her head still pounding, tugged Thad through the open door into the den. "What is the matter with you, anyway? You jumped in front of that wolf demon like you were inviting it to chomp you."

With his face as flushed as hers felt, he retorted, "So I was supposed to let it eat you instead? The hell with that."

"I'm not the one who almost got bitten in half last night." Tears burned her eyes. She threw herself on him, flinging her arms around his neck. She tilted her head back to gaze up at him. "I'm not sure what happens next with us, but I definitely wasn't ready to lose you that way."

He held her close, the solid length of his body hard against hers. "If you think I'm letting you go now, you're living in an alternate universe." He bent to claim her mouth in a ravenous kiss. She welcomed the heat of his lips and tongue, closing her eyes and digging her nails into his shirt. Her head whirled. When the ridge of his shaft pressed against her, she couldn't resist hugging him tighter. She was melting again. A stifled moan escaped her lips.

He pulled away. The abrupt break in contact left her momentarily dizzy. "This isn't the time," he murmured into her hair. He glanced toward the patio.

Following the direction of his gaze, she saw Hiroshi and Yuki standing in a loose embrace with his hands on her shoulders. Val's cheeks warmed all over again. Not that the other two were paying any attention to Thad and her, though. Hiroshi bestowed gentle kisses on Yuki's forehead and lips. He released her, stepped back, and thinned from solidity to translucence. A glowing aura surrounded him, and he became transparent, then faded away like mist. Yuki covered her face, and a tremor swept over her.

A second later, she looked up with her usual serene

expression and walked into the house. "He has ascended to his proper destiny, and I am free. It is for the best." She pulled off her *shakudo* ring and placed it in Val's hand.

"Do you want me to sell this the way we discussed," Val asked, "so you can buy a ticket to Japan? You could be shipped there as a cat, dematerialize to get out of the crate when it's unloaded from the plane, and change to human form long enough to find a new home."

Yuki shook her head. She shifted into feline shape before answering. "Nippon offers no home for me now. Hiroshi is gone, doubtless my shrine has collapsed into ruins, and I saw in your picture box how much I remember there has changed. I would prefer to explore the new world on this side of the ocean." She perked her ears forward and looped around Val's ankles. "I am actually beginning to enjoy this strange place. The ring is yours, my gift in gratitude for helping to save me from the *okami*. You can sell it and use the proceeds to repair your dwelling."

"Wow." Val sank onto the couch. "That's—I don't feel I should take it."

The cat's whiskers twitched. "Please do. What use have I for money?" She vanished.

"This should cover my half of a new roof, all right." Val put the ring in a pocket of her shorts and rubbed her eyes. "I hope she isn't gone forever, too. I'd miss her."

"Same here." He released a long breath. "Those two had been separated a lot longer than we have, and their love survived."

And they didn't let fear of death spoil it, either, Val thought. Not ready to say anything like that aloud, she stood and clasped his hand. "Come help me clean up that mess."

Together they went outside to set chairs and table upright and collect the candles, scraps of paper, and cracked mirror. Val picked up the ivory figurines and carried them to the living room, where she placed them in their customary spot above the fireplace. She left the rolled-up scroll beside them until she could decide on a permanent location for it. "If the magic is used up, I guess I'll have to start cleaning my own bathrooms again."

"It'll be worth it not to have *yokai* besieging your house, won't it?" He caught her hands and raised them to his lips. "God, when that wolf thing charged straight at you...Val, I can't stand the thought of losing you again. Do we have a chance?"

She trembled at the brush of his lips on her fingers. "I don't want to lose you, either."

"But you were so determined not to be a Navy wife."

"I'm rethinking that position." She met his unwavering gaze with one of her own. "Fighting demons kind of puts other stuff into perspective. If we can survive that, we should be able to get through little things like deployments and cross-country moves together." She swallowed. "Even deployments to war zones."

"So you could stand being uprooted after all?"

"They need librarians everywhere, right? Yuki's giving up her roots. A little change like relocating from the East Coast to the West Coast, or wherever the Navy sends you next, would be nothing in comparison to what she's done." She rested her hands lightly on his shoulders. "I think you were right—I've been making excuses to avoid taking the next step. Now that I'll be able to get the roof fixed, I can't hide behind that problem."

"Can we start over now?" He twined his arms around her loosely enough that she could slip free if she wanted to. "All engines full steam ahead?"

"I don't know about *full steam*, but I'm prepared to accelerate, at least."

"Thank God. We have a lot of time to make up for."

She snuggled against him and molded her body to his. His hug made her feel safe and at home. His hands swept from her shoulders down her spine to her bottom, triggering waves of sensation. The pressure of his hardness ignited a flame at her core.

He nuzzled her neck. "Upstairs?"

His lips on the tender skin of her throat made her tingle all over. "Right," she gasped. She was through fighting the magnetism that had drawn them back together. "Upstairs."

They climbed the steps with arms around each other's waists. At the bedroom door, he paused to kiss her. Before yielding to him, she scanned the room, wishing she hadn't left her nightgown flung over a chair and a pair of socks next to the laundry basket instead of in it. *As if he cares how neat the place is!* She let herself flow into his embrace. While his tongue probed her parted lips, she leaned back against his encircling arm, her head spinning. Finally they stopped for breath and moved to the bed. He switched on the nightstand lamp. "I want to see you." With a second glance at the nightstand, he said, "Hey, you unpacked your collectible cards."

"I decided I wanted to remember those times, after all." She flashed him a wicked grin. "Feel like playing a couple of rounds?"

He laughed and nipped her gently on the neck. "Maybe later." Seated side by side on the edge of the mattress, they peeled off each other's shirts in turn.

He'd filled out since the last time she'd seen him shirtless, as a teenager at the pool. She explored his chest, still lean but now solidly muscular. Her fingers grazing the curls of dark hair wrung a shuddering sigh from him. He unfastened and stripped off her bra while nibbling a path up her neck and along her jawline. After another long, deep kiss, he cupped her breasts and skimmed his thumbs over the nipples. Under his avid stare, a blush spread from her cheeks down her neck and torso. He'd never seen her this nearly naked before. Did she measure up to his expectations?

As if reading her mind, he said, "You have no idea how many hours I used to fantasize about looking at these instead of just groping in the dark. It was more than worth the wait."

A giggle bubbled from her at the memory of his fumbling for her bra hooks in parked cars. The laughter segued into a moan as his tongue flicked over her breasts and teased each aching peak. Heat pooled between her legs. While massaging his back and shoulders with one hand, she let her other roam to his lap and discover the hard evidence of his passion. His hips flexed to thrust into her open palm.

He stroked her inner thighs, close to the spot that needed his touch most but not quite reaching it. Instead, he pulled away to flip back the bedspread and sheets. He dug a foil-wrapped envelope from a pocket before shedding his shorts and briefs.

Not sure whether to feel grateful or indignant, she said, "You actually came prepared?"

He shrugged. "Can you blame me for hoping?" He guided her hand to his shaft. "I've been waiting thirteen years to finish what we started on prom night."

"It's not as if either of us has been in stasis all that time."

"I know, but in a way those years don't count—except that everything we've lived through separately since then has prepared us to be together now." Capturing her mouth, he unzipped her shorts and splayed his hand over her stomach. With an eager wiggle, she helped him get the shorts and panties off. She fondled him while he delved between her legs with a touch far more deft than his teenage experimentation. She shoved aside the question of how he'd gained his expertise and let herself drown in the wave of pleasure that crashed over her. Heat radiated from the hypersensitive bud to every part of her body.

Trembling with aftershocks, she clung to him, inhaling his aftershave and the scent of his flesh, tasting salt on his skin. At a gentle push from him, she lay back and opened to him. As she wrapped her arms and legs around his waist and hips to draw him in, a twinge of worry needled her. After so many years of celibacy, would she remember the moves? Would penetration hurt?

The next moment, he entered her, and her qualms evaporated. The snug fit only made her soar to a higher peak. In fact, they interlocked as if created for each other. They rocked together in perfect harmony until a fresh surge of ecstasy suffused her. He shuddered in release and showered feverish kisses over her face and neck.

Finally, they lay face up, hands clasped, her head resting against his shoulder. His heartbeat pounded in her ear. She didn't speak until their breathing slowed to normal. "Welcome home," she whispered.

His lips brushed her cheek. "That's exactly how it feels. Home."

When his eyes drifted shut, she reluctantly raised herself on one elbow and patted his arm. "You have to leave," she said, tracing circles on his chest.

He caught her hand and pressed it to his heart. "Why?"

"Because I'd never be able to look your parents in the face if they saw your car parked here overnight."

He faked a gusty sigh. "You're a cruel woman. Okay, I'll humor you for now." He stretched and sat up.

They scrambled back into their clothes with several pauses for hugs and light kisses. Holding hands again, they headed down to the foyer. As they passed through the living room, she noticed both cats curled peacefully on the couch. *That's new. Toby must've decided she's not so bad compared to all the other magical chaos.* At the front door, Val said, "Come over tomorrow for dinner after work. I'll fix it this time. Wouldn't want you to think I don't know how to cook."

"Then it's a date."

"Yeah, I guess we could call it that."

He cupped her cheeks between his palms. "Have I gotten around to mentioning that I love you? I think I've never stopped loving you."

"Me, too, I think." She gulped a deep breath. "But is that enough?"

"I'm praying you'll decide it is. I believe it can be if we give it a chance." After a lingering embrace that tempted her to change her mind about letting him stay, they parted.

Having locked the door behind him, she walked to the living-room couch, where the cats lay dozing less than a foot apart. "So you like her now?" Val ran her palm over Toby from head to tail, then said to Yuki, "I'm glad you're still here."

The white cat blinked and yawned. "Where else would I go? I enjoy having a human companion who can understand my speech."

"In that case, I have an idea." Val took the scroll and the ivory figurines from the mantel and carried them up to the spare bedroom along with a hammer and thumbtacks from the kitchen. Yuki padded in her wake. Val hung the scroll right above the dresser to drape over the mirror. Having set aside the framed photos in the center of the dresser, she arranged the dragon and octopus in the cleared space with their own reflections visible behind them.

"So they're definitely inanimate for good now?"

"I believe so," Yuki said.

"And the *akaname's* gone? I'll sort of miss it." Val knelt to rub Yuki under the chin. "This can be your room as long as you want to stay. When I sell the house and move out, you're welcome to join me."

Yuki gravely thanked her. "Will you wed Thad-san?"

"If…" Her voice quavered. "If I do marry Thad, we'll be taking these things with us, and you can come along if you want to."

The cat purred. "The idea of traveling your immense country appeals to me."

Suddenly, it appeals to me more than it ever did before.

****

On the way home the next afternoon, Val stopped at the supermarket for salad ingredients, a block of Parmesan cheese, noodles, a loaf of Italian bread, and tiramisu. She chopped up a pile of her homegrown tomatoes for spaghetti sauce and grated the cheese. Water for the noodles was just rising to a boil when Thad arrived with a bottle of red wine.

"How did you guess?" she asked.

"Telepathy. Or maybe fifty-fifty odds between red and white." He pulled her against him and ravished her mouth with a kiss that made her quivery and lightheaded.

With both hands on his chest, she pushed him to arm's length. "Dinner first. Conversation. Civilized stuff."

While the noodles simmered, she showed him the niche she'd designed for Yuki in the spare room. "Neat idea," he said. "I'm glad she's sticking around."

When the kitchen timer beeped, he helped to set the table and dish up the meal. After they'd settled in the dining room and sampled a few bites, he said, "How about that? You really can cook."

Val shot a mock scowl at him. "Don't push your luck there."

"For the record, so can I. We could split the job."

She diverted the conversation to less fraught topics. Over dinner, they chatted about their lives during the past decade. They traded anecdotes about his Navy assignments in various exotic ports and the quirks of state politics she'd encountered in her work for the General Assembly. They discussed books, and she learned with delight that both of them still followed a couple of the same sword-and-sorcery authors. As they finished dessert, he brought up the possibility of a shared future again.

"You know, when we get married, we could buy out your sister's half of the house."

"When, not if? Overconfident much?"

He grinned. "After last night, don't I have a right to a little confidence?"

She lightly punched him on the uninjured arm.

"I'm serious. Between the two of us, we could qualify for a mortgage and afford the payments. We could live here until I get transferred about three years from now, then rent out the place if we can't sell it right away."

"Got it all worked out, don't you? Do you have a timeline planned for this hypothetical marriage? Not that I've definitely agreed." She smiled to blunt the edge of that last remark.

"We could hold the wedding in the Naval Academy chapel as long as it's not during the summer rush right after graduation. Want to try for a date sometime this winter?"

"How much do we really know about each other the way we are now? I don't know whether you sleep with the window open or closed, how high you set the thermostat, or if you squeeze the toothpaste tube in the middle. What if we can't stand living together?"

"We have the rest of our lives to find out that stuff." He reached across the table to clasp her hand. "I want to try. We may not have a love that transcends time and death like Yuki and Hiroshi's, but after what we've just gone through, I'm willing to gamble on a single lifetime."

Why pretend she didn't long for that next step, too? Her heart and her body sang a resounding *yes*. Only her brain hovered on *maybe*. "Okay. I'm ready to take the leap." She refilled the wine goblets and stood, holding her glass. "Let's go relax in the den and talk about it."

They strolled there hand in hand, carrying their drinks. When Thad took a seat at one end of the couch, the papasan chair scooted up next to him.

Val let out a muffled "eek," glanced behind her, and gingerly sat down. "Thanks, I guess. Wow—looks like we'll still have magic in our life, after all."

He leaned over to kiss her. "A bonus. We already have our own magic no matter what."

Kitsune Enchantment

by

Margaret L. Carter

Chapter One

As usual, holding human shape for an entire day in the near-constant presence of other people had strained Ryo's control. He didn't bother changing out of the slacks and polo shirt he'd worn to work but hurried out back as soon as he got home. Alone in the tiny yard behind a six-foot, wooden privacy fence, he unlatched the gate so he'd be able to push it open without hands to go for his evening run. At last he allowed himself to relax. His ears lengthened and perked up, pointed and furry. His teeth sharpened into fangs, while a plumed tail sprouted from his backside. He crouched on the ground. A familiar voice shattered his focus.

"Ryo? You back here?" Footsteps paced around the outside of the house. "I rang the bell, but I guess you didn't hear it. I came by to drop off your courier bag. You must've accidentally left it in the office. I don't live that far out of the way, and I figured you might need it between now and the next time you come in."

Damn. Joel Brady. Can't let him see me. Joel occupied the cubicle next to Ryo's at the company they worked for, Delmarva Game Galaxy. Since Ryo mostly telecommuted and wasn't scheduled to be on site again for almost a week, he couldn't deny bringing him the bag was a nice gesture. Still, damned inconvenient timing. Shapeshifting in this sheltered spot had always been safe enough that he'd obviously become complacent. He forced his mouth to form intelligible words. "Thanks. You can leave it on the front porch."

"What the heck, I'm here now. Let me just give it to you."

The latch clicked, and the gate started to open. "No need." Ryo's voice came out as more of a growl than human language. He struggled to wrench his half-transformed body back into man shape.

"You okay, Ryo? You sound sick." The gate swung ajar. About the same age and height as Ryo, but huskier, the unwanted visitor had a mop of sandy hair trimmed to just above his collar and wore wire-rimmed glasses. Ryo froze and stared up at him.

The blue eyes behind the glasses widened in shock.

The change swept over Ryo like a gust of wind. His clothes vanished to wherever they went on such occasions. He shrank from man-size to twenty pounds as his face became a muzzle, his hands and feet morphed into paws, and a reddish pelt covered his skin. Stunned, both he and the intruder gaped at each other for a second.

Joel broke the silence. "Good God, this is actually happening. You really turned into a fox."

Ryo sprinted for the open gate, tripping Joel in the process. The other man dropped the black courier bag and yelled after him, "Hey, wait, I won't hurt you!"

In blind panic, Ryo rushed around the house with Joel lurching after him. From the corner of his eye, he glimpsed Joel getting into a car and starting it. Ryo ran up the street, pursued by the vehicle—a two-door compact of some light color—his animal vision couldn't distinguish exactly what.

After running two blocks through the quiet neighborhood of sixty-year-old houses similar to his own, he gathered his wits enough to think of leaving the street and cutting through yards instead. *Can't go home now. Need a safe place. Where?*

He zigzagged under trees and through hedges, abruptly shifted course whenever he hit a fence, put on a burst of speed when a dog barked as he ran past its yard, and skidded to a halt at an intersection with a four-lane road blocked by speeding vehicles. Glancing behind him, he didn't see Joel's car. Fragmentary scraps of human thought reminded Ryo to wait until the light changed to let him cross without getting flattened. He imagined drivers and passengers exclaiming to each other, "Wow, look, a fox in broad daylight," and snapping photos with their phones.

Where to now? Inhaling the auto fumes, he abruptly sensed something else, not exactly a smell, yet something beckoned him, wafting on the air. Like magnetism, it drew him across the road onto a tree-canopied, two-lane street that led into a community more upscale than his own, though apparently not much newer. Grateful for the fading of the gasoline and smoke stench, he followed the lure of the strange-yet-familiar energy. Suddenly he knew what he was sensing. *Magic!* He quickened his pace again, to first a trot, then a run. *Got to get to it. I'll be safe there.* He sprinted along the sidewalks, now heedless of the risk that some curious resident would catch a glimpse of him.

Panting, his legs aching, paws sore from the pavement, at last he reached the spot the magical allure emanated from. He found himself on a short, narrow side lane lined with the same kinds of ranch-style and split-level houses as the rest of the neighborhood. Mature trees shaded the yards, and freshly mown grass tickled his nose. One of those houses looked familiar...

I've been here before.

He'd eaten a meal there as a guest not long ago, in his human body. The magical aura didn't glimmer around that dwelling, though. The energy drew him to the house next door.

As he approached it, a tirade of furious barking burst out on the other side of a chain-link fence one house farther down. A dachshund flung itself against the barrier, proclaiming its indignation at the wild beast intruding on its territory.

Ryo's heart raced with fresh alarm. His human mind knew the dog couldn't get through the fence and probably wouldn't be a match for a fox anyway, but his animal self wouldn't listen. *Danger! Dog!*

He dashed to the front steps of the magic-haloed house and stopped to catch his breath. Next door, a woman's voice called, and the dog wheeled around to run toward her. Ryo shuddered in relief.

A small figure materialized on the porch in front of him—a slender, white cat wearing a red scarf around her neck. With a grave nod, she greeted him in Japanese. "Welcome, *kitsune*."

Her melodious voice soothed his panic. With as much of a bow as he could produce in fox shape, he answered in the same language, "Profound thanks, *bakeneko*." Even if she hadn't spoken, he would have instantly recognized her as a cat spirit, just as she'd realized his nature at first glance. Therefore, she understood his speech, which would have sounded like yips and whines to an ordinary mortal.

"Come up and rest." She flicked her tail and sat down next to the front door. "What brings you here in such haste?"

With another word of gratitude, he climbed the three stairs and stretched out on his belly a few feet from her. "A man was chasing me in a car, but I'm pretty sure I've lost him." Now that his animal flight instinct had faded, he reconsidered Joel's unexpected visit. The two of them didn't know each other well enough that Joel would impulsively drive out of his way to return an object that would have been safe enough in the office. And considering the route Joel would have normally taken, Ryo did live out of the way, even if not much. *Does he suspect there's something abnormal about me?* "Until just a minute ago, I didn't know where I was going. I followed the magic I sensed and ended up here." His lips spread in a vulpine version of a smile. "Now it's obvious why."

"It is not only because of me. This house holds a scroll that was once enchanted. Although its power has drained away, some residue lingers." She inclined her head to him again. "My name is Yuki."

Ryo introduced himself. "You live here?"

"The master and mistress kindly share their home with me." A tinge of humor crept into her voice. "As does their cat." At the rumble of a car engine, she glanced toward the street. "Ah, here they are."

A sports car pulled into the driveway behind the hatchback already parked there. Two people got out, a tall, lean man with seal-brown hair, who wore a naval officer's summer white uniform, and a strawberry-blonde woman. Ryo suppressed the urge to flee again. Now that the panic-induced fog was fading from his brain, he recognized Thad and Val Garrett. He recalled they were almost newlyweds, just married in January. On

Memorial Day, he'd met them during a cookout at Thad's parents' house next door. He'd gone as a guest of Thad's cousin Shannon McBain, Ryo's partner on a crowdfunded graphic novel series.

Halfway up the sidewalk, Val stopped short. "What's that? A dog?"

Thad, too, halted in mid-stride. "I don't think so."

She clutched his arm. Even from a couple of yards away, Ryo's vulpine ears picked up the acceleration of her breath and heartbeat. "Um, there's a fox on our porch."

"Roger that, it's a fox, all right. A big one. Yuki's with it, though, so it must be harmless."

Ryo couldn't blame them for their nervousness on finding a twenty-pound fox at their door. He sensed their gradual relaxation as they scanned him, doubtless taking a closer look at his dark copper fur, white-tipped, plumed tail, and black paws, muzzle, and ear tips. It struck him as odd that the endorsement of a bakeneko—spirit cat—made them more comfortable with him.

Yuki greeted the couple as they walked up the porch steps. "Good afternoon, Valerie-san, Thad-san."

Val stared at the fox, her breathing not quite calm yet. "Who's this?"

"He fled here for refuge because he sensed traces of magic. I trust you do not mind."

"No problem, if you vouch for him," she said.

"He is not an ordinary fox. He is a kitsune."

Val translated the exchange for Thad. Ryo wondered why she understood the dialogue while her husband didn't.

"Kitsune—fox shapeshifter," Thad said. "Come on in, no point standing around out here."

"More magic?" Val muttered as she unlocked the door and walked into the foyer. "I thought we'd finished with that." As Thad held the door ajar for Ryo to enter, she blushed and said, "Sorry, no offense meant."

Ryo answered with a yip he hoped sounded friendly.

After depositing his hat, car keys, and briefcase on a small table just inside the door, Thad led the way to the living room. An ordinary cat—a long-haired, silver-gray tabby—lay sprawled across the cushions of an armchair. He bristled at the sight of fox-Ryo, hissed, and ran away. Val and Thad sat on the couch with Yuki between them, her tail curled neatly around her front paws. He said to Ryo, "Can you change to human form? That would make it easier to talk."

In full agreement with that point, Ryo hesitated anyway, since he hardly knew these people. He cast an uncertain glance at Yuki, who said, "Have no fear. They can be trusted."

He willed himself to shift. His two hosts' stunned expressions blurred before his eyes as he made the transition. Having sometimes watched himself in the mirror, he knew they saw his outline waver, expand, dissolve, and re-form, with a pale glow shimmering around him. He knew his eyes kept their amber hue in both shapes, while his triangular, sharp-chinned face hinted at his fox nature. His slightly wavy, short, dark hair had deep red highlights that also reflected the coloration of his animal form. Not that anyone who didn't know the truth about him would guess those connections.

"Ryo Larsen." Thad waved to the armchair opposite the couch. "Good to see you again, though I wasn't expecting it to be in a situation like this. Have a seat."

Taking the offered chair, Ryo allowed himself to relax as he recalled their first meeting. He'd been reluctant to accept Shannon's invitation to the Memorial Day family party. Crowds unnerved him and stressed his ability to control his shapeshifting. To his relief, though, he hadn't needed to face a crowd, only Thad's parents, Thad, Val, and Shannon. The hosts didn't have a dog or cat to react with alarm and hostility to Ryo's hidden animal side. He'd lounged in a lawn chair under a fragrant magnolia tree, enjoying conversation and bloody-rare hamburgers with no unpleasant surprises. Not once had his human shape threatened to disintegrate.

The others had relished the spicy tofu and sweet red-bean rolls he'd brought as his contribution to the meal. Sure, the lore about kitsune having a special fondness for those foods was a cliché, but it was also true. Thad, his folks, and Val asked intelligent questions about Ryo and Shannon's graphic novel series and didn't seem bored by his answers, even when he got carried away and ran on at elaborate length about the complications of translating character and story ideas into e-book form. He left the party wistfully imagining he might someday get closer to Shannon than their current, mostly online, collaborative friendship.

His thoughts snapped back to the present when Val asked, "Can I get you anything? Water or tea or something?"

The question reminded him how parched his throat felt from the frantic run. "Water would be great."

When she returned from the kitchen with a tall glass of ice water, Thad said, "Sorry, but as an engineer I have to ask. How do you have clothes on when you turn human? Where do they go when you're a fox? Not to mention all the extra mass? According to the basic laws of physics, the first time you ever transformed should've set off a nuclear explosion."

Ryo shrugged. "Magic. As far as I can figure out, that stuff disappears into a pocket dimension until I change back." He gratefully accepted the glass from Val and took a long drink. "Thanks. I raced here all the way from my house in Eastport."

"As a fox?" She resumed her seat on the couch. "Why? If you don't mind talking about it?"

"Simple. Joel, a guy I work with, accidentally saw me changing, and I panicked. As Yuki mentioned, I instinctively headed for the magic in your house. I must have subconsciously sensed it when I was next door with Shannon on Memorial Day." He sipped at the water and set the glass on a coaster on the coffee table. "With luck, maybe he'll decide he imagined the whole thing."

Val asked, "So you're like Yuki?"

The white cat herself answered, "Not precisely. I am a cat with the power to become human. Ryo-san is a man who sometimes becomes a fox."

Val translated the reply for Thad. "Makes sense," he said, "from what I know about kitsune."

Ryo recalled hearing about Thad's tour of duty on a ship stationed in Japan, which accounted for his knowledge of the folklore. "Technically, I'm only half kitsune. My dad's a retired American naval officer, and I was born in this country and grew up with ordinary people, so most of the time I think more like a human than a fox." Ryo hesitated before asking a question of his own. "I can't help wondering why you're not more shocked about me and how you ended up living with a cat *yokai*." That word, which had no single English translation, referred to a wide variety of spirits, demons, and other supernatural beings.

"Complicated story," Val said. "Yuki woke up from an enchantment when I accidentally broke the spell on a Japanese scroll I inherited from my grandfather. Next thing I knew, the house became infested by magic and besieged by a wolf demon." She smiled at Ryo's blank stare. "I told you it was complicated."

"That's why Val can understand Yuki's speech and I can't," Thad put in, "because she's the person who activated the scroll."

"So we're surprised to meet a fox shapeshifter," she said, "but not totally mind-blown. Does Shannon know about you?"

Ryo gave an emphatic shake of his head. "No way. Aside from my parents, nobody knows except you two." He sighed. "And now Joel, maybe. I hope he'll decide he was hallucinating."

Val frowned thoughtfully. "You aren't planning to tell Shannon? Not that I know her all that well yet, but she doesn't strike me as the kind of person who'd react well to a guy keeping a dark secret."

"She'd think I was either putting her on or flat-out crazy. If I proved it with a demonstration, she'd probably freak. Either way, I'd lose her. Lose her friendship, I mean." As much as he wanted more, he feared risking even that by pushing for a closer relationship.

Yuki's mouth quirked in a feline approximation of a smile. "He has a point, Val-san. Not everyone shares your openness to the supernatural."

Ryo finished his glass of water and stood up. "I better get going. By now Joel must have given up and left when he couldn't catch me. Thanks for the hospitality."

Thad said, "Let me give you a lift. No point in walking a couple of miles back home in this heat."

"Great, I won't turn down that offer." After farewells to Val and Yuki, Ryo followed Thad out to the car. Their acceptance of Ryo's double nature, an unfamiliar experience for him, warmed him to the core. If only he had any hope of the same response from Shannon, he might consider sharing the truth with her.

****

At 6 p.m. on Friday, Shannon McBain turned the sign on the door of the bookstore to "Closed" and joined the owner, her friend Elena Salazar, in the combination office and break room in the back of Twice-Told Tales. *I wonder what this is about?* They didn't usually hold meetings at the end of the work week. Elena, a tall, slender woman in her thirties with her black hair worn in a single long braid, waited in the chair behind the desk. The grave expression in her brown eyes wasn't reassuring.

"Have a seat. We've got to talk." She gestured to the shabby armchair nearest the desk.

"That doesn't sound good." Shannon moved a pile of paperbacks from the chair to the floor and sat down but didn't relax into the sagging cushions.

"I'm afraid not." Elena sighed. "You must have noticed what's been happening to our profit margin."

Shannon nodded. She could hardly help noticing. In the eleven years since she'd started working at the bookstore, first in summers during college, then as a full-time employee, and now as assistant manager, she'd seen internet businesses cutting into their sales. The store had started as a used book shop before expanding with new titles as well. Without the ability to pass along deep discounts, no quantity of book launch parties and local author signings made them competitive with online convenience. *I guess this means no raise this year.*

She braced herself for that news but gaped in dismay at Elena's next sentence. "There's no viable choice but to close the shop."

Shannon drew a long breath and let it out in a whoosh. "Are you sure? When?"

With a wry smile, Elena said, "Not today or even next week. I'll plan on six months from now, when the lease comes up for renewal—with a probable rent increase."

Only six months to find another job. Shannon's head reeled. "Have you told the others?" Two young men who worked part time between classes, just as Shannon originally had, were their only other staff members.

Elena shook her head. "I'll talk to them on Monday."

"I can hardly imagine this place not being here." Shannon looked around at the fridge, microwave, and lunch table in one corner, and at the comfortably overstuffed shelves on the opposite wall.

"Neither can I. I fully expected to run it for the next twenty or thirty years, then turn it over to the next owner—maybe you, if you were still around."

They'd casually discussed that possibility several times before. A pang of regret pierced Shannon at realizing that future would never come to pass. "What will you do?"

"Sell off as much inventory as possible." Elena waved at the open door to the adjacent stock room. "Then move the business online. That way, I won't need to pay for retail space or staff, but I'll still probably have to get some kind of day job. I'll miss you."

"And I'll miss you."

"Of course, it's not like we'll never see each other. We'll keep getting together for lunch or whatever."

Shannon nodded. Still, she knew their friendship wouldn't stay the same once the work connection ended.

After a subdued goodbye, she picked up her purse and walked out. On the way to the exit, she couldn't resist pausing to inhale the reassuring scent of new books and scan the familiar rows of shelves, with a glance at the archway leading to the used-book section of the store. *Only six more months of this.* The humid summer heat enveloped her when she stepped outside. Still struggling to absorb the shock of the announcement, she headed for her compact car in the parking lot of the strip mall. Not a glamorous location, but a fairly affordable one with the bonus of some impulse traffic from the other stores in the complex. *Not my worry anymore. I'd better start considering where I go from here.*

Chapter Two

As Shannon drove homeward down Route 2 with the air conditioner on the highest setting, her thoughts revolved like a hamster on a wheel. She hadn't applied or interviewed for a job since her sophomore year of college. The prospect of entering the job market, effectively for the first time, at the age of twenty-nine made her pulse race with anxiety. She'd known Elena as a family friend for years before the offer of a part-time position, since their fathers had worked together. Shannon had loved the bookstore work from the beginning, and after deciding against graduate school, she'd segued smoothly into becoming a full-time employee. *What else am I supposed to do with a degree in English lit? I guess I've got six months to figure that out. The clock is ticking.*

She swung into a fast-food drive-through a block from home and minutes later pulled into the parking spot outside her one-story apartment in Severna Park, the end unit in a row of six. A crape myrtle tree, festooned with pink blossoms beginning to shed their petals on the sidewalk, shaded the front door and offered an illusion of shelter from the heat. She hurried into her much cooler apartment. After changing into shorts and a T-shirt, she carried her chicken sandwich and diet cola into the spare bedroom furnished as an office. As soon as she opened the internet browser, she yielded to her worries and ran a quick financial check. The figures in her savings account and IRA looked no more reassuring than the balances on her credit cards. Because of the damage her father's gambling addiction had done to the family in her teens, fiscal security topped her priority list.

I do have one more income source to fall back on, at least.

Not that she could dream of living on the crowdfunded graphic novels she coauthored with Ryo Larsen. However, a recent development gave them a chance to make a significant profit from those works. Six Continents Media had expressed interest in mass-producing their books and had hinted at offering a contract. If that prospect came through, Shannon's half of the advance could provide a comfortable cushion for job-hunting. The deal depended on the meeting she and Ryo had scheduled with Harvey Wright, an editor from Six Continents, next weekend at ContrariCon, a science fiction and fantasy convention held just north of Baltimore. For the dozenth time, she silently prayed to make a good impression on him.

She opened the unfinished file of the latest adventures of her character, Golden Raptor, and Ryo's, Crimson Vixen. Just as Raptor took the form of either a man or a giant eagle, Vixen alternated shapes between woman and bipedal, human-size fox. Shannon wrote the action and dialogue based on plots the two of them brainstormed together, and Ryo, who had a day job with a game design company, created the art. Now she paused on an image of Raptor in mid-transformation from man to bird of prey. As usual, Ryo portrayed the shift in an ethereal style that made her feel the magic could actually happen. The discreet but sensual glimpses of Raptor's nudity in human form didn't hurt. Opening a separate window, she typed the next few pages of dialogue that she'd been mulling over through the afternoon, before Elena's bad news had overridden thoughts of fantastic quests.

Within a few minutes, the signal for a new instant message dinged. *I should've remembered to turn off the sound. Shame on me—distraction bad, concentration good.* She couldn't resist checking, though, and was glad she had when the transmission turned out to come from Ryo.

"About the con this weekend," it started.

Oh, no, he isn't sick or something like that, is he? I can't meet, greet, and negotiate all on my own.

"I don't really have to be there for the whole con, do I?" the message continued. "What if I just drop in on Saturday long enough to meet the editor with you?"

She crumpled a napkin in her left fist, heat flooding her cheeks. *Don't even think about letting me down!* She typed simply, "Why can't you be there the whole weekend?"

"I'm not much for socializing, and I've got a project for work I should be catching up on. I trust you to speak for both of us."

"Not good enough," she tapped out with furious speed. "We can't predict how often or how long Wright will expect to talk with us. How do you think he'd react if you bail? Anyway, you're not leaving me to cover our dealers' room table alone without a better reason than that." *This is all I need, right after I hear I'm about to lose my job.* She considered adding that complaint to her message but decided she didn't want to sound as whiny as she felt.

"You feel that strongly about having me there the

144

whole time?"

"You think?!?!" She let her anger boil over in an eruption of punctuation.

After a long pause, he answered, "Okay, if it means that much to you, I'm in. I'll show up as scheduled on Friday and stay the weekend. Word of honor."

"I'll hold you to that." Did that mean she was important to him as more than a collaborator? Despite all their virtual conversations over many months, she still couldn't be sure.

After that heated exchange, she lost all motivation for composing a heroic scenario. She typed a few more sentences, then closed the word processor. She sighed over Ryo's illustrations for a minute longer before closing that file, too. *What's with him constantly trying to get out of social obligations? Is meeting people that awkward for him?* She could understand if he suffered from agoraphobia, but she'd seen no evidence of such a condition, and surely he could trust her enough to say so instead of inventing excuses.

They'd met at a convention in Washington two and a half years earlier, and he hadn't shown any signs of distress about being there. The video game company he worked for as a graphic artist had assigned him to a shift staffing a sale table. At the adjacent table in the dealers' room, Shannon had been helping a friend sell fanzines, some of which included her own stories about Golden Raptor. Ryo had bought one to read during lulls in customer traffic. To her surprised satisfaction, he mentioned that he'd already read some of her fiction online and become fascinated with Raptor, an eagle shapeshifter who'd accidentally crossed over to Earth from an alternate world after a magical cataclysm.

Casual conversation had led to a late dinner after the dealers' room closed, followed by hours of brainstorming about future adventures. At first Shannon had wondered about ulterior motives on Ryo's part, but he hadn't tried to hit on her at any point during the conversation. He proved himself genuinely excited by the story they'd concocted on the spot, giving Raptor a companion Ryo insisted the character needed. Thus they'd generated Crimson Vixen, a female fox shapeshifter who'd fallen through the same dimensional rift. Although the two characters hadn't known each other in their original world, they'd become first reluctant allies and then friends. The next logical step, according to Ryo, had been a website dedicated to a graphic novel series about the pair. By the time they'd parted at the end of the con, not only had Shannon committed to the plan for *Raptor and Vixen*, she wouldn't have minded a more-than-friendly gesture from Ryo after all. No more than a couple of years older than Shannon's late twenties, he stood only a few inches taller than her own five feet six, just the proper height for the hugs and kisses she caught herself fantasizing about all too often. She also imagined stroking his wavy, short-cropped, sable hair, so like a wild animal's pelt. Most alluring was the unusual color of his eyes, a golden brown that looked amber in certain lights.

Since that weekend over two years earlier, Shannon and Ryo had shared hundreds of e-mails, multiple cloud-based documents, and countless late nights of live chat elaborating their imaginary world. They also spent hours discussing everything but their personal lives—books, movies, TV shows, role-playing games, and the latest internet memes. To her delight, their opinions about such things, as well as politics, meshed well enough to allow lively arguments without hostility.

Yet their face-to-face meetings could be counted on two hands with fingers left over. She couldn't help wondering why, considering they lived less than half an hour apart, he in the Eastport section of Annapolis, she in Severna Park on the other side of the Severn River. Soon after their first meeting, they'd arranged to get together at a comic convention in downtown Baltimore. They'd driven separately and bought one-day tickets for Saturday. Come to think of it, at that event she'd gotten the impression Ryo didn't feel comfortable in crowds. He acted more relaxed when they retreated to the video room, where they spent most of the day binge-watching complete seasons of anime series and munching on popcorn. At the end of the day, they picked up sandwiches to go from the convention center snack bar and ate on a bench outside, dissecting the films they'd seen. Later, though, when she'd offered a tentative invitation to get together closer to home, he'd turned her down. Why did he seem to enjoy video chats and online work sessions with her, yet evade real-world interaction?

Although she suspected he found her as attractive as she did him, he didn't make any romantic overtures. She'd been pleasantly surprised when he actually accepted her invitation to the Memorial Day cookout at the home of her aunt and uncle. Ryo even contributed food to the potluck meal. As far as she could tell, he had fun, with no symptoms of social anxiety. She'd sampled his spicy tofu with some trepidation, relieved to find it had a pleasant zing but not scorching heat. Val, Thad, and his parents—Shannon's aunt and uncle—liked it, too, judging from the empty tray left at the end of the meal.

Ryo instantly connected with Thad over their shared enthusiasm for anime and manga. Shannon basked in the shade next to Ryo, listening to him explain their graphic novel projects to the others more clearly than she'd ever been able to. At least, his presentation riveted their attention in a way she couldn't manage, and the questions they asked reassured her they weren't just being polite. When she drove him home, he said he'd had a great time in a tone that sounded genuine.

When she dropped him off at his place, he leaned toward her, his hands lightly resting on her shoulders, as if about to kiss her. At the last second, though, he drew back. After that, any hope she might have cherished for a breakthrough to a new level in their relationship seemed to have fizzled. A couple of weeks later, she'd invited him to spend an evening at her place outlining the latest book, and again he'd politely declined, on the grounds that he might be coming down with a cold. Since then, he'd continued to insist collaborating over the internet worked fine for him, with the excuse of not wanting to put her to extra trouble.

Doesn't he have feelings for me, after all? Or is he hiding something that has nothing to do with us? Maybe an old breakup that's left him cautious, like me? Enduring her parents' marital strife because of her dad's gambling, even though they'd eventually reconciled, had made her hypersensitive to evasion and possible deception. From her glimpse of Ryo's house when she'd picked him up for the cookout—a single car in the driveway, no hint of a second occupant during her few minutes inside—she was sure he lived alone. Even if he had a significant other, why wouldn't he mention that fact? He'd have no reason to conceal a relationship from her, since they were just friends.

No matter how much I wish we were more. Oh, stop obsessing like a teenager with a crush.

****

All weekend and into the next week, Ryo brooded over the upcoming convention. He couldn't blame Shannon for insisting that he pull his weight at ContrariCon, but the prospect loomed over him like a thundercloud of impending disaster. Representing his company for a few hours now and then, as he'd done at the con where they'd originally met, was one thing. He could put up with a short period of sitting at a display table surrounded by people he would likely never see again. But almost three days in the near-constant presence of a woman who turned him on? There Shannon would be, right next to him, with a snug T-shirt showing off her softly rounded curves, a miniskirt or tight jeans drawing his gaze to her legs, the sharp scrutiny of her hazel eyes focused on him, her auburn hair either tied in a jaunty ponytail or rippling to her shoulders... *Stop that!* He didn't have a snowball's chance of maintaining a continuous grip on his shapechanging power with that kind of distraction. At times like those, his alleged gift, as his mother labeled it, felt more like a curse. Maybe he could think up an excuse to duck out of most of the con without offending Shannon. *Right, who am I kidding?*

When he managed to stop worrying about ContrariCon, his thoughts reverted to the problem of Joel Brady. On the following Wednesday, Ryo's next day at the office instead of working from home, he tried to stay out of Joel's path. He succeeded until he left his desk late in the afternoon and headed for the elevator, only to find the corridor blocked by the very man he wanted to avoid.

"Ryo, just who I need to talk to."

Ryo couldn't quite make himself shove past Joel. "What for? I'd like to hit the road before the traffic gets bad."

"Come on, I'm sure you can guess what I want to discuss—what happened last week at your place. I know what you are."

Ryo's pulse accelerated. "I have no idea what you're talking about."

"Sure you do." The other man smiled as if inviting him to share a joke. "I saw you change into a fox."

"Are you kidding or just losing your mind?"

With a glance down the hall, where two women were rounding the corner toward the elevators, Joel said, "You don't want to talk about this where anybody could hear, do you? Let's go someplace private." He clutched Ryo's arm and steered him toward the nearest vacant conference room.

Ryo let himself be steered, not eager to have his coworker raving on about magical transformations in range of potential witnesses. *What can he do to me right here, anyway? Maybe I can convince him he imagined the whole thing...*

Leaning against the window frame, he warily watched Joel, who took the seat at the head of the table as if preparing to chair a meeting. "Give it up, Ryo. I wasn't high on anything. I know what I saw."

"Sounds like your reality check bounced. You saw me, and then you saw a fox. I don't know what made you imagine some kind of connection." He kept his hands relaxed at his side rather than clenched and drew slow breaths to calm himself inwardly as well as outwardly. *The last thing I need is to sprout ears or a tail with him staring straight at me.*

"We spend most of our waking hours on video games about wizards and monsters. Why shouldn't I have an open mind about the supernatural?"

"You really believe this?" Ryo tried to echo the other man's casual tone.

"I'd rather believe you changed into a fox than think I actually have gone crazy." Joel leaned back in the chair, his gaze fixed on Ryo as if expecting the change to repeat at that very moment. "I've been reading up on kitsune. Fascinating stuff, including little details like their favorite foods being tofu and red bean paste. According to the folklore websites, you've got some amazing powers."

"So work them into a game. Which you seem to be confusing with reality."

Unfortunately, the repeated denial didn't deflate Joel's confident manner. "The legends mention a lot of other abilities besides changing shape. Foxfire, invisibility, possession, and a bunch more."

"If I could turn invisible, the first thing I would've done was dodge you."

As for fox possession, when Ryo had discussed it with his mother, she had warned him as a teenager not to try. "Until you gain much more experience, that would be dangerous for you. It is too easy to lose yourself in the mind of the person you attempt to possess, unless you have a companion to support you—ideally another kitsune."

"But you're the only kitsune I know," he'd said.

"A human partner would do, if you find one you can trust completely." Her wistful tone gave him the impression she'd never found one, even in marriage.

He had little hope of forming a bond with any such

person, and it certainly wouldn't be Joel. Ryo started toward the door, but Joel stood up to block him.

"Don't be that way. I don't mean you any harm. There's something I'm hoping you can help me with, if you have those powers."

"Stipulating for the sake of argument that you're right about what you claim you saw, it doesn't matter, because I wouldn't be able to do most of those things. I'd be only half kitsune." He edged around Joel, who didn't stop him from reaching the door this time. "What do you want anyhow? Planning to sell this wild tale to a tabloid or monetize it on the internet somehow?" He stalked out of the room and headed for the elevators at a brisk walk.

Joel followed Ryo onto the elevator, vacant except for the two of them. "Hell, no. What kind of friend would that be?"

So now we're friends? Funny way to show it. "Again, what do you want?" Ryo jabbed the button for the parking garage.

As the elevator descended, Joel said, "In my research, I ran across the concept of *kitsune-mochi*."

Oh, hell. So that's what he's after. Clinging with an increasing sense of futility to his play-dumb strategy, Ryo said, "You expect me to automatically know what that means?" He did, of course, from the lore his mother had taught him, but he hoped to throw Joel off balance.

No such luck. "I'm sure you know." Joel trailed after Ryo as they got out of the elevator and hurried into the garage. "It's a type of wizard who makes a pact with a kitsune. I'm hoping to do that with you because I need your help."

"Aren't you mixing up Asian legends and that deal-with-demons game we started designing last month?"

Ryo reached his car and paused beside it, key in hand. "Look, if you leave me alone, I'll drop this subject, too. And consider seeking professional help. Or at least get away from the computer more."

"Nice try, but I'm not giving up."

"There's a flaw in your plan, isn't there? To make this alleged pact, you said you'd have to be a wizard, which would require magic to exist."

"Magic does exist." Joel's cheerfully assertive tone turned solemn. "I have reason to know it does. I'll prove it to you soon enough."

To Ryo's relief, his coworker backed off when Ryo unlocked his car door and slid into the driver's seat. As he struggled through Baltimore traffic for the first few minutes after exiting the garage, he panicked at the thought that Joel might follow him home. Turning onto the freeway on-ramp, Ryo released a pent-up breath and laughed at himself. Since his potential pursuer knew where he lived, a car chase would serve no useful purpose.

Which meant he might get an unwanted visit at any time. What did that last pronouncement about magic mean, anyway? Maybe Joel actually was coming unhinged. Ryo revolved the unpleasant possibilities in his mind as he drove around the Baltimore beltway to Interstate 97 and south to Annapolis. He reached home with no sign of Joel's car on his tail. Ryo hurried inside and locked the door behind him, releasing the tension in his chest with a long sigh. He stripped off his clothes as soon as he made it to the bedroom. Sure, he could transform while wearing them, but this way was more relaxing. A minute later, he sat in the middle of the floor as a fox instead of a man.

As usual, smells and sounds instantly sharpened, while colors faded to pastels. The comforting scent of his lair enveloped him.

Can't go out like this now. Have to wait for dark. He'd let himself get lulled into carelessness lately, taking risks like transforming outdoors in daylight. Drained by the stress of the clash with Joel, he curled up on the throw rug next to the bed, covered his muzzle with his tail plume, and fell asleep.

When he woke, the sky visible through the window showed the rose and violet of sunset, and he found himself in human form. He stretched arms and legs stiff from lying on the floor with only a braid rug for padding. *Damn, I really should quit doing this.* Ravenous from expending energy on the change, not to mention that it was past dinnertime anyway, he dressed in gym shorts and a T-shirt, then went to the kitchen to throw a steak under the broiler. With no viable plan for handling Joel, Ryo's mind reverted to Shannon and the upcoming weekend. Between getting harassed by a wannabe magician and spending most of two and a half days in a convention dealers' room, the prospect of helping Shannon staff the sale table sounded better every minute. Maybe Joel, given breathing space, would reconsider what any rational person would dismiss as a harebrained idea. Meanwhile, if nothing else, a couple of days away from home would allow Ryo time to figure out his next step. At least at the hotel he'd be a comfortable distance from his unwanted "friend" and surrounded by other people all day.

Not to mention spending time with Shannon. That proximity could prove either a plus or a minus. Plating the steak with the potato he'd microwaved while the meat broiled, he caught himself smiling at the thought of her bouncing ponytail and all the other bouncy bits. Curved in all the right places, she stood only a few inches shorter than he, so if he ever kissed her, he wouldn't have to bend over too far.

Don't go there! He had good reason to avoid getting close to women, especially one who turned him inside out the way she did. For one thing, sexual excitement, even more than other kinds of emotional stress, was likely to trigger the loss of a grip on his human shape. Not only that, if legends he'd read and the hints his mother had dropped were true, erotic intimacy with a human female could pose a worse problem. Folktales claimed kitsune were irresistibly alluring. If a woman responded to his desire, how could he be sure her feelings were genuine instead of magically induced? In the past, when he hadn't yet learned caution, he'd had some close calls along that line.

Even in the not so distant past, such as the evening when he'd let his office mates talk him into going to a bar with them. Three women, out of the blue, had practically invited themselves home with him, two of them female coworkers and one he'd never met before. Sure, maybe some guys would consider those incidents missed opportunities, but he got no pleasure from the idea of seduction by what amounted to a supernatural roofie power.

So we'll keep the relationship friendly and professional the way we have all along. No problem.

After dinner, he sent Shannon an e-mail reassuring her he'd be at the con hotel Friday morning, as agreed, and stay on task all weekend. As soon as twilight fell, he went into his miniature back yard, opened the gate just far enough for a fox to slink through, and—having first checked that nobody was close enough to peek over the fence this time—changed shape for a pleasantly mindless run through the woods bordering nearby Back Creek.

Chapter Three

A background buzz of conversation hummed in Shannon's ears as she set up her display in the ContrariCon dealers' room around noon on Friday. The large, brightly lit space contained several rows of tables in the middle as well as more lining the walls, many of them not yet occupied. It wasn't quite twelve, and the room wouldn't open for business until mid-afternoon, so the only other people present were fellow vendors who'd also arrived for an early start setting up. As she exchanged smiles and greetings with dealers she knew from previous conventions, she plugged in and switched on her laptop while silently fretting over Ryo's continued absence.

Stop thinking like that, she admonished herself. *There's plenty of time yet. He could've gotten stuck in traffic. He promised he'd be here, and he will.*

Not all guys were like Owen, her college boyfriend. In fact, probably most weren't. She had no reason to expect Ryo to let her down the way that loser had. Elena's voice echoed in Shannon's mind with the often-repeated admonition, "Just because you fell for one man who'd lie about the sun shining on a rainy day doesn't mean you should write off the entire opposite sex." Anyway, worrying about Ryo on that basis would be irrational, because he wasn't a boyfriend, just a friend and partner. *Unfortunately. No, wrong thinking!* Suppose they did develop a closer personal relationship that later cooled off? They would still have to work together on the graphic novels, and how awkward could that get? All the fun would fade from those late-night video chats she looked forward to so much.

Shannon opened the web page displaying the covers of the latest two volumes of *Raptor and Vixen*. The jewelry vendor at the table on her right glanced over and said, "Fantastic artwork."

With a smile and a murmur of thanks, Shannon pulled a stack of print-on-demand paperbacks from the box she'd lugged in earlier. Just as she started setting them out, Ryo strode into the room. She greeted him with a wave she hoped looked casual. *Of course, he showed up. Why wouldn't he?* In high school, infected by her mother's worries about her father's frequent no-shows and late homecomings, Shannon had suffered a perennial fear of getting stood up for dates, a mishap that actually happened once, sort of. The boy arrived an hour late for a Sunday picnic because his family forgot to switch their clocks to Daylight Saving Time. *That was thirteen years ago. Get over it.*

As Ryo walked toward her, she let herself admire his lean form, shown off by tight, black jeans. He wore a black T-shirt with a portrait of Raptor and Vixen, identical to her own. *No harm in looking, is there?* He took his place behind the table and helped arrange the books, propping one copy of each volume on a small stand with others stacked behind it. Working alongside, she sneaked a glance at him, enjoying the way their comparative heights made it necessary to look up but not too far, so he didn't loom over her.

"Did anybody stop by to talk to you yet?" he asked.

"Just a few people I've run into at other cons."

Noticing how he scanned the area and repeatedly paused to stare at each of the two doors, she said, "Why? Are you expecting anybody in particular?"

Ryo shook his head, avoiding her gaze. With a mental shrug, she returned her attention to the task at hand. After fifteen minutes of watching him twitch whenever somebody walked into the room, though, she couldn't resist questioning him again. "What's wrong? If you've got a problem you want to talk about, I'm listening. What are friends for?"

"Nothing, really." He rearranged a couple of books before glancing at her, then looking toward the main entrance again. "Nothing that'll affect our work."

Shannon decided not to push. He had a right to keep his private worries to himself, didn't he? She reminded herself she had no reason to doubt his claim that, whatever the trouble was, it wasn't related to their partnership. After they finished setting up, she suggested getting lunch together, although she half expected him to decline.

"Sure," he said. "We've got almost two hours until we open for business."

She returned his smile, careful not to show her mild surprise at his acceptance. This lunch amounted to only the second time he'd agreed to hang out with her for a purely social rather than professional purpose. Although he acted as if he enjoyed her company, he avoided face-to-face interaction more often than not. *The mixed messages are enough to make me dizzy with the head-spinning,* she thought as they walked down the hall to the hotel's casual bar-and-grill.

****

Ryo sneaked appreciative glances at Shannon's legs

under her denim miniskirt. The way the black T-shirt clung to her breasts also offered a view worth lingering on. He reluctantly dragged his attention away from the alluring sight. Sharing lunch shouldn't be a problem for him, but letting himself dwell on her physical appeal might undermine his control. *We can do friend stuff together. I have to be satisfied with that.* Still, he couldn't avoid inhaling her rose-scented cologne, mingled with her individual feminine fragrance.

In man shape, his sense of smell didn't equal the keenness of his fox nose, but it did exceed an ordinary person's. Well before they entered the bar-and-grill, aromas of beer, fried meat, and human bodies wafted toward him. They overwhelmed Shannon's scent, probably a good thing. The hostess led the two of them to a booth in the rear and left them to scan the brief menus.

As soon as they'd ordered—cheeseburger and fries for him, a light pasta dish for her—Shannon unfolded her copy of the convention schedule. "We'll both want to attend some panels, so we should divide up table-staffing duties ahead of time."

He got out his own copy, and they ran down the chart discussing which sessions each of them couldn't bear to miss. "Same as always," he said. "The programming committee is telepathic." At her quizzical look, he continued, "They know exactly which events I want to see most and make a point of scheduling them opposite each other."

She laughed. "True that!" They agreed they'd attend Friday night's costume contest and Saturday evening's concert together, when the vendors' area would be closed anyway, then roughed out a plan for staffing their table the rest of the weekend. "Remember, our appointment with Harvey Wright, the editor, is tomorrow at eleven. He said he'd meet us in the dealers' room."

Ryo didn't miss the note of anxiety in her voice. He hoped she was worrying only about the meeting itself, not whether he'd show up on time. "Right, I'll be there, bells on. So what do you think—is the contract a sure thing?"

She tapped on the table. "Don't jinx it. But you read the e-mails from Six Continents at the same time I did. They've made a tentative offer. All we have to do is not screw it up."

He imitated her "knock on wood" gesture. "It'll be awesome to have our stuff in bookstores. And the advance will be nice, too, however much it turns out to be. Not that I plan to quit my day job anytime soon."

A troubled expression passed over Shannon's face before she said with a wry smile, "Good plan. Speaking of that, how long have you been doing game design?"

"I started fooling around with graphic design in high school. I took a double major in art and computer science at the University of Maryland, and I got lucky with the job search. Got hired by the company right out of college." Devouring the last of his fries, he noticed she hadn't touched the garlic bread that came with her pasta. "If you don't plan to eat that…"

With a sidelong glance at his empty plate, she pushed the bread over to him. "Feel free. Must be nice to be able to eat anything you want. Typical male high-powered metabolism, I guess."

Actually, it was the shapeshifting that burned calories in such high volume. He squelched the impulse to protest that she didn't have a thing to worry about in the weight department. He might not know much about women in general, but he knew any comment on that topic could lead him into a minefield.

"As far as jobs went, I sort of had the same kind of luck," she said. "I majored in English literature, planned to go to grad school and teach college English, until I woke up to the state of the PhD job market. Something like ten applicants for every opening. Meanwhile, I'd been working summers plus part time during the school year in a bookstore in Severna Park, so when the owner, Elena—a family friend—offered me a full-time salary and benefits, I jumped at the chance. It sounded like a better life choice than mailing out a hundred copies of my CV while quoting Shakespeare in between asking, 'Want fries with that?' I'm the bookstore assistant manager now." She sighed, staring down into her iced tea glass. "That job's evaporating, though."

"Ouch. What happened?"

"Money trouble. Elena can't afford to keep the store going." She added with a faint smile, "So I hope our books turn into bestsellers and get made into a hit animated series."

"Here's to that." He raised his glass, and she clinked hers against it. "But I'm not sure I'd quit the day job even if they did. I'm lucky to have work I enjoy that I can do from home most of the time. If the series took off with Six Continents, though, I could afford to visit my mom in Japan more often, which would be cool."

"Your parents aren't together?"

"Not since I started college. I think the marriage had been going downhill for a long time, and they were just waiting for me to get launched before they officially ended it." Encouraged by Shannon's sympathetic murmur, he continued, "My dad's a retired naval officer. They met when he was stationed in Japan early in his career. They loved each other, for all I could tell—what does a kid know about that stuff?—but the relationship deteriorated over the years because Mom was never completely happy away from her home." He couldn't mention the other, more important reason: His father never seemed to fully accept his mother's nonhuman nature. "They didn't fight, at least not where I could hear them. There was no yelling, just a lot of coldness. Even as a self-centered teenager, I could sense the distance."

"It must be rough, not being able to see her."

"I've flown over there twice, but it's hella expensive." Having long since adjusted to the situation, he didn't mind talking about it. "We keep in touch with video chats and social media. It works out okay."

"I can relate, sort of. My father was a naval officer, too, and my parents almost broke up when I was in my late teens. He had a gambling addiction, but while he was on active duty, he had it under control. After he retired and took a high-paying civilian job, it got worse, maybe because he had money to throw around. Lies, secrets, coming home at all hours, driving the family into debt—" She blinked away tears and took a sip of tea. "Things eventually improved, though. He went into therapy, they got counseling, and they stayed together. They're fine now, living in a senior condo complex in northern Virginia." A flush spread over her cheeks.

She'd never shared so much personal information with him before. Warmed by her gesture of trust, but figuring she was embarrassed at blurting it out, he tried for a lighter tone so she wouldn't regret opening up. "So we've got something else in common. We're both Navy brats. What are the odds?"

"Considering this area and Norfolk are East Coast

ground zero for Navy retirement, not all that bad," she said. "My older brother went into the military, too—Air Force in his case. Joined the enemy, so to speak." She grinned. "He's married and stationed in Colorado now."

Ryo returned the smile, glad to see her relaxed again. *Friends can discuss personal topics without getting uptight, can't they?* "My dad retired to West Coast Navy retirement ground zero, San Diego. We keep in touch online, and I fly out to visit him every year or two." Getting together that infrequently made it easy to avoid forcing his dad to cope with Ryo's kitsune half. Sure, he knew both of his parents loved him, yet even as a small child he couldn't miss how his father sometimes winced at the sight of a little boy involuntarily transforming into a fox cub. Ryo had been as relieved as his folks when he got old enough to develop some control.

Not that he could reliably hold an intended form even then. One afternoon during his first week in public school, he'd found himself changing on the way to class after lunch. He ducked out and hid in an adjacent vacant lot just in time to keep from getting caught in fox shape. When he didn't show up in the classroom, the staff searched for him and finally called his parents. His mother arrived, tracked him down, coaxed him into reverting to human form, and took him home, claiming he was sick. After giving him a couple of hours to recover from the trauma, she'd coached him through multiple cycles of changing back and forth. Later, she'd trained him in breathing exercises to calm himself and hang onto control, a technique that helped a little but never worked as well as the two of them hoped.

He wrenched his thoughts away from the traumatic memories and picked up the dessert menu. "Want anything else?"

Shannon shook her head. "We better get back to the dealers' room." She waved at the waitress, who dropped off the bill a minute later. Separate checks, as Shannon had insisted despite Ryo's offer to pay.

The instant they stood up and started toward the exit, he glimpsed Joel in the doorway. For a second Ryo hoped he was mistaken, misled by his own fears. But, no, that was his coworker, all right. *What's he doing in this hotel? Looking for me? How did he know I'd be here?* Ryo's pulse raced. Of course—during the past few weeks, he'd mentioned the upcoming convention several times at work. He'd even made casual comments about his plan to sell graphic novels in the dealers' room. *That'll teach me not to bring up personal stuff in the office.*

He sprang to his feet and muttered an incoherent excuse to Shannon about needing to go up to his room for something. "I'll join you at our table later."

She scowled at him as he barely restrained himself from sprinting toward the exit. Drawing attention by openly rushing wouldn't do him any good. Luckily, Joel was occupied with talking to the hostess. Ryo skirted the edge of the room and ducked into an empty booth while Joel followed the woman to a table near the bar. Just as Ryo slipped out of the booth and edged toward the door, Joel turned in his direction.

It was too much to hope the other man hadn't glimpsed him. With a startled look followed by a wide grin, Joel popped up from his chair. Ryo picked up his pace, darted between two people waiting to be seated, and emerged into the corridor. There he broke into a trot. With the frequency of eccentric behavior at cons, nobody seemed bothered by a man running in the hall as long as he didn't bump into people. When he reached the elevators, he found a nearly packed one about to close. An obliging man in an ebony panther costume held it open for Ryo, who dashed inside just as Joel rounded the corner in pursuit.

Ryo let out a long breath as the door shut and the elevator started rising. Heat flooded his face, and his ears sizzled with what felt like static electricity. He recognized the sensation as magic. *Damn, my fox ears are growing.* He resisted the temptation to check the transformation by touch, a gesture certain to attract the gazes of his fellow passengers. The panther noticed anyway. "Wow, great cosplay. Those look totally real."

Ryo managed a weak smile and a murmur of thanks. At least, if he had to suffer such a lapse, this was the place for it. The one woman in the elevator scanned him with open admiration. He might have felt flattered if he hadn't known the appeal almost surely sprang from his kitsune pheromones, not his looks or personality.

By focusing on the techniques his mother had tried to teach him—not easy, when he had trouble concentrating from the stress of his plight in itself—he managed to avoid changing any further and forced his breath into a normal rhythm by the time he reached his floor. He hurried to his room, half expecting Joel to pop up and intercept him. *Don't panic, idiot. He couldn't possibly know what floor you're on.*

Convincing himself he was safe for the moment, Ryo stretched out on the bed and willed his ears to revert to human shape. *Sure, I'm safe now, but I can't lurk in here the whole weekend. If I don't get back to Shannon soon, she'll skin me alive and use my hide for a fox-fur stole.*

****

Waiting for the dealers' room to open, Shannon sat at the table with fists clenched in her lap and gritted teeth. *What the heck is wrong with him?* Upset stomach, maybe? She couldn't think of any other legitimate reason he'd rush out like that. She'd give him the benefit of the doubt and trust that he'd either show up or call her soon. He had her number, and her phone was on, so he had no excuse for not communicating.

Under the background hum of conversation, she greeted the jewelry seller on her right and complimented the racks of Renaissance-style costumes the man on her left was setting up. When the venue opened for browsers, she forced an inviting smile and made eye contact with passers-by, trying to strike a balance between welcome and blatant salesmanship.

About half an hour after opening, she was chatting with a girl in an anime T-shirt about the art displayed on the laptop when Ryo walked in. Shannon tossed him a pretend-casual wave and continued the conversation with the potential customer. When the girl meandered down the row with a *Raptor and Vixen* flyer in hand, Shannon stared up at Ryo, keeping her face blank and choking down the words she wanted to snap at him.

"Sorry about running off, back there in the bar. I saw somebody I'm trying to avoid. Nothing you need to worry about."

"Why? You owe him money?" she asked lightly. *Or is it a she? Old girlfriend?* She mentally shook off the random thought. Sure, Owen, her college boyfriend, had been too much of a coward to admit he'd violated their pledge of exclusiveness by dating someone else behind her back. That disaster had nothing to do with Ryo. *Paranoid much? That happened nine years ago. Totally irrelevant now.*

He answered her half-joking question with a wry smile. "Not that simple, unfortunately. But I won't let it affect our project."

"Better not. You know how much the Six Continents deal means to me." She brushed aside her lingering embarrassment over what she'd spilled earlier about her job crisis and her family's dysfunction. What had possessed her to open up that way anyhow? On the other hand, he'd shared bits of his past, too—an encouraging development.

"It means just as much to me. I won't let you down." With a brief squeeze of her forearm, he took his seat next to her behind the table.

He removed his hand quickly, his face reddening. A blush warmed her own cheeks. Evading his glance, she unnecessarily straightened the nearest stack of books.

The crowd of people wandering through the dealers' room brought a welcome distraction. For the next hour, both Shannon and Ryo were kept busy describing their characters and showing off their work to prospective buyers. They even sold three copies of the trade paperbacks, not a foregone conclusion with all the surrounding competition for con-goers' bucks. She noticed, though, that he frequently cast nervous glances around the room, often pausing to focus on the two doors. Maybe he really was worried about avoiding someone. *Well, why should I doubt his word on that? But who could be causing him that much trouble?*

She finally asked outright.

Ryo sighed. "He's a guy I work with, Joel Brady, who started bugging me about confidential stuff I can't go into. He followed me to the con. That's why I ducked out all of a sudden after lunch."

She remembered seeing a man with sandy hair and wire-rimmed glasses enter the bar, then jump up and leave right after Ryo did. "He must be super obsessed with whatever it is, then. Sounds like a real pain."

"To say the least." Ryo's gaze darted over the crowd yet again. "But maybe he's given up for now. If he shows up again, though…"

"You'll vanish again. I get it, but I hope you won't make a habit of it. One of us has to watch the table continuously until dinnertime or risk losing sales. Such as they are." She tapped the far from overflowing metal cash box.

They spelled each other a couple of times to take breaks in turn. After returning from a session on shapeshifters in folklore, Shannon admitted to herself she felt relieved to find him still on duty. She'd half expected him to abandon his post.

At the end of the afternoon, he said, "Sorry again about my flakiness. Let me make it up by treating you to dinner."

For a couple of seconds she hesitated, unsure about accepting a "treat." Didn't that come perilously closely to a date with him? On the other hand, wasn't that what she wanted—to wade into deeper waters than professional friendship? *Heck if I know. What can it hurt to stick a toe in the pool?* She accepted.

"Cool, and we can go to the masquerade afterward."

She nodded agreement with that suggestion. How much trouble could she get into, emotionally speaking, watching a costume contest in a packed auditorium? Yet she couldn't resist an occasional lingering look at him while they packed up their wares and spread a cloth over the table to indicate they were closed for the evening. The bright overhead illumination brought out deep red highlights in his wavy, black hair. He had amber eyes, almost golden, a color she'd never seen in human eyes before. But yummy looks weren't everything. Was she cutting him slack for his erratic behavior because of his physical appeal? Or, on the other hand, was she being too hard on him because of her own hang-ups?

Quit overthinking. She picked up the cash box and her laptop and bade him a casual goodbye before heading upstairs to freshen up for dinner.

Chapter Four

They met half an hour later at the more upscale of the hotel's two restaurants. Ryo had changed into black slacks with an open-necked polo shirt bearing the logo of his game company on the upper left. Shannon noticed his gaze sweep over her, from the V-necked blouse to the denim miniskirt and her exposed legs. *Does he like what he sees?* If so, why didn't he make a move? How could she sort out her own feelings if he didn't make his clearer? She shook off the thought and followed the hostess to a corner booth with an electric candle glowing on the table.

She ordered a shrimp salad, listening enviously as Ryo went straight for the steak and lobster. How did he stay so thin while eating so heartily? "What about wine?" she asked.

He briefly mulled over the wine list. "Well, okay, I guess. White? We both have seafood coming."

Why did he sound reluctant? If he didn't drink at all, he would simply say so, wouldn't he? "Sure. Chardonnay?"

To her mild surprise, he ordered two glasses instead of a bottle, the more economical choice. With the wine, the waitress set a basket of bread between them. Nibbling on a slice, Shannon asked Ryo more about how he'd gotten interested in game design.

"Since I was a typical videogame-obsessed teenage boy and liked to draw, it felt like a natural path. I was always that kid who sat in the back of the room sketching cartoons during class instead of taking notes." He finished his first piece of bread and slathered butter on a second.

"I can imagine. Did Vixen start then?"

"An early incarnation of her, after I got giant robots out of my system."

She laughed. "There's a thought. Maybe in the next story arc Raptor and Vixen should battle an invasion of giant robots."

He chuckled. "That could make a great animated feature."

"Do you think we'll ever get a film version?" she asked. "Or a computer game? Maybe you could talk your company into designing one."

"Or we could create an indie game, but that would take big bucks to produce. If we do decide we want to expand into visual media, we should look for an agent."

"First things first. At this point, the mass market books feel like a dream."

"True dream," he said as the waitress delivered their dinners.

"I'm still trying to convince myself it's real," Shannon said. "I'll believe it when I see our signatures under the publisher's on that contract. For now, where do Raptor and Vixen go from here? We can't let their character development stall, and the fans keep trying to ship them." Although the series had a strictly niche audience, it did boast a core group of avid readers who expressed their opinions with rabid enthusiasm. A significant percentage of those wanted to see Raptor and Vixen in a romantic relationship.

"Granted, we need to move in a new direction. They can alternate rescuing each other from supervillains only so often."

"I'm open to having them fall in love," she said as she drizzled dressing on her shrimp salad.

He cut into his steak, which oozed red. "They're two different species, though."

"Our fans accept the idea of animal-shifting heroes from an alternate universe, and that's a problem?" She'd already dropped ambiguous hints in previous issues that an attraction might exist between the two characters, to lay groundwork for just such a potential development. "We've established they love each other as friends, so why not take the next step?"

"You believe cross-species mating could work?" He asked the question in a surprisingly serious tone.

"Why not? Even if they can't interbreed, they could share romantic love. Anyway, if they did have sex, we wouldn't have to worry about the details. It would happen offstage, since we're not writing erotica." Blushing, she shifted her gaze from his face to her plate, but not before noticing a flush redden his cheeks, too.

They talked about future story ideas through the meal. When she finished her wine, Shannon ordered a second glass. After an instant of hesitation, Ryo did the same. "Here's to living dangerously." When the refills arrived, she caught herself watching his mouth as he sipped from the glass. Their eyes met, and heat flooded her skin. He immediately looked away. She deflected the awkwardness with a random remark about the hypothetical game their series might spawn. Ryo's answers became more absent-minded, while he scanned the dining room as nervously as he had during lunch.

"Are you that worried about the guy, whosis, you were trying to escape from earlier?"

Ryo replied with a jerky nod, "Joel Brady. I keep expecting him to materialize from thin air."

"Exactly why is he stalking you, anyway? I mean, aside from the confidential parts you can't discuss."

"We have a fundamental disagreement about a project he's pushing and I'm not in favor of. He won't let it go."

"Wow, to follow you to the con, he must be really obsessive."

Another furtive glance toward the exit. "About this, he definitely is."

At Ryo's request, the waitress handed them dessert menus. Shannon sighed. "This flourless chocolate cake looks yummy, but…"

"Oh, come on, you can live dangerously, too, for a change." He gazed into his empty wineglass, then directly at her. "I'll get one, too. Let's order them to go and eat dessert in my room. No worries about Joel interrupting us there."

Does he mean more than he's saying? Probably not, she decided. At a convention, a hotel room served as a meeting area as much as sleeping space. Glad for anything that might stop Ryo from acting like a road runner on the lookout for a coyote, she agreed to his suggestion.

After they'd left the restaurant with their boxed cake slices and made it to the elevator, he let out an audible breath of relief when the doors hissed shut. She didn't comment, figuring if he wanted her to know further details about why that Brady guy worried him so much, Ryo would share them without prompting. They rode up to the fourth floor and walked to his room in silence.

The room mirrored her own, with a king-size bed,

flat-screen TV, mini-fridge, desk, easy chair, coffee table, and small couch. The open drapes displayed the evening sky fading toward twilight, streaked with rose and violet. She settled on the couch beside him, grateful for the imaginary border between the bed and the sitting area. Between bites of cake, they talked more about the chances of their work expanding into other media.

"We can daydream to our hearts' content," she said after a while, "but you know we won't get much if any input into games or films. Not unless we make them ourselves."

"Games, I can do. Movies, not so much. If I could sell the idea to my company, I might get to design the game." He paused to lick a fleck of chocolate off the corner of his mouth.

A shiver coursed through her. How would his tongue feel on her lips? *Danger ahead!* As she'd considered more than once, if their relationship heated up but cooled later, the working partnership could fall apart. "Listen to you," she said with a nervous giggle, "counting our eaglets before they hatch."

"What kind of babies would Raptor and Vixen produce if they did mate? Winged fox cubs hatched from eagle eggs?" He polished off the last of his cake.

"I'm almost tempted to write that scenario just to see you draw it." To avoid the sight of Ryo licking chocolate from his fork, she concentrated on finishing her dessert, too.

"Considering the fans of a certain major film franchise don't seem to have a problem with dragon-donkey hybrids, it's not so farfetched."

He set his empty box on the coffee table, then took hers from her and did the same with it. Turning toward her, he clasped her hand before she could withdraw it.

His skin felt fever-hot, a heat that radiated up her arm. *On the other hand, like he said, sometimes we should live dangerously.* She swayed closer to him.

"Magic," he murmured. "Magic can do almost anything."

He cupped her cheek with his free hand. He leaned in, giving her plenty of time to draw back if she chose.

She didn't. Instead, she parted her lips, waiting. His lips brushed hers. The heat spread over her whole body and flared at her core. His tongue teased hers, and she twined one arm around his neck. Her nipples peaked and tingled. Twisting sideways to close the space between them, she couldn't suppress a sigh of pleasure when he drew her into a loose embrace that tightened as she snuggled up to him.

Her eyes drifting shut, she ran her fingers through the dense pelt of his hair while he deepened the kiss. Waves of sensation rippled through her. As she moved her hand downward to skim over his cheek, fuzz tickled her palm. Whiskers? Surely she would have noticed if he'd been unshaven. Besides, this growth felt more like velvet than sandpaper. She opened her eyes.

Ryo flinched and pulled back. In the twilit dimness relieved only by the light from the overhead fixture just inside the door, his skin definitely looked lightly furred. Not only that, his teeth looked, well—*sharp*. She scooted to the end of the couch.

Ryo snapped his mouth shut and covered it with one hand. Springing to his feet, he mumbled, "Sorry—not feeling well all of a sudden. I'll see you tomorrow morning. Sorry!" He scurried to the bathroom and slammed the door.

Staring after him, Shannon stood up, suddenly lightheaded, and gripped the back of the couch to steady herself. *What's gotten into him? And his ears—why do they look the wrong shape?*

Did he expect her to leave just like that? Assuming he was actually sick, he would have asked for help if he'd wanted it. So, yes, he apparently did expect her to clear out. Well, she wasn't about to beg him to let her stay. Tears prickling her eyes, she grabbed her purse and stomped out.

In her own room a few minutes later, she flopped face up on the bed and waited for her pulse to slow and her head to stop buzzing with hurt and confusion. When she'd calmed down, she forced herself to consider the situation rationally. Either he'd told the truth about a sudden attack of sickness or he hadn't. If so, he would probably call her when he felt better. If not, what had possessed him to act that way? He'd been as into the kiss as she had, no doubt of that. If he had some issue that prevented him from taking their relationship to the next level, why wouldn't he come clean about it? For that matter, why would he initiate a kiss in the first place?

Silly question. Same reason I responded, even when I know mixing collaboration with romance could be a recipe for disaster. That problem aside, if her previous record was any indication, she had a talent for picking the wrong guy.

She was evading the bigger question. What had she seen in those last few seconds? *He had fur and fangs. His ears were turning pointy. What is he? A vampire or werewolf or something?*

With a humorless laugh, she sat up, wrapping her arms around her knees. *Been reading a little too much fantasy?*

She had to have imagined or hallucinated what she'd thought she saw, but why? Two glasses of wine wouldn't have that effect. The idea that Ryo might have drugged her drink was too absurd to contemplate. For what motive? Furthermore, if he had, he wouldn't have run away from the result of his nefarious deed. Okay, she'd simply spaced out for a second and over-interpreted an optical illusion. Chalk it up to neurotic ambivalence about getting involved with him.

She'd suffered a freakish reaction unlikely to repeat itself. The more immediate concern was that their plan to attend the masquerade together was a washout. *The heck with him. I'll go by myself.*

In the main auditorium a few minutes later, she snagged a seat near the front for a good view of the contest. Overheated from the clash with Ryo followed by the rush to get to the auditorium before the program started, she welcomed the chilly draft from the air conditioning on her bare arms and flushed cheeks. Chatter from the audience blurred into a dull roar like waves on a beach. Ten minutes after the scheduled starting time, a burst of music quieted the crowd, and the MC walked up front to welcome them. While he rattled off a succession of SF-themed jokes, costumed competitors lined up on the right side of the large room. Shannon watched with only half her attention as mythical beasts, anime characters, fairy-tale creatures, and heroes and villains from various film franchises strolled, marched, shambled, or danced across the stage.

Maybe next year Ryo and I should enter as Raptor and Vixen. That is, if we're still working together then. She couldn't get her mind off that final disastrous minute in his room.

In the intermission while the judges retired to decide the winners, and a musical group performed parodic songs about currently popular fantasy and science fiction TV shows, her gaze wandered around the auditorium. She caught sight of a man who looked familiar, walking slowly down the center aisle.

Isn't that Ryo's nemesis? Yes, she couldn't mistake the husky, sandy-haired man in wire-rimmed glasses, especially since he wore a shirt with the game company's logo, like Ryo's. Among all the other people milling around, he didn't draw any particular attention as he paused to scan each row of chairs. He roamed the room in a meandering search pattern for a while, then walked out a side exit.

He did seem to be looking for Ryo. *Persistent, isn't he? But is that enough to send Ryo running for cover at the sight of him?* Surely the trouble between them must consist of more than a disagreement over a work project. *Unless Ryo's just being neurotic about the whole thing. Not that it's any of my business.* He had labeled the problem "confidential," so he must have solid reasons not to discuss it with her.

His nagging presence in her thoughts left her too preoccupied and depressed to care about the outcome of the contest. Instead of waiting to hear the winners announced, she retreated to her room. Just as she reached it and bolted the door, her cell phone rang in her purse.

****

Barricaded in the bathroom, Ryo listened to Shannon storming out of the room. His ears, now completely pointed and furred, twitched at the noise of the door closing behind her. Doubled over, he shuffled out of the bathroom, as the change swept over him. With a groan, he released his grip on his human form and melted into animal shape. He ran in circles between the armchair and couch, lashing his plumed tail, until he exhausted his pent-up frustration. He flopped down on the rug, panting, and forced his body to transform from fox to man. Although he still had vulpine ears and teeth, he stripped off his clothes as soon as he had the appendages to do so. In the process, his tail vanished, and his ears shrank and re-formed.

He stretched on the bed, naked, and clenched his jaws, willing the fangs to revert to blunt, human teeth. The fragrance of Shannon's rose cologne still lingered in his nose, along with the sweet musk of her natural scent. With a sense of smell more acute than an ordinary man's even in human form, he'd been unable to avoid noticing her arousal. She wanted him, maybe as much as he craved her, but how could he know whether that desire sprang from within her or from his innate kitsune allure? Of course, she'd opened up about her personal life more than ever before. Didn't that mean something beyond mere physical attraction? *Damn, I should never have drunk that second glass of wine. I should know better by now.* The blend of alcohol and sexual excitement inevitably dissolved his self-control.

How much had she seen in that last minute or two? With luck, she would convince herself she'd imagined whatever anomalies she'd glimpsed, as most people usually did when confronted with the impossible. He would learn her reaction soon enough anyway, since he couldn't hide from her the rest of the weekend. He owed it to her to lend his support in the meeting with the editor.

Rolling over, he buried his face in his arms. *I'll be*

lucky if she ever speaks to me again. After wallowing in misery for a while, he sat up and scowled at his phone, hooked to the belt of his discarded slacks. Dealing with her wouldn't get any easier if he put it off. The longer he delayed, the worse impression he'd make. He pulled on his undershorts, grabbed the phone, and scrolled to her number.

She answered on the third ring, squashing his cowardly hope to leave a message instead of plunging into a conversation. "Well?"

He flinched at the ice in her voice. "I just want to apologize. I had a sudden attack of upset stomach. Maybe it was the lobster."

"Sorry to hear that." Her clipped tone sounded far from sympathetic. "Will you be okay for the meeting tomorrow?"

"For sure. Wouldn't miss it. This collaboration means too much to me."

"Fine. See you then." She hung up without waiting for a goodbye.

She was obviously getting fed up with what she probably considered lame excuses for erratic behavior. Come to think of it, maybe he shouldn't have run away after lunch. Going straight to the dealers' room with Shannon would have kept him in a public place, surrounded by people. In that environment, Joel wouldn't openly bring up shapeshifting foxes unless he had become completely unhinged.

If the man showed up again, Ryo would stand his ground and stay cool. *That is, if I don't start sprouting fangs or a tail.*

He couldn't expect Shannon to let another sudden exit pass with a vague apology, yet he couldn't allow himself to be seen half-transformed. *On the bright side, if she stays mad, I won't have to worry about accidentally enchanting her with my supernatural charms.*

Watching his parents' relationship disintegrate should have warned him against making any kind of romantic gesture toward her, much less kissing her. The seductive aura of kitsune lovers was real, as demonstrated by the numerous men who hit on his mother with no encouragement from her. Ryo's father, sadly, had grown more jealous over the years, more prone to see deliberate enticement that didn't exist. Worse, he'd reached the point of accusing his wife of using that enchantment on him, luring him into marriage against his true will.

Almost all the mythology about their kind warned against cross-species liaisons. Sure, there were a few tales of fox women who became loving, devoted wives. In most of the stories, though, the kitsune seduced the human partner, gave him or her an interlude of dreamlike joy, then ruined the hapless lover's life and vanished. The archetypal legend of a man who thought he'd spent years sharing ecstasy with a beautiful bride in a luxurious mansion, but returned to his right mind only to discover he'd been living in a burrow with a fox and a litter of half-human cubs, was only the most extreme of such stories.

Not that Ryo needed to worry about luring Shannon into such a plight. He didn't have the power to create a magical retreat outside normal space and time. No matter how hard his mother had tried to teach him to use the gifts she thought he should have inherited, the results never measured up to her expectations.

Which is probably a good thing on the whole, considering how I keep screwing up the powers I do have.

****

Hanging around the entrance to the dealers' room Saturday morning, waiting for a staff member to unlock it, Shannon let out a pent-up breath in relief when Ryo walked into view. Irritated at herself for expecting him to bail and at him for inciting that expectation, she answered his greeting with a curt nod. Like her, he wore a T-shirt bearing the cover image from the first volume of their series. He'd remembered their agreement to coordinate their outfits for today. In most ways, he'd constantly proved himself dependable, and then he'd pulled those disappearing stunts on the previous day.

When he commented on the sunny weather outside and made a casual remark about the concert scheduled for that evening, she shut him down with a brisk reply. "No time for chitchat. Let's concentrate on setting up the table to make a good impression on the editor."

The disappointment on his face at her rebuff saddened her, but she hardened herself against that feeling. *All business, right?*

At their table, they folded up the cover and got to work. While he rearranged the books at her direction and unlocked the cash box she'd brought with her, she powered up the laptop. After opening several windows with covers and sample pages from multiple issues of the series, she showed him the result. He complimented her on the display, and she returned a brusque word of thanks. With a barely audible sigh, he took a seat behind the table and assumed a mask of bright-eyed welcome.

By now potential customers were starting to wander in. Both Shannon and Ryo made eye contact with each passerby and pitched the series to anybody who paused long enough to listen. As usual, they had to tiptoe along a fine line between friendly enthusiasm and overbearing hard-sell tactics. In the next forty-five minutes, they made three sales and handed out countless flyers to whoever would accept them. Shannon kept checking her watch, counting the minutes until eleven, when Wright was due to appear. Ryo, she noticed, was glancing around the room the way he had the day before, flinching whenever anyone who roughly resembled his alleged stalker came within their field of vision.

Finally she voiced her exasperation. "Are you still worried about that guy from your office?"

He nodded with a sheepish half-smile. "I know he's not likely to make a scene in front of you and all these other people, but I don't want the hassle of dealing with him anyway."

"Can I count on you to stick around until Wright gets here?"

He glanced at his watch. "I'll do my best. I won't make an ironclad promise, but that's the plan." He looked up, his eyes widening in alarm. "Damn, there he is now."

She followed the direction of his gaze. Sure enough, Brady had just entered the room and was heading toward them.

Ryo cursed under his breath again. "Look, I'll be back to meet Wright on time if I can, but I have to get out of here now. Try to stall Joel."

Before she could sputter out an objection, he slipped from behind the table and retreated at a rapid walk in the direction opposite the main entrance. She spun around to glare after him. What was that hanging from his backside? A russet plume of fur that looked like—

A fox tail? Where did he get a tail? Surely if he'd been wearing it when he'd arrived, she would have noticed. She hadn't been *that* distracted. When did he have a chance to put it on?

When she turned back to the table, Joel Brady was standing in front of it. He scanned the books on display. "Cool covers."

She returned a cautious word of thanks.

"I need to talk to Ryo Larsen. Do you happen to know where I can find him at the moment?"

Resisting the urge to glance toward the side exit, she said, "Sorry. No idea." Ryo must have escaped into the corridor already. Anyway, it was perfectly true she didn't know where he'd gone.

Brady apologized for bothering her and walked away, headed for the main door.

He doesn't look very scary. Why does the sight of him turn Ryo into a nervous wreck?

Chapter Five

Weaving among the stream of people in the hall, Ryo fled toward the elevator at a near-trot while he internally fumed at himself for his lapse. So much for his plan to stand his ground at the vendor table. If Joel saw Ryo this way, there'd be no hope of persuading him to disbelieve in the transformation. Ryo could hardly believe his tail had spontaneously popped out in public. At least here the witnesses assumed it was a costume accessory. He cringed to think of the disastrous results if he ever lost control like that at work.

Mom was right. I'll never measure up to full-blooded kitsune standards. Not that she ever said anything like that aloud, but he couldn't miss the implications of her overly patient instructions. She gave up after trying to teach him to construct a pocket dimension. She created a garden outside normal space, complete with a lotus pool arched by a small footbridge, stepping-stone paths winding through green landscape broken up by bamboo growth, and a stone lantern beside a miniature waterfall. She'd expected him simply to expand the boundaries of the garden. His most diligent efforts produced only patches of mist. If he couldn't even master his shapeshifting, of course he couldn't do complicated things like building a secret world. His fox nature was only a handicap, an alleged superpower that got him nothing but trouble.

In her unguarded moments, he'd thought he sensed more sadness than surprise in her reaction to his efforts. After all, he was half human, not a real kitsune. No wonder he'd disappointed her, even if she tried to hide that feeling.

These furious ruminations got him as far as the elevator, just as he glimpsed Joel at the end of the hall. Ryo squeezed in right before the doors closed, forcing a vague smile in acknowledgment of murmured compliments on his realistic-looking tail and ears.

Ears, too? Damn! He got off one floor below his own and dashed up the stairs.

The moment he reached his room and inserted the key card, Joel popped out of the ice machine alcove and rushed to his side. Ryo dodged around him, darted into the room, and slammed the door.

Joel hammered on it.

"What the hell do you want?" Ryo drew several shuddering breaths as he struggled to make his tail recede and his ears revert to normal.

"You don't want me to stand out here yelling through the door, do you?"

Might as well listen to his rant. What can he do to me, anyway? Ryo let in the unwanted visitor, pacing across the room and flinging himself onto the couch without offering Joel a seat. "How did you know where to find me?"

"With this." Without waiting for an invitation, Joel sat in the armchair and plucked a thin, silver chain from under his shirt. A bronze, pentagonal pendant about the size of his palm hung from it.

He held it up, and Ryo leaned forward to peer at the amulet. It was etched with the image of a tentacled creature—whether octopus, squid, or jellyfish, he couldn't tell. "What's that? And make it snappy, please. I've got places to be." If he didn't show up for the meeting at eleven as Shannon expected, she'd never forgive him.

"It's a long story, so I may not be able to manage *snappy*." Joel lounged back in the chair. "First off, I told you I knew magic was real, and this is why."

"Cut the crap. I don't have time for this." Ryo stood up.

Joel brandished the pendant. "Freeze. Except for breathing and so on."

Ryo did. He couldn't move, except to open his mouth to yelp in protest.

Before he could get out another sound, Joel said, "You can unfreeze. But if you give me any grief, remember I can stop you anytime."

Sinking onto the couch, Ryo said, "Okay, talk." *I'm the last person who should be surprised at authentic magic. But how did he get hold of what's obviously a powerful talisman?*

"You probably know I've gotten into the habit of browsing thrift stores, antique shops, and so on for unusual objects to base game items on."

Ryo nodded, recalling several mentions of such items in brainstorming sessions.

Joel went on, "I ran across this amulet in a tray of miscellaneous costume jewelry a couple of weeks ago. It was rattling around loose without a chain, so I bought this one separately later." He fingered the silver necklace, then went on, "I discovered the pentagon's qualities by accident."

"How?"

"The day I bought it on my lunch break, I came back

to the office and caught Brenda, who has the cubicle on the other side of mine, sneaking a candy bar out of my desk. When I told her to stop, she not only stopped, she froze. I experimented with a couple of other commands—don't worry, nothing painful or humiliating—and she obeyed them."

"Whoa, freaky," Ryo said, fascinated despite his anger over being trapped.

"You bet. Finally, I ordered her never to snitch from my stash again and to leave without remembering anything that happened."

"Did that work?"

"Sort of," Joel said. "Later I noticed her giving me funny looks, like she was confused, so I think it might've worn off. Anyway, she must have been shaken up knowing she'd been caught, if she did remember, because no more candy went missing."

"I bet you experimented on other people after that." Ryo doubted anybody could resist such a temptation.

"Sure. Not at work, though. I discovered I have to focus on the person I'm commanding, and if I stop concentrating, the orders don't stick for long. I haven't totally figured it out yet. How long the effect lasts seems to vary widely. Still, it would be super convenient if I wanted to take up a life of crime."

"Which you don't, I gather." Ryo allowed a tinge of sarcasm to creep into his voice. "You have a perfectly ethical motive. You just want to turn me into your familiar because you read somewhere about kitsune-commanding sorcerers. Even if that stuff were true, do you seriously think I'd effectively agree to become your pet? What do you want from me, anyhow?" As Joel had mentioned earlier, a kitsune-mochi formed a pact with a fox shapeshifter to wield power for him. Even if Ryo had possessed the gifts of a full-blooded member of his mother's species, he didn't have the slightest interest in binding himself to someone that way.

"That's a little complicated." Joel leaned back on the couch. He took off his glasses, polished them on the hem of his shirt, and put them back on. "Almost a year ago, my uncle died. He never married and didn't have any nephews or nieces other than me, so he left me his house on the South River in Edgewater."

Ryo estimated that would be located only twenty minutes or so from his own home.

"It's a huge, rambling place built around 1900, and when I moved in, it was stuffed to the rafters with, well, *stuff*. Uncle Tim wasn't exactly a hoarder, but he was an accumulator. He collected all kinds of things— gemstones, fossils, art works, you name it—but never classified or organized them in any systematic way." With a wry smile, Joel said, "I probably inherited that gene. After I started scouring secondhand shops for game inspiration, I kept up the habit just for the fun of it. Anyway, I've been sorting through the house all these months."

"Which has what to do with magically binding me?" With a sidelong look at the door, Ryo speculated on the chance of making a break for it, but Joel pointedly kept one hand near the dangling amulet.

"I'm getting to that. I've whittled down the piles little by little, getting significant items appraised, donating some things, keeping some, selling others. The main interest Uncle Tim constantly returned to was books, thousands of them. I'm talking floor-to-ceiling shelves in almost every room, closets overflowing. I've sorted a lot of the valuable volumes, and when I'm sure I've exhausted that category, I'll sell most of the rest in bulk to a secondhand book dealer. There's one particular collectible I'm looking for, though, and I can't find it."

Is he ever going to get to the point? "Are you sure it exists?"

Joel nodded. "Uncle Tim showed it to me once and said he especially wanted me to have it. A first edition of H. P. Lovecraft's collection *The Outsider and Others*. It was easily the most valuable book he owned."

"And you want to sell it for big bucks."

Joel shook his head emphatically. "I don't need money that badly. I plan to keep it as a memento of him. What I want is to make sure I don't accidentally let it go with the bulk sale."

While Ryo sympathized with that motive, it didn't make up for Joel's highhanded behavior. "I still don't see where I come in."

"Remember that time a few weeks ago when we went to a bar after work to celebrate Mark's birthday?"

"Oh, that." Ryo had let himself get talked into downing one drink more than he usually risked. He thought he'd escaped the consequences. *Obviously I was a tad too optimistic there.*

"I don't think anybody else noticed your ears getting pointed and furry right before you rushed out, but I did. So, just out of curiosity, I researched kitsune myths. When this amulet fell into my hands, I couldn't help but think it was serendipity."

"Sure, the first thing anybody in that situation would naturally think of would be using magic to enslave a coworker like your personal genie."

Joel grimaced. "Please—nothing like that. I just need

help."

"To do what?" Ryo sneaked another glance at his watch—past eleven. *Yep, I'm doomed.* In confirmation of those qualms, his cell phone rang.

"Turn that off," Joel snapped.

Ryo's fingers automatically carried out the order.

Smoothly reverting to the main conversation, Joel continued, "From what I've read, kitsune have a wide range of powers beside changing between fox and human. I mentioned some the other day, and you denied having any." He counted them on his fingers. "Invisibility, foxfire, superhuman strength, irresistible sexual magnetism, retrieving desired objects, making people get lost, possessing them, even speaking through them like a medium. Not to mention creating an illusion or reality— it's not clear which—of a place outside normal space. Like one legend I read about a beautiful, mysterious woman who lured a man to her luxurious mansion for a night of passion. When he woke up the next morning, he found himself on a pile of rotting leaves in a graveyard. So did the house exist, or was it a hallucination she generated?"

"You believe all that?" From his mother's words and actions, Ryo knew the truth of the legends. It surprised him a bit that his coworker swallowed the mythology whole, though.

Joel shrugged. "Some of the stories may be exaggerated, but I figure a lot of it's true. The beliefs have to come from somewhere, don't they? What interests me is the part about finding desired objects."

"I get it now. You expect me to track down your missing book like a bloodhound or something."

"Right. If you have that ability, it should be a breeze

for you."

Ryo sighed. "And as I told you when you brought it up the first time, I don't. I'm only half kitsune. Like I said, if I could become invisible or hide in a pocket dimension, you wouldn't have caught me this easily. I can change shape and create foxfire, not that I have perfect control over either one. That's all. You'll have to figure out another way to unearth your first-edition Lovecraft." He started to get to his feet.

Joel brandished the amulet. "Stay."

"What, now you think I'm a dog instead of a fox?" Ryo involuntarily resumed his seat.

"Maybe you've never tried hard enough. If I gave you a direct order to use that power, maybe it would work."

"Interesting concept. I have no idea. Keep in mind, you're not exactly putting me in a mood to cooperate."

"You'll want to," Joel said, "if you remember you're stuck under my control until I decide to let you go." He made the threat in an almost apologetic tone rather than the gloating voice of a comic-book villain.

"Are you sure? Didn't you say you have to focus on your target for the magic to keep working? Maybe you can march me down to your car and drive to your house, but it sounds like the minute you take your attention off me, I'll be free to move." Despite his frustrating predicament, Ryo smiled as the funny side of it occurred to him. "Haven't quite thought through your cunning plot, have you?"

Joel frowned, mulling over that point. "Okay, so I'll have to keep giving you fresh commands. I'll manage somehow. Look, why not agree to help me and save us both the trouble? Once I've got the book, I'll leave you alone."

Yeah, right. He'll get a taste of magical power and then just give it up. "Let me go, leave me alone from now on, and I'll forget this ever happened. You're wasting your time anyway."

"You keep insisting you don't have the powers. What if you're wrong?" He held up the pentagon and intoned, "I hereby order you to believe that if you need to, you can do anything a full-blooded kitsune can."

For a second, Ryo wondered whether that harebrained stunt might actually work. He suspected his own doubts about his abilities, combined with his mother's disappointment, had hampered the flourishing of his gifts. His constant fear of exposure if he let his kitsune nature run wild probably didn't help, either. Joel's command didn't make him feel any different, though. "Nice try, but no dice. What's your next move, mighty sorcerer?"

Joel glared at him. "Shut up and let me think."

****

Harvey Wright strode up to Shannon's table promptly at eleven and introduced himself, insisting she call him "Harv." Apparently in his forties, he was a man of average height and build, with sable-brown hair and beard, brown eyes, and tortoiseshell-rimmed glasses. His black polo shirt bore the Six Continents Media logo, a stylized Mercator projection map of the world. She shook hands with him, hoping her palm wasn't clammy with nervousness. "Ryo suddenly felt sick and had to leave. He should be able to meet with you soon, though." *I hope. It could even be true.*

The editor suggested they adjourn to the bar to discuss the proposed deal. He admired the laptop display and the book covers while she left a message on Ryo's cell phone and also wrote him a note stating where she'd gone. As she locked the cash box and covered the table with the cloth drape, the editor said, "I've noticed you have an attractive, well-established web platform and a solid reader base. Those are definite pluses."

She thanked him for the compliment, and they strolled to the bar, where they managed to grab one of the last open tables. Clearly, lots of people tried to beat the lunch crowd, thereby defeating the purpose. She got a soft drink, while Harv ordered a beer. "I'm in favor of buying your series for e-book and print," he said, "and the rest of the staff is on board, too. We just need to work out the details." He mentioned a surprisingly generous advance payment.

She managed to express her gratitude without babbling effusively.

"Don't worry. We're not planning a rights grab. We like to deal with animation studios ourselves, but you two can keep control over audiobooks, translations, and merchandise like T-shirts, action figures, et cetera. If I were you, I'd get an agent for that kind of thing."

"We've been thinking about it."

If I can pin Ryo down long enough to think straight about anything. She squelched her simmering exasperation over his flaky behavior and forced herself to focus on the conversation.

After a free-ranging discussion of the proposed contract, Harv checked his watch and said, "I have to get ready for a noon panel. This evening Six Continents is hosting a party along with a couple of other companies. Can you and Ryo attend? I'd like to get his input firsthand."

Shannon didn't miss the hint that non-attendance by Ryo would make a negative impression. "We'd love to. Let me try him once more before you go." She called Ryo's cell, which went straight to voice mail again. She left a terse message about the party invitation.

Harv jotted the location and time details on a business card he handed to her, and they strolled out of the bar. "I'm surprised your partner isn't answering his phone, even if he doesn't feel well."

"Maybe he had to lie down for a while and turned it off." *That's all it better be.* "I'll go up and check on him."

"Good idea. I need to meet him in person before making a final decision. He does fantastic work, but the company would have reservations about signing an artist who's not completely reliable."

Acid welled up in her throat. "He'll come to the party. I'll make sure of that."

"Great, see you there." After a farewell handshake, he strode down the hall toward the program rooms while Shannon hurried to the elevator. If Ryo was genuinely sick, she would apologize for disturbing him. If not, she wouldn't leave without a complete explanation.

****

For a minute Joel stared at Ryo, who simply stared back, magically compelled to silence. Finally, Joel said, "Cancel that command. Answer truthfully: You really can't do most of those things mentioned in the legends?"

"I've never been able to so far. My mother had many of those gifts, but she's a full-blooded kitsune and a two-tailed one, at that. Like I said, casting foxfire is about the extent of my ability. Burning your house down wouldn't be much help, would it?"

"Shut up again already." After a moment's thought,

Joel said, "Well, it can't hurt to try anyhow. Let's go."

Unable to speak, Ryo arched his eyebrows. Joel said, "We'll go to the garage, pick up my car, and drive to my house. You'll do your level best to conjure up that object-finding power. Once we've found the book, I'll release you."

Ryo gave him a skeptical look. Joel sighed. "Okay, you can talk, but don't even think about yelling for help."

"Have you figured out how to keep me from escaping the minute your concentration lapses?" Ryo followed his captor into the hall. He wasn't tempted to test whether that last clause constituted an order, since he knew if he tried to disobey, he'd only get silenced again.

"That's my problem."

"So it is," Ryo said in an assumed carefree tone. In fact, he wasn't too worried yet, certain the other man would eventually get distracted enough to let him break free.

Joel glared at him. "Go to the elevator."

Walking on, Ryo said as they turned the corner at the end of the hall, "Won't you look sort of conspicuous waving that thing around and giving me orders if we run into other people on the way down?"

Hesitating several paces from the elevator, Joel cast a dubious glance in the direction of the stairs.

"Maybe you should have taken elementary villain lessons before starting this project."

Scowling, Joel opened his mouth, probably to bark another order for silence. At that moment, one of the elevators down the hall opened, and Shannon stepped out.

"Ryo? What on earth is going on?"

At the sound of her voice, his heartbeat accelerated, and heat surged through him. His ears and buttocks sizzled with electricity as the former elongated and the latter sprouted a tail. Joel, brandishing the amulet, glanced wildly from Ryo to Shannon and back again.

Freed from the magical compulsion, Ryo dashed for the stairway entrance. Both Shannon and Joel yelled after him. Fortunately, with her calling his name, he couldn't distinguish the words Joel was shouting, which doubtless consisted of an order to halt. Ryo wrenched the heavy door open and ran down the steps. Seconds later, the other two clattered behind him.

****

Shannon gaped at Ryo's ears and tail. *He didn't have those a minute ago. Where did they come from?*

Deciding to shelve that question for now, she rushed downstairs alongside Joel Brady. "What are you doing? Why are you chasing him?" Maybe Ryo's reluctance to deal with this weirdo wasn't so irrational after all. When they reached the first stairwell, she jumped in front of the man. "Hold it right here and explain yourself." Not that she knew how she'd stop him if he chose to shove past her.

He grabbed her arm. When she batted him with her free hand and tried to jerk loose from his grip, he raised the pendant he was wearing and said, "Freeze."

To her amazement, she couldn't move. Her arms even stopped flailing around, petrified in the position they'd held when he had spoken. She swayed, off balance with one foot on tiptoe.

"You can stand straight," he said, letting go of her, "and breathe and blink, but not talk or scream."

Her leg muscles obeyed. She gulped a breath and swallowed.

Halfway down the next flight of stairs, Ryo pivoted,

ran back up, and knocked Joel sideways. Joel released the pendant to catch himself, landing on hands and knees. Shannon instantly regained the ability to move. She retreated to wedge herself in a corner, her head spinning. As Joel scrambled to his feet, Ryo sprinted down the stairs.

As he ran, a pale glow shimmered around him. His outline wavered and melted, then coalesced into the shape of a small animal with dark copper fur, a white-tipped, bushy tail, and black paws, muzzle, and ear tips. *A fox? He turned into a fox!*

Joel gripped the pendant and opened his mouth. Without pausing to consider, Shannon thumped him in the side with her purse, then shoved him against the wall. Although dizzy with confusion, she figured the thing Joel wore had to radiate some kind of magic, crazy as that sounded. She couldn't let him shout a command before Ryo got out of range, however far that might be.

When she looked for the fox, he'd fled out of sight. *Good, he's probably safe for the moment.* It apparently didn't take much to break Joel's control over his victims, so it seemed likely he needed to be near people to command them. She ran in the direction fox-Ryo had gone, hoping to get a head start before Joel gathered his wits. Two landings and flights down, she caught up with the animal.

"Ryo? Is that really you?" *Am I dreaming? Hallucinating?*

The fox yipped and wagged his tail. With an inviting look over his shoulder, he scurried down the next stretch of stairs. Hearing Joel's footsteps on the landing above, she hurried after Ryo. *What the heck, if I've fallen down the rabbit hole, I might as well go with the flow.* On the chance that this was actually happening, she couldn't leave him to fend for himself. He picked up speed, and she raced after him.

Chapter Six

Panting, she caught up with him at the ground floor exit. He pawed at the door. The pursuer's clatter on the staircase grew louder. She pushed the door open far enough to squeeze through it along with the fox, and they emerged into the garage. "Hold on! Explain yourself!"

He replied with an impatient-sounding bark, as if to say there wasn't time, and kept running.

She followed, darting around parked cars and dodging vehicles in motion.

I hope he knows the way out. I also hope nobody notices there's a fox loose in the garage. Pausing behind a pillar, she peeked around it in search of Joel. He'd halted two lanes over to scan the area. At her side, Ryo whined for attention and trotted away. She kept pace with him, crouching as low as possible while looking around for an exit sign. When she sighted one, she alerted the fox with a low whistle and pointed.

Together they raced toward it. Joel must have noticed the movement, for he yelled, "Hey, stop," and broke into a run.

To her relief, neither she nor the fox became paralyzed. The wielder of the amulet must need to be closer, maybe right next to them, for the magic to work. He was catching up, though. She lost sight of him as he circled around the rows of parked cars. When he reappeared, Ryo changed course, and Shannon followed.

Joel cut across their path. Gasping, her legs aching, she angled away from him. Out the corner of her eye, she glimpsed Ryo charging in the opposite direction. Joel hovered indecisively for only a couple of seconds. Instead of chasing the fox, he ran toward Shannon. He was panting, too, she noted with satisfaction, but he still managed to block her at the end of a lane.

Ryo pivoted and dashed toward them. "No! Run away!" she cried. No sense in both of them getting trapped.

He ignored her. Instead, he charged at Joel, who instantly ordered him to stop.

Ryo screeched to a halt. When Shannon advanced on Joel, he said, "You stop, too—what's your name?"

Immobilized, she choked out, "Shannon McBain."

The fox's lips curled back from his fangs in a snarl. With a sidelong look at him, Joel said, "If you don't want her hurt, behave yourself."

Ryo froze.

Joel continued, "You're both coming home with me. Okay, I can't command both of you at once, but I can control Shannon, and I know you won't let anything happen to her. After you do what I asked, I'll release both of you."

Yeah, sure you will. As if he'd let them go free, knowing he possessed a magical artifact. Still, it seemed safest to pretend to comply for the moment. Although he didn't strike her as the violent type, he sounded stubborn and desperate enough that provoking him wouldn't be wise.

He gestured with the amulet. "Shannon, go that way."

Her legs moved in the direction he indicated, parallel

to the wall, while her muscles quivered in a vain effort to break the compulsion. "Where are we going?"

"To my car. Like I said, we're driving to my house, where I've got a job for him. If I have to renew control over you at every stop and turn on the way, I will."

"Why? What job?"

"Never mind that for now. The point is, if he wants you safe and free, he'll discover how to use those powers he says he doesn't have."

Baffled, she considered asking him to explain himself—*what powers?*—but, knowing he probably wouldn't answer, she decided to conserve her energy.

Fox-Ryo kept pace with them, his teeth bared in a soundless growl. When they reached a two-door compact car parked in the lane nearest the wall, Joel dug in his pocket for the key. The tension in Shannon's muscles slackened. She turned to flee.

Joel instantly snapped, "Stop. Get on the floor and stay there."

As the magic forced her to her knees, the fox lunged at Joel, bumping into his legs. The man staggered and almost fell, barely catching himself by leaning on the car, but kept hold of the amulet. Shannon sprang to her feet. The fox vanished.

Huh? Did he just disappear into thin air?

An invisible hand grabbed her arm.

****

A furious growl rumbled in Ryo's throat. *Hurt her, will you? Not if I have any say in it.*

A wave of energy surged through him. At the same instant, he shifted from fox to man—and became invisible.

Well, go figure. He commanded me to be able to use

my gifts when I needed them. I need them—by my standards, not his—so now I can.

He grasped Shannon's arm, and she shrieked in surprise, while Joel looked wildly around. Ryo launched a baseball-size sphere of foxfire at his legs.

The other man screamed and fell, landing on his side, and let go of the amulet. With Ryo still holding onto her left forearm, Shannon lunged at Joel, jerked on the delicate chain with her right hand, broke it, and snatched the amulet. As Ryo pulled her a couple of paces back, out of the other man's reach, she pointed at Joel and ordered, "Stop there. Sit down, don't move, and be quiet."

Scowling, he obeyed. Ryo willed himself to become visible. He vaguely realized he had a fox's tail and ears, but that was the least of his current problems. Shannon gaped wide-eyed at him. A scent of fear wove through her natural fragrance. "What's going on?" She tugged her arm out of his grip.

"Don't freak out. I'm still me." He glanced at the far end of the lane, where a car was creeping in their direction. *That's all we need, witnesses.*

"Now what?" She stared at Joel, who started to heave himself up from the floor.

"Damn it, give that back." He lurched toward her, one hand clawing the air.

She again yelled at him to stop, which he did with an inarticulate growl of protest.

A fresh wave of anger swept over Ryo. It uncovered another layer of gifts he'd suppressed. Without needing to pause for thought, he clutched Joel's collar and dragged him toward the corner where two walls joined. Ryo visualized what he wanted, and it appeared—a door, mahogany with a brass doorknob shaped liked a fox's head.

With Shannon next to him, he wrenched the door open and shoved Joel inside. When Joel turned to flee into the garage, Ryo blocked the way and threatened him with a deep-throated snarl. Joel ran down the corridor, around a curve, and out of sight. The door behind them swung shut. Ryo beamed a silent command at it, and it vanished. *Can't have people in the garage noticing it.*

In response to Shannon's look of alarm, he said, "Don't worry, I'll make sure we can leave when we need to." Clasping her hand, he took a step forward.

She held up her free hand in a "halt" gesture. "Hold it. Time out." Her breath came fast and labored. "Is there another exit where he can escape?"

Ryo shook his head. "I don't know exactly what's in here, but there won't be a door unless I make one."

"Then you can take a few minutes to explain what's going on. I'm trying really hard not to panic, but help me out here." She pulled free of his grip and sat on the floor against the nearest wall. "What are you, exactly, where is here, and what's with that weirdo harassing you?" As he took a seat beside her, she pressed the amulet into his hand. "You better take care of this. You're the one who's got experience with magic."

"Not much." With a half-smile, he stashed the pentagon in a side pocket.

"Um—you have clothes on. How do you do that?"

Why is that the first thing everybody asks? "Whatever I'm wearing plus any small objects I'm carrying go into some kind of magic virtual storage space until I change back to human. At least, that's how my mother explained it."

"Your mother is a kitsune?"

205

He nodded. "It wasn't just the cultural differences that broke up my folks' marriage. Dad never fully adjusted to her nonhuman side."

"That must have been rough on you." She patted his hand. "I know a kitsune is a fox shapeshifter in Japanese folklore, but not much else. This is a little scary, but also kind of cool."

He suppressed a sigh. Would *scary* eventually win out, as it had with his father?

At the moment he no longer smelled fear on her, an encouraging development. "You didn't tell me the truth about yourself," she said. "You let me think, well, all sorts of crazy things."

"And this isn't crazy?"

"I haven't made up my mind about that yet. Half of me expects to wake up any second now."

"I've hidden the truth from everybody all my life, for good reasons. This isn't the kind of thing I could just blurt out. Anyway, would you have believed me?"

"We'll never know, will we?" She reached for his head. "May I?" When he nodded, she ran her fingers over the tip of his right ear. "Wow. It's real," she whispered.

A shiver coursed through him. Catching her hand, he forced words past the tightness in his throat. "We'd better find Joel."

"Why has he been stalking you?"

"Short version: There's a valuable book somewhere in his late uncle's house, and he wants me to unearth it with my alleged kitsune powers."

She arched her eyebrows. "That's all this is about? He's mislaid a book and expects you to find it by magic?"

"I think there's more, even if he believes that himself." Ryo spoke slowly, articulating the idea to himself for the first time, as well as to her. "I think he's fascinated with the idea of magic and excited about seeing it in action. I figure this demand is only a test. So I doubt he'll stop bugging me even if I track down the book."

"He said you told him you didn't have the ability to do that." Her voice held a hint of a challenge.

"I didn't, before. Now I do. When he threatened you, something snapped. Also, I've always worried someone would discover my kitsune nature if I used my alleged powers, and here that ship has sailed." He got to his feet and helped her up. "It's as if a locked cabinet full of the gifts I'm supposed to have suddenly got opened."

"Like throwing fireballs and turning invisible?"

"Among other things," he said, "though I could already make fire. Maybe now I could even unearth Joel's lost book, not that I want to do anything to reinforce this obsession he's developed. Speaking of him, let's get moving. There's only so far he could have gone."

As they followed the corridor around the bend, she scanned the curving walls of dark, polished wood. "You haven't explained what this place is yet. How did you find it? Another feature of your fox magic?"

"I didn't find it. I made it. Mom could create pocket dimensions with whole houses and gardens. Until a few minutes ago, I couldn't do anything like that. She'd be amazed to know I managed this much."

Shannon came to an abrupt stop. "Hang on while I process the mind boggle. Making virtual spaces is standard kitsune stuff?"

He shrugged. "For purebred kitsune, it is."

She shook her head, apparently in amazement rather than denial. "How long will it last?"

"Like I said, I'm new to this. Mom's secret

hideaways were permanent until she decided otherwise."
Scenting a spike of alarm from Shannon, he added,
"Don't worry, this place won't evaporate with us in it.
It'll stay put at least as long as I'm here."

"What's in it besides a long hallway?"

He took her hand. "Let's find out."

Around the next curve, they came upon five
branching corridors. "What now?" she asked.

"We try one and see what happens, I guess."

He led her down the rightmost hall, which dead-
ended in a T intersection. Glancing to the right, he
glimpsed Joel turning left at the next branching point.
Ryo hurried in that direction, followed by Shannon. That
path led to a square room with an opening in each wall,
including the one they'd entered through.

"This place is a maze," she said. "You didn't plan it
this way?"

"Hardly. You saw what happened. I conjured it up on
the spur of the moment. For all I know, it's a reflection of
my subconscious or something."

"The walls all look alike. We could wind up where
we'd already explored without realizing it."

"Yeah, scurrying around at random won't get us
anywhere. I need to track him systematically, which
means shifting into fox form."

She raked her fingers through her hair as if to scrub
away confusion. "I'm maxed out on freaking at the
weirdness for now, so go for it."

A few seconds of concentration shrank Ryo's body
and morphed it from biped to quadruped. The colors of
Shannon's clothes faded to pastels, while her aroma and
the noise of her breathing sharpened. He trotted around
the square space, sniffing along the walls. Joel's spoor,

sour with fear, assailed his nose. Ryo traced it to the door the man had passed through.

He glanced back at Shannon with an encouraging yip. She followed close on his heels as he trailed his quarry. Three more turns brought them to a spot where Joel's scent saturated the air. Multiple openings led to passageways that each curved out of sight within a few feet. Ryo pawed the floor in frustration and sniffed the air.

Wait—I don't have to track him this way anymore. I know where he's going. The heart of the virtual space would draw the intruder, just as it drew Ryo himself.

He shifted back to human form, noting that the transformation flowed more smoothly than usual, and grabbed Shannon's hand. "We're near the center. He's very close. Shut your eyes."

"Huh?"

"Trust me, it'll minimize the weird." When she obeyed, he closed his eyes, too, and stretched his inner perception to trace the shape of the maze. *Yes, there's the center.* Taking three paces forward, he sensed a ripple in the substance of the wall. With her hand still in his, he stepped through the portal that formed around them.

When he opened his eyes, they stood in an octagonal chamber lined floor-to-ceiling with mirrors. He led Shannon across the gleaming hardwood floor, about ten feet wide, to the opposite wall. Their multiple reflections flickered around them. "You can look now."

She opened her eyes and stumbled at the visual barrage. "What's this?"

He steadied her with an arm around her shoulders. "We're in the middle of the pocket dimension. Joel will show up anytime now." Ryo stared at the oval gap where they'd entered. As he'd expected, seconds later Joel, gasping in barely controlled panic, staggered through it. Ryo silently commanded the portal to vanish. Next he summoned invisibility to conceal him, wrapping an arm around Shannon to shelter her. She flinched for an instant when he faded out of sight but then relaxed into his embrace.

Joel spun around and pounded on the mirrored wall. When no escape route appeared, he lurched along the perimeter, knocking on the unbreakable mirrors and shouting curses. He didn't seem to notice Ryo and Shannon, who sidled out of his path as he completed the circuit. *My invisibility must be shielding her from him somehow.*

"What's wrong with him?" she whispered.

"This place belongs to me, and he wasn't invited. Maybe that's why he's going nuts."

"I can't see you, but I can see myself, and he acts like he can't. See me, I mean."

"This use of the magic is new to me, too. Somehow I'm blocking his sight of both of us. Which is a good thing even if I'm not sure why."

Still whispering, she said, "What now? Staying stuck in here with him doesn't seem like a viable strategy."

"I can get us out anytime. I have to do something about him, though."

Joel, sweaty, his chest heaving, stumbled across the middle of the chamber. He continued to ignore them. When Shannon spoke in a normal tone, he didn't react. "Now that your kitsune powers are working, isn't there some way you can calm him down and make sure he won't hassle you with crazy demands again? If you can conjure a maze out of thin air, it seems like you could do that."

After mentally riffling through the list of abilities Joel ticked off earlier, Ryo said, "Maybe so." His mother had confirmed the reality of the fox possession lore but, after his failure to manipulate magical space, she'd decided the other advanced magics weren't worth trying. Now he seemed to have leveled up in power, though. He canceled the invisibility. What he planned would take all his concentration. "I think I can do this if you support me. Don't let go. I'll need you as an anchor so I won't lose myself." He clasped Shannon's hand in a firm grip.

She squeezed his fingers and edged closer to him. "What are you going to do?"

"If it works, I'll explain afterward." He fixed his gaze on Joel. "Look at me. Sit down and listen."

Exuding a miasma of fear, Joel stared at him. "What? Where did you come from? How the hell did I get here?"

Ryo imagined extending invisible tendrils to envelop the other man and exert pressure on his mind. "Sit down and be quiet. Everything will be all right."

Joel retreated to the nearest wall and slumped to the floor. He shifted his fear-widened eyes away from Ryo.

"Look at me," Ryo repeated. "I won't hurt you. Open your mind." He visualized twining those tendrils around Joel's head and lulling the storm of panic. Closing his eyes, he imagined himself painlessly slipping inside the other man's skull.

A chaotic swarm of emotions buzzed there. For a second Ryo recoiled in shock. *It worked! I touched his thoughts. Can't stop now—have to go through with it.*

He decided to alter the visualization. Not tentacles, cables. He linked his mind and Joel's together like a pair of computers. A flood of sensation and emotion rushed along the link. Confusion, fear, avarice, and guilt threatened to swamp Ryo's awareness. The other man's heartbeat hammered inside his head, and for a moment Ryo couldn't distinguish that pulse from his own. Overwhelmed, he flailed against the tide.

I'm drowning!

A warm embrace drew him from the depths. A firm handclasp steadied him—Shannon's. He clung tightly to that support.

I can do this.

He channeled his consciousness down the link again. *Calm, quiet, peace.* The tumult receded.

Listen to me, Joel. Magic doesn't exist. There's no such creature as a kitsune. Forget what you did with the amulet. It was an ordinary medallion with no special qualities. You've misplaced it, but that's not a problem. You didn't need it after all.

The waves crashing through the other man's mind smoothed away. Ryo continued the gentle reshaping process: *Forget you had any reason to believe I'm a kitsune. You don't believe in the supernatural. You didn't witness anything unusual this weekend. When we meet again, you'll see me as a casual work acquaintance, like always.*

Joel's thoughts settled into placid acceptance. *Rest now,* Ryo told him. *When you leave here, you won't remember anything weird, and you won't be upset or worried. Now go to sleep.* The other man's mind went blank.

Link by link, Ryo detached the connections and dissolved the cables. When he finally withdrew into his own head and opened his eyes, Shannon was still clasping his hand. After a couple of deep breaths, she said,

"Incredible. For a minute I felt like I merged with you, as if I was inside your mind." Just before the remnants of the link dissipated, he felt her pulse racing with a blend of excitement and fear.

"It was a little scary for me, too, but mainly it was good. You grounded me the way I asked you to." With hands joined, they walked over to Joel and gazed down at him. He slouched in a heap against the wall, apparently asleep as Ryo had ordered.

"What did you do?" she asked.

"Got into his head. I changed his mind—literally."

"Is he okay?"

Ryo nodded. "Just sleeping. He'll be all right, and he won't remember any of the supernatural stuff."

She studied his face with a sidelong look. "You sound awfully sure."

"It worked." He was surprised himself at how confident he felt. "Something clicked, you might say."

She scanned their surroundings. "No door. What now?"

"That's no problem. Stick with me." Holding onto her, he gazed at the nearest wall. The mirrored surface melted. In three paces, he led Shannon through it.

They stood in the wood-paneled corridor. At a wave from him, the opening behind them flowed shut.

"We have to retrace our path through the halls to get out?" she asked.

He smiled at her with new confidence. "No, we can use a shortcut." He touched the wall, and a door appeared. They stepped from the corridor into the parking garage. With no need to puzzle over what to do next, he waved at the door, and it vanished, leaving only the gray cinderblock wall.

Margaret L. Carter

Chapter Seven

Her head spinning, Shannon sagged against Ryo and wrapped her arms around his waist for support. His heartbeat thumped reassuringly in her ear. She drew a quivering breath and sighed it out. "The door's gone." *Was it ever really here? And did he really turn into a fox?*

"Well, yeah. It's not like I could leave it for random people to discover."

She rubbed her eyes and gazed up at him. He didn't have fox ears anymore. "I'm not sure I didn't dream this entire incident."

"Does this feel like a dream?" He enfolded her in a tight embrace and lowered his mouth to hers.

She gasped, involuntarily parting her lips. His tongue teased hers. A rush of heat surged over her. Reeling with the flood of sensation, she clung to him to keep from being swept away. Her pulse pounding in her head and her chest tight from lack of air, she finally had to break off the kiss and gulp for breath.

He stepped back and held her at arms' length. "If that's a dream, let's not wake up."

Slipping out of his grasp, she had to swallow before she could speak. "We have to wake up. Places to go, things to do." She couldn't let herself get carried away by passion until she had answers for the questions of her rational side.

He switched on his phone, glanced at the time display

with a dismayed expression, and showed her the numbers. After 5 p.m.

Her pulse stuttered. "Seriously? There's no way we've been inside that magic space—or whatever—all afternoon."

"Most of the legends say time inside a kitsune's lair runs slower than time outside. Apparently that's true. I should've remembered."

His quick shift to cool acceptance of the anomaly annoyed her a bit. "What about Joel? You're just leaving him in there, wherever *there* is?"

"Without my input, the virtual space will eventually disintegrate, and he'll go free."

"How soon?" she asked.

"Since I've never done this before, I'm not sure. It was all mainly theoretical for me until today. Hopefully not until after we leave here tomorrow."

She looked dubious. "Will he be okay for that long?"

"If time runs on a different scale in the maze, it's not as if he'll feel like he's been trapped inside all weekend. Plus, I ordered him not to worry." Uncertainty flickered in his eyes. "At least, I hope it works that way. He's a pain, but I don't want to do him any real harm."

As they crossed the parking garage toward the entrance to the hotel, the reason she'd come after Ryo in the first place surfaced in her mind. "I don't want that either, but I'm glad he's not likely to harass us tonight. We have to meet Harvey Wright at a party."

"Say what?"

"That's what I came up to tell you. On top of that, we have lots to talk about. You not telling me you're a fox shapeshifter, to start with." They hurried through the halls to their dealers' table. "No point in reopening for sales now, so let's go up to my room." She retrieved the cash box from under the cloth and led the way to the elevator.

"Way to take charge. I like it," he said as they rode up to her floor.

She blushed at his teasing grin. "I'm not letting you run off this time."

"I don't want to run." He squeezed her hand.

In her room, they sat together on the small couch between the desk and the window. After catching her breath, she blurted out the first thought that popped into her head. "So that's why you're so good at visualizing beast-people. And why you suggested a fox for Raptor's partner."

He nodded.

"So why didn't you trust me enough to tell me?"

"Was I supposed dump it on you out of the blue? And as I said before, would you have believed it? You'd have thought I was putting you on or out of my mind."

"Well, I almost thought I was out of my own mind when I saw you change. Earlier, I wondered if I was losing it when I saw you with fox ears and a tail at random moments, too." Her stomach churned with a blend of outrage, astonishment, and excitement. *The transformation thing is kind of thrilling, in a way. There's magic in the world!*

"Look, I understand why you didn't want to reveal your secret at first," she went on. "But you could've shared it with me when you started half-changing in front of me. More important, you could have come clean about why you kept vanishing instead of letting me think of you as flaky or worse."

"I didn't want to risk destroying our relationship by freaking you out. I was afraid you'd panic or be repulsed.

I can't forget how Dad never completely got used to Mom's…differences. Deep down, he wanted her to act as human as possible, like on that old TV sitcom about the nose-twitching witch." He took her hand. "I didn't want something like that to get between us."

Shannon pulled away. "Now we'll never know how it would have worked out, because you didn't trust our friendship enough to take the risk."

"Give me a break on that, can't you? You're the first person except Joel who's ever found out since I was a kid. Well, plus Thad and Val."

"What? You told my cousin but not me?" That detail felt like a slap in the face, just when she'd begun to accept his rationale for secrecy.

Ryo sighed and covered his eyes for a second before gazing into hers. "It wasn't like that. They accidentally saw me in fox form the same day Joel did, only a couple of weeks ago." He sketched the highlights of an incident when Joel had caught him transforming and Ryo fled to Thad and Val's for refuge. "The magic in the atmosphere of their house attracted me." When Shannon opened her mouth to question that new revelation, he cut her short. "It's complicated. I'll explain that part later. Now, what were you saying earlier about a party?"

She told him about the editor's reaction when Ryo hadn't shown up for the appointment and about the event the two of them were invited to. "He implied his decision depended heavily on meeting you tonight, so don't flake out this time." She smiled to take the sting from the words.

"I won't, now that I don't have to hide my true nature from you. I do worry about the fox traits popping up at awkward moments, though. That's why I avoid groups of people as much as possible. Not to mention going easy on the alcohol."

"You don't have to worry this time. We'll figure out how to handle it together." Now that the most anxiety-stirring parts of the conversation were done, her stomach growled a reminder of the long stretch since lunch. "How about ordering dinner from room service?"

They called for burgers, fries, and soft drinks from the menu. While waiting for the food, she quizzed him further about his double nature. "How long have you known you were a kitsune?"

His eyebrows arched. "As long as I can remember. How long have you known you're human?"

She acknowledged the retort with a self-conscious laugh.

"Mom started teaching me to control the change as soon as I was old enough to understand. When I'd stopped transforming at random, around five, she let me play with other kids under her supervision." He gazed into the distance as if watching a video of his memories. "Sometimes I felt it made Dad uncomfortable to see me frolicking around the house as a fox cub."

Shannon patted his shoulder. "That must have been tough for you." *Maybe I shouldn't have been so hard on him about keeping this stuff secret.*

He shrugged. "It was what it was. Little kids don't know the world should be any different from their experience." A knock on the door interrupted him, so he paused to collect the food and tip the delivery person. Arranging the items on the coffee table, he continued, "Sometimes my ears or tail, or both, popped out while other kids were around, but of course nobody believed them. Mom taught me at home until middle school, and by then I could suppress the changes pretty well except when I was stressed."

"Judging from the way you've acted this weekend, I guess keeping it under control isn't always easy."

"True that." He took a sip of his drink. "It tends to happen when I get upset for any reason, and of course lapses cause more stress, which leads to more lapses. Vicious circle."

"I'm starting to understand why you avoid people so much." She nibbled on her fries, watching him take two large bites of his burger. "Hey, I bet transforming burns a ton of calories."

He nodded with his mouth full.

"Sounds like a plus to me. Any chance I could learn to do that?"

He laughed. "Sorry. I'm not a movie werewolf. It isn't contagious."

She sighed. "That's what I figured. So before today you couldn't do most of those magical things?"

"Right. Only the fireballs. I think part of my problem was unconsciously living down to my mother's ideas about my half-human limitations. When I saw you in danger, though, something snapped. It didn't matter anymore how many times I'd proved I couldn't make full use of my kitsune gifts. I had to do whatever it took to protect you."

Warmth suffused her at that remark. *Then he does care about me.* Her first impulse was to snuggle up and wrap her arms around him, but she thought better of it. *Talk first, then get physical—maybe.* "How do you feel about your powers now?"

He paused in thought for a moment before answering. "Better. Discovering what I could accomplish without those ingrained inhibitions gave me confidence."

"Great, so you should have confidence we can work things out between us."

"I've wanted that for a long time, more than I can say." He clasped her hand. "I didn't dare try to get closer as long as you didn't know about my—my other side."

"Well, if you'd tried," she said, "think where we might be right now."

He flushed, released her hand, and looked down at his plate. They finished off the food in silence.

After they stacked the plates on the tray and took a break to wash up, she rejoined him on the couch and made the request she'd been working up to. "I want a demonstration. Before, in the middle of being attacked, all I saw was a blur and then a fox."

"You're not afraid?" he asked in a hesitant tone.

"Why would I be? You'd never hurt me." True, her pulse was racing, but not with fear. "I need to watch you transform so I can convince myself for sure it absolutely happened."

"All right, if that's what you really want." His hands shook a little as he stood up and peeled off his shirt. "I can change while fully dressed, but it's easier this way." Toeing off his shoes, he emptied the contents of his pockets onto the coffee table. Again a faint glow emanated from him. His shape melted and dissolved into mist. A second later, the fox stood in the man's place.

Shannon exhaled a tremulous breath. "Wow." She reached out, palm up, to hold her hand under his muzzle. She suppressed a nervous giggle as she realized she was treating him like a dog. "May I touch?"

He gave an affirmative-sounding yip. With a tentative brush of her fingertips, she stroked the side of his neck. The dark russet fur felt dense and soft. *Like his hair in human form,* she realized.

When he leaped onto the couch beside her, she ran her hand down his back and along the plume of his tail. He felt almost feverishly hot to her fingertips. "It's real. I didn't imagine any of it. I wonder how it feels to turn into an animal? I'm almost sorry I'll never know." She stroked him once more, and his body quivered under her touch. *What am I doing? This is still Ryo.* She folded her hands in her lap.

The air shimmered around him again, and he flowed back into the form of a shirtless man. When their eyes met, he glanced away and hastily pulled on his shirt. "Hard to say how it feels," he said, "because it comes naturally to me. Adjusting to four legs and a lower visual vantage point takes almost no time after changing. As a fox, I don't see colors so vividly, but smell and hearing become sharper. A side effect of having a double nature is that those senses are keener in human form, too, though not nearly as much as when I'm transformed." He captured her hand. "Either way, you smell delicious." He leaned over to graze her lips with his.

Swaying toward him, she yielded to the melting warmth that radiated from the point of contact. She rested her free hand on his shoulder to steady herself.

"You taste great, too," he murmured, then deepened the kiss.

She figured she tasted like hamburgers and fries, as he did, which was fine with her. She clung to him as her head seemed to float above her tingling body. When he abruptly pulled away, she winced at the shock.

Touching her only with his hands clasping hers, he said, "Sorry, I don't know what came over me to say that—or do that."

"Why are you apologizing?" She barely managed to avoid screaming. "It was fine with me, or didn't you notice?"

"I don't want to put pressure on you, which I could do without even meaning to." He released her hands and sat back against the cushions.

"What do you mean, pressure?" She shook her head in bewilderment. "I don't get it."

"That's one main reason I haven't tried to get closer to you, even though I wanted to. Well, aside from the problem of revealing my true nature." His lips quirked in a rueful smile. "Believe me, I really wanted to get close."

"So what stopped you?" Exasperation sharpened her voice.

"Kitsune emit an erotic aura that's irresistible to some humans. How could I be sure you weren't responding to me for that reason instead of sincere attraction?"

Wavering between annoyance and amusement, she folded her arms and glowered at him. "Think a lot of yourself, do you?"

"It's not me as an individual. It's a kitsune gift—if you want to call it that—common to all of us and not under our control. I saw it with my mother. Men pursued her even when she did her best to discourage them. That was one of the reasons she and Dad broke up, I think."

Shannon couldn't help sympathizing with Ryo on that point. While an involuntary erotic lure wasn't the same as her father's gambling addiction, she knew how it felt to watch her parents' marriage disintegrate.

"It's happened to me, too. I've been hit on by women I hardly know."

"And from that you jump to the conclusion I can't control my own response to you? I haven't thrown myself at you, have I?" *Not for lack of desire, though. Maybe he has a valid concern.* No, she wouldn't believe a mindless magical aura could warp her free choices.

With a half-smile, he said, "Not so I've noticed. But how could I ever be sure how you really feel?"

"You can be sure because I'm telling you I kissed you of my own free will. Don't you trust my ability to make decisions for myself?" She held his gaze with a challenging stare.

His cheeks reddening, he looked away briefly, then met her eyes again. "I trust you to be honest."

"I hope I can trust you the same way. No more secrets." She scooted closer to him. "Now kiss me." She almost choked on the bold demand, but she had to dismantle his belief that an outside force was compelling their mutual attraction.

He took a deep breath and drew her into a loose embrace. "You're sure?"

She answered with a jerky nod, "What do you want, a written guarantee?" She tilted her head in invitation.

He accepted, first tentatively nibbling her lips, then claiming them in a deep kiss. She twined her arms around him, delighting in the lean firmness of his shoulders and torso. Heat flooded her body, with a tightness in her breasts and a flutter in the pit of her stomach. After a long moment, they broke apart, both gasping for breath.

He had fox ears.

He sprang to his feet and backed away. "You see why I was afraid to get too close to you before? The transformation tends to run wild when I get—uh—excited."

"Not to worry." She struggled to suppress the tremor in her voice. "That's no problem now that I know the truth anyway, is it?"

"You're not repulsed?"

"Of course not. I think it's awesome, even if in a weird sort of way."

"We probably shouldn't rush this, though." He closed his eyes as if concentrating, and his ears melted into their normal shape. "We need to get ready for the party, right?"

She nodded, reluctantly grateful for the respite. "Drop by here at eight, and we can go together."

"Sounds like a plan." He hastily stuffed his things back into his pockets. After a quick hug, as if he still feared lingering over it, he left.

She bolted the door behind him and leaned against it, breathing hard, her pulse racing. She touched her tingling lips.

I'm falling in love with a fox-man.
****

Ryo knocked on the door promptly at eight. Her internal sigh of relief surprised her. *Was I afraid he wouldn't show? I should start trusting him.*

Like her, he'd chosen to wear a T-shirt with one of his illustrations on it. "Great minds," she said, pointing to his chest and then her own.

As she stepped into the hall, he said, "I can't help being nervous about meeting this guy in the middle of a crowd of strangers. Whenever I have to do anything like that, I worry about suppressing the ears and tail, not to mention fangs and random fur."

"Worrying makes control harder, right?" She offered her hand as they walked, and he accepted it. "So don't obsess. Go with the flow."

"Just like that?" He glanced at her with a rueful smile before scanning the corridor as if concerned about being overheard. "Easy to say."

"Have you tried partially changing on purpose and stabilizing it that way? Around here, anybody who doesn't actually see the transformation happening will assume they're fake."

"I never thought about doing that. Holding it stable would be the hard part."

"You've got me to help you now, though." She thought back to what they'd done in the last few minutes before exiting the maze. "Before, I felt as if I were channeling psychic energy to you. If that wasn't an illusion, I could act like an anchor, keep you from losing your grip on the shape you want to maintain."

"It's worth a try." Leaning against the wall, still holding her hand, he closed his eyes. His fingers, at first cool, grew warm, then hot.

I'll bet transforming revs up his metabolism. The outlines of his ears wavered, and they dissolved from human to fox. On the lower part of his body, a plumed tail lashed from side to side.

"Way to go," she said.

He turned his head to check out his tail. "I've never changed selectively like this on purpose before."

"I knew you could do it." *Well, I hoped so, anyway.* "How about an experiment? Could you transform one but not the other?"

"I never tried." He narrowed his eyes in concentration. A second later, the tail vanished.

"Cool! See, you do have control over the process."

The tail reappeared while the ears reverted to human.

Next, tail and fox ears appeared together. "I guess you're right."

"Of course I am. If you feel it slipping, just concentrate on me. I'll be right beside you the whole time."

He squeezed her hand. "Thanks."

They rode the elevator up to the designated party floor. They easily found the suite they wanted by the roar of conversation overflowing through the open door. Inside, a wall-to-wall pack of people shouted to be heard over each other, ramping up the overall volume. Science-fiction-themed music played in the background. Ryo visibly winced at the noise. *His ears must be extra sensitive even when he's mostly human.*

With at least a third of the guests in costume, Ryo's animal appendages drew only an occasional glance. She noticed, with an absurd twinge of jealousy, that women's gazes did tend to linger on him. *Could that supernatural allure really be why he turns me on? No way!* While she had to concede that might have sparked the attraction, now she knew and appreciated him as a whole person.

Shannon caught a glimpse of Harvey Wright on the other side of the room next to a desk that displayed publications from Six Continents Media and the two other publishers co-hosting the event. Noticing her, he waved and started threading a path through the crowd. Shannon and Ryo met him halfway. When they got close enough to hear each other, she introduced him and Ryo.

"Nice ears. Very realistic," Harv said when they shook hands. "Good to finally meet you."

"Sorry I had to bail earlier. I'm fine now."

"Grab a drink, and let's find a quiet corner."

Beverages and nibbles covered a pair of tables

against one wall. Ryo passed up the wine and beer for club soda, so Shannon did the same. The three of them retreated into one of the adjoining bedrooms, Harv claiming the desk chair while she and Ryo took seats on the edge of the bed.

The editor reviewed the terms he'd already proposed to Shannon. Next, they discussed the logistics and timing of taking the self-published volumes off the market in preparation for release of the Six Continents reprints. Harv laid out a tentative timeline for several new graphic novels, a schedule she knew Ryo would have no trouble meeting. He'd always displayed the drive of a hardcore workaholic, and now she realized why. With his understandable aversion to socializing, he had an abundance of time and energy for creative pursuits. When the advance figure came up, he was as delighted with the amount as she had been.

Finally, Harv stood up and shook hands with them. "I'll recommend a contract on these terms, and you should hear from us within a week." He rejoined the throng in the main room, while Ryo and Shannon, heading for the exit, picked their way around the edges of the clustered conversation groups.

"You don't want to stay for a while?" she asked him.

He bent to speak directly in her ear, the tickle of his breath sending a delicious shiver through her. "No, thanks, crowds of people still make me jumpy."

With a glance at his vulpine ears, she hooked her arm in his. "You're doing fine. But leaving is okay with me. I can hardly hear myself think."

They cleared a path to the door and stepped into the relative quiet of the corridor. By unspoken consent, Ryo rode to her floor with her. "We're in," she said as they strolled toward her room. "We're going to be rich and famous."

He returned her grin. "I'll be thrilled if we manage one of the above. At the very least, Six Continents is big on pushing for film adaptations, so we might see an animated Raptor and Vixen some year in the not too distant future."

At her door, they both hesitated for a second after she pushed it ajar. She took the initiative to step inside, waving him ahead of her. "You made it through without slipping. I knew you could." Okay, that expression of confidence might be exaggerated, but considering how well things had gone, she figured she could be excused for shading the truth.

"And I think I can undo it at will now." As soon as he finished the sentence, his ears and tail poofed out of existence.

"Do it again."

With a rakish smile, he conjured up the ears and instantly made them vanish.

"See, you don't have a thing to worry about." She hugged him around the waist.

When he wrapped his arms around her to draw her into a tighter embrace, her heart pounded at the pressure of his taut body against hers. With a sense of inevitability, she tilted her head in invitation. He accepted with obvious eagerness. The heat of his lips on hers radiated throughout her body, making her nipples and other, more sensitive areas ache. She closed her eyes to savor the melting sensation deep within her. When she became conscious of his hardness pressing against her, she ended the kiss, struggling to catch her breath.

"Wow." He pulled away to put a few inches of space

between them, although his arms remained loosely around her. "You're not afraid of me?"

"Are you kidding?" Disentangling herself, she took his hand and led him to the couch. When they were both seated, she said, "Does this feel like fear?" This time she initiated the kiss.

Endless minutes later, her head reeling, she drew back. He had a tail, fox ears, and a velvet layer of russet fur on his chin. "Oops," he said with a lazy smile. The vulpine features disappeared.

"Way to go." She ran her fingers along his jawbone. "I'm getting to like the ears, though."

His smile faded. "You have no idea how good that makes me feel. But how can we be sure your attitude won't change the way my father's did?"

She leaned back against the cushions with a thoughtful frown. "We can't, can we? How can anybody be sure how they'll feel after ten or twenty or fifty years? All we fallible mortals can do is make promises and try to live up to them." Her parents had fought to heal their damaged union and succeeded. Maybe she should focus more on the healing than the damage.

"I don't know about you, but I definitely fall into the fallible mortal category." As if he'd read her mind, he added, "I'm sorry I thought I had to lie to you, especially now that I know your father failed your mother that way."

She exhaled a long breath, as if dispelling the pent-up mistrust she'd clung to. "We don't have to be like our parents, do we?"

"Right. You can trust that I won't lie to you again, and I can trust that you won't turn against me because of what I am." He raised her hand to his mouth and bestowed a lingering kiss on her curled fingers. "You know I want to stay with you tonight, don't you?"

"I did sort of guess that," she said with a shaky laugh. She couldn't resist a quick glance downward at the visible bulge.

Do I want that? So soon? While her body shouted an enthusiastic affirmative, her brain urged caution.

"The last thing I want is to leave you like this, but I feel we shouldn't rush it."

Torn between disappointment and relief, she nodded agreement. "This is all so new and strange. It's true I'm not scared, but my mind is still boggled."

He got to his feet, still clasping her hand. "We can take all the time we need to process what's happening between us. After all, waiting builds anticipation." He flashed her a smile. "If you need to work through the concept with somebody besides me, you could talk to Thad or Val."

"Because they already know about you?"

"More than that. They had the supernatural in their life before they found out about me."

Shannon stood and walked with him to the door. "Really? How so?"

"Not my secret to share, like mine wasn't theirs to tell." He brushed his lips lightly over hers. "See you tomorrow in the dealers' room."

She hugged him but forced herself not to linger over the embrace.

"I'd better go before I weaken and change my mind."

Squashing the persistent wish that he would, after he left she bolted and chained the door behind him before she could weaken instead.

Chapter Eight

While staffing their table Sunday morning and packing up at noon, Shannon and Ryo kept their conversation light. Only when they had an illusion of privacy in the garage, loading her car, did she feel free to mention the events of the previous day.

Scanning the bare concrete walls, she asked, "What about Joel? You think he's still in that dimensional pocket?"

"If he weren't," Ryo said, hefting a box of books into the trunk, "I think we'd have seen him. I'll check up on him after I get home. I just hope I can do it without making him suspicious about why I'm suddenly interested in what he's up to."

Shannon paused to brush stray hair out of her eyes. "You're sure he'll forget all about the supernatural phenomena the way you told him to?"

Ryo shrugged. "With luck. I can't be sure, never having done this before."

After they'd finished stowing the boxes and laptop, he dug into his pocket for the pentagonal amulet and offered it to her. "You should have this, in case you have second thoughts and feel you need protection."

"From you? No way."

"Take it anyhow. I'm not totally cool with having used fox possession on Joel, even though I didn't have much choice. I can understand if that creeped you out a little. I'll feel better knowing *you* know I can't have any power over you."

Warmth radiated through her at the tenderness in his eyes. She closed her hand around the amulet. "That's not a worry, but thanks."

He gave her a quick kiss on the cheek, turned away, and strode briskly across the garage. Watching him, she fingered the burning spot he'd kissed.

****

Over the next couple of days, the only contact Shannon had from Ryo consisted of brief e-mails about their current project. Without the amulet, she might have relapsed into dismissing the weirder parts of the weekend as a dream. The conversations with the editor had really happened, anyway. The generous advance made the looming prospect of unemployment and job-hunting less grim. She researched kitsune, astonished to read about the wide array of magical gifts legend attributed to fox shapeshifters. Their power level was linked to the number of tails they had, with nine-tailed kitsune being almost godlike. As far as she'd noticed, Ryo had only one, maybe because of his half-human background.

By Tuesday evening she finally worked up the nerve to phone Val, her cousin Thad's wife. Shannon had misgivings about broaching the topic of animal shapeshifters with someone who wasn't much more than a friendly acquaintance.

After identifying herself on the phone, she said, "Ryo Larsen suggested I should talk to you about him. This is going to sound crazy, I know…" She trailed off, groping for a rational way to phrase her question.

"You found out he's a kitsune," Val said in a casually cheerful tone.

"Then I'm not crazy? I was starting to wonder."

"You must have a ton of questions. Want to get together and talk about it? We could meet at lunchtime someday soon, if that works for you."

They made an appointment for the next day. Shannon could hardly wait to find out the meaning of Ryo's remark about Val and Thad's experience with the supernatural.

****

Shannon took a long lunch hour on Wednesday and drove to downtown Annapolis to meet Val, who worked in the historic district on State Circle. She found the other woman waiting at the Main Street coffee shop they'd agreed on. Val, around Shannon's own age, with shoulder-length strawberry-blonde hair, bangs, and silver-rimmed glasses, wore a light summer dress and carried a small paper bag. They each bought an iced coffee, and Shannon chose a veggie wrap from the display case.

At Val's suggestion, they sat at an outside table on the brick-paved sidewalk next to the narrow, one-way street. The awning of the coffee shop provided cover from the summer sun, and a light breeze mitigated the humidity. She produced a sandwich and an apple from her bag. "I'm a little surprised you know about Ryo. When we learned his secret, he mentioned he didn't want to tell you."

"He didn't. He bent over backwards to keep me from knowing. That's why I was a little shocked when he told me you and Thad knew." Also indignant at first, but Shannon didn't intend to mention that shameful reaction.

"It happened totally randomly. A man who works in

the same company accidentally witnessed him changing into a fox."

"Joel Brady," Shannon said. "He was stalking Ryo at the convention."

"Really? I'd like to hear more about that. Anyway, Ryo ran in a blind panic and ended up at our place. We decided he must have been attracted by the magic in our house."

"Ryo said you already knew about magic, but he wouldn't explain why."

"Yeah, we've known things like that really happen for about a year. We have a spirit cat living in our house."

Shannon almost choked on the bite she was chewing. After swallowing, she said, "A what?"

"She's an immortal white cat who can take human form at will for limited times. I accidentally woke her from a spell she was under."

Val's casual tone boggled Shannon's mind. "Do you often have interesting accidents like that?"

Val laughed. "Believe me, at the time I was completely blown away. At first I thought I was going bonkers, the way you must have felt when you saw Ryo change. It's a long story. Short version, Yuki—the cat—was under a curse, and Thad and I helped break it. Several other yokai—miscellaneous spirits—were involved, including a wolf demon."

"Compared to that, one shapeshifting fox seems almost routine. So your live-in spirit is like Ryo, only a cat?

"Not exactly." Val paused to sip her coffee, as if gathering her thoughts. "Yuki is mainly a cat, and she was never human. She just takes the shape of a woman now and then. Ryo's human, or half human anyway, so he's mortal, and that's his primary form."

"I guess I get it." Shannon's head was spinning by now. She finished her veggie wrap and took a drink of iced coffee while watching the mundane view of crawling Main Street traffic and strolling tourists. "How do you deal with knowing reality is so different from what science teaches, what our whole culture believes?"

"As I said, we've had a year to get used to the idea. Once the crisis with the curse ended, having Yuki around became just a part of our lives. It's not as if the occult pops up at every turn otherwise." Val caught and held Shannon's gaze. "You're worried about adjusting to the supernatural if you get more deeply involved with Ryo?"

Shannon nodded. "I'm falling in love with him." *There, I said it aloud.* About time she admitted she'd been half in love with him since long before their "date" on Memorial Day. "But I don't know how to feel about his nonhuman side."

"Is he a different person now from who he was before you knew this? Did you see any indication he'd ever hurt you? In principle, is this so different from discovering he has a chronic disease or something like that?—except being a kitsune is more of an advantage than a liability. It inspired him to create his Crimson Vixen character, didn't it?"

"Oh, are you a fan of Vixen already?"

"Sure, Thad and I have been following your work for quite a while."

Shannon cast her thoughts over the events of the past weekend. "I know he'd never hurt me. He saved me from Joel." She sketched a quick overview of what had happened at the con. "But that showed me Ryo has powers I don't have and couldn't have imagined. Though

236

I'm sure he wouldn't use them against me, they're still hard to wrap my head around."

"On a mundane level, most men are physically stronger than most women. Yet in good relationships we don't sit around worrying about that discrepancy."

"You've got a point there. I just have to find a way to accept that there's a whole other world underneath the one we know. It's mind-boggling that almost anything could happen, like in Wonderland or fairy tales."

"It's not that extreme," Val said, stuffing her sandwich wrapper and apple core in the paper bag. "After all, since last year Thad and I haven't met any new supernatural creatures except Ryo, which was a positive experience, nothing scary."

"If other ordinary people, like you and Thad, can accept it, I guess I can learn to."

Val stood up and tossed her bag into a nearby trash can. "Why don't you and Ryo come to dinner at our place this Friday? Just casual. You can pass on the invitation to him and let me know."

"Thanks, I'll do that. And thanks for the unique perspective." *It's my job to invite him? Clever way of throwing the ball into my court.*

****

Unable to nerve herself up to phoning Ryo, Shannon transmitted the dinner invitation by e-mail. He instantly replied with an acceptance, and she confirmed the specifics with Val. Late Friday afternoon, he picked Shannon up at her home to drive to Thad and Val's.

"Do you know anything about Joel's status?" Shannon asked as she buckled her seat belt.

"I know he escaped from the pocket dimension," Ryo said, backing out of the driveway, "because he called out sick from work part of this week. I don't know what he remembers, if anything, though."

"What are you going to do?"

"Already did it. Right before leaving home just now, I e-mailed him asking how he's doing. Missed you at the office yesterday, that kind of thing. I used a question about a current project as an excuse."

"Sounds good. If he doesn't mention anything supernatural, you can assume your command to forget it stuck." She shared Ryo's misgivings about letting the issue slide, along with his obvious relief that his coworker hadn't stayed trapped in the maze.

When they got to Thad and Val's home and walked up the front steps, a white cat with a red scarf around her neck was seated on the porch. With a meow that sounded almost like a greeting, she strolled to the door, tail waving. Ryo spoke to her in what Shannon assumed was Japanese.

"That's the spirit cat you mentioned?"

He nodded. She had a momentary flash of doubt— was that detail some kind of put-on after all?—before Thad opened the door to let them in, and the cat vanished. *I was looking right at her. She didn't run inside. She just suddenly wasn't there.*

Mentally shaking off the down-the-rabbit-hole feeling, she concentrated on greeting Thad and Val. A long-haired tabby stalked into the living room, hissed at Ryo, and sprinted out of sight. Val said, "Sorry. You probably smell like a predator to him."

She's so casual about that, Shannon thought. *Will I ever get that blasé about believing six impossible things before breakfast?*

"No problem," Ryo said. "I'm used to it. Dogs react

the same way, only worse. That's why I've never had a pet."

"So what can we get you to drink?" Thad asked. "And how do you like your steaks grilled?"

Dinner prep and serving proceeded with general conversation about everything but shapeshifters and magic. Thad and Val asked questions about the convention and the graphic novel series to draw out Ryo, with Shannon tossing in occasional comments. The white cat didn't reappear until they adjourned to the den with dessert, strawberry-topped cheesecake. Curled up in the center of the couch that faced the sliding glass door onto the patio, she stretched and moved to a corner to make space for Shannon, Ryo, and Val.

A high-backed, bamboo papasan chair scooted into the middle of the rug and positioned itself for Thad to sit on. Shannon dropped her fork on her plate and sputtered for several seconds before she could manage articulate words. "Did that chair move by itself?"

Thad nodded, patting the chair arm. "You're not hallucinating. Believe me, I reacted the same way the first time I saw it."

Val said, "It's residual magic from the enchanted scroll that broke the spell on Yuki. It's complicated."

After a bite of cheesecake and a fortifying sip of wine, Shannon said, "And the cat—Yuki—is really an immortal, shapeshifting creature?"

The cat arched her back and meowed in what sounded like a slightly indignant tone.

"She says of course she is," Ryo translated, "and please don't speak about her as if she isn't here."

Shannon murmured an apology. "You understand her?"

"Yeah, I hear her sounds as Japanese. It must be because I'm half yokai—supernatural creature—myself."

"And I hear them as English," Val said, "because I'm the one who accidentally activated the scroll."

Thad flashed a smile at Shannon. "Welcome to the null-magic club." All four humans laughed.

"I do have possession of a small piece of magic," she said, fishing the amulet out of her purse. "We took it from Joel when he tried to control us with it, and Ryo gave it to me for safekeeping." She passed the bronze pentagon to Val, who showed it to Yuki.

The cat pawed it and vocalized.

Val handed it back to Shannon. "She confirms that it's a powerful talisman. Do you know where it came from?"

Ryo explained how Joel had found the object by chance in a secondhand shop.

Yuki emitted another string of meows. "She says we should be careful with it," Ryo said, "which I already figured out on my own. Even if the effects don't last long, it's still a dangerous temptation, being able to compel people to obey you. That's why I gave it to Shannon."

"Like I'm guaranteed temptation-free, huh?" She asked Thad, "As one null-magic to another, how did you adjust to all this? You obviously aren't freaked by it now."

"After we defeated the wolf demon threatening Yuki, with a lot of help from the spirit of her long-dead boyfriend, we settled down to a new normal." The cat's whiskers twitched at the word *boyfriend*, as if objecting to it. "People can get used to just about anything. Once you accept that things you thought were impossible can happen, you stop worrying about your sanity and move on with your life."

After dessert and further conversation about their respective paranormal experiences, they strolled around the back yard in the twilight, admiring Val's vegetable garden. She sent Shannon and Ryo off with a sack of early tomatoes for each of them. By the time they said goodnight to their hosts, lightning bugs were twinkling in the shrubbery.

In the car, Ryo switched on his phone to check it before starting the engine. "Hey, I've got an e-mail from Joel. He answered my question about the game project, then said this about the con." He read aloud: "I didn't feel great after that convention, so I went to the doctor Monday. He didn't find anything wrong, but I took a couple of days to rest up anyway. My memory of the whole weekend is patchy. Truth is, I don't remember a thing between exploring the dealers' room on Saturday and finding myself in the garage Sunday night. Did I do anything flaky, stupid, or obnoxious? If so, don't hold it against me, okay? Maybe I had a prolonged blackout for some obscure reason, like an attack of forty-eight-hour flu. Meanwhile, on the bright side, I came up with an idea for a new game, a maze with mirrors and shapeshifting monsters."

"So your forget-everything command took effect," Shannon said. "That's a relief."

"Without permanently warping his brain, apparently, thank God." Ryo turned on the dome light and typed a reply, which he showed her: "No problem, you acted normal every time I ran into you. You did mention you were worried about a book you inherited from your uncle that was misplaced somewhere in his house. What if I come over sometime soon and help you look for it? Two sets of eyes are better than one."

"Do you think that's a good idea? It won't trigger the buried memory?"

"I don't think so," he said, sending the message. "I don't have to explain how I find the book. If stray memories did surface, I could wipe them again, but I hope that won't happen. Messing with his head once was more than enough."

"And you think you'll be able to use your kitsune finding gift to dig up his lost book?"

"I'm pretty sure I can." Ryo turned off his phone, started the car, and pulled onto the street. "It's got to be easier than constructing a pocket dimension. Anyway, for the first time in my life, I have solid faith in my abilities. You give me confidence." He reached over to touch her hand.

When they arrived at her apartment complex, she invited him in. She managed to suppress a sigh of relief when he readily accepted. He'd never visited her before. Too late, as they walked into the foyer of the one-story end unit, she remembered the newspapers scattered on the coffee table and the unmade bed and basket of unfolded laundry in her bedroom. *Not that he'll necessarily see the bedroom.* A blush warmed her cheeks at the thought.

In the living room, she swept the papers into a pile and offered him a drink. He'd restricted himself to one glass of wine at dinner.

"I'm not sure I should."

"One more won't interfere with your driving, and you don't have to worry about accidentally changing in front of me, do you?"

He smiled. "Granted. Okay, one drink."

She poured two glasses from the bottle of Riesling she had open in the refrigerator. Seated beside him on the couch, she took the amulet out of her purse and handed it to Ryo. "Now I know I'll never need this. You should keep it." From the way he'd dealt with Joel, she had faith that Ryo would never misuse his inborn mind-control ability, so he could certainly be trusted with the amulet.

"If you insist." He put it in his pocket. "But rather than risk temptation, I'll rent a safe deposit box and lock it up, first chance I get."

"I admit I'd feel better knowing a thing like that isn't rattling around loose for anybody to pick up."

They drank their wine while discussing the terms of the publication contract and their plans for the next story arc in their series. When Ryo finished his drink, he leaned toward her, his fingers lightly curling around the nape of her neck. He stopped with his face inches from hers. "May I?"

"What are you waiting for?"

"Hell if I know." His arms tightened around her, and he claimed her mouth in an ardent kiss.

She opened her lips to welcome the flicker of his tongue. From that point of contact, waves of fire and ice chased each other along her arms and down her spine. When he shifted one hand to her breasts and brushed his fingertips across the taut peaks, electricity zinged through her nerves.

Too soon, they had to stop and breathe. "We can move to the bedroom if you want." Her pulse pounded in her head, and her voice trembled despite her struggle to sound calm.

"Oh, I definitely want. Can't you tell?" He stood, drawing her to her feet. He hugged her to him, letting her feel his hardness through their clothes. "I've craved this practically since the day we met."

Inside, she melted from the heat of his embrace. "I have, too, almost as long. So why didn't you say anything?"

"Like I explained, because I was afraid of influencing you to do things you didn't really want." He massaged her back in expanding circles. "Now I know we've moved past that."

Holding his hand, she led him down the hall to the bedroom. She folded the covers all the way down and sat on the bed. Her gaze fixed on his eyes, she unfastened the top two buttons of her blouse.

He perched on the edge of the mattress a few inches from her. "There's something I need to confess before we go too far. The few times I made love to women in the past, it always ended in disaster. Seconds after the climax, or once right in the middle of it, I started transforming. I had to jump up and run away to keep from getting unmasked. Needless to say, that wrecked any chances of intimacy. So I'm not totally inexperienced, but close."

She suppressed an irrational twinge of jealousy at the idea that he'd been with other women before she'd ever met him. "You lost your grip because you panicked. There's no risk of panic now, is there? Anyway, if you do change involuntarily, we'll work around it."

"You really think we can?"

Her belief didn't rest on thought in the analytical sense, but on the emotion that welled up as she gazed into his eyes. "Trust me on this."

"I do." He scooted closer. "Because you trust me. I never dared to feel this way before."

Between kisses, they unbuttoned and unzipped each other's clothes. An awkward pause followed as both of them peeled off the layers of garments, each getting briefly tangled up in sleeves or leg openings. The draft from the air conditioner cooled Shannon's flushed skin. Her heart racing with a blend of excitement and nervousness, she lay face up, her head propped on a pair of pillows, and scanned Ryo's naked body. He was lean and trim, with a sprinkle of dark hair arrowing down to his groin.

What did I expect, a fur coat? Heat pooled in her core at the sight of his erection.

Lying above her, he skimmed one hand down her side and over her hips while they shared still more ravenous kisses. She couldn't help squirming with impatience as their hands roved eagerly over each other's bodies. His skin felt feverishly hot. Running her fingers through the dense pelt of his hair, she encountered something unexpected and widened her eyes to examine what she'd touched.

He had fox ears. She stroked their velvety tips and felt his responsive shudder down the full length of her body. A plume of fur brushed the backs of her legs—his tail. He flinched and rose onto his elbows. "Sorry."

"Relax, it's okay." She twined her arms around him. "You won't change any further."

He nuzzled her neck. "It doesn't bother you?"

She laughed softly at the tickle of his breath as he spoke the muffled question. "No way, I think it's kind of sexy." Actually, the caress of the restlessly lashing tail on her thighs sent a wave of sensuality sweeping over her. "Whatever you were about to do, don't stop now."

His hands and mouth explored everywhere, making her desire spiral higher by the second. He seemed to brand every place he touched. She whispered and moaned, first in encouragement, then entreaty. When he reached her most sensitive spot, ecstatic sensations flooded her whole being. She clung to him as the tide crashed over her.

When she opened her eyes, he leaned on his elbows above her, hesitating. She eagerly arched her hips. "Aren't you ready?"

He ran a hand from the V between her breasts to the triangle of her mound. "More than ready." His hard shaft grazed her thigh. "But what about protection?"

She rummaged through the nightstand drawer for one of the just-in-case condoms she'd stocked up on, with fantasies of a moment like this lurking in the back of her mind. After sheathing him, she opened her arms in invitation. He stretched on top of her again, nibbling on the corners of her mouth. As that playful gesture morphed into a devouring kiss, she let her eyes drift shut as she wrapped her arms and legs around him. He plunged deep inside. As he drove to his peak, another wave swept her away.

At last, panting, he turned on his side, bringing her with him. She noticed that at some point the vulpine appendages vanished. "Sorry it was so rushed."

She gripped his shoulders and gave him a gentle shake. "Quit apologizing. It was great."

"It should be more relaxed next time." He planted a kiss on her bare shoulder. "Assuming there's a next time." Her heart fluttered at his tentative tone. "Because I realize I've been in love with you since—I don't know, half of forever."

"And I've felt the same way. I just didn't admit it until it ambushed me last weekend." A giggle escaped her, which he cut short with a quick kiss. "So I hope we'll have too many next times to count."

Kappa Companion

by

Margaret L. Carter

Chapter One

The final dismissal bell jangled. Minutes later, as Heidi Clarke finished shutting down the main library computer, her son Adam clattered in from the corridor.

"Don't slam the door," she automatically ordered. She stepped from behind the desk and leaned over to hug him and tousle his hair.

"Hi, Mom." He waved to the auburn-haired woman shelving the last of the day's returned books. "Hi, Mrs. Larsen."

Shannon Larsen, the assistant librarian, in her early thirties like Heidi, returned the wave.

"Mrs. Larsen is giving us a ride home because the car's still in the shop," Heidi said.

Shannon trundled the empty book cart back to its corner. "Ulterior motive. I can't wait to see your new house."

Heidi posed her usual after-school question to Adam. "What interesting thing happened today?"

"My friend Window hit a home run in tee-ball at recess."

Heidi exchanged glances with Shannon. "Window?" her assistant echoed.

Recalling Adam's introduction of another friend as "Tomorrow," a girl actually called Tamara, Heidi riffled through her mental file of his second-grade classmates. "Maybe you're thinking of Wendell?"

Adam pondered for a second, then nodded. "Yeah, that's him."

She collected her purse and took his hand to walk out of the rambling, late-Victorian mansion that housed Eastport Sunrise Academy. By now, most of the departing horde of children had cleared away. Only a few scattered clumps of students, clad in the private school's royal blue polo shirt with sunburst logo, still waited for their parents. Heidi held tightly to Adam's hand as they crossed the parking lot. Sure, at the age of seven he knew not to run between cars, but better safe than sorry. Muggy heat pervaded the atmosphere, typical of a mid-September afternoon in Maryland. As he clambered into the back seat, Shannon switched on the air conditioner along with the ignition. Heidi checked his belt before buckling her own.

"Can we go to the park so I can feed the ducks and play with the turtle boy?"

Shannon cast a quizzical look at Heidi. "Turtle boy?"

"No clue." To Adam, she said, "No time for the park on a school night. But I have a different treat for you. Mrs. Larsen and I decided it's okay for you to read *Raptor and Vixen*. I'll lend you the first volume as soon as you're ready."

"I'm flattered that he's so wild about wanting to read our graphic novels, even if they aren't really targeted at children," Shannon said. "Ryo"—the artist, her Japanese-American husband—"will get a kick out of it, too."

"Adam's crazy about the idea of shapeshifting superheroes, and your comics—excuse me, graphic novels—don't have any over-the-top violence, so what harm could they do?"

"Thanks for the seal of approval." Shannon glanced over her shoulder with a smile at Adam. "I hope you'll enjoy the book."

"Yay!" He bounced in his seat. "Can I read it before bed tonight? I mean, may I?"

"Fine with me," Heidi said.

Guided by her directions, Shannon drove along narrow, tree-shaded streets to their destination, less than ten minutes away. "It must be great to live so close, after your old commute."

"For sure," Heidi said. "No more hassles with Route Two traffic and morning backups on the Severn River bridge. The location's perfect in other ways, too, like that pocket park on Spa Creek Adam mentioned. It's less than a five-minute walk from the house."

As soon as they pulled into her driveway and the car switched off, Adam unfastened his belt and flung the door open. Heidi disembarked at a sedate, end-of-workday pace, watching her son dash ahead of them along the sidewalk and the four steps up to the porch. He had her naturally curly hair, which she thought looked better on him than her, but raven black like his late father's instead of her walnut brown. He also had Doug's puppy-dog brown eyes instead of her blue. The mental comparison no longer pierced her with an automatic pang of grief. Instead, wistful regret momentarily shadowed her before dissolving like a mist in a breeze.

"Nice trees." Shannon glanced at the crape myrtle on one side of the sidewalk and the magnolia on the other.

"Thanks, they were the first thing that attracted me about the place."

Shannon swiveled around to scan the front of the house—gray-blue siding, detached garage, and a four-foot, wooden privacy fence marking off the back yard. "I love those gable windows on the second floor, too. It must be at least a century old."

"About a hundred and ten years, according to the real estate agent, like a lot of houses in this neighborhood. Being so close to the downtown historic district, it cost a bundle, but it's worth every penny." Heidi ran her fingers along the railing as she climbed up the porch steps. *Home. All ours.* A wry smile quirked her lips. *Well, and the bank's.*

"Big change from your townhouse in Severna Park."

"Yeah, I love having room to spread out, not to mention an actual yard for Adam instead of a patch of grass about the size of a tablecloth in front and an enclosed patio in back. Doug never had any interest in trading up from the condo to a house." Heidi added, "Want to see the inside?"

"I thought you'd never ask." As Heidi unlocked the door, Shannon took another look at the front lawn and the "Jeff Austin for Alderman" sign. "You and Jeff must be getting pretty close, if you're boosting his political career."

Heidi glanced aside from Shannon's teasing grin. "Why not? He'll be great on the Annapolis City Council. He's so honest and reliable, and he really cares about things like the environment. He was doing that public service stuff long before he decided to run for office, all on top of teaching eighth- and ninth-grade biology."

"Reliable?" Shannon gave her a mock slap on the arm. "You make him sound like the faithful family dog. What about *hot*?"

A blush warmed Heidi's face. "Oh, come on."

"You're telling me you've been dating him for a year now, and you don't think he's hot?"

"I'm not sure I'd call it officially dating, but okay, maybe he's a little hot."

"Thought so." With a sly smile, Shannon added, "And I don't know what you'd call going out every weekend, even during school vacations, if not dating. Not to mention eating lunch together every day."

"That's no big deal. We've been eating with a group at the same table in the cafeteria the whole six years he's been on the faculty."

"Yeah, but lately you always sit next to each other. And don't think I haven't noticed how often you go out to lunch one-on-one." Shannon gave her a playful poke in the arm.

Heidi froze, her fingers tightening on her purse strap. "Really? Do you think other people notice? When you put it that way, it sounds unprofessional."

"Take it easy." Shannon patted her shoulder. "There's no rule against consenting adult staff members getting close on their own time. Relax and enjoy."

Heidi changed the subject to tame the flutter of her pulse. "Come on in, and I'll give you the grand tour."

She opened the door, and they stepped inside with Adam in the lead. She stopped short in the foyer and gaped at the living room couch. The throw pillows she'd left in a neat row that morning lay on the floor and the coffee table. "What in the world?"

Shannon looked around at the otherwise tidy space. "I gather it's not usually like this."

"Ha, ha." Heidi strode into the center of the room and picked up one of the cushions. "I wonder if Ebony knocked them off somehow. She's never done that before, though." The sleek, all-black cat was nowhere in sight.

Joining her to help straighten up the couch, Shannon said, "Would a cat even be strong enough? Maybe it was an earthquake."

Heidi answered the joking remark half seriously. "Earthquakes happen in this area, but less than once in a blue moon. Besides, we would've felt it at school. Also, things would be knocked off shelves, too."

"Speaking of shelves, the cat or a quake couldn't do that, could they?" Shannon pointed to the bookcase beside the television cabinet.

A cushion lay on top of the bookcase, where Heidi herself could barely reach while standing on the floor. Her stomach knotted as she retrieved the misplaced object. *What kind of craziness is going on here?* Only one halfway plausible notion occurred to her. "For weeks I've been running around like a decapitated chicken between getting ready for the fall term and unpacking. Maybe I did it without thinking."

"Unless you've got a poltergeist." Shannon punctuated the suggestion with a laugh.

Adam spoke up. "I bet Zashi did it."

"Who's Zashi?" Heidi asked as she stepped over to the far wall to turn on the central air conditioning.

"She's my new friend who plays with me in the yard."

Recalling "Window" and "Tomorrow," Heidi asked, "Are you sure that's her name?" Not that offhand she could come up with a real name "Zashi" resembled.

"I think so."

"Well, there's no way she could have gotten into the

house while we were gone. Is she a friend from school?"

"No, she hangs around here. She can be anywhere. She's magic. May I take my dinosaurs outside to show her?"

"I guess so." As soon as he headed for the stairs, an alarming idea struck her. "Oh, no, what if somebody did get into the house?" Her heartbeat surged into overdrive. Followed by Shannon, she checked the living room windows, then hurried along the hall with a detour into the dining room. Ending up in the kitchen, they found no broken or open windows on the way. Both outside doors in the kitchen were locked and deadbolted. Nothing aside from the couch cushions looked disturbed. Heidi leaned on the kitchen counter to catch her breath.

"There you are," Shannon said. "Cat, poltergeist, or Zashi, whoever she is. Maybe she's an imaginary friend like the turtle boy. If he is imaginary."

"Most likely. This is the first I've heard of either one." Heidi unlocked one of the two kitchen exits, the door to the screened back porch. "There aren't any kids his age on this block that I know of, just adults and teenagers."

"Then he probably made her up, since he says she's magic."

"Should I be worried that he suddenly has imaginary friends? I thought he had plenty of real ones at school."

"That's normal for bright kids, especially with no siblings. Don't sweat it." Shannon mused, "Zashi sounds familiar. Maybe Japanese? I'll ask Ryo."

"Before I bought the house, a Japanese family rented it. The husband was a visiting professor at the Naval Academy. But Adam coming up with the name has to be a coincidence, I'm sure." Heidi led the way through the screened porch to the back yard, shaded with several mature oaks and maples. A dense row of shrubbery lined the fence that divided the lot from the neighbor behind it.

Pausing to inhale the fragrance of yellow blossoms on a late-blooming rosebush beside the porch, Shannon commented, "Beautiful yard."

"Thanks. I'm thrilled with it—plenty of room for Adam to play. I even bought my first lawn mower and weed whacker."

Shannon grinned. "Joys of homeownership, huh?"

"It'll be worth it. Plus, I'm thinking about putting in a vegetable garden next year. Maybe I'll go ahead plant some winter vegetables this fall, like kale."

After a stroll around the yard, they turned back toward the house. Adam emerged in shorts and a superhero T-shirt. He carried his toy dinosaurs in a net bag. "I'm going to show my dinos to Zashi."

"Have fun." Heidi resolutely squelched her unease at his remark. The two women walked through the kitchen again, where Shannon admired the state-of-the-art appliances. "The place looks in great shape for its age."

"Mostly, though it's not perfect. Some of the rooms need repainting, and I want to get new rugs and other stuff. But it's been updated with modern bathrooms and closets, and the previous owner had lots of work done on it within the last few years, since he was keeping it as a rental. New roof, new windows, rewiring, waterproofing the basement, upgraded heating and cooling system—yeah, I was really lucky to find it." The black cat, Ebony, strolled into the kitchen, and Heidi bent over to stroke her. "If you batted those pillows off the couch, don't make a habit of it."

Heidi led Shannon on a quick tour of the upstairs, with two bedrooms on each side of the hall. She paused at the threshold of one of the rooms across from the master suite. "I use this for an office. Haven't decided what to do with the other one yet. Right now it's a stash for boxes I haven't gotten around to unpacking." Before stepping away from the office, she cast a nostalgic glance at her wedding picture on the wall above the desk. *God, I looked so young and naïve.*

"Hey, you've gotten an amazing amount done in only a month," Shannon said.

They made a brief stop in Adam's room, with the bed covers pulled up straight, toys in boxes, books on shelves, and no clothes strewn on the floor. Heidi had often given silent thanks for producing such a neatnik kid. Shannon paused to examine the ant farm and the terrarium next to it, which housed a cricket. "You let him have a bug for a pet?" She punctuated the remark with a mock shudder.

Heidi laughed. "If he heard you say that, you'd get the lecture on ants and crickets not being bugs. Bugs are a special kind of insect with sucking mouth parts, which is a verbatim quote from Jeff. He's the one who talked me into letting Adam keep insects and helped me order an escape-proof ant farm."

"Ant farm advice, huh? Sure sounds serious to me."

An annoying blush warmed Heidi's cheeks. "Oh, stop it, already. Do you have time for a glass of iced tea before you go?"

"Okay."

In the kitchen, Heidi poured tea for both of them, and they took seats at a table in the tiny breakfast nook beside a window facing the next-door neighbors' yard. "Jeff gets along great with Adam. Giving him that set of dinosaurs, for instance. They're even educational—names and sizes stamped on their undersides."

Shannon laughed. "That figures. Just what you'd expect from a science teacher."

"I'm not sure how I feel about things like presents when it's not even his birthday. Maybe they're getting too close. If Jeff and I developed a more serious relationship and it fizzled, Adam might be traumatized."

"Don't overthink it. Good grief, isn't it premature to worry about breaking up a relationship you claim doesn't even exist yet? For that matter, do you think it will ever exist?"

Heidi squeezed lemon in her tea, stirred it, and took a long drink while mulling over the question. "I'm not sure what I want to happen with us. Is two years soon enough to consider that? It's been only a few months since I finally got over feeling guilty about Doug."

"Why, for goodness' sake?" Shannon stared at her in obvious amazement. "It's not like you had anything to do with his death."

"Of course not. The aneurysm ruptured while he was jogging. Totally surprising and random." Heidi's stomach churned at the memory of that call from the hospital just as she'd been headed out the door to work. "But we'd argued almost constantly in the last few weeks of his life. In fact, we had a spat right before he left the house that morning. He was seriously considering an assistant professorship at a college in Colorado. That position would've meant a higher salary and a better chance at tenure. When I objected, he said I should have known he hadn't planned to spend his entire life on the

Naval Academy faculty."

Shannon grimaced. "Ouch."

"And I said he should've known I wouldn't want to leave the job I'd had since before he met me, not to mention my parents."

"They live pretty close, don't they?"

"Yeah, a senior community less than an hour away, so I could get there fast if they needed me. Doug couldn't understand how important I felt that was."

"So not exactly a meeting of minds," Shannon said.

"Hardly. He insisted we could fly back east to see them anytime, just like we could visit his mom and dad in California anytime. He kept telling me I needed to dig out of my rut." She shook her head, stirring the ice in her tea with emphatic clunks of the spoon. "His father is a retired Marine, so Doug moved around through his entire childhood and didn't get the roots thing that mattered so much to me. Plus, he has a brother who lives closer to his folks, and I'm an only child. I wouldn't want to take Adam away from all his friends, either, and he's been effectively going to that school since he was born."

"That's almost literally true, isn't it? I remember you mentioning you put him in the staff daycare center straight off your maternity leave."

"Right. So naturally I worried about how he'd adjust if we had to move, and Doug didn't sympathize with that, either." She sighed. "Sometimes I wonder if I knew him well enough before we got married. We'd only been going together for a year. Maybe the 'tall, dark, and handsome' vibe fogged my brain."

"But you were happy up to then, weren't you?"

"Mostly, until we started fighting over his career plans. Like on that last morning."

"So that's a reason to feel guilty? As if the argument caused the aneurysm to burst right then?"

"When you put it that way, it does sound silly." Heidi stared down at her glass and started tearing a napkin into strips. "I finally managed to talk myself out of the guilt thing. But for the longest time I couldn't stop brooding over the way I got what I wanted because he died. Which is the last thing I'd have ever wished for, of course."

"You mean the house?"

Heidi nodded. "He was perfectly happy where we were, and it turned out that was because he thought of it as temporary. Also, his death was the only reason I had enough money, between life insurance and selling the condo, to put enough down on this place so I could afford the monthly payments—barely—plus have a nest egg left over for Adam's college fund." She rolled strips of shredded napkin into pea-sized spheres. "I didn't have to make a choice between loyalty to Doug and leaving my parents, job, and home state. We could even get a cat, which Adam and I always wanted but couldn't have before because Doug was allergic. Hence the guilt."

"Granted, I never met him, since he died just a few weeks after I started working with you. But I'm pretty sure he wouldn't want you to feel that way, no matter how much you disagreed toward the end. He'd want you to move on and have a good life."

"You're probably right." She swept the napkin bits into a pile and wadded them up in a ball.

Shannon drank the rest of her tea and got up to leave. They walked out through the screened porch so she could say goodbye to Adam. As he turned at her call and waved, the shrubbery along the fence in the rear of the yard rustled.

At the same moment, a flash of red flitted through the bushes. "Hey, is that a person back there? A child?"

"I don't see anything."

Heidi touched Shannon's arm and pointed with her other hand. "Right there, next to Adam."

"Wait, I do see something." Shannon shook her head. "No, whatever it was is gone."

Heidi didn't see it anymore, either. She rubbed her eyes. "Never mind. Probably shadows." A breeze must have stirred the branches. And the glimpse of red, if not an optical illusion, might have been a cardinal fluttering among the leaves.

She walked Shannon around the house to her car, then called Adam in to start his homework. As they started inside after he'd bagged his dinosaurs, he asked permission to sleep on the screened porch.

"Okay, soon, but not on a school night, and anyway it's supposed to rain. Tomorrow night," she said, trying to sound casually confident even though her throat tightened and her pulse accelerated, as they had the previous time she'd allowed him that treat. As Jeff had pointed out when they'd discussed it, that routine was no different from camping in the back yard, only without mosquitoes. He noted that he'd slept outside plenty of times as a child, and she had to admit she'd occasionally done the same. As far as risks were concerned, she couldn't ask for a safer neighborhood. *I can't turn myself into an overprotective mother hen and my son into a scaredy-cat. Even though his father did drop dead out of the blue, he still deserves a normal life.* Replaying what she'd just told herself, she had to giggle at the image of a hen mothering a cat.

****

After the customary routine of dinner, a couple of cartoons on DVD, and the addition of a chapter from the *Raptor and Vixen* graphic novel, Adam took his bath, old enough to complete that task on his own now. In pajamas, he went into his bedroom and said goodnight to the ants and crickets in their enclosures on a table next to the window. He'd already lined up his dinosaurs in their usual place on the dresser, largest to smallest.

He blew a kiss at two framed photos next to the row of toys, one a family portrait of himself with Heidi and Doug, the other a candid father-son pose beside the community pool at their old place. Heidi did her best to keep those memories alive for Adam, although he'd been barely five when Doug taught him to swim and coached his neighborhood tee-ball team. Finally, Adam petted Ebony, who'd already curled up on the foot of his bed, and commanded her to sleep tight. Heidi chimed in, although she knew the cat would leave the bedroom to wander around the house during the night, as cats did.

She read aloud a few pages from *The Wonderful Wizard of Oz*, the way she'd done every night for a couple of weeks. Adam was a big fan of the movie, so she wanted him to enjoy the full experience of the original story as well.

Lightning flashed behind the curtains just as he was snuggling into bed, and thunder rumbled. "That's electricity jumping between the clouds, right? That's what Mr. Austin says."

Although she suspected that remark to be a simplification of Jeff's statement on the topic, she nodded agreement. Again she fretted about whether it was desirable to let Adam get too attached to him. The closer they grew, the more upset Adam would be if she and Jeff stopped dating. *Yes, that's what we're doing. As Shannon says, don't overthink it.* Furthermore, Heidi didn't want to stop seeing Jeff. If anything, despite what she'd said to Shannon, she had to admit to herself that she wanted a deeper relationship. "My grandmother used to say it was angels bowling."

He giggled. "Angels can't bowl on clouds. They're too soft."

"Right, it's just pretend, like your friend Zashi."

"She's not pretend," he insisted.

Since trying to discover where the alleged friend lived hadn't gotten anywhere, Heidi asked, "How old is she?"

"I don't know. Littler than me."

That data point didn't do much to establish age, for Adam was the tallest student in his second-grade class. He got his height from his father, Heidi herself being of average height, and his slim build from both parents. She knew some of her friends envied her capacity to eat what she wanted without gaining weight. On the other hand, she sometimes wished for Shannon's curvy figure in place of her own B-cup bosom. "Well, you said Zashi's not in your class, didn't you? So she must be younger."

He shrugged, clearly bored by this line of inquiry. Wiggling deeper under the sheet, he said, "A storm can't really carry a house to Oz, can it?"

Did the thunder or the book scare him? Heidi hated to think of anything frightening her son. On the other hand, the graphic scenes in the movie hadn't disturbed his sleep. "Of course not. That's magic, like in fairy tales, not real life."

"Zashi is magic, and she's real." His face scrunched

up in a frown.

Rather than upset him, she dropped the subject. "Lights-out time."

Adam folded his hands and recited his "God bless" litany, naming Gramps and Grammie (Doug's parents in California), Granddad and Grandmamma (Heidi's parents), Heidi herself, "Dad in Heaven," Mrs. Larsen, Wendell, Tamara, Zashi, the ants, Hopper the cricket, Ebony, and Mr. Austin. Unsure whether she should encourage adding his probably imaginary friend to the list, Heidi decided belaboring the issue would make him even more fixated on it. *Let it blow over. Like Shannon said, it's no big deal.* Maybe it was only a side effect of adjusting to a new home. *He just has to be happy here. This move has to work for us.*

When she walked into her own bedroom, she found both pillows out of place, one on the floor, the other on the dresser. She'd forgotten to close the window. Its curtains flapped while rain pounded outside. *So the wind blew the pillows off the bed,* she told herself as she shut the window.

And one of them landed on the dresser on the other side of the room? she answered herself. What else, though? Blame it on the cat again? She recognized both explanations as farfetched but preferred them over the alternative, that Adam had sneaked in and played a prank to confirm the existence of his alleged playmate.

She collected the pillow from the dresser and set up the framed photo it had knocked over. It pictured her with Jeff at the previous November's annual Annapolis-Eastport tug-of-war across Spa Creek. She let herself linger on the image of his broad-shouldered but lean physique, blue eyes, boyish sprinkling of freckles, and tawny hair with shaggy bangs. Aside from his slim waist and hips, he reminded her of a huggable teddy bear. She caught herself sighing with pleasure as she gazed at the photo.

So maybe he is sort of hot.

Chapter Two

After school the next day, Friday, Jeff gave Heidi and Adam a ride to the auto shop to pick up her car. When Jeff dropped them off, he asked, "We're still on for dinner tomorrow?"

"Sure. It's your turn to pick the movie." After their dinner dates, they often watched a DVD at her house. He did his best to turn her on to science fiction thrillers, especially the cheesy monster films from the forties and fifties, while she tried to educate him about vintage screwball comedies.

"How do you feel about radiation-mutated, man-eating giant ants?"

She frowned, pretending to ponder the problem. "I'd feel like calling an exterminator. Or maybe getting a radiation-mutated giant anteater."

He laughed and kissed her lightly on the cheek before she could dodge. She wished she could suppress her blush at the contact, which was only a casual gesture, of course. Never mind that her face tingled from it.

When she and Adam got home, he asked permission to ride his bike up and down the street. Now that he'd discarded the training wheels, he seized every chance to practice his new skill. Heidi reminded herself that she'd ridden her own bike around the neighborhood at the same age. "Okay, but stay on the sidewalk and watch out for traffic." Fortunately, their residential side street didn't have much of that to worry about. With a long-suffering sigh, he agreed.

After she'd changed from her working outfit of skirt and blouse, started a load of laundry, and replaced magazines that had been knocked from the coffee table onto the floor—this time the cat must've been the culprit for sure—she thought to check on Adam. At first, she wasn't alarmed at not glimpsing him right away. Mature trees and dense shrubbery made it hard to scan the whole block at a glance. When she walked down to the curb, though, she still didn't see him. Her throat constricted, and her heart raced. She called his name, looking up and down the street. No sign of a little boy on a bicycle.

At that moment, Arturo, one of the two middle-aged men next door, pulled into his driveway. She waved frantically to him as he got out of the car. "Have you seen Adam? He was riding his bike."

"I just passed him going that way." Arturo pointed up the street toward the Spa Creek waterfront.

"Thanks!" Her stomach roiling, Heidi raced in that direction. Didn't Adam know better than to go near the water alone? Sure, he'd had swimming classes, but there was no comparison between an artificial pool and a natural creek. *This is exactly why I wouldn't have bought a waterfront lot even if we could afford it.*

Panting, her legs and lungs aching, she'd almost reached the pocket park at the foot of the dead-end street when she caught sight of him crouched on the grass under a tree. For a second another small figure stood next to him, but she blinked, and it wasn't there. She yelled Adam's name. He mounted his bike, pedaled toward her, and skidded to a halt a couple of yards away. The guilty look on his face confirmed his awareness that he was in trouble.

Heidi lunged forward, grabbed the handlebars, and glared at him. "What did you think you were doing, young man?"

His lips quivered. "I went to the park to play with the turtle boy."

"I don't want to hear about your imaginary friends now. Get off that bike."

He obeyed, and she pushed it along as she marched homeward so briskly he had to scurry to catch up. "You knew you weren't supposed to go there without me."

"But you didn't tell me not to," he said in a tiny voice.

"I said you could ride up and down the street. In what world does that mean you're allowed to go to the park without even asking?"

Speechless, he trudged beside her, his head hanging. When they reached the house, she wheeled the bike into the garage. "I'll consider how soon you might be allowed to ride again. Also if you still get to sleep on the back porch tonight."

"But, Mom—"

"Not another word. Get inside right this minute." After entering the house, she ordered him to his room. "Stay there and think about what you did until I tell you to come out." *Good grief, I'm channeling my mother.*

He stomped upstairs, tears trickling from his eyes. Fortunately, he didn't have a TV, computer, or video games in his bedroom. He sometimes used her computer in the office under supervision, and he played other game systems on the main household television in the living room. So she hoped he would spend at least part of his confinement actually meditating on his disobedience. On the other hand, now that her pulse had stopped pounding, she had to admit to herself she hadn't explicitly forbidden him to visit the park alone. Trust a kid to wiggle through any available loophole.

By dinnertime, she grew calm enough to summon him to the living room. Ordering him to a chair, she sat on the couch across from him and stared into his eyes with what she hoped looked like a stern glower. "Do you understand why I'm mad at you?"

"I guess." He rubbed the back of a hand across his eyes. "Because I might fall in the creek?"

She sighed. Obviously he didn't grasp the hazards of his escapade. "That's part of it."

"But I didn't go near the water, and anyway I know how to swim."

"Falling in the creek isn't the same as swimming in a pool. We don't even know how deep the water is there. But that isn't the main thing. You disobeyed me." She held up a hand to cut off his protest. "It doesn't matter whether I told you not to do that in so many words. You knew you weren't supposed to run off anywhere by yourself without asking. We have rules for a reason—to keep you safe."

He nodded, wide-eyed.

Deciding he'd taken the scolding to heart, she said, "I won't confiscate your bike—this time. But no campout on the porch until you've had time to think about what you did, wandering off alone. Maybe tomorrow." After all, within a month or so the nights would get too chilly for that treat. She sent him to wash up for dinner while she finished the meal prep by grilling hot dogs under the broiler.

Afterward, she let him go outside to play until dark.

271

With sunset coming earlier, he wouldn't be able to do that much longer, either. As she finished loading the dishwasher, he popped back inside. "Do we have any cucumbers?"

"Uh—no." He'd never shown the slightest preference for that vegetable before. "Why?"

"Cap wants one. I'm going to get my dinosaurs to show him." He disappeared into the front of the house before she could ask who Cap was. *Another imaginary friend?*

"Can we buy some cucumbers tomorrow?" he asked when he dashed through the kitchen again on the way out, his net bag of toys in hand.

"I guess. Don't slam the—" She winced. "—door." She mentally shrugged at the cucumber request. At least eating them to preserve the illusion of a phantom friend would add fresh veggies to Adam's diet.

Jeff would probably remind me cucumbers are actually fruits because they have seeds. She shook her head in exasperation at her wandering mind, which tended to devote entirely too many brain cells to Jeff lately.

****

When Heidi went upstairs later to check on Adam's bedtime preparations, she found him in pajamas drawing at his desk. Peeking over his shoulder, she saw a picture of a green, bipedal creature. Although he had better art skills than an average seven-year-old, she didn't expect photographic realism. Still, the sketch didn't resemble anything she could identify. "Can you tell me about this picture?" All the child-rearing books advised against asking outright, "What's that?"

"It's Cap, the turtle boy," he said in an offhand tone.

"But he doesn't know any ninja moves. He followed me home from the creek."

"Really?" She picked up the drawing to study it. The figure did look vaguely like a green-skinned child with a sort of shell on his back, plus webbed feet and hands. The top of his head was flat.

"Yeah, he wanted to play with me, and you wouldn't let me stay at the park."

"And he wants a cucumber."

"Uh-huh, that's his favorite food."

Adam had certainly concocted a peculiar selection of traits for his invented playmate. Well, imagining a humanoid turtle with no ninja skills was better than obsessing over boogeymen in the closet. "We'll see about that when we go shopping tomorrow."

"I have to be nice to him because being green is hard, right?"

"So I've heard." *How can I argue with the life lessons of a singing frog?* "But next time you see him, tell him you're not allowed to go to the park by yourself."

"Okay."

After reading the night's Oz chapter, listening to Adam's prayers, and tucking him in, she crossed the hall to the office for a final check of her e-mail. A message from Jeff popped up, confirming the time of their date for Saturday dinner. He signed it "Luv, Jeff," as he always did. Not quite "Love," but hinting at more than friendship. They hadn't progressed beyond kisses and occasional, fleeting below-the-neck caresses, but the memory of those was enough to warm her cheeks. She glanced at the wedding portrait of Doug and herself on the wall above the computer. Shannon was probably right that he wouldn't begrudge her a fresh start with a new love. Wherever he was now, he'd surely moved beyond petty jealousy. *Am I ready for the next step, though?* Did a solid friendship combined with a frisson of excitement whenever Jeff touched her add up to lasting love?

As if the thought of Shannon had conjured her, at that moment the e-mail in-box refreshed itself with a message from her, subject line "Zashi." Heidi opened it and read, "I mentioned Adam's new friend to Ryo, and the name reminded him of *zashiki warashi*. It's a kind of ghost child, sometimes mischievous but in a harmless way. In fact, the folklore says it's good luck to have one in your house." She included a link.

Heidi replied, "I don't think I want a ghost in my new house, lucky or unlucky." She added a smile emoji. "How could Adam have heard that word? I know it isn't in any of the manga or anime I've let him have, because I always read or watch them first."

Shannon wrote back, "Maybe some other kids at school came across it and mentioned it in front of him? Or it could be pure coincidence, a nonsense word he made up. There's only a finite number of syllable combinations possible in any human language, after all."

Heidi thanked her and closed the e-mail program after clicking on the link and bookmarking it to study later. Mention of a ghost brought to mind her one brief meeting with the previous tenants of the house, the Naritas. Shortly before closing on the purchase, she'd done a final walk-through with the real estate agent. The Japanese couple and their teenage son had been in the process of loading a rental car with the last of their luggage. Mrs. Narita had paused on the way out to introduce herself to Heidi. She'd said in a tone that sounded more dubious than optimistic, "I hope you will have good fortune with this house." She'd strode down the sidewalk to the car without giving Heidi a chance to react to the oddly phrased wish.

Was that meant to be a subtle warning? That the house is haunted, maybe? Heidi shook her head, laughing at herself.

Later, just before turning off her bedroom light and lying down, she paused for another look at the photo of Jeff on the dresser. Anticipation of their date for the following night made her stomach flutter with a mix of delight and nervousness, all out of proportion to the prospect of spending time with a man she saw five days a week at school. In the past few months, he'd awakened feelings in her that hadn't stirred in way too long. She swept her hands down the length of her aching body, her nipples perking up as her palms skimmed over them. *Okay, I admit it, he's definitely hot.*

****

Heidi woke to a bloodcurdling yowl. Heart pounding, she sat up in bed. After a second, she realized the noise wasn't a remnant of a monster in a nightmare, but a cry from the cat. She'd never heard Ebony make a sound like that before. *Maybe she's protecting us from a wild, fierce mouse.* She hoped not. The pre-sale home inspection hadn't reported any pests. The caterwauling receded along the hall and down the stairs, then stopped.

Heidi lay back and closed her eyes, waiting for her breath and pulse to slow to normal. Now that Ebony had fallen silent, though, a different sound wafted from the hallway. Singing.

Sitting up again, Heidi strained her ears. A child's soprano voice sang in a language she didn't recognize.

"Adam?" No answer. The voice grew fainter and faded away.

She extracted a flashlight from the nightstand and crept to the closed bedroom door. Leaning against it, she didn't hear anything. She stepped into the hall and switched on the flashlight, not wanting to wake Adam with the overhead light if he'd slept through the cat's cries and the song, assuming he hadn't done the latter himself.

Tiptoeing toward his room, she glanced at the floor, which showed traces of water at regular intervals. At first sight, they looked like child-size wet footprints. Had Adam made the tracks after his bath? Surely she would have noticed them before, though, and anyway they would have dried by now. She nudged his partly open bedroom door farther ajar and peeked in. In the faint glow of the night light, he lay sprawled on his side, breathing deeply and evenly, with no sign of faking sleep. Also, when she thought to check the floor inside his room, that space showed no wet marks. Withdrawing into the hall, she found the tracks already drying.

After going downstairs to check all the doors, which were locked the way she'd left them, she returned to her own bed, shaking her head in bewilderment. *If he wasn't singing, what did I hear? The TV?* She didn't think she'd become so absent-minded at the age of thirty-four that she would leave the set on and forget doing it. Maybe the cat had stepped on the remote control in the living room just long enough to switch the TV on and off. And if she'd been pawing in her water bowl and then taken a stroll upstairs, that could explain the wet spots. *Sure, blame it all on the cat.* Considering the hypothetical identification of "Zashi" as the name of a ghost child,

Heidi emphatically preferred blaming the cat over suspecting a mischievous spirit.

She'd poured every dollar she could spare into the house. What would she do if it was actually haunted? Sue the home inspector for missing that problem? Abandoning her investment like a hysterical heroine in a horror movie wasn't an option. She dismissed the whole idea with a shaky laugh. *This place is our fresh start. There can't be anything wrong with it. No way would I accept that—even if I did believe in ghosts, which I don't.*

****

Upon entering Adam's bedroom early the next morning, Saturday, Heidi found one of his two pillows on the floor ten feet from the bed. Two dinosaurs were missing from the lineup on the dresser. Scanning the room, she discovered them balanced on top of the window curtain rod, high above his reach. Even if he'd climbed on the desk, he wouldn't have been tall enough. She had to stand on a stool herself to retrieve the toys.

"Why did you throw your pillow across the room?" she asked, replacing it on the bed. "And how did you get your tyrannosaurus and brontosaurus way up there?"

"It's an apatosaurus, remember?"

"Right, I keep forgetting they've changed the name. So how did you do it?"

"I didn't." He gave the cheerful reply with no sign of guilt or evasion. "Zashi must have."

She sighed. "You can't blame everything on your pretend friend."

He scowled and clenched his small fists, his face reddening. "She's not pretend. She's real."

"Then bring her to the house and introduce her to me. Right now, get dressed so we can eat breakfast and go shopping."

He hopped out of bed. "Can we buy cucumbers for Cap?"

"We'll see."

While fixing breakfast, she brooded over Adam's imaginary friend obsession. Did he miss his few playmates from the townhouse complex that much? He had plenty of living friends his age in school and at church, and he knew she'd arrange play dates if he asked. Granted, make-believe childhood friends were common enough, but such emphatic insistence on their reality didn't seem normal. What about the minor pranks like pillow-flinging, which he might or might not have perpetrated? He sounded sincere when he claimed Zashi had committed those. Heidi was reminded of a comic strip in which the kids blamed their misdeeds on a phantom child named "Ida Know." If Adam wasn't simply caught up in his fantasy games but really believed in Zashi and Cap, how worried should she be? Would buying vegetables for the "turtle boy" encourage a delusion?

Get a grip, she admonished himself. *He acts perfectly normal every other way, and what could it hurt to stock up on cucumbers? At least we can eat them.*

After breakfast, they drove to the supermarket for the week's groceries, including a package of mini-cucumbers. When they got home, Adam went out to play while Heidi unloaded groceries and zipped through her Saturday cleaning routine. She then turned to the off-and-on task of unpacking the moving boxes she'd stashed in the spare room.

Upon walking into the room, she discovered the closet door already open. *Funny, I don't remember leaving it that way. Isn't thirty-four too young to start losing my marbles?* Adam might have done it, but what could he have been searching for? He should have known the closet was empty.

It wasn't quite, though. An eight-by-eleven manila envelope lay on the otherwise bare floor. Heidi knew she'd left the packet on the closet shelf. *So it fell off, big deal, and Adam wandered in here and opened the door, if I didn't do that myself and forget about it.*

Curiosity diverted her from the unpacking chore. She picked up the envelope, which contained three paper rectangles she'd found hanging beside the three exit doors when she'd moved in. She'd stored them away in case the previous tenants had left them by accident and eventually wanted them returned. Sitting on the floor next to the closet, she drew the objects out of the envelope to study more closely. The pieces of heavy paper, about nine inches by three, each bore a vertical column of what she assumed to be Japanese characters, in black ink. Each had a symbol of some kind in red at the top.

What did the writing mean? She had a go-to source for information about Japanese culture, so she might as well inquire. Abandoning the box she'd started to empty, she went into the office, scanned the papers into the computer, and e-mailed the images to Shannon. Probably Ryo could explain Heidi's find.

Just before lunchtime, Adam came in to ask for a cucumber for Cap. After giving him one, she followed him through the screened porch and watched as he ran to the back of the yard. Something moved in the shrubbery—or did it? She blinked. Maybe the wind had stirred the bushes. The leaves rustled again. Adam scampered to that spot and held out the cucumber. Was that shadow next to the fence a greenish figure almost his size or an optical illusion?

Heidi rubbed her eyes. *There's nothing there. What's it called when your brain makes shapes out of clouds and so forth? Oh, yeah, pareidolia.* Better that than to believe worrying about her son's pretend playmates was causing her to have hallucinations. Nevertheless, she walked outside to look around. Adam was alone, of course, and no longer holding the cucumber. Had he eaten it that quickly? She didn't see it discarded on the ground. A whiff of a fishy odor drifted to her nose. The neighbors in the house behind theirs must be cooking seafood. "It's almost time to eat," she told Adam. "You might as well come in and wash up."

As she served his lunch a few minutes later, he said, "Cap liked the cucumber. May I give him another one tomorrow?"

"Sure. Why didn't he stick around?"

"Maybe because I told him Zashi might be coming over." With a thoughtful frown, he spooned up a mouthful of canned chicken soup. "She doesn't like him."

"Why not?"

Adam shrugged. "She thinks he's mean. I don't know why."

Heidi sat down across from him with the salad she'd prepared for herself. *Great, now he's got a whole drama going on between his imaginary friends.* "Tell me more about Zashi. What does she look like? All you've said so far is that she's not as big as you."

"She's just a little bit littler. She has black hair."

"Like yours?"

He shook his head. "Not curly like mine. It's in two round knots on the sides of her head."

"Buns?"

"I guess so. And she's always wearing a long, red dress with floppy sleeves and pictures of flowers and birds on it."

The description sounded oddly specific for a made-up companion. Could the little girl be real after all? "Are you sure her name is Zashi?"

"I think so. I'll ask her."

"While you're at it, ask her to come up to the house so I can meet her. I want to find out where she lives and who her parents are."

"I'll try. She's kind of shy, though."

After he finished lunch and went out to play again, Heidi mulled over the conversation while clearing the table. Suppose Zashi actually existed? She still couldn't have disarrayed toys and pillows while the house was locked up.

Chapter Three

Late Saturday afternoon, Jeff Austin phoned his widowed mother, as he always did about that time every week. She lived in a senior-only complex in northern Virginia. As she always did, she first asked about the progress of his campaign for a spot on the city council.

Seated at the front window of his second-floor condo unit in Eastport, with a panoramic view of the surrounding residential neighborhood, he summarized the latest citizens' group meeting he'd attended. "Basically same old, same old," he concluded. "The usual balancing act between environmental groups, local businesses, and the Historic Preservation Commission, while trying to keep any of them from getting too mad at me. So what's up with you?"

"Yesterday I found a quarter on the sidewalk in front of the beauty salon, with the year of your father's death on it. I'm sure it's a message from him."

Not again, Jeff silently groaned. How could a rational woman like his mother, a retired accountant, believe in this crap? "What kind of message?"

"Well, since he died five years ago last month, maybe he's trying to cheer me up, reminding me that he's happy."

She didn't spend her life mired in obsessive grief, by any means, but it made sense that she'd be thinking of her husband at this season. More often than not, his mother reported these alleged communications from beyond the veil in a perfectly cheerful tone. Although she'd always shown an interest in the paranormal, reading her horoscopes every day and hanging crystals all over her home, she'd plunged into full-blown flakiness on the subject only after her husband's death. She seemed to take it as obvious fact that her late spouse would send consoling messages through what most people would consider random coincidences.

Despite Jeff's awareness that arguing with her had about as much impact as pouring water on a fish, he couldn't resist trying again. "If he's happy, he must be in Heaven, right? So why would he hang around on Earth tossing coins on sidewalks?"

"Of course he's in Heaven," she said in a serene tone. "But why shouldn't he be watching over us from above?"

He stifled a sigh. At least she'd stopped paying fake mediums to reach out to the other side on her behalf. The "channeler" she nowadays visited once a month performed that alleged service gratis and seemed to be a sincere believer—or, to put it less charitably, a sincere nutcase. "He might be, at that." Jeff figured he could make that concession without dishonesty. Although not a regular churchgoer like his mother, he did believe in Heaven in some form, and he couldn't claim to know the conditions thereof any more than she could.

He glanced at the time display on the DVR on top of the television. "I've got to go now. I have a date."

"With Heidi?" His mom's voice brightened up.

No use evading the question, since she knew he wasn't seeing anyone else. "Yeah, I'm taking her to dinner again." His lips curved in the goofy grin that often surfaced when he thought of her.

"When will I get to meet her? Not to mention that little boy you've told me so much about?"

He'd told her a lot about Adam because he didn't trust himself to talk much about Heidi without exposing his feelings. The last thing he needed was to encourage his mother's wishful assumption that a wedding was imminent. *Even if I hope so myself.* "No rush, Mom. I wouldn't want her to feel pressured."

"How much pressure could there be after you've been friends for six years already?"

"During four of which her husband was alive. We've only been dating for a year."

"Only? Are you trying to act like the tortoise in the race, slow and steady, or what?" Her voice held a gently scolding tone.

"Since I don't have competition from any hares at the moment, why not?" He managed a patient tone as he tossed her a crumb or two in hopes of appeasing her curiosity. "We go out one evening a week and eat together in the cafeteria almost every school day." Sitting side-by-side, their thighs almost touching and her hand grazing his as they passed salt or ketchup, often ignited fantasies too vivid to indulge in the workplace. "Believe me, I'm just waiting for the right moment to take it to the next level."

"Well, don't wait too long." He had no trouble imagining the coy smile that accompanied the advice. "Seize the day."

Wouldn't I love to, he thought as he drew the conversation to an end. *Meanwhile, it's cool just hanging out with her and Adam.* Jeff would have enjoyed spending time with such a bright kid for his own sake even if not for his mother's. His previous year's first-grade project about the evolution of dinosaurs into birds had shown an enthusiasm for research not typical of six-year-olds. *Of course, his cute, fun, intelligent mom is definitely a bonus.*

Thoughts of Heidi made a pleasant backdrop to showering and dressing. Buttoning his shirt in the bedroom, Jeff paused to contemplate the snapshot of her on his dresser, downloaded from his phone, printed, and framed. It showed her on the waterfront at City Dock downtown against a background of sailboats in the narrow inlet. Her curly, brown hair framed her heart-shaped face and barely brushed the collar of the V-necked blouse she wore with a pair of shorts that enticingly displayed slender legs. From unguarded remarks she'd dropped, he knew she wasn't completely happy with her less-than-lavish B-cup endowment—when were women ever content with their looks? To him, though, her trim figure looked exactly right, including the dimensions of her perky breasts. Which, so far, he'd sampled only with light touches, just enough to discover their perfect fit for his hands. That memory flooded his body with a surge of heat. She seemed to relish sharing kisses as much as he did, but could he assume she'd welcome deeper intimacy? He caught himself hardening in anticipation. *Down, boy. All in good time.*

Before he left to pick up Heidi, he checked on his Venus flytrap in the sunny windowsill of the kitchen. He dropped a couple of freeze-dried mealworms into the red petals, which snapped shut. To stimulate the digestive process, he tickled the sensitive "hairs" with a toothpick. He smiled at the memory of Heidi's creeped-out reaction to her first sight of the plant. She would come around to appreciating it eventually, he was certain. Hadn't he managed to talk her into accepting a cricket and a colony of ants as pets for her son?

Jeff retrieved a package that had arrived earlier that day, a new dinosaur for Adam's collection. When he'd ordered the set for the boy's birthday, the iguanodon had been out of stock. Although Jeff understood Heidi's misgivings about too many gifts and treats, what harm could he do with an extra prehistoric reptile more or less? *They're educational, right? Also a bonding experience.* He'd have done the same if the boy were his own son. Jeff caught that same sappy grin spreading over his face again. With luck, he hoped to become a surrogate dad to Adam soon enough. Having already resolved to ask Heidi to marry him, he was just waiting for the right moment. *Maybe it's time to switch tactics from tortoise to hare.*

****

After dressing for her dinner date, Heidi sat with Adam while he ate grilled cheese sandwiches in the kitchen breakfast nook. "Can I still sleep on the porch tonight?"

"It's not supposed to rain, so you may if you behave and do everything Gina says."

"I will. She's nice."

Heidi considered herself lucky to have found a reliable babysitter living practically across the street, especially one Adam liked. After he finished eating and placed his dishes in the sink, they went upstairs together. When she followed him into his bedroom to lay out his pajamas, he emitted a howl of dismay. Her stomach clenched as she darted across the room to grab him in her arms.

"Mom, look!" He pointed at the terrarium. The fine-mesh screen lid lay beside it instead of on top.

She let out a long breath. "Take it easy. Let's see if your cricket is still in there."

A quick but methodical examination, though, showed that the insect wasn't lurking in a corner or under a leaf. "Why did you take the top off, anyway?"

"I didn't!" he almost wailed. "Zashi must've moved it."

"Well, don't let her do it again." Heidi saw no point in arguing about that impossible claim when he was already so upset.

"We have to find him. Ebony might eat him." His voice sounded clogged with tears.

"Don't panic. If he's hiding in this room somewhere, we'll make sure she can't do that." She led Adam into the hall, closed the door, and left him on guard while she got a towel from the linen closet. Rolling it into a tight cylinder, she wedged it against the crack at the bottom of the door. "Okay, if he's in there, he can't escape."

Adam rubbed his eyes. "But what do we do now?"

Darned if I know. Assuming the cricket didn't wander off, how do we find him? She had to sound confident for her son, though. "We'll think about it and make a plan."

The doorbell provided a welcome excuse not to follow that vague statement with a practical suggestion. Jeff had shown up almost fifteen minutes early. Used to that habit of his by now, she'd made sure to finish dressing in plenty of time. Scampering downstairs after her, Adam flung himself at Jeff. "Mr. Austin, Hopper escaped. I'm afraid Ebony will kill him!"

"Whoa, slow down. How did he escape?" Jeff disentangled himself from Adam's clinging arms.

Watching them enveloped Heidi in an aura of comfort, as if Jeff's mere presence guaranteed things would turn out all right.

"Zashi took the top off the tank," Adam said.

"Who's Zashi?"

"My magic friend. Come on!" Clutching Jeff's hand, the boy tried to tug him up the steps.

While Adam was distracted, Heidi whispered to Jeff, "Imaginary. I'll explain later."

Jeff briefly draped an arm around her shoulders like a sheltering cloak. *Yeah, he'll fix this.*

Upstairs, after scanning the hall for any sign of the cat waiting to pounce, she ushered the other two into the bedroom and replaced the towel at the bottom of the door. Jeff put down a box he was carrying and gravely inspected the terrarium. "Yep, he's gone, all right. When did this happen?"

"While Adam was eating supper, I guess," Heidi said. Given the probable nonexistence of magical little girls, he must have removed the lid himself, but when would he have gotten the chance? She was certain the tank had been covered until she'd called him for the meal.

"If Hopper's still in this room, we'll find him," Jeff said. "We all have to be very quiet and listen carefully."

Heidi and Adam obediently froze. Less than a minute later, she heard a chirp. Then another. The sound came from the direction of the closet. "Crickets like dark places," Jeff said. "Do you have a flashlight in here?"

Fortunately, Adam had a pocket-size one in his

nightstand drawer. She handed it to Jeff, who emptied the contents of the trash can onto the floor. "Okay, you shine it into the closet, and I'll be ready to catch the cricket."

She switched on the light, grateful he hadn't assigned her the insect-grabbing task. Training the beam on the closet floor, she gingerly picked up one object after another. The cricket leaped out of a shoe. With a stifled yelp, she dropped it, and the insect sprang into the middle of the room. Jeff swooped to the rescue, trapping the escapee under the can. He then lifted one edge far enough to catch Hopper before he could seek refuge in a new hiding place.

Cupping the cricket in his hands, Jeff lowered him into the terrarium and settled the lid firmly on top. "There, all safe. Be sure not to leave it open again."

"I didn't. Zashi did. Thanks, Mr. Austin." He gave Jeff a brief but emphatic hug.

"You see why I've always taken a dim view of bugs in the house," Heidi said while retrieving the towel and opening the door.

"Crickets aren't bugs," Adam reminded her.

Jeff grinned. "He's got you there. By the way, I brought you something." He picked up the discarded box and handed it to the boy.

Adam opened the package and pulled out a quadrupedal reptile with a tapered tail and a thin neck. "Wow, an iguanodon. Thanks!" He hurried to his dresser and placed the new toy in the proper size slot in the dinosaur parade.

Just as Jeff was replying to him, the doorbell rang again.

"That'll be the sitter," Heidi said.

Jeff walked down with her. On the way, she said, "You really shouldn't keep giving him presents when it's not his birthday or a holiday."

"Come on, I've hardly ever met a less spoiled kid. Anyway, that's just to fill up the set. The iguanodon was out of stock when I gave him the others." At the bottom of the stairs, he curved an arm lightly around her waist and kissed her on the cheek. "I wish you'd let me do more for both of you."

Her skin tingled where his lips had touched. Blushing, she slipped out of his light embrace and hurried to open the door. Gina, a slender teenager with long, straight, black hair, glitter-painted fingernails, and a butterfly-patterned T-shirt over cut-off jeans, stepped inside and greeted them with a wave of the hand that wasn't carrying a tablet. "Oh, I'm not late, am I, Ms. Clarke?"

"No, you're fine." Heidi strolled up to Adam's room with her, reminding her of bath and bed schedules and mentioning the DVD he'd picked to watch. "He's allowed to sleep on the porch tonight, and I've already spread out the air mattress and sleeping bag." After once again admonishing Adam to behave and kissing him goodbye, she assured them the evening wouldn't run very late and detoured into her room for her purse.

Gina headed downstairs with her. While pointing out ice cream bars and other available snacks, Heidi asked in what she hoped sounded like a casual tone, "Do you happen to know if a little girl named something like Zashi lives around here? She's about six years old with black hair in a pair of buns, I think."

Gina shook her head. "Doesn't ring a bell."

Jeff was waiting by the door to escort Heidi to his

car. On the way out, she noticed Arturo and his partner, Craig, working in their yard next door. She thought of asking them about Zashi, too, but decided she'd obsessed over the problem enough for the moment. Jeff drove the short distance to the seafood restaurant they'd chosen. They could have walked the few blocks in the mild evening, but considering it would be after dark by the time they finished she was glad to ride instead.

After they got seated and ordered appetizers, Jeff asked about the conversation with Gina he'd overheard. "Who's this Zashi you and Adam mentioned?"

Heidi sighed. "Adam's imaginary friend who, according to him, pulls all the mysterious pranks that've been happening around the house."

"Like what?" Jeff picked out a dinner roll and pushed the basket in her direction.

"Oh, throwing pillows around, rearranging toys in weird locations, leaving wet footprints in the hall in the middle of the night. Stuff like that." She decided not to mention the child's voice she'd heard singing. That must have been a stray dream fragment.

"That doesn't sound like anything to worry about."

"Suppose it's a sign he's having trouble adjusting to the new house?" She tore bits off her roll and dropped them on her bread plate. "If there's something wrong with either Adam or the house, I don't know how I'll cope. I can't casually walk away from a five-figure down payment and a thirty-year mortgage."

"He's as well-adjusted as any seven-year-old boy I know. Imaginary friends are a perfectly normal phase. Heck, my little brother had one. A talking dragon that took all the blame he couldn't squirm out of. Mom played along if it didn't involve anything dangerous."

"Maybe you're right. That's basically what Shannon said."

"See, we have a consensus. And you should know by now I'm usually right. After all, I'm the science guy." He laughed, and she joined in. Maybe she was making too big a deal out of a "phase."

Jeff went on, "Remember the movie about the man who hung around with a six-foot-tall, invisible rabbit? That friendship was harmless enough."

"But his family spent most of the film trying to commit him to an institution. And in the end the rabbit turned out to be real. Probably."

"Do you think Adam's imaginary friend is real?" Why did Jeff's voice suddenly go flat?

"The shy little girl, Zashi, might be, even if she can't be responsible for everything he blames on her. Letting the cricket out, for example. I'm almost sure the turtle boy is made up, though." Watching Jeff's face, she buttered the remains of her roll.

Smiling, he echoed in a lighter tone, "Turtle boy?"

"Adam says his name is Cap, and in the picture Adam drew, he's green with webbed feet and a shell on his back. Supposedly he lives near the creek or maybe in it." She summarized Adam's excursion to the mini-park. "That escapade was definitely not harmless."

"That's a separate issue. He has to learn not to wander off without permission whether he invents a creek-dwelling creature to share the blame or not." Jeff opened his menu. "The waiter's headed this way. Ready to order?"

During the meal, they talked about his campaign for alderman. "I saw your picture in the paper earlier this week, serving dinner at the homeless shelter, which I know you don't do just to impress voters."

He shrugged. "No, but I can't deny it's good for the image. I'll be running the 5K charity race for the shelter in a couple of weeks. Want to come and cheer me on?"

Her stomach fluttered. Even after two years, mention of jogging or racing reminded her of Doug's final hours. She forced herself to draw a deep breath and let it out slowly, expelling the negative thoughts with it. Running hadn't killed him. That aneurysm could have burst anytime. "Sure, wouldn't miss it. I'm definitely ready for a step up from that .05K 'race' in May."

Jeff grinned. "Yeah, you aced the three-minute stroll across the Spa Creek drawbridge."

"This time, I'll be strictly a spectator, though." She raised her wineglass in an exaggerated flourish. "Today, alderman. Tomorrow, mayor—governor—President!"

With a chuckle, he shook his head. "No, thanks. I have absolutely no desire to let politics take over my life. Annapolis City Council, okay, maybe County Council, but that's the limit. I'll stick with public service I can do part time and not have to quit my real job."

A glow of warmth blossomed inside her, knowing she didn't have to worry about his rushing off to fulfill some higher ambition in a remote location. He would be right here as long as she wanted him around.

Am I seriously thinking I want him around permanently, as more than a friend?

After a leisurely dinner and dessert, they strolled along the pier behind the restaurant for a few minutes, his arm around her. A cool night breeze blew off the creek where dozens of sailboats and power craft lay at anchor, and the water reflected the lights of downtown Annapolis. "Looks like a postcard, doesn't it?" she said.

He murmured agreement. "Living here, it's easy to forget to appreciate the place the way tourists do."

"On the other hand, considering what the tourists do to traffic in the summer, would you want to be lumped in with them?"

"True that." His arm tightened around her waist in an affectionate squeeze, making her breath quicken.

With some reluctance, they walked to the car and drove back to her house, where Gina greeted them with a report that Adam was asleep. Heidi confirmed that fact with a quick peek onto the screened porch before paying Gina and watching her cross the street to her own home, where the girl paused at her door and waved. Heidi waved back and went inside.

She started a bag of microwave popcorn and poured two glasses of flavored seltzer, since Jeff still had to drive. Minutes later the two of them settled on the couch to watch the giant ant movie. With the cat on her lap and the popcorn on his, they snuggled up with his arm around her shoulders, their thighs pressed together. Heat radiated through her as if she sat in front of a cozy fire instead of in an air-conditioned living room.

The film provoked them to alternate gasps at the suspenseful moments and giggles at the old-fashioned special effects. "You realize this is total nonsense," Jeff said at one point. "Invertebrates can't grow that big on land. It violates the square-cube law. They'd collapse under their own weight."

"If you feel that way, why do you like watching it?"

Laughing, he tossed a popcorn kernel at her. "Half the fun of these movies is deconstructing the scientific fallacies. Wait until you see the killer shrews, the giant bunnies, and the vicious monster tomatoes."

She said with a suspicious frown, "You made up that last one."

He raised his right hand. "Truth. I swear."

Finally, flamethrowers wiped out the last of the ants in the Los Angeles storm drains. Heidi cleared away the glasses and empty popcorn bag, then walked Jeff to the door. He'd never asked to spend the night, to her gratitude. Knowing she wouldn't advance to that stage of intimacy with her son sleeping in the same house, Jeff considerately spared her the need to refuse. In the foyer, he lightly wrapped his arms around her and drew her close.

She slipped her arms around him in an equally tentative touch. When he bent toward her, she tilted her head in invitation. His mouth covered hers, his tongue teasing her lips. Closing her eyes, she leaned into the embrace. Lightheaded, she basked in the rosy cloud that enveloped her as the kiss went on and on.

At last he pulled away and released her, both of them gasping for air. "If I'm leaving, I'd better go now."

She nodded, struggling to breathe evenly. "Good plan."

He caressed her hair in a long, gentle stroke before opening the door. "I hope I won't always have to," he murmured. He'd never expressed that desire so openly before.

She had to swallow before she could speak again. "We'll see." With a faint smile, she brushed her fingers over the curve of his jaw, then stepped back. After he walked out, she leaned against the closed door, pressing her palms to her flushed cheeks until her pulse steadied.

I hope you won't always have to leave, too. She'd never quite admitted that to herself before, either.

Still floating in a haze, she meandered up to the office to check her e-mail before bed. Shannon had sent a message about the scanned images Heidi had sent.

"Ryo says they're *ofuda*. They're for protection and luck. People get them at shrines, blessed by a priest like charging a battery, and the writing on these is the name of the shrine where they were made. They're supposed to hold spiritual power. If you found them hanging beside the doors, they were meant to keep the house safe from evil forces."

Heidi mulled over that information while powering down the computer and undressing for bed. Why had the former tenants felt their home needed protection? Was that what Mrs. Narita had meant by expressing the hope that Heidi would have "good fortune" in the house? Had the remark been intended as a subtle warning?

If so, I wish she'd been more explicit. Surely she couldn't have meant the house is haunted.

Chapter Four

The next morning, Heidi had managed to shake off her concerns of the previous night. In the light of day, viewing any number of oddities, ambiguous remarks, and even apparent poltergeist phenomena as signs of the supernatural seemed absurd. By the time she and Adam got home from church, she'd decided Mrs. Narita had expressed good wishes with no deeper meaning, had hung the ofuda as a routine cultural custom, and had simply forgotten to take them down. With a mind unburdened by superstitious qualms, Heidi sent Adam out to play.

Then she finally saw his "imaginary friend."

After an hour, she stepped outside to call him to lunch. Adam was sitting on the grass in the middle of the back yard showing his new iguanodon to another child. A little Asian girl crouched in front of him, gravely contemplating the toy. She had a bun on each side of her head, as he'd described, and she wore a red kimono adorned with a floral print and what looked like peacocks.

She's real. I've been wrong all this time.

Heidi had to gulp a couple of deep breaths before she could speak. "Adam? Come on, time for lunch. Would your friend like to ask her parents if she can join you?"

He stood up and turned in her direction. The girl

sprang up, glanced at Heidi, whirled around, and scurried toward the fence.

"Wait! You don't have to leave."

The child ran without looking back and wiggled into the shrubbery at the rear of the yard. Heidi dashed after her. Catching up, she pushed aside branches to comb through the bushes. Nothing.

She turned to face Adam, who'd walked up behind her. "Where did she go?" Could the girl have climbed over the fence that fast? Or scaled a four-foot barrier at all?

"I don't know. She always goes away all of a sudden like that." He didn't sound troubled by that disquieting habit.

On her way back to the house, Heidi brushed torn leaves off her shirt and bare arms. "Well, I wish she'd stayed for at least a minute. I want to meet her."

"Like I said before, she's shy."

"Are you sure you don't know where she lives?"

He shook his head. "She's just here."

"I'm sorry I didn't believe you when you said she was real."

"That's okay."

"I asked Gina if she knew Zashi, and she didn't. So her house can't be on this block," Heidi said as they walked inside.

In the kitchen, Adam washed his hands at the sink without being reminded. "I found out I was mixed up about her name. Zashi is just what she is."

"You mean it's her last name?" Heidi served him a glass of juice to go with his lunch and poured iced tea for herself. They sat together at the small table in the kitchen nook.

He shrugged. "I guess. She told me to call her Kiku."

So now not only do I have to adjust to her being real, I have to get used to thinking of her by a new name. "Thanks for clarifying that. Regardless, you still can't keep accusing her of doing stuff she couldn't possibly do, like moving things at night when the house is locked up."

He said with a stubborn pout, "But she does too do them."

She sighed. "That's impossible. Even if her parents would let her wander around the neighborhood in the dark, she couldn't come inside unless you're getting up to let her in, and I think I'd notice that."

"I don't have to. She's magic."

Heidi stifled the impulse to bang her head on the table and took a big bite of her sandwich to keep from saying something she'd regret. Arguing would only make matters worse by inciting him to defend his flights of fantasy.

Later that afternoon, while unpacking a box of blankets to stow in the spacious linen closet in the upstairs hall, she found another item left by the Naritas. At least, she couldn't think of anywhere else it could have come from. Standing on tiptoe, she shoved a folded quilt onto the top shelf. Something wobbled, then sailed off the shelf and floated onto the floor.

It did not float. I spaced out for a second, that's all. She leaned over to pick up the object. It turned out to be a framed, eight by eleven, black-and-white snapshot.

She blinked at the picture, willing it to change from what it seemed to be at first sight. It showed a little girl in a full-length kimono with a pattern of flowers and peacocks. With her two tightly wound buns, she looked exactly like Adam's elusive playmate. She stood beside an arched footbridge over a pond surrounded by flowering shrubs.

It couldn't be the same girl, in a black-and-white photo hidden or forgotten on a high shelf. Realizing she'd caught only a quick glimpse of the child, Heidi insisted to herself that the resemblance had to be coincidental and not nearly so close as she'd initially thought. She set the picture aside, leaning against the wall where she wouldn't knock it over, and finished emptying the carton.

She passed Adam's room with the box and the photo just as he exited into the hall. "What's that?" he asked, pointing.

Unable to think of a reason not to let him see the snapshot, she wordlessly showed it to him.

"Hey, where did you get a picture of Kiku?"

"In the linen closet. But this can't be her. The people who used to live here must have left it."

"I think it's her," he said. "I'll ask her. May I watch cartoons?"

"Okay, sure." He hurried downstairs, while Heidi took the picture into the office and tucked it into a half-filled drawer in the file cabinet for safekeeping. Wiping her sweat-dampened forehead with a tissue, she considered Adam's claim. The photo was faded, not even very clear. He might have identified the image of any little girl with the right dark hair, hairstyle, and costume as Kiku.

Anyway, this picture must have belonged to Mr. and Mrs. Narita. Heidi had to make an effort, at least, to return it to them. After washing up from her bout with dusty boxes, she e-mailed the real estate agent to ask about getting the tenants' contact information from the previous owner.

****

When she tucked Adam into bed that evening, he asked, "Mom, are you and Mr. Austin going to get married?"

Her face heated. "I don't know. We haven't talked about it." She couldn't honestly either deny or affirm the possibility. "What would you think about that?"

"It would be okay. He's cool."

That verdict cheered her, although Adam might develop a different idea of Jeff's coolness if he transformed from an adult buddy to a parent figure. As she undressed for bed later, she imagined a future with him in that room and bed beside her. Her pulse quickened, her nipples peaked, and heat flooded her. She stroked her aching body, indulging in fantasies she'd resisted for too long, until at last she sank into fitful sleep.

In the middle of the night, she woke to the noise of Ebony's insistent meow. When Heidi shuffled, half-asleep, into the corridor to shush the cat, a singsong tune in a childish voice drifted to her ears. She flicked on the overhead light. Ebony, at the top of the steps, lashed her tail and ran downstairs. Heidi glanced at the floor, where she spotted traces of wetness—again, diminutive footprints. As she tiptoed to Adam's door, the singing faded away. One glance confirmed he hadn't awakened.

The tracks detoured across the hall to the office. Just as she reached the entrance to the room, the lights in there flashed on and off. "Who's there?" she asked in a harsh whisper. No answer. Brandishing the flashlight like a club—*as if I could knock out a burglar with it*—

she crept into the office.

She turned the ceiling light on. Nobody there. Releasing pent-up breath, she scanned the room. Again the lamps, overhead and on the desk, flashed. *Great, now I've got electrical wiring problems. Why didn't the home inspector find them?*

She froze, waiting for the next glitch. Instead, the ceiling light stayed on, while the desk lamp stayed off. Making a circuit of the room, she found the black-and-white photo on the desk beside the computer. *I know I put this away in the file drawer. I'm not that flaky.* At a second glance, she gaped in disbelief. The picture was balanced upside down against the front of the printer. Gingerly picking it up, she turned it around and stared at it.

Unless she'd suddenly started wandering in her sleep, she hadn't moved it. Adam hadn't even seen her put the photo in the drawer, so he couldn't have taken it out. His assertions that Zashi—no, Kiku—could sneak into the house and play pranks at will were obviously unbelievable. *Either that, Adam's somehow doing those things and lying about them, we have a poltergeist, or I'm losing my mind and playing tricks on myself. Take your pick.* She stowed the picture on the shelf in the closet and stalked off to bed, wondering which of the alternatives would be worst.

****

At lunch in the school cafeteria on Monday, Heidi told Jeff about learning the truth of the "imaginary friend." "I saw her playing with Adam, as clear and solid as I'm seeing you now. So I was wrong."

"But you still don't know where she lives?"

She shook her head. "Definitely not in any of the

houses nearest ours. Maybe she belongs to a family on the block behind us." She hesitated before describing her other discovery, which might make her sound a tad wacky. Fortunately, they had the table to themselves, so she didn't have to feel self-conscious about being overheard. "The funny thing is, I found a picture Adam claims is of her. He says her real name is Kiku, by the way. I guess Zashi is her last name."

After she finished narrating the incident, Jeff asked, "What do you think about it, then?"

She took a bite of her sandwich to stall while framing an answer. "The renters must have left it by accident, and the resemblance to Adam's friend must be a coincidence. It probably isn't that close anyway. After all, I got only a quick look at her."

"Makes sense. He might mistake a photo of any Asian girl with a similar outfit and hairstyle for her," Jeff said, echoing Heidi's own thoughts.

"He keeps insisting she's magic and sneaks into the house to move things around, though."

"You're not still worried about that, are you? It just proves he has a great imagination."

She frowned, nibbling on a potato chip. "I can live with his exaggerations about Kiku, but I draw the line at the turtle boy. Adam regularly feeds him cucumbers. Apparently that's the favorite food of humanoid turtles."

"If Adam's eating them himself, at least he's getting vitamins and fiber." With an indulgent smile, Jeff patted her hand. "Anybody can see he's a bright, normal kid. Remember, being a worrywart doesn't eliminate tomorrow's problems. It only wrecks today's peace."

She relaxed enough to laugh. "Thank you, O great dispenser of wisdom."

"Not wise, just rational. Science guy, remember?" He checked his watch, stood up, and gave her a mock bow. "Right now I have to rationalize a bunch of eighth-graders into getting excited about flatworms."

She cleared her tray and returned to the library in a lighter mood.

****

Her serene frame of mind didn't last long after she got home that afternoon. In the spare room cluttered with boxes of books she planned to shelve in the new bookcases she'd recently bought, three of the cartons lay open. The volumes they'd held were stacked in a tidy pyramid in the center of the floor. *When could Adam have gotten a chance to do that between last night and now? Or have I taken up sleepwalking and sleep-unpacking?* If so, why hadn't her subconscious done something useful, such as arranging the books on shelves?

After that shock, the pre-dinner hour continued smoothly enough at first. A message from the former owner of the house, following up Heidi's request to the real estate agent, provided her with Mrs. Narita's e-mail address. She immediately dashed off a note to the ex-tenant, describing the photograph and asking how to return it.

When she stood up to stretch and glanced out the window to check on Adam, who'd taken a cucumber outside a few minutes earlier, she caught her breath, stunned by what she saw.

A small figure stood beside him. Not Kiku this time, unless the little girl had changed into a green outfit and put on a mask. This visitor, slightly shorter than Adam, had a grass-green body, bluish-green arms and legs, and a shell-like hump on his back. A costume, obviously, complete with mask. From this distance, Heidi couldn't see the features clearly, but it did look vaguely turtle-like. Oddly, his head appeared flat on top. Did he dress like that all the time? Halloween was a month and a half away.

He's been real all along, too.

As she watched, another person ran out of the shrubbery toward Adam and the turtle boy. Definitely Kiku this time, dressed in the same kimono as before. *Where did she come from all of a sudden? She wasn't there a second ago.*

Waving her arms, Kiku dashed between Adam and the other child. She shoved the turtle boy, who staggered backward, tripped, scrambled to his feet, and lunged at the girl.

If the children were fighting, Heidi had to stop them before somebody got hurt. *That's all I need, two neighbor kids whose parents I've never met beating up each other on my property.*

She sprinted downstairs, through the house, and into the back yard. She rushed up to Adam and halted, panting. There was no sign of either visitor. A faint odor of fish stung her nose but faded within a second or two. "Where did they go? Kiku and the boy?"

Adam gazed up at her with a puzzled expression. "They just left. What's wrong?"

She grabbed him by the shoulders. "What do you mean, what's wrong? They were practically hitting each other. Why?"

He shrugged. "Like I said before, Kiku doesn't want me to play with Cap. She chased him away because she doesn't like him."

Heidi struggled to slow her breathing and stifle the scream of exasperation that threatened to burst out of her. "Why not?"

"I don't know for sure. I think he hurt her once."

"Then maybe he's not safe for you to play with." One hand still on his shoulder, she steered him toward the house. "Better come in and start your homework."

"He wouldn't do anything to hurt me," Adam said, glancing backward while trudging beside her. "He just wants somebody to play with. He's lonesome. And he likes the cucumbers."

"Glad to hear that." She scrubbed her free hand across her eyes as if to clear her mental vision. "So where does he live? In one of the houses on the next block, maybe?"

"Nope. He lives in the creek."

****

The next afternoon, Heidi received an e-mail reply from Mrs. Narita:

"Thank you for notifying me of the photograph you found. It is a picture of my great-grandmother's sister, Kiku, who died in 1900 at the age of six. She drowned in the pond in her parents' garden. Our family has several prints of this photograph. You need not take the trouble to return it."

Heidi printed out the message and reread it twice over. *Kiku? You think that's a coincidence, too?* Springing out of the chair, she paced up and down, clutching the paper in one hand. How could Adam have known the girl's name when Heidi herself had learned it only this minute? No, she was evading the main issue. Was the child who played with him a ghost from over a century ago?

306

I don't believe in ghosts. But how else can everything fit together to make sense? She shook her head with a bitter laugh. *Sense? What's that?*

Marching to the window, she looked out at Adam in the back yard. Kiku was with him. *If she's a ghost, what's Cap?* A chill prickled Heidi's spine at the memory of what Adam had said—Cap lived in the creek. Had she been wrong to let the subject drop? Or would nagging Adam for an explanation of that ridiculous claim make matters worse?

She sprinted downstairs and ran outside. This time she wouldn't let that child, whether mortal or phantom, get away without providing answers. Adam and the little girl glanced up as Heidi crossed the lawn toward them. Kiku darted toward the back fence.

As sternly as she could manage, Heidi ordered, "Stop right there, young lady." The next second, it occurred to her to wonder whether the child understood English.

Either way, the tone seemed to convey her command. Turning, Kiku froze with a wide-eyed stare.

"Adam, bring your friend over here. I want to see her up close."

Clasping the little girl's hand, he led her across the yard, halting a few feet from Heidi. "I'm glad to meet you at last, Kiku," she said, softening her voice. "Where do you live? Do your mom and dad know you've been visiting Adam?"

Kiku silently gazed up at her, showing no sign of comprehension. Her face blushed a rosy pink.

"Why don't we go inside? Wouldn't you two like some lemonade and cookies?"

Adam tugged on Kiku's hand. "That sounds great,

doesn't it?"

Heidi reached for both children's free hands. Kiku drew back, shaking her head with a look of alarm.

"It's okay. Nobody's going to hurt you. I just want to get to know you."

The child turned translucent, clothes and all. As Heidi blinked in disbelief, Kiku faded to transparency, then vanished.

Heidi's legs went weak. She plopped down on the grass, covering her face with trembling hands. Adam patted her on the shoulder. "It's okay, Mom. There's nothing to be scared of." He sounded tolerantly amused at her shock.

She uncovered her face to meet his calm gaze. "Your friend just—disappeared."

"It's okay. She does that sometimes. She'll come back later. Like I said before, she's magic."

"Well, if she does come back anytime soon, you'll be in the house." She stood up, grabbed his hand, and half-dragged him onto the screened porch.

"What's wrong? Why can't I wait for her out there?"

Heidi sank into one of the lawn chairs on the porch. Pulling him in front of her, she gripped his shoulders and stared him in the face. "Listen to me. Disappearing into thin air is not normal. Either I'm going crazy, or I saw that happen, which means she might be a ghost."

Tears welled up in his eyes. "Then she's a nice ghost. She just wants somebody to play with."

"That's what you said about Cap, too." *So who is Cap? Or what?* "Now go do your homework and let me think."

If Kiku was a ghost, did her presence explain Mrs. Narita's ambiguous remark the one time she and Heidi had met? Had the ofuda been hung up to keep the child spirit out of the house? If so, Heidi had blundered by taking them down. She marched into the house, dug out the envelope containing the paper talismans, and thumbtacked them to the doorjambs of the three exits. Ridiculous as she felt for yielding to superstition, the protective charms couldn't hurt.

Recalling the internet link about child ghosts she'd never gotten around to checking, Heidi opened the web page and read about zashiki warashi. They appeared as children five or six years old with blushing red faces. The boys wore child-sized warrior costumes, the girls patterned kimonos. They enjoyed making harmless mischief. Signs of their presence included small footprints, phantom noises, and objects being moved, especially pillows. Her skin prickled with chill at the list that so closely matched her experiences.

Mischievous or not, zashiki warashi were considered good luck, welcomed as guardians of the house. She reread that sentence with a dubious sniff. *Sorry, I'm not convinced a ghost is a safe playmate, much less a trustworthy guardian.* Only children and the owner of the house were supposed to be able to see them. If Mrs. Narita had known about the haunting, "owner" must include "tenant." *So if the bank loan officer dropped in for a visit, would Kiku appear to him?* Heidi remembered how Shannon hadn't shared Heidi's own glimpse of the phantom playing with Adam, except when Heidi and Shannon had been touching each other.

Heidi closed the page with a sigh. *Great, some houses have termites, but mine has a supernatural creature infestation. Imagine calling a pest control company for that.*

When she went across the hall to check on Adam's homework, she noticed several crayon drawings of Cap on the desk. She asked to borrow one, and he agreed without looking up from his arithmetic paper. She'd take it to work so Shannon could look it over. If Kiku was a spirit from Japanese legend, maybe Cap was, too. Or, at least, a boy dressed as one.

Heidi felt she'd better reserve that topic for a live conversation, since she would have to describe the encounter with "turtle boy" in detail and hope she wouldn't sound deranged. For the moment, she decided just to update Shannon on the ghost child. After all, they'd both seen her, if only a momentary glimpse in Shannon's case. Heidi sent an e-mail describing that afternoon's incident. She concluded, "She vanished before my eyes. She checks all the boxes for a zashiki warashi, stuff I didn't know until I read it a few minutes ago. So am I hallucinating? And if so, how do I see the same disappearing girl Adam does? Are we both nuts?"

Shannon answered almost immediately: "You aren't any nuttier than the rest of my friends, and Adam acts perfectly normal. If you say you saw the little girl vanish, I believe you. 'More things in Heaven and earth,' as Hamlet says. Unless contrary evidence turns up, I'm willing to accept that Adam has a ghost friend. I have reasons to be open to the supernatural, which maybe I'll tell you sometime. Remember, zashiki warashi are supposed to be benevolent, so don't freak out. I know, easy for me to say." She punctuated the sentence with a smile emoji.

After exiting her e-mail, Heidi skimmed her media feed and stopped short at a local news item—"news" in its broadest sense. Five alleged witnesses in the Eastport and downtown Annapolis area claimed they'd sighted a small, green, web-footed, humanoid creature on the banks of Spa Creek. One of them had posted a snapshot, so blurry it could be anything greenish and bipedal. She closed the page, her heart racing. *That blows the hallucination theory, anyway. If he's a kid celebrating Halloween early, he sure gets around.*

She reminded herself that she didn't have to cope with this weirdness alone. Tomorrow she would show Adam's drawing to Shannon, who at least wouldn't dismiss or laugh at her. That resolution brought the ghost issue to mind again. Heidi had no use for spirits lurking around the house, supposedly benevolent or not. She ran a search for methods of repelling them. One web page suggested simply asking the ghost to leave. She doubted the effectiveness of that ploy, considering Adam had welcomed the phantom child. Would the ofuda keep her out of the house? The point was to banish her from the entire lot, outdoors as well as inside.

Other methods included marking the boundary of the desired safe zone with holy water or salt. Since her own church didn't use holy water, Heidi tried to visualize explaining to a Catholic or Orthodox priest why she wanted enough to pour around the edge of her entire yard. Definitely a non-starter. If she chose salt instead, she'd need a ton of it, and either one would wash away in the first rain anyhow. Next, she read about smudging the area by walking the perimeter with a container of burning sage. That procedure sounded practical and couldn't do any harm. She might apply that remedy, hoping to pick a time when nobody would notice and wonder what she was doing.

Later that night, she again woke to the sound of a

childish voice singing. When she tiptoed into the hall to peek in Adam's bedroom, where he lay sprawled on his back sound asleep, running water gurgled in the distance. She followed the noise to the kitchen and discovered the sink faucet on. As she turned it off, the light above the sink flashed.

"Stop that." Her voice came out as a thin squeak. "Leave us alone. Or at least quit waking me up in the middle of the night."

The water turned on and off in three short bursts. "I'll take that as a yes."

So much for the magic of ofuda.

Chapter Five

During a lull in the next day's work, she mentioned to Shannon how enthralled Adam was with the *Raptor and Vixen* graphic novels. "He even asked if there's a movie of them."

"Don't tell him yet, because it's a long way off," Shannon said, "but our agent just signed a deal for an animated series with a streaming service."

"Fantastic! So I guess you'll quit your day job." Although Heidi spoke lightly, she was only half joking.

"No way. We're not likely to get rich off it. Besides, I love the work."

Heidi didn't even try to hide her relief at that answer. "Speaking of Adam, I want to show you something he made." She sat with Shannon at a table in the school library and handed her the crayon drawing of Cap. "This is what he says his other imaginary friend looks like. Or maybe not imaginary. Does it ring any bells for you?"

After a quick glance, Shannon said, "I don't even have to ask Ryo about this one. It's got to be a *kappa*." She spelled the word. "It's a sort of water monster. They're all over the place in Japanese popular culture— not just anime and manga, but advertising, toys, even public service announcements. Like, you might see a cute kappa on a sign warning kids to stay away from a body of water. Kind of ironic."

"How so?"

"Because one of the main themes in the folklore is that they lure or drag people into lakes or whatever and drown them. They're not always malicious, though." She went over to the nearest computer and typed in a link.

Heidi stood at her shoulder to skim the website that opened. Kappa were said to be about the size of human children but much stronger, with scaly, green or blue-green skin, turtle-like shells, and webbed hands and feet. They usually reeked of fish. *Didn't I catch a whiff of fish when Cap was nearby?* They loved cucumbers and would sometimes help people in exchange for that food. So, yeah, they weren't always dangerous, but it sounded as if any sensible person would avoid them, given their habit of dragging victims underwater for prey or just for kicks. *Cap lives in the creek, and he wants Adam to play with him there.* Her stomach knotted with anxiety. *But Cap has to be an ordinary boy in a costume, right?*

She read on. A kappa had a flat head topped with a shallow dish, which held water. Since the creature depended on this water for its strength, a surefire way to defeat a kappa was to make it spill the water. This trick turned out to be laughably easy. If you bowed to the monster, it had no choice but to bow in return. If it lost all of its water, it couldn't move. Once you defeated the kappa, you could force or persuade it to make a deal, pledging you its lifelong loyalty. Apparently offerings of cucumbers helped. One reassuring factoid—kappa never broke a promise. In addition to the water-spilling ploy, they were vulnerable to iron, sesame, and ginger. *Okay, I should keep the spice rack stocked.* She shook her head. *Am I actually taking this stuff seriously?*

"So apparently Adam's other friend I thought was imaginary is a kid who's such a big fan of kappas that he dresses like one all the time."

"Kappa," Shannon said. "The word's both singular and plural, like ofuda."

"If that's what Cap is, why would his parents put up with it?"

Shannon shrugged. "Maybe they don't think it's a hill worth dying on. In first grade I had a friend who wore her fairy princess outfit, complete with wings, every day for three weeks after Halloween."

"I just wish I could find out where he comes from. Not from a house on our block, for sure. Adam says he lives in the creek." Again a shiver went through her at the thought. "Have you seen any posts like this?"

She pulled up a chair, and Shannon scooted over to make room. Heidi entered a search phrase to call up the photo of the creature supposedly lurking around Spa Creek.

Shannon stared at the page. "Weird coincidence."

"And this isn't the only sighting."

After a few seconds of hesitation, Shannon said, "Please don't think I've gone off the deep end—oops, pun, sorry—but what if it's a genuine kappa?"

Heidi stared at her. "You believe in that stuff?"

"As I mentioned before, I have good reasons to keep an open mind. You said Kiku might be an actual ghost, so why not a kappa? They might have come here together."

"He does seem to pop up out of nowhere, and I remember smelling fish when he was around. But a legendary water monster? I'd sooner believe anything other than that."

"Hallucinations? Insanity?" Shannon said, echoing Heidi's own earlier thoughts. "You'd have to believe

315

Adam and you shared the same delusions. That sounds more farfetched than supernatural phenomena to me."

Although not sure she agreed, Heidi did find comfort in discussing the inexplicable events with someone who took them seriously. "So you think Kiku is a zashi-whatever and Cap might be a real kappa?"

"Those wouldn't have been my first assumptions, but I wouldn't dismiss them, either. Here are these sightings, for one thing." She tapped the computer screen.

"What should I do, then?" The previous night's notion of burning sage around the boundaries of her lot sounded a bit silly in a well-lit school library.

"Good question. All we have to go on is folklore. Who knows which of the superstitions are based on truth?"

"I know one thing," Heidi said. "I do not approve of letting Adam play with ghosts and water monsters."

****

Jeff ended that Saturday's phone call with his mother on an affectionate note, resisting the temptation to argue with her about her daily newspaper horoscope. At least those "predictions" always offered uplifting, generally optimistic advice that couldn't hurt anybody. Nor had he mentioned the prospect that goaded him to pace from room to room in jittery restlessness as he got ready to leave. If he'd told her he planned to broach the subject of marriage to Heidi, his mother would have bubbled over with excitement he didn't need to confront right now. He didn't intend to propose formally on the spot, only open a discussion leading, he hoped, to a positive response.

What is this, the preliminary trial in a science

experiment? he chided himself. *I'm in love with her. I want to spend my life with her, starting the sooner the better.*

He had a strong feeling Heidi wanted the same thing. *Can't risk scaring her away by rushing her though.* He drove to her house with a loaf of Italian bread and a bottle of Chianti in the front passenger seat. They planned to eat at her place this time, a homemade spaghetti dinner. He was also bringing an electric model boat to show Adam. Jeff resolved to find a quiet moment alone with Heidi after dinner to ease into the conversation he'd waited so long to have.

When he pulled into her driveway and rang the bell, Adam flung the door open with his mother several paces behind him. "Hi, Mr. Austin. Did you bring the boat?"

"Sure." Jeff held up the boat in his left hand, while carrying the wine in his right and the bread in the crook of his elbow.

After a quick, light hug that left him craving more, Heidi took the bread and wine from him. "Come in, and I'll put these in the kitchen."

"Mom says we can go to the park and sail the boat," Adam announced.

"I thought we'd feed the ducks, too." She disappeared in the direction of the kitchen while Jeff waited in the foyer with Adam, discussing the cricket and the ants. Shortly Heidi returned with her purse and a small paper sack. "Stale crackers. It's a nice afternoon, so I figured we'd walk."

Since Adam wanted to ride his bike, she got it out of the garage for him. The two adults strolled the couple of blocks to the creek while he pedaled slowly along. Jeff clasped Heidi's hand and watched her from the corner of his eye, admiring her slim figure in snug capri pants and a loose, V-necked blouse. A cool breeze off the water ruffled her curly hair.

The pocket park had a grassy open space, a few trees, benches, two picnic tables, and a short fishing pier. Kneeling on the pier, Jeff set the boat in the water, started the motor, demonstrated the steering technique, and turned the remote control over to Adam. His navigation was clumsy at first, but he soon caught on. Heidi hovered over the two of them, her fingers intertwined in front of her as if forcibly restraining herself from dragging her son away from the edge of the pier.

Glancing at her, Jeff murmured, "He's fine. It's not over my head near the bank at this point. If he falls in, I'll wade in and haul him out." He kept his tone light.

"I know he probably won't, but it's hard not to worry."

Well aware of her fretful tendencies, he suppressed the reassurance he wanted to add. Ordering her not to worry would only focus attention on her qualms. He heard her gasp of indrawn breath as Adam leaned closer to the water's surface, frowning in concentration. The boat veered from its circular path toward the center of the creek. Jeff reclaimed the remote. "Here, let me bring it back for you." He guided the craft to shore and plucked it out of the water. "Suppose we feed the ducks now. They look hungry."

Heidi cast a grateful glance at him when he led the way from the dock to the grass. A small flock of mallards waddled along the bank about three yards away. She retrieved the paper sack from the picnic table, doled out crackers to Jeff and Adam, and tossed a handful toward the ducks. Amid a chorus of quacking, the birds shuffled over to gobble up the snack. "Remember, don't try to feed them from your hand. Even if they're pretty friendly, they might bite by accident."

"Can I take one home?"

"No, you not only may not, you can't. They're still wild animals. They wouldn't be happy in a fenced yard with no pond."

Adam gazed up at her wistfully. "Not even a wading pool?"

"Definitely not."

He sighed. "I wanted to take one to get blessed with Ebony and Hopper."

She laughed. "For sure they wouldn't like that."

Jeff echoed, "Blessed?"

"The Blessing of the Animals in early October. I told him he could take the cat carrier and the cricket's tank but not the ant farm. One lady brings her horse every year, but at least he'd be easy to catch if he escaped."

Jeff arched his eyebrows. "Sounds—interesting."

"It's a short, simple service, held outside weather permitting."

"If it doesn't permit?"

"We move inside the social hall and hope for the best."

"Not including the horse, I hope." He smiled, trying to visualize the potential menagerie.

"Most likely not. Would you like to come with us this time?"

"Sure." The event sounded like a painless way to ease back into regular church attendance, something he'd have to get used to if they married. His pulse accelerated at the thought. "Let's go sit down."

She glanced at Adam, surrounded by demanding

ducks.

"He'll be okay. We'll have him in plain sight." Jeff lowered his voice. "Hopper will probably still be around for the blessing, though I can't guarantee it. I haven't figured out a way to break it to him that crickets don't live very long."

Heidi passed the rest of the bag of crackers to Adam, aside from a handful she kept for herself, and let Jeff steer her to a bench. The two of them sat close together, Jeff's arm around her shoulder. She tensed for a second, then relaxed against him, sending a fresh surge of warmth through his body. "Mom will be glad to hear about me going to church in October instead of waiting for Christmas Eve. I think she's afraid I've turned into a heathen."

"How's she doing?"

"Fine, same as ever. When we talked today, she told me about her latest horoscope and the new channeler she's consulting with." He shook his head, mentally replaying the conversation. "Woo-woo crap, as my father would've called it. At least this new woman sounds like a sincere nutcase, not a mercenary con artist. She doesn't ask for money or give investment advice, just vague messages supposedly from Dad in the great beyond."

Heidi squeezed his free hand. "That must be uncomfortable to listen to."

Jeff shrugged. "I've long since gotten used to it. It seems to make Mom happy, so I shouldn't let it bug me. But I can't swallow the idea of the dead hanging around on Earth to carry on trivial conversations with the living. Aren't they supposed to ascend to a higher plane of existence?"

She gazed into his eyes and asked in an unexpectedly serious tone, "So you do believe in life after death?"

"In some sense, but I reserve judgment on exactly how it would work. After all, I'm a science nerd. I can't come to a conclusion without concrete evidence. Especially if you want me to believe my late father sends messages by dates on coins, which is what Mom was going on about last weekend." He laughed. "I'd hate for the voters to find out my mother's a flake on that subject."

"Really?" Heidi's voice sounded strained.

"Well, half seriously. I doubt it would scare away my support base, but it wouldn't exactly enhance my image as, you know, environmental science guy."

Heidi nibbled on a cracker, then tossed the rest of it to a duck that waddled up to her. "So no ghosts in your world, huh?"

"As a scientist, I guess I'd have to consider changing my opinion if I witnessed credible evidence, but I've never seen or heard of any."

"I have. Maybe." She stared at Adam for a moment, then turned back to Jeff. "You know those imaginary friends I mentioned?"

"Don't tell me you've decided one of them is a ghost?" He tried for a light tone but didn't quite manage.

"The little girl, Kiku. I saw her up close, and she vanished into thin air right in front of me." She held up a hand to stop him from interrupting. "No, listen. I know how this sounds. I would've felt the same way about it less than a week ago." She summarized a series of incidents involving poltergeist activity and a picture over a century old. "I tried hard to explain everything to myself rationally, and that doesn't work anymore. If I'm not going crazy and Adam, too, his little playmate is the ghost of a child who died at the age of six in 1900."

He removed his arm from around her. "You're serious."

"I know what I saw. I have to accept either the existence of a zashiki warashi or an even more incredible cluster of coincidences and shared hallucinations. Are you going to claim the second choice makes more sense? How is that scientific?"

His chest tightened. How could he consider spending the rest of his life with a woman who believed this stuff when he couldn't stand to listen to his mother natter on about it for fifteen minutes? Furthermore, he hadn't been completely kidding when he speculated about how the intelligent voters he hoped to influence would react to such nonsense. *But I love her!* "Stipulating for argument's sake that your house is haunted, how did the ghost get there?"

"If she's really a spirit, she came with the Japanese family who rented the place, obviously. Maybe she was attached to the picture." Her anxious gaze silently pleaded with him to understand.

Instead, he stood up. "Shouldn't we head back to the house?" He walked over to Adam. "Are the crackers all gone? We have to get going."

Adam crumpled up the empty bag. "Can't we sail the boat some more?"

Jeff shook his head. "I'm sure your mom has some dinner prep to finish. We can help her, right?"

"I guess." He waved in the general direction of the creek as the ducks, realizing the handouts had ended, ambled toward the shoreline. "Bye, ducks. Bye, Cap."

"Cap?" Heidi had mentioned that maybe-not-imaginary playmate, too.

"The turtle boy. He's here somewhere."

The nape of Jeff's neck prickled. True, the notion of shared delusions had dubious validity, but he wasn't ready to embrace the alternative of a supernatural infestation.

He knew one thing. He wouldn't introduce a discussion of marriage tonight. He had to think through this issue first. After Heidi took the bag from Adam and tossed it in a trash can, she told him to pick up his bike. Jeff didn't reach for Heidi's hand. Her baffled expression shot a pang through him, but he pretended not to notice. Although he wouldn't bail on dinner, he didn't feel right about showing affection while his brain roiled with confusion about their relationship.

****

Just as Adam started toward the spot on the grass where he'd left the bicycle, a greenish biped rose out of the creek. Literally rose, as if riding on an underwater elevator. Adam waved to the creature. Its beaked face looked too mobile for plastic. *That's not a mask,* Heidi thought. *Hollywood-quality makeup, maybe, but why would a little kid be wearing it?*

She flapped her arms at the—kappa? "Get away from him!" The green, web-footed humanoid backed away. A fishy odor emanated from it.

Jeff turned toward her. "What's wrong?"

"Right there!" She pointed toward the creature. It leaped into the creek and sank out of sight. The fish smell evaporated. After waiting a few seconds while the surface of the water remained unruffled, she muttered, "Nothing. Sorry." *That thing didn't act human. Up close it doesn't even look human.*

She grabbed Adam's hand, and he shot her an accusing look. "Mom, why did you scare Cap away? He wanted me to go swimming with him."

"In the creek?" she asked, her voice trembling, as Jeff stared at her with raised eyebrows.

"That's where he lives. Why can't I?"

"We discussed that before. The creek is not like a pool. Now, let's go."

With Adam pushing his bike, they started the homeward walk. "Who's Cap?" Jeff asked.

"My friend who lives in the water," Adam said before Heidi could answer.

"One of the imaginary friends I told you about before," she said, "but now I think he might not be so imaginary. Didn't you see him just then?"

"I thought I saw something, but it moved too fast to be sure what it was," Jeff said, not looking at her.

As they strolled up the block, she cast sidelong glances at him. Why the sudden coolness? *He probably thinks I'm deranged, and no wonder. If I'm starting to believe in the kappa, I've got my own doubts about my sanity.*

At home, she started boiling water for noodles, took out the spaghetti sauce she'd cooked earlier to heat on the stove, and popped the Italian bread Jeff had brought into the microwave. While tossing the salad, she assigned him to open the Chianti. Throughout the preparation, they didn't converse except for necessary questions and instructions. *Why did I try to tell him about Kiku and Cap? I should've known how he'd react.* His remarks about his mother's superstitions had made it amply clear how irrational he considered such beliefs.

On the other hand, shouldn't a scientist examine the evidence instead of automatically dismissing a strange phenomenon?

After setting out the meal and calling Adam to dinner from his video game, she forced herself to pretend enthusiasm for the food, although her appetite had faded. The aromas of tomato sauce and garlic made her stomach gurgle with tension instead of hunger. The wineglasses, candles, and white tablecloth on the dining room table felt like a waste of effort when she couldn't discuss the incidents that preyed on her mind. It was a relief when Jeff unbent enough to talk about the school science fair, a project they could work on together as professionals even if their personal relationship hit potholes in the road.

Having exhausted that topic, he brought up the 5K charity race for the homeless shelter she'd already agreed to watch. "My next event after that will be the Bay Bridge run and walk in November. You should sign up for it. You don't have to train for the running part. Hundreds of people will be doing the walk."

"Eek. I don't even like to drive over that thing. Too high" Her heart constricted at the thought of watching anybody, especially Jeff, run across the span that arched above the Chesapeake Bay. Echoes of the shock at the moment when she'd learned about Doug's collapse reverberated through her. *Get a grip. It's not the running that killed him, remember? I have to let go of that sometime.* "But I'll think about it. Walking, basic skill, been doing it most of my life."

"Good to hear." His voice, which had held a spark of animation for a moment, flattened again.

After clearing the table, she dished out scoops of

spumoni ice cream to avoid disappointing Adam. She had to force herself to swallow nibbles of hers until the bowl was empty, and Jeff showed no greater interest in his own dessert. Adam wolfed down his share and rushed outside. Since Jeff refused another glass of wine, she corked the bottle and moved it to the kitchen counter.

When she returned to the dining room, she found Jeff standing, poised to leave. "I'd better get going. Monday we should set up a time to start the prep for the science fair. I'll touch base with you then."

"Okay." She blinked to suppress the tears that threatened to fill her eyes. *Damned if I'll beg him to hang around.* "Want to say goodbye to Adam?"

"Sure," Jeff answered with a smile, if only a brief one.

They headed to the kitchen and out through the screened porch. Scanning the yard for her son, Heidi caught sight of him kicking a soccer ball to his playmate—Kiku.

Chapter Six

Jeff resolved to put on a cheerful face for Adam. It wouldn't be fair to take out his emotional turmoil on the kid. As Jeff stepped outside with Heidi, she halted abruptly and stared at her son, who was chasing a ball around the lawn. "There she is," she said in a harsh whisper.

"Who?" Adam was alone in the fenced yard.

"The little girl, Kiku. You can't see her, can you?"

A sour lump congealed in the pit of Jeff's stomach. How could he bear it if the woman he wanted to spend his life with was delusional? The strain in her voice proved her sincerity, and anyway she wasn't the type to perpetrate a sick joke. He shook his head. "I don't see any girl."

Heidi clasped his hand. "There," she said in a tone shrill with impatience. She pointed toward Adam.

Yes, there was a child standing next to Adam—an Asian girl in a red, floral-print kimono. She hadn't walked out of the bushes or otherwise arrived in a normal manner. She'd simply popped into existence. Jeff's head reeled.

"I see." He could barely hear his own hoarse voice. Clearing his throat, he spoke louder. "Adam, who is that girl?"

"My friend Kiku." A serene smile accompanied the answer.

Jeff struggled to keep his voice from shaking. "But she just—appeared."

"Yeah, she's magic. Sometimes she appears and disappears. But she's nice, so don't be scared."

Heidi said, "Bring her over here."

Holding the girl's hand, Adam led her to within arm's reach of the two adults.

With a sharp sidelong look at Jeff, Heidi said, "Well? Still think she's imaginary?" She let go of his hand.

Kiku vanished.

He gasped. "She's gone."

"Then it works the way I thought," Heidi said. "You can see her only when I'm touching you." She grabbed his hand again.

The child reappeared. A second later, she retreated a few paces and disappeared again.

Jeff blinked and shook his head to dispel a wave of dizziness. "Wait, she's gone again."

"Really gone this time. I don't see her now either."

Adam said with a disapproving frown, "You must have scared her away. She's shy."

Jeff staggered to the nearest lawn chair and sank into it. "What's going on?"

Folding her arms, Heidi glowered down at him. "Didn't I mention that only children and the owner of the house she's haunting can see her? Also anybody who's touching one of those people, apparently."

He rubbed a hand over his face. "So that's your ghost. Unless hallucinations are contagious."

She glanced at her son. "Adam, go inside." After he did, she glared at Jeff again. "So that's what you thought? That I was crazy?"

"I admit it was the first thing that came to mind."

"That's why you suddenly acted all distant and wanted to leave early? I don't think much of your friendship if you have that little faith in me. Good thing I didn't tell you the turtle boy—the kappa—is real, too, not a kid in costume. I saw him at the creek right before we left. I guess you would've called the men in white coats on the spot."

He stood to face her. "How did you expect me to react? Until recently, didn't you think Adam was pretending or imagining things?"

"Yeah, but I'm not seven years old. I thought we knew each other better than that. You should've given me some credit for using my mind before you decided I'd lost it."

"And you should cut me some slack after a shock like that." A defensive note crept into his voice. "You've had a while to get used to being haunted."

"Well, when you've had time to get used to the idea, too, we can talk." Her tone pierced him like an icicle in the heart. "You said you needed to leave. I think you'd better."

With a blend of guilt and indignation simmering inside him, he stalked through the house, picked up his model boat, and strode out to his car. Driving home, he mulled over what he'd witnessed. Otherwise stable people didn't suddenly develop psychoses and see things that didn't exist. As far as he'd heard or read, mass hallucinations were more mythical than real. If they did happen, they affected mobs caught up in group hysteria, not two or three people in a calm, domestic setting. Given the unlikelihood of those explanations, the most credible hypothesis was that he, Heidi, and her son had actually met the ghost of a child dead for over a century.

Does this mean I have to buy Mom's entire load of occult crap? Pulling into his parking space at home, he emphatically shook his head. *No way!* He refused to start watching for messages from his late father in every random coincidence. Granted that some spirits apparently did roam the earthly plane, they had to be exceptions to the general rule. Otherwise, the world as he knew it would be disintegrating.

A few minutes later, with an open beer can beside his computer, he browsed for information about hauntings. Skimming a dozen websites started a headache throbbing between his eyes. Legends and superstitions contradicted each other at least as often as their lore coincided. A page on Japanese folklore confirmed and expanded on the background about the child ghost, zashi-whatever, that he'd heard from Heidi. The belief that this kind of spirit bestowed good luck on a house didn't reassure him. *I just want my reality to revert to the status quo.*

He abandoned the subject and opened his media feed. A local news-of-the-weird item jolted him out of his absent-minded scrolling. People on the waterfront in Annapolis and Eastport claimed to have seen a small, blue-green, vaguely turtle-shaped biped. Photos of the alleged creek monster displayed greenish blurs. One snapshot, however, caught a distorted view of the thing diving into the creek, barely clear enough to show it as a child-size creature with a shell on its back and a flat head. The caption read, "Maybe it's a kappa that got lost by a few thousand miles? Somebody should buy it a plane ticket to Japan."

Kappa. Now that Jeff reflected on his argument with

Heidi, he recalled she'd mentioned that word. And hadn't Adam called his other "imaginary" playmate Cap? Jeff ran a search for the creature. Drawings of the water monster on the pages that popped up did resemble the photo, so far as that picture looked like anything in particular. He leaned back in his chair and chugged from the beer can. *What's next? Do I have to believe in mermaids, dragons, and unicorns, too?*

No, he'd stick with one impossible phenomenon at a time or at most two. Even in the realm of the supernatural, logic and evidence had to mean something. He woke his cell phone and opened the photo folder. Sipping his drink, he brooded over images of Heidi and Adam. They'd enjoyed too many happy times, bonded too deeply to throw away their chance at a life together. If he had to accept ghosts and monsters as the price of winning that chance, he'd go for it. He conceded she had a right to be outraged at the conclusions he'd jumped to, even if he did think she'd overreacted a tad.

I totally blew it. His chest ached with the fear of never holding or kissing Heidi again, losing all hope of spending his life with her.

How could he make up for instantly rejecting the truth she'd tried to share with him?

****

By the time she'd cleaned up the remains of dinner, Heidi managed to calm down. Maybe her indignation at Jeff hadn't been fully justified. How would she herself have reacted only a few weeks before if anybody else had told her the neighborhood was infested with supernatural beings? Still, she couldn't yet bring herself to forgive Jeff's lack of trust in her rationality. Wanting a second opinion and maybe some support, she e-mailed Shannon about the sightings, although with no details about the blow-up with Jeff. Four people had seen Kiku by now, and Jeff and Heidi as well as Adam had glimpsed Cap, not to mention the alleged witnesses on social media. Heidi linked to the most coherent of their posts in her message. "I believe Kiku is a real ghost, and Cap is probably not human. Jeff thinks I'm nuts, of course. I wouldn't blame you if you agreed." She sent the e-mail before she could lose her nerve. True, Shannon had expressed openness on the subject before, but it had been mainly hypothetical then.

Now that Heidi's belief in the ghost child had solidified, she couldn't stand the idea of letting a spirit have free run of her property. Even if, as Adam insisted, Kiku simply wanted to play, Heidi didn't trust a phantom guest who played pranks with electricity and plumbing. *Enough, I'm banishing her.*

With Adam busy watching cartoons so he couldn't witness her bizarre behavior, Heidi dumped half a jar of ground sage into a bowl wrapped in a dish towel, carried it outside, and lit the dried herb on fire. She glanced from side to side, hoping no neighbors happened to be looking her way. *What's to worry about? They'd probably think I've taken up New Age spirituality.*

She sneezed from the smoke and considered how to order the ghost to vacate the premises. Obviously the ofuda hadn't barred Kiku from the house. Would a ritual that didn't even come from the same cultural tradition work any better? *Can't hurt to try.* Heidi began by crossing the front lawn about six feet out from the bottom of the porch steps. "Stay away, Kiku," she murmured every few paces. "Move on to your next life or wherever you should be. You don't belong here."

Although she felt silly speaking into the void, she continued that procedure into the back yard and around the inside of the fence. "Leave this house alone. You aren't welcome here anymore." By the time she completed the circuit, the flame in the bowl had sunk to smoldering, crimson ashes. Nothing else happened. No ethereal fragrance blossomed in the air, only the residue of sage-tinged smoke, and no reassuring glow of celestial light illuminated the path she'd traced. She would just have to wait and see whether the spirit returned.

Later in the evening she received a reply e-mail from Shannon: "Like I said before, I don't have any trouble believing in zashiki warashi or kappa, given enough evidence, and as far as I'm concerned, your witness to them is evidence. You're not a liar or a ditz. Remember, the ghost child is supposed to be good, not evil. She might play tricks, but she won't hurt Adam."

Her friend's calm acceptance dissolved the knot in Heidi's chest. With someone who believed her, she could discuss practical solutions. "I'm not convinced of that. She might not mean to do harm, but tricks with the electric wiring and throwing stuff around could be dangerous. I've already done a ritual to banish her." She described it.

"That might work, if you really want her gone," Shannon wrote in response. "As for the kappa, I don't know what to tell you, except that I've never heard of one coming inside a human dwelling."

"It comes in the yard, though, and I can't keep Adam in the house 24-7 when we're home. If the kappa's real, how did it get here?"

"Same way Kiku did, maybe?" Shannon suggested. "The picture you found probably brought her to this country with the family who lived in the house before you. After all, they're related. Maybe the kappa tagged along somehow?"

"But isn't a kappa a solid creature, not a spirit?" Heidi could hardly believe she was analyzing an impossible entity as if it were natural. On the other hand, from all she'd read about folklore and fairy tales, supernatural creatures had to obey rules, too.

"Got me there. Who knows why it even relocated here, let alone how. Anyway, keep me updated." After a final sentence of reassurance, Shannon signed off for the night.

Soon afterward, the landline phone rang as Heidi was getting out of the shower. Wrapped in a towel, she sat on the edge of her bed to answer. Seeing Jeff's number on the caller ID, she almost let the call go to voice mail. No point in putting off the inevitable, though. "Yes?" she said as coolly as she could manage.

"You're still mad," he said.

"How perceptive of you."

"Look, I was wrong to shut you down earlier. I'm really sorry."

She struggled to resist his plaintive tone. "But now that you've seen the ghost for yourself, you've changed your mind."

"Well—yeah, among other reasons."

"Including because you trust my judgment the way you should've to start with?"

"I deserve that. I'm not sure what I believe about the supernatural, but I believe in you. I should have known better after six years of friendship. It's the classic trilemma—lies, insanity, or fact. You don't tell pointless lies or make malicious jokes. You're a stable person, and people don't suddenly go mad overnight like in horror movies. Please, let's get together and talk about it."

What good would it do to remain stubborn? She couldn't deny she yearned to reconcile as much as he did. Her chest ached at the thought of losing him. *Wait, losing?* That word implied its opposite—that they belonged to each other. *I think I love him. When did that happen?* She already knew the answer, though. It had been happening for months, yet she hadn't wanted to recognize the change in her feelings because that acknowledgment would require a decision she hadn't been ready for. But now...

"All right. When?"

"How about an early dinner tomorrow?"

She agreed, stressing "early" because of school on Monday, and ended the conversation. After a glance at the clock, she phoned Gina to ask for last-minute babysitting. With that arrangement settled, Heidi picked up the novel she'd been reading but laid it aside when another task occurred to her, a step she should probably have taken months earlier.

She walked into the office and gazed up at the wedding photo on the wall. *Rest in peace, Doug. It's time for me to move on.* She took down the picture, wrapped it in tissue paper, and tucked it away in the top of the closet. Previously unnoticed tightness in her neck and shoulders melted away as if she had shed a physical burden.

Back in her room, she reclined in bed with her book, wondering whether her attempt at sage-burning magic would guarantee peace in the house overnight. *Doug thought I needed digging out of my rut. If anything would accomplish that goal, this will.*

****

Although she heard no singing in the night and found no loose items upset the next morning, she'd spent most of the day jumping at random noises by the time Gina arrived to babysit at five p.m. The doorbell set Heidi's heart racing, and her shoulders sagged with an instant of letdown when she opened the door and didn't find Jeff on the porch. She escorted Gina to the kitchen to outline instructions for Adam's supper. "I've ordered pizza, vegetarian for you. He's allowed ice cream and a cookie after, and feel free to have some yourself."

Gina thanked her and turned on her tablet to play a game at the kitchen table as Adam walked in. "Hey, dude, how's it going?"

"I don't know," he said. "Mom, why didn't Kiku come to play today?"

To Gina's quizzical look, Heidi mouthed, "Imaginary friend." She didn't feel up to explaining that the house was haunted. To Adam, she said, "I asked her to stop coming. We'll talk about it later."

His chin quivered. "Why did you be mean to her?"

"Later, I said." Softening her tone, she continued, "Would you like to sleep on the porch tonight for a treat while I go out with Mr. Austin? The weather's supposed to stay nice for now, and soon it'll get too chilly."

He brightened up. "Okay. May I play games on Gina's tablet, too?"

"If she'll let you. But tomorrow's still a school day, so you have to go to sleep on time."

Gina mentioned that her parents expected her home by ten for the same reason. Just then the doorbell rang again, and Heidi hurried to greet Jeff. He'd made a reservation at a French restaurant in downtown

Annapolis. As they got into his car after bidding goodbye to Adam and Gina, she said with a sidelong glance at Jeff, "Sounds pretty fancy for a last-minute Sunday date."

He answered with a wry smile, "I figured a grand gesture might boost my chances at forgiveness."

"Yeah, right. Good luck with that." But she couldn't help smiling in return. Her insides fluttered as their eyes met.

In the downtown historic district, they snagged a parking space directly on the narrow, brick-paved Main Street and strolled half a block to the restaurant. "So you're willing to accept Kiku as a ghost now?" she asked after they'd been seated with menus and water glasses.

Jeff glanced around the half-empty dining room and said in a low voice, "Now that I've seen her vanish myself, I don't have much choice, do I? As a bona fide science guy, I can't ignore the evidence."

"Why are you practically whispering? Even if one of your prospective voters overheard us, they'd think we're talking about a movie or TV series."

"Fair point," he said with a faint smile. "Exactly what I'd think if I heard a tale like this from anybody else. But I have to yield to logic. Either you and Adam are making the whole thing up, you're having delusions or hallucinations, or you're reporting true events. Like I said last night, you're not a pathological liar, and I've never seen any evidence that you're mentally unbalanced. Plus, the second hypothesis would mean I saw the same hallucination you did, which is beyond unreasonable. So…ghosts exist, or at least this one does. I just have to adjust."

"I tried to exorcise her, sort of." She explained about

the poltergeist phenomena and the sage burning. "I don't know whether it'll work, of course. How can I tell which legends and superstitions have any truth in them? Adam keeps saying she only wants somebody to play with, but he's just a kid. What if she wants something not so harmless?"

She broke off as the waiter delivered salads and bread. When he'd gone, Jeff said, "Ghosts usually have an agenda, don't they? How did you say she got here?"

"Shannon and I think she must have been carried, so to speak, by the old photograph I mentioned."

"Wait, you told Shannon, and she believes in the haunting?"

"Gee, imagine that. She believed me right away."

He raised his hands defensively. "Okay, I surrender. I grovel in remorse."

She reluctantly laughed, and he joined in.

"And the former tenant didn't want the photo shipped to her," he said. "That implies she might've left it on purpose because she didn't want her—what would it be? great-great-aunt?—following her back to Japan."

"So Kiku was lonely and attached herself to Adam as a playmate. The legends do say children can see this kind of spirit. But even if she doesn't mean harm, I don't want her fooling around with things in the house. Ghost or not, she's perpetually six years old. Maybe she doesn't know what's harmful and what isn't."

After munching on his salad in silence for a few minutes, Jeff said, "I don't get where the kappa comes in. From what I read online, that isn't a spirit. It's a physical being."

"Good question." Since her e-mail exchange with Shannon, she hadn't devoted any further thought to that point. "Hmm—maybe it somehow hid in a moving crate and got shipped overseas with the household property?"

"Assuming the reality of the thing, that could almost make sense. Reptiles can hibernate, and since it looks like a humanoid turtle, maybe it can be classified as a supernatural reptile." He shook his head with a rueful grin. "If anybody had told me two days ago I'd be seriously considering this, I'd have wondered what they were smoking."

"Okay, it curled up in a box in Japan, went into suspended animation, and woke up here when Mrs. Narita and her family weren't watching." From personal experience, she knew how chaotic moving days could be. Assuming that had been how the monster got into the house, it could easily have crept out and found the way to its preferred aquatic habitat.

"Hey, is there any chance it might be a natural animal, a rare species turned into a cryptid by popular legend?" Jeff visibly relaxed as if relieved at the hope of a rational explanation.

She reluctantly quashed the hypothesis. "I don't see how. From the way it looked and behaved, it's either a small person in disguise or exactly what the mythology claims."

He pushed away his empty salad bowl, moved the decorative candle aside, and leaned his elbows on the table to stare into her eyes. "Listen, don't get me wrong. I don't mean to doubt what you saw, but are you a hundred percent sure it couldn't be a child in costume after all?"

"I'd like to believe that, but it doesn't add up." Shredding a slice of bread, she returned his steady gaze. "You didn't watch it jump into the creek and vanish the way I did. There's a clear line of sight along the shore in that spot, nowhere it could have climbed out without being seen. Besides, up close that face couldn't be mistaken for a mask. If it isn't a real creature, it's wearing professional makeup, and if a kid had it in the first place, why would he be allowed to roam the neighborhood dressed like that day after day?"

"Not to mention the multiple posts about widely scattered sightings in Eastport and near City Dock. They probably aren't all attention-seeking fakes, at least not the earliest ones. Okay, I accept the provisional conclusion that it's an authentic Japanese water monster."

He broke off when the waiter came to collect their bowls. A couple of minutes later, the entrees arrived.

After making a start on her boeuf bourguignon, she said, "No wonder Mrs. Narita wished me luck and left the ofuda hanging by the doors."

"The what?"

Heidi explained about the paper charms. "She must have been worried about the kappa as well as the ghost."

"From what I read online, no wonder. Some kappa are just mildly mischievous or even helpful, but other legends say they're into drowning people. They drag victims underwater and suck out their internal organs." When she made an involuntary "yuck" sound, he hastily added, "Sorry, that's gross. And we don't have any way to know which legends are based on fact. At least, according to what I read, they're easy to defeat. All you have to do is bow to them."

She remembered that detail on the website she'd consulted, too. "Right, it has to bow back, and the water in the hollow of top of its head spills out."

"Which I don't get," Jeff said. "Why would the kappa be dumb enough to return the bow? Shouldn't they have caught on to that trick after hundreds or thousands of years?"

Heidi frowned in thought. "Another good question, but fairy tale and folklore creatures have to obey the rules of their nature. Even if it doesn't make sense from a scientific viewpoint, that's how the world works in those stories."

"So we have to accept an alternate category of rules. The kappa bows, its water reservoir empties, and it instantly becomes weak." He shook his head and took a fortifying sip of wine. "Aquatic magic? Next, I guess I'll have to accept the four classical elements as the fundamental components of the universe—the folklore universe, anyway. Well, I'll try to get used to toggling between two systems of reality."

The mention of aquatic magic netted a stray memory. "That reminds me, Adam said Kiku didn't like Cap because he hurt her once. Kiku drowned in a pond. I wonder if the kappa killed her." The full implications of that idea seeped through her veins like ice water. "It drowns children. It wants Adam to play with it in the creek."

She dropped her fork and half stood. Jeff clasped her hand. "Easy. Even if this is all true, there's no reason to rush home."

She lowered her voice to a furious whisper. "How can you say that?"

"First off, kappa hang around bodies of water, right? That's the point of their existence. They don't invade houses."

"Not that we know of." She settled into her chair,

fighting to force her ragged breath under control. "It came into our yard, though."

"Without doing any harm so far. You don't have a pond on your property, and Gina won't let Adam wander away, will she?" He gave her hand a gentle squeeze before releasing it.

Heidi picked up her fork. "I guess you're right. But he did sneak to the park by himself once. Who's to say he won't try it again? How am I supposed to protect him from a creature that shouldn't even exist? Do I have to watch him every minute?"

"You know you don't. You can't protect him from everything. In principle, is this different from any other kind of danger? He'll eventually grow up like all children and have to rely on himself. You can't let fear run your life, not to mention his."

She swallowed a lump in her throat. "Easy for you to say."

"You know I care about him." He covered her free hand with his. "By now you must know how I feel. I want to take care of both of you—and more than that."

Warmth spread up her arm and thawed the chill that had crept over her. *Is he working up to the L-word? I'm not ready to hear it right this minute.* She eased her hand away to grip the stem of her wineglass and tried for a light tone. "Let's hope you won't have to fight monsters for us."

"Here's to that." He raised his own glass and took a sip. "Let's also hope it won't be *monsters*, plural. One is almost more than I can wrap my brain around, not counting the ghost girl. Do I have to start believing in unicorns, leprechauns, trolls under bridges, God knows what?"

She rejected the idea with a nervous laugh. "You're the logical one here. I count on you to keep my world sane or mostly so. Let's talk about something else for a while. Old movies, the science fair, anything."

So they ranged over those and other topics through the rest of the meal. After dessert crepes, they strolled in the cool evening past boutiques and souvenir shops to the car. When they reached it, he paused to take her hand. "Have you totally forgiven me for doubting you?"

She nodded. "If the positions had been reversed, I'd probably have rejected the whole idea, too."

"In that case—" He glanced away for a second, then looked straight at her. "It's still early. Will you come home with me?"

Chapter Seven

Heat flushed her cheeks and radiated through her core. *Do I want this? Whom am I kidding? Of course I do. But am I ready?* On the other hand, would she be any more ready next week or next month? "Okay," she whispered.

They passed the ten-minute drive to his home in silence. She'd visited his second-floor condo apartment before, but only for casual drop-ins. This time, climbing the stairs to his door felt like hiking up a mountain. Once inside, they walked through the living room straight to the bedroom. There was no point in pretending either of them doubted what would happen next.

The room was tidy, the bed made. Jeff paused to open the window, letting in the night air. Hands clasped, they sat on the edge of the bed. The fragrance of his spicy aftershave wafted toward her. He leaned in for a long, gentle kiss. Resting her free hand on his shoulder, she parted her lips on a sigh as his tongue teased them. He tasted like wine and coffee.

Drawing back, he said, "Are you sure?"

She nodded, already short of breath. To confirm her willingness, she undid the top two buttons of his shirt and splayed her palm on his bare chest. He kissed her again, deeper this time, and grazed her breasts with one hand while wrapping his other arm around her. Electricity sizzled through her.

While he began unbuttoning her blouse, she trembled with a stomach-churning blend of excitement and anxiety. She was wearing a plain cotton bra, not the lacy lingerie she would have chosen if she'd expected this interlude. And would her modest endowment disappoint him? She tensed when he completed the unfastening process.

He kissed her neck and looked up to meet her gaze as if sensing her qualms.

"I'm afraid I'm out of practice." She clasped his wandering hand, not sure whether she meant to stop him or encourage him.

"It's probably like the proverbial riding a bicycle. Muscle memory doesn't forget."

A nervous giggle escaped her. "I was never very good at bike-riding."

"It's been a long time for me, too." He brushed his lips over her hair. With a low chuckle, he nuzzled the hollow of her throat, tickling the sensitive skin. "Oh, but I'm sure the procedure will come back to us."

They stripped off each other's clothes bit by bit, pausing to kiss and fondle between each step. To her delight, when he cupped her bare breasts and bent to lap each one in turn, he murmured something that sounded like, "Beautiful." Her nipples perked up, and she arched her back, silently begging for more. She melted inside, waves of heat rippling over her.

They hurried to finish undressing, with frantic moments of untangling twisted garments. He flipped back the covers, and they stretched out side by side on the bed. When his hardness brushed her thigh, she felt him shiver. She gripped his shaft, thrilling at his renewed quiver of response. He stroked the length of her body and roamed to places no hand but her own had touched in over two years. She closed her eyes and, trembling, caressed him in return while her release shuddered through her.

He covered her mouth with his to catch her cry of fulfillment. She lay back, panting, and he said in a hoarse near-growl, "Now?"

"Yes, now!"

Eyes slitted open, she watched him open a nightstand drawer, remove a packet, and sheath himself. "You were prepared?" she murmured.

"I hoped." His teasing smile vanished as he braced himself above her.

She twined all four limbs around him and drew him in. After a second of awkward tightness, he filled her, and they found their rhythm. Her excitement mounted higher with each of his urgent thrusts. Together they soared to the peak and spiraled down.

With his head on her chest and his hot breath on her damp skin, she clasped him still tighter as her pulse and breathing calmed.

He murmured something unintelligible into the V between her breasts.

"Hmm?"

He spoke again, enunciating clearly. "I'm in love with you. I've loved you for a long time."

Dizziness surged over her. She had to draw a deep breath before she could answer. "I love you, too. Even if I wasn't ready to admit it before now."

He kissed the hollow of her throat. "Good to hear." He rested his head on her shoulder with a drawn-out sigh.

She drifted in and out of a doze, luxuriating in the warmth of his body covering hers.

When at last she floated out of the rosy mist of half-sleep, the bedside digital clock showed almost 9:30. Jeff lay face down beside her. Jolted fully awake, she sat up and shook his shoulder. "Hey, Gina's curfew!"

"Huh?" He rolled over and stared at her.

"She has to be home by ten. I can't risk losing my babysitter."

"Okay, no need to leap to battle stations. It's less than ten minutes away."

Both of them hastily washed up and scrambled into their clothes. After one last ravenous kiss, they hurried to the car. They arrived at Heidi's home several minutes before 10 p.m. Gina greeted them at the door, in the process of taking out the earbuds umbilically attached to her tablet. "Adam got into his sleeping bag on the porch right on time. I checked on him about fifteen minutes ago, and he was sound asleep."

After paying her, Heidi stood on the front steps with Jeff to watch Gina cross the street to her house. Holding the door open for him, Heidi gestured for him to come inside. "You can stay for a little while if you want," she said, avoiding his eyes with sudden self-consciousness.

"I'd love to—a little while. It's a school day for us, too." He grinned.

"Have a seat. I'll make coffee. I want to check on Adam first, though."

In the kitchen, she switched on the single-cup coffeemaker as the cat wound around her ankles. While waiting for the machine to heat, she opened the door to the screened porch. At first sight, her brain didn't register what she saw.

The outside door hung open, and the sleeping bag lay disarranged and empty. Her stomach roiled.

She flipped on the backyard floodlight and dashed outside. "Adam?" No sign of him as far as the lamp illuminated. "Adam, answer me this minute!"

Nothing but the scent of cut grass from a neighboring yard and the buzz of nocturnal insects.

Rushing into the house, she called for Jeff, who hurried to her. "Adam's gone!" She grabbed a flashlight from a kitchen drawer and ran out back again with Jeff at her side. Even as panic threatened to swamp her, his nearness anchored her. *Jeff is with me. It will be all right.*

"Let's be systematic," he said. "Start at one corner and work around."

She gulped a breath. "Okay." Holding hands, they paced to the intersection of the fence with the farther end of the garage and picked their way along the side of the yard. As she pointed the flashlight beam into the shrubbery, they examined the perimeter foot by foot. Every few seconds she called Adam's name. By the time they reached the back of the lot, it seemed obvious he wasn't nearby. They proceeded anyhow, walking faster. After completing the circuit, they exited through the gate into the front yard.

In the middle of the sidewalk leading from the porch steps to the curb, Kiku stood waiting for them. A silvery glow haloed her. She started toward them but halted abruptly, as if hitting an invisible wall.

Jeff squeezed Heidi's hand painfully hard. "That's an actual ghost. I mean, I believed it before, but now I really believe it."

"The sage-burning ritual did keep her out of the house," Heidi said. "But if Adam didn't wander off with her—"

"Are you thinking the kappa lured him away?"

Lightheaded, she clung to him, drawing deep breaths to dispel the dizziness. "Maybe I was wrong trying to banish her."

The phantom child glided to the curb, then turned and beckoned to them.

"I think she'll guide us to Adam," Heidi said.

"We'd better drive." Jeff led her to his car, where he had to let go of her hand.

Scraps of information from her research on kappa popped into her head. "Wait a second. I need to get some things just in case." She ran into the house. In the kitchen, she snatched up a jar of powdered ginger and the smaller of her two cast-iron frying pans, then hurried out to the car.

"What are those for?" Jeff asked as she got into the passenger side.

"Kappa are repelled by ginger and vulnerable to iron, or so the legends claim."

She'd barely buckled her belt when he started the engine and backed out of the driveway. "I can't see the ghost now. You'll have to tell me where to go."

Heidi placed her hand on his shoulder to let him share her vision and pointed up the street where Kiku floated ahead of them. "That way, toward downtown." She'd already made a tentative guess about where Adam had gone.

A minute later, she was sure of the destination. "No need to wait for Kiku. She's leading us to the park."

After a brief burst of speed, they pulled into the gravel parking lot next to the creek. Tracking the ghost child's glimmer, Heidi sprang from her seat and ran to the patch of grass beside the fishing dock. She trained the flashlight on Adam, who stood less than a yard from the bank of the creek. The kappa hovered at the verge of the water. Between the flashlight's beam and Kiku's glow, Heidi made out Adam's dazed expression as he took a hesitant step toward the kappa, which extended a webbed hand.

"No. Stop," she whispered. She wanted to scream and run toward them, but what if startling the creature provoked it to plunge into the creek with her son?

Kiku glided up to Adam and thrust out an arm to break the contact between him and the kappa. "Cap," Adam muttered. He stepped sideways away from the ghost child, while she and "Cap" spoke to each other. At least, their mouths moved. Heidi couldn't hear anything but faint, unintelligible murmurs.

Jeff stepped to Heidi's side. "So that's the kappa. It's real. Where's the ghost?"

Without looking away from the tableau on the bank, she clasped his hand.

"I see her. What now?"

"She must be trying to protect Adam," Heidi said, keeping her voice low. "She was never evil at all, just mischievous. But she can't defeat the kappa in its natural element. You have to distract it by bowing, like the folklore says."

"Sure, but why me?"

"Because the trick is more likely to work than if I did it—I hope. The thing might recognize me and be cautious."

"Okay." Jeff took one step forward.

"Wait, throw this at it while it's supposedly helpless." She unscrewed the lid from the spice jar and handed it over.

Nodding, Jeff strode toward the kappa, which had

returned its focus to Adam. It grasped one of his hands, ignoring Kiku, who waved her arms between Adam and the kappa with no effect. *Its power must increase near a body of water.* With the flashlight beam pointed at the ground in front of her feet, Heidi tiptoed to the verge of the creek and edged around to creep up on the monster from behind. Acid welled up in her throat as she almost gagged at the fishy reek of the thing.

With its stare fixed on Adam, the kappa paid no attention to Jeff, either. He marched up to them and shouted, "Hey, you, turtle-face, over here."

Good try, but it probably doesn't understand English. Regardless, the noise alone might divert it. Adam looked up, but his eyes still held a trancelike blankness. The kappa slowly turned toward Jeff.

"Yeah, I mean you." Jeff locked stares with the creature and executed a profound bow.

Releasing Adam's hand, the kappa bowed low in response. Heidi elevated the flashlight beam to watch as water spilled from the shallow bowl that formed the top of its skull.

Jeff froze as if stunned that the ploy had actually worked. When the kappa took a backward step toward the verge of the creek, Heidi yelled, "Jeff, the ginger!"

He dumped the entire jar of powdered spice on the creature's head. A pungent blend of cookie fragrance and fish odor permeated the air. Batting at its face with webbed hands, the kappa collapsed to its knees.

At the same instant, Adam stumbled, his feet slipping on the damp ground. He slid toward the bank. A scream burst from her mouth.

Jeff lunged forward, grabbed the boy's arm, and yanked him away from the shoreline.

With a howl of rage, Heidi was astonished to hear erupting from her own throat, she sprinted the short distance between herself and the others, swung the cast-iron pan like a tennis racket, and bashed the kappa on the head. The thing crumpled in a heap on the grass. Her insides lurched. *I didn't kill it, did I?* She didn't want that image stuck in Adam's head, not to mention her own.

Adam blinked, ran to her, hugged her, and cried, "Why did you hurt Cap? Is he dead?"

To her relief, the kappa stirred, snarling under its breath. Heidi brandished the frying pan. "Don't even think of getting up." She turned to her son. "No, honey, he'll be all right. I had to hit him because was trying to drag you into the creek."

Adam glanced at the kappa, who spoke an incomprehensible line. "He didn't mean to hurt me."

"You can understand him?"

"Sure," Adam said, knuckling tears from his eyes. "I can talk to him and Kiku."

Heidi pressed against Jeff's side to enable him to see the ghost, who lingered next to Adam, glaring at the kappa. "According to the legends on the internet," Heidi said, "kappa have to obey the person who defeats them, and they always keep their promises. Maybe we can force it to behave."

"You trust that guarantee?" Jeff asked.

Heidi shrugged, making the flashlight beam waver. "What choice do we have? I doubt we can actually kill a supernatural creature." She said to Adam, "So he didn't mean to hurt you like he didn't mean to hurt Kiku when he drowned her?"

Adam stared first at the ghost, then at the kappa. "He did do that, but he just wanted her to play with him. He didn't know people can't live under the water like he can."

"I'm not sure I buy that excuse. He should know better by now, but he tried to lure you into the water anyway."

"That's why Kiku tried to keep him away from her and me. But Cap didn't understand it was bad to turn her into a ghost. She's still here, isn't she? She can still talk and do stuff, right? He wanted her to play with him again."

"That almost sounds logical." Jeff glanced from the cringing creature to the spirit, then at Heidi. "You plan to bind it, or him, with promises? Such as?"

She mulled over the question, keeping the cast-iron pan ready for action. "First off, he has to stay in the creek. No more coming to our house. Adam, make him promise that."

Adam pursed his mouth in a pout. "Do we have to?"

"Absolutely."

He recited the words she'd dictated, his gaze fixed on the kappa's face. "Okay, he promises."

"He also has to promise not to hurt anybody else and especially not to try to take anybody into the water."

After a similar repetition, Adam said, "He promises that, too."

From her limited research, she had the impression that a kappa would obey more reliably if offered a reward. "Tell him if he keeps those vows, we'll leave cucumbers on this dock for him every Saturday." She gestured at the fishing pier with the flashlight. As an afterthought and safeguard, she added, "Unless the weather turns terrible or some emergency comes up."

Adam relayed that message, too. "Okay, he says it's

a deal."

"Make him swear." Although she didn't know whether that step would seal the creature's vow more firmly than a simple promise, she didn't want to take any chances.

Adam nodded. "He swears by everything."

"Fine." She lowered the frying pan to her side. The weight was making her arm sore anyway. "He can leave now."

At her brusque wave with the flashlight, the kappa dove into the creek and disappeared. The fishy odor evaporated.

Heidi's shoulders sagged, and she breathed out a long sigh.

Jeff wrapped his arm around her waist. "So now you're committed to weekly cucumber donations. Could be worse."

Trembling, she returned the hug and leaned against his solid bulk. For a second she rested her head on his chest, taking comfort from the steady pounding of his heartbeat. "I hope that creature can be trusted. As you said earlier, who knows which legends are reliable?" She asked Adam, "Does Kiku think Cap will keep his promises?"

After a brief exchange of glances with Kiku, Adam nodded vigorously. "She says he can't help it."

"That's reassuring, I guess."

"Which raises the second-order question of whether you can trust the ghost," Jeff said. "Good God, I can't believe I'm saying that with a straight face."

"I think we can. She tried to save Adam from the kappa." Heidi turned to Kiku. If the barrier hadn't stopped the ghost from entering the screened porch, maybe she could have prevented him from being lured away. "I'm sorry I didn't understand. I shouldn't have banned you from the house. I revoke my prohibition. You're welcome in our home."

"She says thanks," Adam reported.

"But please stop moving things around and messing with the electricity and plumbing."

Adam touched the ghost child's glowing hand. "She doesn't have to do that stuff now. It was to get you to pay attention because Cap was dangerous, and he won't bother me anymore."

"Glad to hear that. Let's go home."

Kiku vanished. With only the flashlight for illumination, Heidi blinked until her eyes adjusted. Since she had her hands full, Jeff got a firm grip on Adam's arm and led him to the car.

With a glance at the empty shoreline in the headlights as they backed out of the parking space, Adam said, "Will I get to see him again?"

Not if I have anything to say about it! "Maybe when we drop off the cucumbers. You're never to come here by yourself, though? Got that?"

He sighed. "Yes. I promise."

To Jeff, she said, "Come to think of it, I bet that's why Mrs. Narita left the photo behind. She didn't want the kappa chasing her family back to Japan, and he seems bound to Kiku."

At home, she gathered up the sleeping bag and blankets from the screened porch, lugged them inside, and locked the kitchen door. "You'd better spend tonight in your own room after all." The next time she saw Shannon, she would ask whether Ryo could get them another ofuda to guard the porch.

Adam agreed without the fight Heidi had half expected. Even if he'd stayed in a trance for much of the incident, it must have scared him at least a little when he woke to consciousness far from his sleeping bag at home. After she tucked him into bed, Jeff came in to say goodbye.

"Say goodnight to Hopper and the ants," Adam said.

Jeff complied, then patted Adam on the shoulder by way of farewell. Downstairs, he and Heidi shared a lingering kiss in the entryway. "Will you be okay now? I could stay."

"No, thanks." She softened the refusal with a hug. "We'll be fine, and I wouldn't want to confuse Adam with you being here overnight on top of everything else."

"Understood. Tomorrow, then." He claimed one more kiss before leaving.

After locking the door behind him, she ducked into her home office to send a quick e-mail to Mrs. Narita, who probably had a right to know the ghost of her great-great-aunt had found a welcome. As an afterthought, Heidi added, "We also dealt with the kappa, so everything is fine."

She then returned to Adam's room for a final goodnight. He was snuggled under the covers with Ebony curled at the foot of the bed. "Kiku likes pillows. Is it okay for her to still play with the pillows?" The question trailed off in a yawn.

"Well—I guess that's harmless enough, if she's careful where she throws them. But nothing else." *Doesn't seem like much to ask after she tried to protect my child.*

"Mom, Mr. Austin helped you save me, didn't he?"

"That's right."

"I think you should marry him."

Her face warmed, and her pulse stuttered. "I think that's a very good idea."

****

Next morning between his class sessions, Jeff popped into the library and invited Heidi to lunch. At midday she left with him, to the accompaniment of a teasing smile and thumbs-up from Shannon.

Jeff and Heidi drove across the Spa Creek drawbridge into downtown and picked up crab cake sandwiches to go. They sat on a bench at City Dock, with a cool breeze blowing off the water, and unwrapped their food under the covetous stares of a flock of gulls. "Go away." She shooed them with a wave of a hand. The birds squawked, flapped their wings, and stayed put.

"Why don't they ever give up? People aren't supposed to feed them." She gestured at the sign forbidding that action.

"But enough do anyway to encourage them. Intermittent reinforcement. Strongest type." He took a bite of his sandwich and gazed across the sailboat-clogged inlet for a minute, then turned to her. "So. How's Adam doing?"

"Fine, as far as I can tell." He'd eaten breakfast and dressed for school as casually as ever, mentioning the night's adventure only to assure her he would remind Kiku not to disturb anything except pillows. "He knew the ghost and the kappa were real all along, and he doesn't seem to understand why we got freaked about them. After all, he's seven. He still believes in Santa Claus and the Tooth Fairy."

Jeff shook his head with a faint smile. "At this point, I wouldn't rule them out, either."

"My mind boggles, too, but I'm not ready to go that far."

"I want the world to make sense," he said. "After five years of giving my mother a hard time about her alleged messages from beyond, I have to start believing in ghosts and monsters? But it really happened, didn't it?"

"We both remember it, so it must have. That makes sense, doesn't it? Otherwise, we have to fall back on the shared hallucination theory, which is even less believable."

"Right, use logic on me." He nibbled a French fry. "To think the main thing I was worried about two days ago was how my future constituents would react if I got involved with that woo-woo stuff."

"Are you still worried?"

"Nah. It's not as if either of us is going to spread this around. And if the word did get out, well, I'd lock in a majority of the woo-woo vote."

Both of them laughed. After eating in silence for a while, as she finished her own sandwich and watched the boats, ducks, and seagulls, he said, "I phoned Mom and asked for the latest update on her favorite channeler. Talking about it makes her happy, and I figured it couldn't hurt to listen."

"An open mind is a good thing," she said. "I've discovered that myself in the past week."

"If you can knock down a humanoid turtle with a frying pan, I can expand my mind to accept it."

She sipped her diet cola as a couple of teenagers ambling along the dock in twin "Save the Bay" T-shirts jogged her memory of an earlier conversation. "I've made up my mind. I'll do that Bay Bridge walk in

November with you. After defeating a mythical monster, what's a four-point-three-mile hike across a bridge 350 feet above the water, give or take a few feet?"

"Way to go." With a broad smile, he clasped her hand, making her pulse quicken. "We'll rise to the challenge together."

After gathering up their trash and dumping it in the nearest waste can, he returned to his seat beside her.

"Speaking of challenges," she said with a glance from side to side to check whether anybody was close enough to wonder about the strange conversation, "we supposedly restricted the kappa to the creek, but the ghost can still drop in for a visit if she wants to. Can you live with that?"

"The important thing is I can't live without you. And I care about Adam like my own." He took her hand again, laying his other arm across her shoulders. "If being with both of you means moving into a haunted house, I'll adjust."

Her skin tingled at his touch. "Are you saying what I think you are?"

The tenderness in his eyes warmed her like the midday sun on her bare arms. He lowered his voice. "You must know I've been working up to this for a long time. I love you. Last night we established that goes both ways, right?"

She nodded, her face flaming again at the memory of his lips and fingers exploring her body.

"So let's take the logical next step." His voice turned husky, resonating with more passion than rationality. "I've been waiting almost forever to ask this. Will you marry me, Heidi?"

Her nerves humming, she exhaled a shaky breath.

"How can I argue with logic, science guy?"

"I'll take that as a yes."

In a tremulous voice, she said, "Please do."

He shifted his hand from her shoulder to cup the back of her head and leaned in to brush his lips with hers.

After a gasp of surprise at this gesture in broad daylight in view of every passing tourist, she relaxed and parted her lips in invitation. Her head was spinning by the time he ended the kiss and stood up. Still holding her hand, he drew her to her feet.

He bent his head to whisper in her ear, his hot breath rustling her hair. "I wish we had time to stop by your house and celebrate."

Another rush of blood scorched her cheeks. "So do I. But we'll have all the time in the world for that."

****

Back in the library, she couldn't hide her excitement from Shannon, who said with a sly smile, "Ah, hanky-panky on the lunch break."

Heidi shook her head, annoyed at how readily she blushed at the teasing. "No panky and only a little bit of hanky. But he did propose, and I did accept."

"You go, girl. About time."

"Promise to keep this between us for right now."

"Sure." Shannon hugged and congratulated her.

As the dismissal hour neared, Heidi fretted about whether Adam would feel the same way. Sure, he'd expressed eagerness for her to marry Jeff, but she still wondered whether her son might have a different reaction when the hypothetical became real and the "cool" grown-up transformed into an authority figure. She and Jeff had agreed he would come over to eat that evening, when they would break the news.

When she and Adam got home, they found the throw pillows on the couch stacked in a neat tower. A quick survey of the house didn't reveal any other disturbance. "See," Adam said, "Kiku is being good like I told her you wanted."

"Glad to see that." *So now I have a tame ghost. Better than a mischievous one, I guess.* Heidi changed the subject to mention they'd be expecting Jeff for supper.

Adam asked why that was happening on a Monday. She evaded the question, sending him to his room to do homework. He'd finished by the time Jeff rang the doorbell promptly at five, carrying two flat boxes redolent of pepperoni. Her pulse quickened at the sight of him.

Adam clattered downstairs into the entryway right behind Heidi. "Hi, Mr. Austin. Did you bring the electric boat again?"

"No, but I come bearing pizza."

"Yay! Want to come to my room and see Hopper and the ants?"

"Sure." Jeff kissed Heidi on the lips, warming her from head to toe, and handed her the boxes.

She glanced at Adam, who gave the affectionate gesture only a fleeting glance. With the pizza, she headed for the kitchen as Adam grasped Jeff's hand to tug him upstairs. While waiting for them, she tossed bagged salad mix into bowls, which she set on the table in the screened porch along with drinks, paper plates, and other accessories.

"We might as well eat out there," she said to Jeff and Adam when they walked into the kitchen together. *They already look like father and son.* Blending into a new family unit might not flow as smoothly as a vintage sitcom, with every glitch repaired in thirty minutes minus commercials, but they'd made a fair start.

After gobbling his first slice, Adam asked, "Why are we having pizza on a school night?"

She exchanged glances with Jeff. *Well, here goes.* "We have something important to tell you."

Adam looked from her to Jeff and back again. "Are you going to get married?"

Heidi nodded. "That's right."

Jeff cast a wry smile in her direction. "So much for the big surprise."

"Cool," Adam said. "What are we going to do with our house?"

Heidi's chest constricted. She hadn't thought that far yet. *How could I give it up so soon after going to all that trouble to get it?*

Before she could frame an answer, Jeff said, "Live in it, I hope. Is that okay with you?"

"Sure. You can move in with the Venus flytrap. But don't let it eat Hopper."

"Of course not."

Heidi let out her breath in a sigh. "Then that's settled." Of course, plenty of technicalities remained unsettled, such as whether Jeff would sell his condo or rent it out. They would hash out all those details at the proper time, though.

Adam had yet another question. "Mom, how come you don't have a diamond ring like in the movies?"

"We'll have to go to a jeweler downtown and pick one out soon, won't we?" Jeff clasped her hand and raised it to his lips.

Sparks danced up her arm. "Sounds like a good

plan."

"We have a big yard with a fence now," Adam said, "so can we get a dog?"

Heidi laughed. "Slow down. Let's take time to get settled first. We already have a cat, a cricket, an ant farm, and a ghost."

"Yeah, but she's nice." After a few more bites of pizza, Adam looked outside. "Hey, there she is."

The phantom child hovered just beyond the porch, peering at them through the screen. Adam waved at her, and she waved back.

Touching her fingertips to Jeff's so he could see the spirit, too, Heidi raised her free hand in a tentative greeting.

"She's really a good ghost, right, Mom?" Adam said.

"Right. She helped us save you, so she's definitely a good ghost."

Jeff curled his fingers around hers. "Yes, and if we can believe the legends, a good omen for our new life together."

A word about the author...

Reading *Dracula* at the age of twelve ignited Margaret L. Carter's interest in a wide range of speculative fiction and inspired her to become a writer. Vampires, however, have always remained close to her heart. Her work on vampirism in literature includes four books and numerous articles. She holds a PhD in English from the University of California (Irvine), and her dissertation contained a chapter on *Dracula*. In fiction, she has written horror, fantasy, and paranormal romance, as well as sword-and-sorcery fantasy in collaboration with her husband, a retired naval officer. Her short stories have appeared in various anthologies, including the "Darkover" and "Sword and Sorceress" series. She and her husband live in Maryland and have four children, several grandchildren and great-grandchildren, a St. Bernard, and two cats. Please visit Carter's Crypt:

http://www.margaretlcarter.com